CHRISTMAS SCARF MURDER

Books by Carlene O'Connor

Irish Village Mysteries
MURDER IN AN IRISH VILLAGE
MURDER AT AN IRISH WEDDING
MURDER IN AN IRISH CHURCHYARD
MURDER IN AN IRISH PUB
MURDER IN AN IRISH COTTAGE
MURDER AT AN IRISH CHRISTMAS
MURDER IN AN IRISH BOOKSHOP
MURDER ON AN IRISH FARM
CHRISTMAS COCOA MURDER
(with Maddie Day and Alex Erickson)

A Home to Ireland Mystery
MURDER IN GALWAY
MURDER IN CONNEMARA

Books by Maddie Day

Country Store Mysteries
FLIPPED FOR MURDER
GRILLED FOR MURDER
WHEN THE GRITS HIT THE FAN
BISCUITS AND SLASHED BROWNS
DEATH OVER EASY
STRANGLED EGGS AND HAM
NACHO AVERAGE MURDER

CANDY SLAIN MURDER
NO GRATER CRIME
BATTER OFF DEAD
CHRISTMAS COCOA MURDER
(with Carlene O'Connor and Alex Erickson)

Cozy Capers Book Group Mysteries
MURDER ON CAPE COD
MURDER AT THE TAFFY SHOP
MURDER AT THE LOBSTAH SHACK
MURDER IN CAPE COTTAGE

And writing as Edith Maxwell

A TINE TO LIVE, A TINE TO DIE
'TIL DIRT DO US PART
FARMED AND DANGEROUS
MURDER MOST FOWL
MULCH ADO ABOUT MURDER

Books by Peggy Ehrhart

MURDER, SHE KNIT
DIED IN THE WOOL
KNIT ONE, DIE TWO
SILENT KNIT, DEADLY KNIT
A FATAL YARN
KNIT OF THE LIVING DEAD
KNITTY GRITTY MURDER
DEATH OF A KNIT WIT
CHRISTMAS CARD MURDER
(with Leslie Meier and Lee Hollis)

Published by Kensington Publishing Corp.

CHRISTMAS SCARF MURDER

Carlene O'Connor
Maddie Day
Peggy Ehrhart

Kensington Publishing Corp.
www.kensingtonbooks.com

KENSINGTON BOOKS are published by

Kensington Publishing Corp.
119 West 40th Street
New York, NY 10018

All Kensington titles, imprints and distributed lines are available at special quantity discounts for bulk purchases for sales promotion, premiums, fund-raising, educational or institutional use.

Special book excerpts or customized printings can also be created to fit specific needs. For details, write or phone the office of the Kensington Special Sales Manager: Kensington Publishing Corp., 119 West 40th Street, New York, NY, 10018. Attn. Special Sales Department. Phone: 1-800-221-2647.

Kensington and the Teapot logo is a trademark of Kensington Publishing Corp.

Library of Congress Card Catalogue Number: 2022938416

ISBN: 978-1-4967-3722-9

First Kensington Hardcover Edition: October 2022

ISBN: 978-1-4967-3724-3 (ebook)

10 9 8 7 6 5 4 3 2 1

Printed in the United States of America

Contents

CHRISTMAS SCARF MURDER

Carlene O'Connor

This book is dedicated to my cousin, Heather Kraus. Although your journey is not going to be easy these next few years, I am with you all the way and so proud of you. Sending all my love and light to you.

Acknowledgments

Thank you to my editor, John Scognamiglio, my publicist Larissa Ackerman, my agent Evan Marshall, and all the wonderful staff at Kensington Publishing who work so hard behind the scenes on our books.

Chapter One

Siobhán O'Sullivan stood in the kitchen of her new stone farmhouse, leafing through holiday recipes and insisting yet again to her younger brother Ciarán that Santy wasn't bringing him a tractor for Christmas, when her husband opened the front door and poked his head in. She grinned. *Her husband.* Six months of marriage and it still didn't feel real. Cold air blasted in from the outside but when Siobhán caught the worried expression on Macdara's handsome face, she dropped all plans to scold him. "The Grinch paid a visit to the elder care home," he said. "The residents have all been robbed."

"You're joking me." The Kilbane Elder Care Home was small and exclusive, catering to wealthy clients. It was located outside of town in a beautiful Victorian-style house painted a cheerful yellow. They had immaculate gardens and every year the grounds were decorated to the hilt for Christmas. Mechanical reindeer, Santy and his sleigh, and every tree on the property would be wrapped in colorful lights. It was so lavish it nearly made Siobhán wish she was old enough to move in. Siobhán had been looking forward to visiting this year, only she was worried her younger siblings Ann and Ciarán would insist they decorate their new fields in the same over-the-top fashion. Although they certainly had the room, and Siobhán loved decorating for Christmas, she wanted something rustic and cozy. White lights and a gorgeous wreath for the door—maybe a candle or two in the window. And this year she wanted them to cut down a live Christmas tree. It was their first Christmas in their new house, and she wanted that Christmas tree smell. Macdara's news was troubling indeed. Who would rob an elder care home a fortnight before Christmas? "The poor pets," Siobhán said. "Is everyone alright?"

"Thank goodness no bodily harm to anyone, but I hear some very dear items have been taken and everyone is in quite the state."

"It's a frightening thing when you're robbed," Siobhán said. "They must feel so vulnerable."

Macdara nodded. "I know it's your day off, but nearly everyone has taken their holidays."

"Say no more, Detective Sergeant," Siobhán said. "I'll get me uniform on."

Macdara nodded. "I'll be out here, Garda O'Sullivan." He leaned in for a kiss.

"You promised you'd stop doing that before brekkie," Ciarán said. "I've lost me appetite. Again."

They broke apart and laughed. "You already had two Irish breakfasts," Siobhán said.

"It's a good thing I horsed them into me before all the mushy stuff then isn't it?" Ciarán responded. Macdara clapped Ciarán on the back. Ciarán shook his head. "I deserve a tractor for this."

Siobhán wished she could bottle this moment, their first Christmas as husband and wife, as a family. The entire brood would fill the house to celebrate. Even James, Gráinne, and Eoin, Siobhán's siblings who were now independent and free, would camp out for the holidays. Her minor siblings, Ann and Ciaran seemed to be adjusting to living at the farm house, and chuffed to the bits that they each had their own room. James, Gráinne, and Eoin were still living above the bistro, with a lot more room to spread out. Was it only seven months since they moved from above their former bistro in town to the farm house? The time had flown by. Siobhán's five siblings had lived with her ever since their parents had been killed by a drunk driver in a road accident eight years prior. There were times she wanted to keep them with her forever. Luckily, Eoin and James were building a farm-to-table restaurant on their new farm, and Grainne was chomping at the bit to help decorate it. Siobhán saw them nearly every day. Family was everything, and yet change was inevitable. But this year, they would all be together. And to top it off they had invited their friend Doctor Jeanie Brady, an esteemed state pathologist, to join them for Christmas dinner. She had let it slip that she was taking the holidays off this year and had lamented not having a big family to share it with. Siobhán was thrilled when she accepted the invitation. She handed Ciarán back his Christmas wish list. *Tractor* was the only item on it. "Better add to this," she said. "Unless you want a toy tractor."

Ciarán shook his head. "Typical."

His voice was so low now, puberty well underway. And she still wanted to squeeze his cheeks until he howled. "Isn't it enough we get to decorate our very own tractor for the parade?" Siobhán asked. Before they'd moved outside of town Siobhán was barely aware there *was* a Christmas tractor parade. James had grown close to some of the lads participating and had volunteered the rest of the O'Sullivans to decorate a tractor, most of them either a

Massey Ferguson or a John Deere. They were due at Bill Casey's farm this weekend to map out a route and start decorating.

"Not unless I get to drive it home after," Ciarán said. "I could mow the field."

He said "mow the field" but she could see it now. Ciarán O'Sullivan speeding down the road in a tractor, mowing everything in his path but the grass. *Never.*

"There will be plenty to keep you busy when Eoin breaks ground on the new restaurant," she said. "You'll forget all about tractors." Their property used to contain an old dairy barn, and although it had burned down as a result of arson, Eoin was going to rebuild and open a farm-to-table restaurant. Luckily, the property was zoned for both home and business. Not that the O'Sullivans were turning into instant farmers, none of them had the experience for that, but Eoin was already making connections with local farmers to source the needed ingredients, and in the spring they were sure to at least have a vegetable garden and chickens. It was crazy how swiftly one's life could change, and although somewhat dizzying, Siobhán was finding it an absolute thrill.

"I'll never forget about tractors," Ciarán said. "I was born to ride."

"What about a hoverboard?" Macdara asked. "Santy might be able to spring for one of those."

Ciarán shook his head. "What about a Vespa?"

"No," Siobhán said.

Ciarán put his hands on his hips and lasered her with a look. He was nearly as tall as she was. "You have one."

"I'm an adult."

Ciarán threw his arms open. "Where am I going to ride a hoverboard? In the field?"

Siobhán sighed. The truth was, they were probably eventually going to have to get a tractor. But it would be the family tractor and not teenage transportation.

"You need new hobbies," Siobhán said. "Why don't you do some brainstorming to see what you fancy?"

"I'd rather do some *barnstorming*," he said. "With my new tractor."

Siobhán laughed. "No planes, tractors, motorcycles, cars, or scooters."

"Fine," Ciarán said. "I'll take the hoverboard."

Siobhán threw Macdara a look and he was smart enough to grimace. "We'll have to see what Christmas morning brings. Why don't you get out our decorations while we're gone?" She went to pat Ciarán on the head, but he ducked and she swiped air. It was starting to look like there was going to be more than one Grinch in Kilbane this year.

As they pulled into the lovely manicured grounds for the elder care home, Siobhán found herself wishing it was under happier circumstances. The yellow Victorian house with blue trim popped against the green fields. Lush hedges and gardens created a virtual Eden that blossomed in the spring, but during the Christmas holidays the grounds were transformed into a winter wonderland, complete with a snow machine. Everyone was hoping it would snow for real this year, although most likely it would not, and Siobhán had a feeling the snow machine would be on the ready. Lovely paths curved through gardens featuring sculptures, birdbaths, and benches. A gardener stood near a hedge with clippers, shaping the first row into large candy canes. The residents were so lucky to live in such a magical place—the thought of anyone robbing them infused her with anger. Respect for one's elders was an ironclad principle for the O'Sullivans, something the young ones of today seemed to be sorely lacking.

The house sat on a high elevation with sweeping views of hills and valleys, topped off by the curves of the Bally-houra Mountains. Christmas decorating was full steam ahead, with large plastic bins lining the drive and in the gardens, overflowing with garland, lights, and bows. Despite the cold, residents stood outside in hefty robes and slippers clutching mugs of tea or coffee, some with winter coats, others with just hats and scarves. The minute the pair exited the vehicle they could hear the excited hum of voices. It seemed the break-in had infused the home with a bit of excitement. "The guards are here," an old man shouted, waving both his hands at them as if he was stranded on an island and they were circling above in a plane. Siobhán waved back; it was nice to feel appreciated. Soon they were surrounded by the elderly residents, all speaking at once.

"They stole Oscar's cane, it was a lovely carved wood with a golden handle."

"And Nuala's precious emeralds."

"Nuala doesn't have precious emeralds, she's messing with us!"

"I did so have emeralds and they've been stolen!"

"Maybe it was your grandson. He's always poking around."

"Wash that filthy mouth out with soap, you old grouch you, or I'll do it for ya."

"Don't forget Rory's money."

A short man with black spectacles stepped forward, brown eyes blinking rapidly. He looked like an adorable little owl. "Five hundred euro they took. All me Christmas shopping money." He held his hands palms up as he shrugged. "What am I going to do now? This may be me last Christmas and I have to buy gifts for all me grand-kids."

Siobhán's heart squeezed. "I'm so sorry. We promise ye, we'll get to the bottom of this."

"Don't forget me scarf!" A plump woman in a flowered bathrobe and a bulky winter coat shoved her mobile phone at them, forcing them to look at the screen. On it was a hideous red scarf with green shamrocks.

"Beverly, Beverly, Beverly. Didn't you hear the lads warn you about that scarf?" an old man said. His winter coat was zipped up but he was wearing pajamas and slippers. He pointed to a spot in the distance. Siobhán followed the trajectory to a birdbath where a pair of twenty-somethings were standing, a lad and a colleen. It was nice to see young people on the grounds. He turned back to the plump woman. "That scarf is too long. You could wrap a giraffe's neck with that yoke and still have bits hanging off him. Did they not warn you about long scarf syndrome?"

"Bah humbug," Beverly said. "It was a work of passion. You can't stop knitting when you're filled with passion!"

"Excuse me," a small voice next to Siobhán piped up. She turned to find a tiny older woman clasping her hands together. She was dressed in a lovely fawn coat and had a red bow pinned in her hair. Her lips were heavily lined in a matching red. "I'm missing me Virgin Mary statue. It isn't very dear, but my mammy bought it at the very first Christmas Market in the town square, with money she'd been saving the whole year. It has great sentimental value. I can't bear the thought that it's gone."

Siobhán placed her hand on the woman's shoulders. "What's your name, luv?"

"Sinead."

"Sinead, your statue sounds most dear to me."

Sinead nodded, her eyes filling with tears. "It makes me feel connected to her. It's like a piece of her."

Siobhán nodded. She understood very well. They had

items from her late parents that felt like an extension of them. "We'll treat your missing statue with the same value we do the missing emeralds." She turned to the crowd. "I promise ye, we are going to do everything we can to sort this out." They all started talking at once. "Give us a minute to speak with the director," Siobhán said. "We'll soon have a proper sit-down with each one of you." The residents stopped jabbering and stared, their faces stamped with hope. Siobhán wondered if she should warn them that it's very rare to recover items in a robbery. The thieves could be long gone by now.

As they took a step toward the house, an exuberant border collie bounded their way, a small stuffed elf in his mouth. He dropped it at Siobhán's feet and looked up expectantly.

"Aren't you a wee dote," she said.

"That's Max," the man with the black spectacles said. "He's visiting us for the holidays. Insanely intelligent that dog."

"And adorable," Siobhán said, leaning down. "Who's a good boy?" The dog, tongue hanging out, swung its head in Macdara's direction.

"Did you see that?" Macdara said. "He's smirking at me." Macdara bent down to pick up the elf. The dog snatched it and laid it at Siobhán's feet. "Cheeky dog," Macdara said. "He only wants you to throw it."

Siobhán picked up the elf. "Do you hear that, love? Me husband is jealous of a dog."

"I think we might be looking at our thief right here," Macdara said, wagging his finger at the dog.

Siobhán laughed, then tossed the elf. The dog bounded after it. Macdara gave her a look. "You're like a magical woodland creature," he said. "Beloved by all your subjects."

She punched him in the arm. "Sort yourself out, maybe you'll grow on him."

"Look at that complexion," a sweet old woman to her right said, reaching for Siobhán's face. "Like a bowlful of cream."

"And that gorgeous red hair," another cooed. "You must have all the lads after ya."

"And all the woodland creatures," Macdara repeated, ducking as Siobhán went in for another swipe.

Her hair was really auburn but it was futile correcting people. Some saw the world in a variety of shades, others couldn't be bothered. Siobhán didn't dare look at Macdara, she knew he was struggling to contain a cheeky response. She'd give it twenty-four hours before he made a "bowlful of cream" remark.

"What a handsome detective," a woman cooed at Macdara. "How can you catch criminals with that sweet face?" Siobhán rather enjoyed watching his sweet face turn red and wondered if that made her a terrible person.

"They've designated a meeting room inside for our inquiries," Macdara said, clearing his throat and trying to regain a sense of order. "But first we need to speak with the director."

"Are you going to take fingerprints?" Sinead said. "I've only seen it on *Law & Order*."

"It's highly likely that the thieves wore gloves," Macdara said politely.

"What a pity," she said, smacking her lips together. "I so wanted to see how you do it." Sinead seemed to shrink with disappointment, her little red bow dipping lower and lower.

"I'll see what I can do," Macdara said. "It never hurts to arrange a little demonstration." She grinned, stood on her tiptoes and planted a kiss on Macdara's cheek. He turned red enough to make the lipstick marks blend in with the rest of his face.

"You can handcuff me too," she said. "I don't mind." She held up her wrists for inspection. Macdara took out his mobile and walked a few feet away to make a call. He returned moments later with a satisfied grin on his face. Before Siobhán could ask him what that was all about, a middle-aged man in a gray suit was hurrying up the path toward them, his hand extended.

"I'm Cathal Ryan. You must be DS Flannery, we spoke on the phone." He was a handsome man with salt-and-pepper hair feathered back and light blue eyes accentuated by his blue tie and pocket square.

"That would be me," Macdara said. "And this is Garda O'Sullivan. Otherwise known as me wife," he said with a wink.

Siobhán groaned. Cathal raised an eyebrow. "Six months so far," Siobhán said.

"Congratulations." He flashed perfectly straight and white teeth.

"So far?" Macdara said.

"Do tell us about the break-in," Siobhán said.

"Follow me," Cathal said. They headed up the path toward the house, and soon stepped onto the grand front porch. More bins were stacked, one on top of the other. Some had their lids off, revealing a mountain of garland and lights. A pair of lads, also in their early twenties, stood nearby, listening to opposing decorating instructions from a nearby cluster of residents.

"String them up along the roof."

"No, not the roof, are ya mad? String them along the windows."

"What about the porch rail, lads? Do you think ye can manage that?"

Max, stuffed elf in his mouth, sat happily watching the hubbub.

Cathal nodded to the younger men. "We have a small group of lads from the tractor parade helping us decorate this year."

"Grand," Siobhán said. She hated her next thought—it was cynical—but she had a job to do. Could one of them be the thief? There were four of them, a lad and a lass by the birdbath and two lads on the porch. Were they good-hearted young people giving their time to their elders at Christmas, or scheming thieves out to swindle them? It was the nature of this job that one had to explore all possibilities. Cathal pointed to the front door. It was made of oak, with a small stained-glass window and a lion knocker. Siobhán loved it. "Isn't this gorgeous," she said to Macdara, pointing out the lion. "Maybe Santy will bring me something similar."

"Maybe you should be happy with your bowlful of cream," Macdara retorted.

She gently punched his arm and he laughed. That hadn't taken long at all. Why hadn't she placed a bet with someone?

Potted holly bushes flanked the door, and a pair of gas lamps were situated on either side. She could imagine how gorgeous it looked in the evening, with the flames dancing.

"This is the main entrance," Cathal was saying. "There were no signs of a break-in per se."

"When did the robbery occur?" Macdara asked.

"Residents only discovered their items missing this morning after breakfast. But we assume it took place yesterday when most of us were on an outing."

"An outing?" Siobhán asked.

He nodded. "We helped decorate the town square for the Christmas market," he said. "It was a grand day." His grin soon faded. "Followed by a wretched morning."

"Wait," Siobhán said. "Why did you add—per se?"

"Pardon?"

"You said there were no signs of a break-in *per se*."

Cathal nodded. "Yes. I'd rather show you once we go inside."

"Did you have any items stolen?" Macdara asked.

Cathal shook his head. "I live off-site, and nothing in my office seems to be disturbed. To be honest, I'm puzzled. Only five residents had items stolen, and coincidentally they were the five residents that remained behind."

That didn't sound at all like a coincidence to Siobhán. "Their items were nicked yesterday but you're only reporting it today?"

"I'm afraid it was chaos here last night—in a good way. There was the excitement of the residents who returned from the market showing off their wares, along with the items we shopped for the five who remained behind, and then we had carolers pay us a visit. A few residents said they had been looking for their items, but misplacing things is a common occurrence around here. It wasn't until the next morning, when they started looking in earnest and comparing stories that we realized this was more than just misplacing their things, that they had indeed been robbed."

"Do these same residents usually stay behind?" she asked.

"As a matter of fact they do," Cathal said. "Are you saying the thief knew that? That this was an inside job?"

"Anything is possible," Macdara said. "We've a long ways to go before we make any declarations."

"Perhaps he or she was interrupted before they could steal from anyone else," Siobhán said. "But why start with the five residents who were still on the grounds?" That seemed very risky. Was this a thief who thrived on the risk of being caught?

"Downright nonsensical if you ask me," Cathal said. "The money and emeralds—if they exist—makes sense alright. But he also steals a cane, a scarf, and a Virgin Mary statue? Who does that?"

"What makes you so sure the thief is a he?" Siobhán asked.

"Pardon me, Garda," he said. "You're quite right. The thief may be a member of the fairer sex."

Inwardly she groaned at the phrase, but she wasn't here to school others on their parts of speech. "How long was the outing to the Christmas market?" Macdara asked.

"We were there for most of the day," Cathal said. "From ten a.m. to four." The town square hosted the Christmas market every year, attracting nearly the entire village. It was a grand place to find Christmas gifts, drink hot cocoa, and sample desserts. It was also where the yearly Christmas pantomime was held. Every year the pantomime was based on a fairy tale and given a comedic twist. The panto, as everyone called it, was a cherished tradition. Siobhán's own brood had starred in one a few years back, a hearty rendition of "Jack and the Beanstalk."

"All but the five residents who had items stolen attended the outing?" Siobhán asked.

"That is correct," Cathal said. "Our front office manager, Nancy Martin, remained on-site as well."

"And what about our four young volunteers?" Siobhán asked. "Where were they?"

"They accompanied us on the outing as well," Cathal said. "Although I did not have eyes on them the entire time. They're young, they come and go as they please."

"And no one saw any strangers on the property?" Macdara asked. "Or did anyone hear anything odd?"

Cathal sighed. "Unfortunately, aside from the one room in the house I need to show you, no one reported hearing or seeing a single thing out of the ordinary. It was as if we were robbed by a Christmas mouse!"

"More like a Christmas rat," Macdara said.

One of the young lads approached. He had a mop of blond curls and intense blue eyes. He wagged his finger at them. "If you wanted someone to blame, look no further than the house manager, Nancy Martin."

Chapter Two

Cathal stepped toward the young man, a look of panic stamped on his face. "Blame Nancy Martin? Whatever do you mean?"

"I was at the Christmas market but returned early," the young man said. "None of them heard a thing because Nancy was blasting Christmas songs." He glanced at Siobhán and Macdara. "Nancy is a mad one for the Christmas music." He grinned, stuck out his hand. "I'm Finn Doyle, Nuala's grandson."

Cathal leaned in. "Nuala is the resident who claims she's missing precious emeralds."

Finn's face clouded over. "If me granny says her emeralds were stolen, then her emeralds were stolen."

"Of course, of course," Cathal said. "It's just . . . none of us have ever seen these emeralds."

"I've seen them," Finn said. "We were just arranging to have them valued."

"Then why hasn't she shown them to anyone else?" Cathal asked.

"Because they're too valuable to flash around." Finn tapped his forehead with his index finger. He turned to Macdara. "That's why she kept them in her safe. And now they're gone."

Cathal turned to Siobhán and Macdara. "He's right about one thing. Nancy does like to blast her Christmas tunes."

"Who doesn't?" Siobhán said. She loved everything about Christmas.

"How many residents and staff do you have in total?" Macdara asked.

"We only have twelve residents at a time," Cathal said. "Our waiting list is very long."

Macdara leaned into Siobhán's ear. "Should we put our names in now?"

"Definitely yours," she said. His chuckle warmed her insides.

"As far as staff goes, we have myself and Nancy, the kitchen staff, and housekeeping." He began to count on his fingers. "Fifteen of us in all."

"Fifteen," Macdara said. That was a lot of suspects.

"But many are on their Christmas break," Cathal said. "Leaving three kitchen staff and three housekeepers." That certainly helped. "We're lucky to still have Nancy." He leaned in and lowered his voice. "Her husband is running for mayor of Cork in the spring. Isn't that exciting?"

Siobhán didn't get particularly excited about politics and was trying to come up with a polite response when they were interrupted. "Don't plug it in yet!" They turned to see a red-faced old man berating a young lad with red hair and spiked fringes. He jumped at the reprimand, jostling the string of Christmas lights in his arms. He wrapped the string around his neck and mimicked hanging himself. Max barked and began tugging on the Christmas lights.

"I'm only messing, Max," the redheaded lad said. "Let go." The dog immediately let go. "Good boy." He removed a treat from his pocket and the dog snatched it up.

"Quit horsing around," the old man yelled. "Do you think this roof is going to decorate itself?"

"I'm not deaf." The young man removed the string of lights from his neck. He towered over the old man. "You don't have to shout."

"Ease up," Macdara said. The young man shot a withering look at the detective sergeant but took a step back.

Cathal, eager to move on, pointed once more to the ornate front door. "As I've mentioned, there were no signs of a break-in at our front or our back doors. They are the only two means of entry."

"Except for the roof." The comment came from another young lad stepping onto the porch. His head was shaved, but he had a baby face and fawn-brown eyes. "Down the chimney?" he added. "Santy and his sleigh?"

"Shall I introduce you to our helpers?" Cathal said.

"Makes us sound like elves," the one with the shaved head said with a laugh.

"No one would ever mistake you for an elf, Shane Boyd" Cathal said. "And that's your introduction sorted." He pointed to the redhead. "Michael Walsh." Still holding the lights, Walsh bowed. Max barked, then dipped down.

Macdara pointed at the dog. "Did he just bow?"

"He's fierce intelligent," Michael said. "Meet my wonder dog, Max."

"And I'm Bonnie Murphy." The one female of the group of young ones stepped onto the porch. She had gorgeous black hair cascading down her back in waves. She was probably six years younger than Siobhán. Bonnie flashed a million-dollar smile at Macdara and he blushed. Siobhán cocked her head, mostly surprised at the ripple of jealousy that went through her.

Macdara turned to Cathal. "Is there no security system on the grounds?" He glanced at the dog.

"He's not a guard dog," Michael said. "But I do believe he would have barked if he sensed a criminal around." He paused. "Unless they had biscuits. Then I'm afraid he would have let the Grinch himself rob everyone blind." He winked.

"Thanks for the tip," Siobhán said. She would have to buy some for Trigger, their Jack Russel terrier. He could use a little training.

"Right so," Finn said, looping his arm around Michael Walsh and nodding to Shane and Bonnie. "It's off to Casey's with us."

"Bill Casey?" Siobhán asked. He was the farmer hosting the tractor parade. Her brood would be there as well. Had they not been interrupted by this theft, she would have been there herself.

"Aye," Finn said. "The four of us are going to have the best-dressed tractor in Kilbane." Max barked. "Make that the five of us," Finn said, ruffling the dog's head. "Isn't that right, Max?" Max barked enthusiastically and everyone laughed. The foursome bounded off the porch, whooping and singing as they headed off the grounds. Max trotted along behind them.

"To be young again," the old man on the porch said as he watched them go.

Cathal removed his pocket square and dabbed around his mouth as if trying to prevent the wrong words from coming out. "Back to the security system," he said. "Someone shut down the main panel." He gestured for them to come closer, then opened the front door and ushered them in.

The first thing that struck Siobhán when she stepped inside, was that it really did look like a proper home. The floors matched the lovely dark wood in the front door, as well as the moldings and the rails of a curved stairway just past the foyer. Parlor doors flanked the left and the right sides, and both were thrown open. A cozy sitting room was situated to their right, and a grand library with a crackling fireplace to the left. A pair of binoculars sat on a coffee table in the library room. Siobhán could imagine how lovely it would be to sit by a cozy fire and gaze out the large windows with the binoculars. She was starting to think the golden years were the ones for her. Cardboard boxes were stacked everywhere you looked. Writing in thick black marker gave away their contents: XMAS DECO-RATIONS.

Cathal closed the door and pointed to an electronic panel on the wall. "Yesterday morning before we left for the market, this security panel was working fine. When the thefts were reported, I ran to check it, and it was turned off. As you can see it's back on now, but the security company confirmed that it was off for twenty-four hours."

"How many people know the security code?" Macdara asked.

"All of the employees." Cathal bowed his head. "I know you'll have to investigate everyone but in my opinion, not a single one of my employees would ever be involved in something so heinous."

"What about the windows?" Macdara said, stepping into the library and approaching the panes. "Do they open from the outside?" He gave a little tug. They did not open.

"We seal them shut in the winter," Cathal said. "Otherwise it gets too drafty."

Macdara nodded. "Is it possible our thief had a key to the house?"

Siobhán wandered over to the table and picked up the binoculars. Heavy curtains obscured most of the windows so she put them down again. She turned and stared across the way at the security panel. Had this been an inside job?

Cathal chewed on his lip. "I'm afraid it is possible. We usually change the locks after a resident leaves. But it's been a very chaotic year with a lot of changeover and I've been waiting for a locksmith. Everyone is busy these days, it's taking forever."

"As soon as we're done having a nose about, I'll call a locksmith for you," Macdara said. "If you didn't need the locks changed then, you certainly do now." He stepped closer to the front door and carefully examined the edges and the lock. "No signs of distress." He turned to Cathal. "What is the usual procedure for visitors to gain entrance?"

"You ring the bell," Cathal said, stepping back onto the porch and pointing to a buzzer to the right. "One of the staff will greet you and sign you in."

"Were there any visitors during the break-in?"

"I'm afraid you'll have to check with Nancy. She keeps the visitor log."

"What about other types of visitors?" Siobhán asked. "Deliverymen and the like?"

"They're not required to sign in," Cathal said. "But we do have a security camera." He dropped his hand. "Unfortunately, it only works if the panel is powered on and I've already mentioned someone had turned it off."

"We'll need to look at your visitor log for the entire week leading up to the theft," Macdara said as they all stepped back inside.

Cathal nodded. "As I said, Nancy Martin keeps track of all that."

"Guards are on their way to dust for fingerprints," Macdara said. "Let's make sure that lovely lady with the red bow gets a demonstration."

"That's Sinead," Cathal said with a nod and a smile.

Siobhán looped her arm through Macdara's. "That is very giving of you, Santy," she whispered.

He winked. "You can thank me later, Mrs. Claus."

She gently pushed him off. "I'm way too young to be Mrs. Claus."

Cathal glanced at his watch as if wondering how long all this banter was going to take. Siobhán stepped away from Macdara and straightened her spine. "Shall I show you why I said that nothing has been disturbed *per se?*" Cathal asked.

He headed down the hall and they followed. He passed a grand kitchen filled with people in white aprons rolling out dough. The scent of sugar wafted out. "They're making Christmas biscuits," he said. "To die for." A few of the bakers waved and Siobhán waved back.

A woman pushing a cleaning cart blocked their path. Her dark hair was ensconced in a white headband, salt-and-pepper tendrils spilling out of it. "Christmas biscuits, bah humbug!" She thrust her index finger into the air. "Did you not hear me say that ever since this Christmas biscuit craze started up, I've seen ants in the residents' rooms?" she said. "Ants!"

"The residents know not to eat in their rooms, Mrs. Grady," Cathal said.

The woman shook her head. "Well, they're still doing it. I've found ants in several rooms, carrying crumbs back to their queen!"

"It is Christmas," Macdara quipped. "Even the ants are

getting into the spirit." Mrs. Grady gave him a withering look. "Horrible," he said. "Ants are a horrible, horrible nuisance."

She nodded and let out a puff of air, disturbing a tendril of hair, making it fly up. "They certainly are."

"I'll have another word with the residents," Cathal said.

"You do that," she said. "I'm a housekeeper not an exterminator." She shoved the cart forward, muttering as she left.

"Here we are," Cathal said, stopping at the last room on the floor. "This is the recreational room—the main place where our residents come to relax, play games, watch telly." It was a generous room with plush sofas, a large television mounted to the wall, comfy chairs, and tables—but they were all pushed back against the walls, leaving the middle wide open. "This is why I said *per se*. When we left for the market, this room was set up as per normal—nothing was pushed against the walls. At first I thought it was Mrs. Grady, that she wanted to vacuum the center of the room—although I thought it was quite puzzling—I couldn't imagine her moving all this furniture on her own. And when I brought her to the room to show her—she was furious. She insists she didn't leave it like this and I believe her."

It was very odd indeed. What kind of thief would take time out to shove all the furniture to the back of a room?

"It's befuddling," Cathal said. "We leave for a few hours to do some Christmas shopping and the whole place goes mad!" They returned to the foyer. Cathal pointed to the formal sitting room on the right. "I'll go find Nancy. Please have a seat."

Siobhán and Macdara waited in the sitting room, listening to the sound of the cuckoo clock ticking precious minutes away. It felt like an eternity before they heard the sound of heels clacking on the floorboards. Moments later a smiling woman with chestnut hair and a flowery dress appeared. "I'm Nancy Martin," she said, extending her hand as Siobhán and Macdara stood. "Welcome to the Kilbane Elder Care Home." She was a beautiful woman with light brown eyes and a generous smile.

They shook hands and introduced themselves. Cathal Ryan popped up behind her. His hair was mussed up and there was red lipstick next to his mouth. Macdara and Siobhán exchanged a quick look, then composed themselves. Were the two having an elicit work affair? Nancy gestured for them to sit again. "Shall we?" The moment they sat a young woman in an apron and a sunny grin entered with a golden tray. On it perched two cups of tea and a generous plate of Christmas biscuits. She set them on the coffee table. Sugar cookies with colorful icing, they were in adorable shapes: trees, Santy, and reindeer.

"That's so kind of you," Siobhán said. "You shouldn't have." Macdara already had half a Santy stuffed in his gob. He finished two more before the group of five came in, insisting it would be rude not to sample one of each. Introductions were formally made: Nuala, Rory, Beverly, and Sinead. Oscar, the man who looked like an adorable owl, was the last to enter, slamming his walker down with each step.

"I. Want. My. Cane." He spit out the words, accentuating it with a *thunk* of the walker hitting the floor. "It was from my pilgrimage in Spain. It was a gorgeous dark wood with a golden head. When you find the thieves and our stolen property, I'm going to take me cane and beat them over the head with it."

"There's no need for any of you to take matters into your own hands," Nancy said. "The guards are here to sort that all out."

Cathal patted the pockets of his blazer. "My keys," he said. "Has anyone seen my keys?"

"I completely forgot," Nancy said. "The morning chef mentioned finding a set of keys in the kitchen this morning."

"I'll go speak with him."

Nancy grimaced. "I'm afraid he's gone for the day."

"What?" Cathal's voice flashed with anger. "Where did he leave my keys?"

"I can't say for sure they were yours," Nancy said. "I didn't get a good look at them."

Cathal raised an eyebrow. "Who else is missing keys?"

"You're right, of course," Nancy said. "They must be yours. Everything happened so quickly—the chef mentioned the keys and then one by one residents discovered their items missing. I completely forgot. I'm sorry."

Cathal straightened up and he seemed to be wrestling with his response. "You'll have to be a bit more organized when you're the mayor's wife," he said with a wry smile.

Nancy frowned for a moment and then laughed. "Don't tell me husband. He's a nervous wreck as it is."

"Do your missing keys include your car keys?" Siobhán said.

"Yes," Cathal said. "Why do you ask?"

Macdara nudged forward. "Where do you park your car?"

Cathal's eyes widened. "Are you saying my car might have been stolen? A getaway car?"

"Did you drive it to the market this morning?" Macdara asked.

Cathal shook his head. "No. We had a rental bus."

"Let's see if we can find the keys first," Nancy said. "Then look for your car."

"I'll check with the kitchen staff," Cathal said.

"I'll help." Nancy turned to Siobhán and Macdara. "You'll be alright on your own?"

"They've got us," Beverly said. "What do you think we're going to do? Bite them?"

Oscar eyed the dwindling plate of biscuits. "Are you sure they're here to help?" he asked.

Macdara slouched in his chair; Siobhán knew he'd been poised to go in for a fourth. Nancy and Cathal exited the room and the residents began to gab. And gab. And gab. And gab. She glanced at the clock on the wall. Nearly an hour and a half had passed, and although Siobhán and Macdara's heads were now filled with stories of their children and grandchildren, and days of yore, they were getting nowhere. She assumed Cathal had found his keys and his car, for he had completely disappeared. She felt for these folks, they were dying for a bit of company, and this was an exciting day. But she was itching to get out of here. Perhaps she wasn't quite ready for her golden years after all.

"It's been lovely chatting," Siobhán said. "But we must focus on the case now."

"Absolutely," Macdara said. The relief in his voice was palpable. He too had been having a hard time cutting them off or getting the residents to focus, and the plate of cookies had been reduced to crumbs.

"I don't know what you're doing here," Nuala said to Beverly. Siobhán recognized Beverly as the plump woman in the flowery house coat, the one who had shown them the photo of the uber-long scarf. "All you had stolen was an ugly scarf."

Beverly gasped. "It was not ugly. It was handmade."

Nuala rolled her eyes. "Obviously the thief didn't think it was ugly, now did he?"

Before Siobhán and Macdara could put a stop to it, four residents were once again yelling over top of each other. Sinead sat quietly, working her rosary beads. Suddenly, "Silent Night" blared through the room. *Ironic.*

All heads turned to Nancy, who was planted next to the stereo. When she had their attention, she turned the volume down. "Now," she said. "You're behaving like spoiled children. The guards need to file their report and they don't have all day." Apologies went around the room.

"Did you find Cathal's keys?" Siobhán ask.

Nancy nodded. "The housekeeper had them."

"And his car?" Macdara said.

"Safe and sound."

That was a relief. But Nancy and Cathel had been gone an awfully long time. Siobhán was starting to wonder if the missing keys was a ruse, an excuse to be alone. It was risky to get romantically involved with work partners. Then again, given she and Macdara worked together, she was one to talk. However, Nancy was married. To a possible future mayor, no less. An affair wouldn't just be messy, it would be reckless. Hopefully there was nothing going on between her and Cathal. It was the nature of her job that made Siobhán suspicious of everything. She had to be careful not to jump to conclusions. "We just need each of you to write down the items that were stolen from you, and anything else you can remember from the time of the theft."

"You want us to write all of that?" Oscar held up a gnarled hand.

"We can write it for you," Siobhán said. "We'll be setting up individual interviews."

From somewhere in the room a phone rang, making them all jump. It was Nancy's. She moved into the foyer as she answered. Siobhán could still hear her talking. "Yes. Who? Oh, yes. Yes, they're still here. What? My word!" When Nancy returned to the room her face was a portrait of a woman about to panic.

"That was Bill Casey—"

Macdara stood. "From the tractor parade?"

Nancy nodded. "The tractors were on a dry run for the parade, and there's been a terrible, terrible accident!"

Chapter Three

It was not something they saw every day, an entire country road lined with tractors in all shapes, sizes, and colors at a complete standstill. A few sported the beginnings of Christmas decorations, lights, bows, and garland, but most of them had not yet been adorned. There were twenty tractors in all. The tragedy became evident when they reached the fifth tractor in line, a green and yellow John Deere. A man was lying on the road directly behind the tractor. Lying on his back, his head was tilted at an unnatural angle. A red scarf with green shamrocks was wound around his neck, the end disappearing into the wheel well. Witnesses said he had been lifted off the tractor and slammed down onto the road. The scarf must have become entangled with the wheel. The victim had spikey red hair. "It's Michael Walsh," Macdara said.

"Michael Walsh," Siobhán repeated. Sorrow gripped her as she stared at his red fringe. No matter how many times she'd seen death, it always jarred her. Just hours ago this lad had been on the front porch of the elder care home, messing around with his friends and introducing them to his dog. Siobhán edged forward and stared at the scarf as a refrain ran through her mind. *Long scarf syndrome.* She recognized the scarf immediately. Long enough for a giraffe, as hideous in person as it was in the photo. "It's Beverly's stolen scarf," she said.

Macdara stared at the scarf, then at their victim. "Do you think he's our thief?"

"I don't know. Why would he flaunt the stolen scarf when he knows we're on the case?"

"Perhaps he liked the danger," Macdara said. "Or he had little faith in our detecting skills."

"We'll find out soon enough. At least Jeanie is in town." They'd already placed a call to Doctor Brady and she was on her way.

A burly man approached, covered in layers of flannel, sporting a tweed cap and handlebar mustache. His eyes were red, and he was still trying to wipe tears off his face with the back of his hand. When he composed himself, he wiped his hand on his trousers and stuck it out. "I'm Bill Casey."

Macdara shook hands and introduced them.

"Mr. Casey," Siobhán said. "You're the host of this year's tractor parade."

"Call me Bill. Indeed, Garda. And before you begin your investigation there's something you need to know."

"Go on," Macdara said.

"He wasn't wearing that scarf this morning, or when we started on the route."

"You mean he put it on during the ride?" Siobhán asked.

"I don't see where he would have put it," Bill said. "You can see his coat isn't that bulky."

They all looked down at his coat. He was right. It was a mere jacket. "You're sure he didn't have it tucked inside and you just didn't notice?" Macdara asked.

Bill shook his head. "I've been doing this tractor run for years. I always warn them about any loose bits of clothing, especially scarves. I definitely would have noticed."

"What are you saying?" Siobhán said. "He obviously had the scarf stashed somewhere."

Bill Casey nodded. "That's the other troubling bit to the story. We'd just begun the practice route when a blue Toyota came flying past, driving on the field. They screeched to a halt in front of yer man, here." He gestured to the victim. "The driver exited the vehicle, and others could see them head-to-head having a chat. After a minute, the driver got back into the car. It was after that yer man was wearing the scarf. The car screeched away and your one started his tractor. And then . . ." He slapped his hand over his eye. "I'm lucky I was in the front and didn't have to see it. The ones who were directly behind him are in shock. The minute he moved the tractor forward, he was yanked out of his seat, flipped into the air, and landed behind the tractor. The only saving grace is that he went quick."

Siobhán crossed herself. "Was it a man or a woman who got out of the car?"

"That's another odd thing," Mr. Casey said. "We don't know."

"Pardon?" Siobhán tilted her head.

"The person was dressed in costume. I thought it was one of the panto actors. But usually those costumes are colorful fairy-tale creatures and whatnot. This person was head to toe in a long brown robe, like a monk. His or her face was completely obscured by a brown hood."

"Tall or short?" Macdara said.

"Medium," Casey said. "Or was he short? I don't know. I didn't see him myself. The fella behind Michael just said he saw a brown hooded robe. It happened so fast."

"This person got out of the car, approached our victim, and chatted for a moment?" Siobhán asked. She was trying to picture it.

Casey nodded. "And we believe this pretend-monk placed the scarf around his neck."

Michael Walsh must have known the person. If a total stranger tried to place a long ugly scarf around her neck, she certainly wouldn't have worn it. And Michael Walsh knew all about Beverly's stolen scarf, she'd been showing pictures of it to everyone who would look. Why on earth would he flaunt it in the tractor parade?

Siobhán turned to Macdara. "Did you hear one of the residents say something this morning about long scarf syndrome?"

"I certainly did," Macdara said. "And I know you do not like coincidences."

"I do not like coincidences," Siobhán confirmed. Not a bit.

"I'm lost," Bill Casey said.

"This scarf was made by a resident of the Kilbane Elder Care Home," Macdara said. "It was reported as stolen."

"Everyone was talking about how long and dangerous it was," Siobhán said.

Bill Casey shuddered. "It's bad enough if this was a terrible accident. But if it was deliberate?" He shook his head. "Who would do such a thing? A fortnight before Christmas?"

Siobhán and Macdara remained silent. It was a question that had a depressing answer. Nearly everyone, given the right circumstances, was capable of doing such a horrible thing.

"We'll need to talk to the drivers of the tractor directly behind and in front of Michael Walsh to see exactly what they observed," Macdara said.

Casey nodded, then pointed to a cluster of folks up ahead in the field. "They're all there. Everyone is in shock."

"I'd never met Michael Walsh before this morning," Macdara said. "Was he new in town?"

"Visiting from Monaghan, I believe," Bill said. "Shane Boyd and Finn Doyle invited him."

"Were they friends?" Siobhán asked.

Bill shook his head. "I asked the group to nominate someone as our special guest this year. Every year we have a guest tractor for the parade. They read about his wonder dog, Max, in the local paper and contacted him. He seemed thrilled with the idea. And that dog is something else."

"Where is the dog?" Siobhán asked.

"He's riding in my tractor at the head of the parade," Bill said. "I have an enclosed cab; we felt it was the safest place for him." He bowed his head. "A dog that smart? He's going to know his owner is gone."

They paused for a moment of silence.

Shane and Finn. All three of them had been at the elder care home. Did this have anything to do with the theft? Were the three unwise-men in it together? Had this murder been a long time in the making? Why would they want him dead? Was he threatening to tell on the others or trying to claim a bigger share of the stolen goods?

"To tell you the truth, I should have told him he couldn't participate," Bill said. "I should have trusted my gut."

Macdara edged forward. "What did your gut say?"

"Michael took the tractor for a joy ride yesterday and ran over my neighbor's hedges. Me neighbor was livid." Bill shook his head. "He was a bit too cheeky and impulsive. I should have disqualified him."

"What is the name of this neighbor?" Macdara asked.

Casey looked startled. "I don't think he wants his name dragged into this mess."

"I'm afraid he won't have a choice in the matter," Macdara said.

"Cathal Ryan," Bill said.

"The elder home director?" Siobhán asked.

"The one and the same," Casey said.

"Odd. He didn't mention it and we were standing on the same porch with Michael."

"I'm telling ye, he was quite livid. He threatened the lad." Casey looked stricken. "I don't mean he threatened to do anything like *this*. He just warned him that if he did it again he'd answer for it. Michael enjoyed trouble. You could see it in his eyes." He stopped then shook his head. "I'm not saying he deserved it. He was just a young lad with a troubled past. He could have sorted himself out. 'Tis a terrible, terrible day."

"A troubled past?" Macdara asked.

Bill nodded. "Apparently, he'd been released from jail a year prior."

"Jail?" Macdara said.

"Some trouble after a breakup. A bit of stalking, I believe," Casey said. "The type of lad that when he becomes fixated on something or someone, he just can't let go. At least that's what I heard."

"Hold on," Macdara said. "With that kind of past he was allowed to volunteer at the elder care home and be a special guest for your parade?"

"I swear to ye, I had no idea he was volunteering at the elder care home," Bill said. "But even so—he was supposed to have turned over a new leaf. There was a whole article on him in the newspaper. The jail he was in paired lads with homeless dogs, so they could rehabilitate each other, like. Yer one's dog turned out to be brilliant. Walsh was featured for teaching the dog over a thousand words. Can you believe that?"

"A thousand," Siobhán said. She turned to Macdara. "How many words do you think Trigger knows?"

Macdara gave her a look and turned his attention back to Bill Casey. "Listen," he said. "We have to cordon off this scene. I want the tractor in front of Michael's and behind Michael's to remain where they are. But we'll need the other tractors to disperse. The ones in the front should continue straight ahead, and the ones in the back should turn and exit in the other direction. Even if they have to take the long way back to your farm."

"Does this mean the tractor parade is off?" Bill looked sheepish, but there was concern in his voice. "All the money we collect goes to local charities. It's been a tough year for a lot of folks and they're really counting on us."

"Let's take it one step at a time," Siobhán said.

"Such terrible business," Bill said. "I don't know how I'm going to break the news to his family. They had such high hopes that he was really turning his life around."

"We'll contact his family," Siobhán said. "But I'm sure they'll need and appreciate your support."

"And we're going to need everyone to write down their account of the car that stopped," Macdara said. "Any detail, no matter how small."

"Absolutely. We'll go back to the farm and do it."

"There are no CCTV cameras in this area," Macdara continued. "But check to see if anyone happened to be using their mobile phone during the route—maybe someone got a photo of the number plate, or even better a shot of the person who got out of the car."

"They weren't supposed to be on their phones whilst driving the tractor," Casey said.

"We all know people don't always follow direction," Siobhán said. "Let's hope that's the case with their phones."

Understanding dawned in Casey's eyes. "Right, right. George Halligan was the fella in the tractor behind Michael. I did give him my permission to keep his phone on him. He's expecting his firstborn any day now. He texts with the wife nonstop."

Macdara nodded and jotted down the name. "Did everyone show up this morning for the practice run?

Casey shook his head. "All but three."

"And who were they?" Macdara asked.

Bill Casey was ready for the question. "Finn Doyle, Shane Boyd, and Bonnie Murphy," he said. "They were supposed to be on Michael's team but they never showed up."

Chapter Four

Finn Doyle, Shane Boyd, and Bonnie Murphy.
Macdara's face did not show his surprise and Siobhán did her best to hide hers. At the elder care home Finn had announced he was going to the tractor-parade rehearsal and the foursome had exuberantly left together. If Michael was the only one who participated, where had the other three gone? But maybe the better, and more troubling question, was—*why*?

Macdara gave a nod to Bill Casey. "Have the lads to clear out now."

"What about Max?" Bill asked.

"Can you mind him for now?" Siobhán asked. "I'm sure Michael's family will want to take him home."

"Of course." He gave a shy smile. "He's a great dog." Casey called out instructions to the tractors and soon all but the one in the front and the back of the tractor Michael had been operating were pulling away from the scene. Garda cars had arrived, the road was being blocked off, and a cordon was set up around the body.

"Here's Doctor Brady now," Macdara said, nodding as she emerged from a guard car.

"Greetings," Jeanie Brady said. Her eyes landed on the

body. "This wasn't what I had in mind when ye invited me to Kilbane for me Christmas holidays."

They all exchanged a wry smile; humor was a healthy way of dealing with the horror of murder probes. Jeanie Brady was looking fit and slim. Normally a mad one for pistachios, she had adopted a "clean eating" lifestyle and was no longer tempted by the nibbly things in life. Her curly brown hair had been cut short, accentuating her cheekbones. She may have lost several stone but she still had the same vibrant personality, and wicked determination when it came to her work. Siobhán had no idea what to buy her for Christmas, for her original plan, a lovely scarf, was now completely out of the question.

"What do we have here?" Jeanie approached the body and knelt. Siobhán and Macdara stayed at the edge of the road and remained silent. Having worked with Jeanie Brady for years they knew it was a rhetorical question. She took her time studying the scene, then shook her head and crossed herself. She gestured them over. "My exam will need to confirm it, but he appears to have broken his neck. At least his passing was relatively quick. Why on earth was he wearing a scarf this long?"

"It gets stranger," Siobhán said. She filled Jeanie in on their visit to the elder care home, the thefts, the discussion of long scarf syndrome, Bill Casey vowing that Michael was not wearing a scarf when they started the procession, and the monk-costumed stranger that pulled alongside him in a car.

"That does make for a very strange day indeed," Jeanie said. "Long scarf syndrome is no joke. The most famous case being that of Isadora Duncan."

"I'm not familiar with the case," Macdara said. "Was it one of yours?"

Jeanie Brady threw her head back and laughed. When she composed herself, she wagged her finger at Macdara. "Are you joking me?"

Macdara shifted uncomfortably. "I want to say yes. But . . . no."

"You're too young, although that's no excuse for not educating yourself." Jeanie gave him a stern look before winking at Siobhán.

Siobhán laughed along with her. Macdara poked her in the side. "An expert on Isadora Duncan, are ya?"

"Not quite an expert," Siobhán said. She turned to Jeanie. "Why don't you give us a refresher."

Macdara tapped Siobhán on the shoulder. "You could always start us off. I'm sure Doctor Brady will forgive you for being 'not quite an expert.' "

"Now," Siobhán said, "I wouldn't want to steal Jeanie's thunder."

Jeanie stepped back in. "She was an American dancer. The tragedy occurred in Paris, in September of 1927—"

"Hold on," Macdara said. "You expected me to be familiar with a case in Paris from 1927?"

"She was quite famous," Jeanie said. "Talented, and some say ahead of her time."

"Go on," Siobhán said. "I want to hear the story."

Jeanie glanced at Macdara as if to see if he had anything to add. He kept his gob shut. "She was in Nice, France, visiting a friend who was a mechanic and some say a paramour. She wore a long handprinted silk scarf made by a Russian artist and given to her by another friend, Mary Desti. It was a cold night and just before they departed Mary tried to convince Isadora to wear a cape to keep warm. Isadora refused but said she would wear the scarf instead. Her last words were: 'Goodbye. I am off to love!' When the scarf became entangled in the axle of the motor vehicle she was traveling in, she was yanked from the car. Like our poor fella here, she broke her neck and was killed instantly."

"My word," Siobhán said, gently touching her neck. "I may never wear a scarf again."

"One does need to be careful," Jeanie said. She turned her attention back to the body. "Because of the length of this particular scarf, our victim here wouldn't have felt the tug on his neck until it was firmly ensconced in the wheel and it was too late. By then it was enough to lift him out of his seat and deposit him on the road." She shook her head. "It's a very sad day indeed." They all bowed their heads for a moment, honoring the gravity of the moment. "But we have a job to do, don't we?" Jeanie said. She looked deep into the wheel well. "I'm telling you right now, strange visitor aside, I don't see any way to prove this was anything other than a horrible accident. Even if someone admitted to handing him the scarf, it's not murder unless they also admit to depositing the end of the scarf into the wheel well of the tractor." She turned to the wheel well and peered down into it. "Although . . . given the apparent length of the scarf, it could have been done easily and quickly." She sighed. "If this was foul play, it was very clever indeed."

"A perfect murder," Siobhán said.

Jeanie nodded. "Without a witness, there's no way for me to prove it." She turned to look at the tractor behind Michael's. "How did the fella on the tractor behind him not see anything?"

"According to Bill Casey, his wife is expecting a baby

and apparently, he's been glued to his phone," Macdara explained.

"You'd think if a car stops and a monk gets out, that would catch your attention," Jeanie said. "Can we speak with him now? See what he witnessed?"

"Let's do it," Macdara said. He pointed up ahead where a small cluster of people remained. "We asked him to stay behind, let's hope he listened." They headed up the road toward the group.

"I'm so sorry to interrupt your holidays," Siobhán said. She'd meant for this Christmas to be special, a celebration.

Jeanie waved her hand as if it was nothing. "Yours are interrupted too and I still have an invitation to Christmas dinner, do I not?"

"You certainly do," Macdara said.

"You'd better catch this killer then," Jeanie said. "I intend to break me diet for Christmas Day."

"But you said there's no way to prove this was anything other than an accident," Siobhán said.

Jeanie held a hand up. "I said there's no way for my postmortem to prove it. What you need is a full confession from a killer."

"Is that all?" Siobhán said. Macdara patted her on the back.

"It's the least we can do now for the poor lad," Jeanie said. "Is he a local?"

Siobhán shook her head. "He's from Monaghan."

"He's an ex-stalker with a famous dog," Macdara added. "Max."

"Ex-stalker?" Jeanie said.

"Apologies," Macdara said. "That's not confirmed. Bill mentioned he'd been brought up on past charges for not leaving an ex alone. Rumor is he often had unhealthy fixations. Then Max came along and it gave him something productive to concentrate on. He was turning his life around."

"Max supposedly knows over a thousand words," Siobhán said. "That's a few more than me husband." She gently shoved Macdara as he laughed.

They reached the huddled group. "George Halligan?" Macdara called. The shortest man in the group turned. He was in his early thirties with a thick dark fringe feathered back.

"That's me."

"We'd like to speak with you for a moment," Macdara said.

"Can you join us back at the scene?" Jeanie added. "I'd like to do a reenactment."

"Not a bother." George headed back with them to the tractors. "I wish I could have done something. It happened so fast. I'm still in shock."

"That's understandable," Siobhán said. "Take a deep breath."

They reached the scene of the accident. The body was now covered, but from the look on George's face, he was still reliving every bit of it.

"This is Doctor Brady, the state pathologist, and I'm Detective Sergeant Flannery, along with Garda O'Sullivan."

The man nodded. "George Halligan."

"We hear you're expecting a baby any day now," Siobhán said. "Congratulations."

"Thank you. It's our first. My wife and I are over the moon."

"Can you please take us through the events leading up to the incident?" Jeanie said.

George motioned to his tractor. "Michael seemed to be enjoying himself. Looking around with a grin on his face. I saw him on his phone a few times too, taking selfies."

"Phone," the professionals all said at once.

Jeanie knelt next to the body again. She turned to George. "You might want to turn away." He gulped and did just that. "Shall we have a look through his pockets?" Jeanie removed gloves from her pockets, slipped them on and did a quick search. She produced a wad of euro tightened by a rubber band, a key, and a receipt. "It looks as if he was staying at the Twins' Inn," Jeanie said, dangling the key. "There's no phone."

"Could it be on the tractor?" Macdara approached the John Deere. There was nothing on the seat, or the floor of the tractor. He got on the ground and looked underneath. "No phone here either."

"He definitely had one," George said. "I wanted to tell him to pay more attention, but given I was using my phone, I kept me gob shut."

Siobhán removed her notebook from her pocket. *Phone. Selfies. Did the Monk take it?* Macdara glanced at her note and nodded.

"If there's something incriminating on that phone it could help us prove this wasn't an accident," Jeanie said.

"I wish I'd been paying more attention, but me wife texted me just as the blue Toyota pulled up."

"Can you pretend to be the person in the car?" Macdara said. He climbed onto George's tractor. "I want to see what you saw."

George nodded. He stood by the side of Michael's tractor. "The car pulled up here. Michael stopped his tractor. Lucky I was going slow or I would have crashed into him. I was on the phone, then of course I saw the car, and looked up. The person left the car running, but it must

have been in park. He got out, and stood right here."
George positioned himself at the back wheel of the tractor.

"That exact spot?" Macdara asked. "Are you sure?"
George nodded. "My view of the wheel well is now
blocked," Macdara said. "If our monk slipped the end of
the scarf into the wheel well, George wouldn't have noticed."

"Did you see the monk hand Michael a scarf?"

George dropped his head. "My wife texted again—she
thought she was having contractions. I was absorbed in
me phone again. Next thing I know, the monk is getting
back into the car, and Michael is taking off again. I noticed the scarf at the same time as Michael was airborne."
He shuddered. "But I tell you one thing. That car screeched
away incredibly fast. It was as if they knew what was
going to happen."

"Thank you," Macdara said. "I don't suppose you got
any of the number plate?"

"I wish I had. It was a blue Toyota Corolla. Looked like
a newer model."

Macdara jotted that down right away. It was a common
enough car, but it did help narrow down the field.

"Any sense of whether it was a man or a woman?"
Siobhán asked.

George shook his head. "I figured it was a man, but the
robe was oversized. It could have been a woman."

"Did you hear any of their exchange?" Siobhán asked.

"I'm afraid not. When you have twenty tractor engines
running, you can't hear a thing." He frowned. "Wait," he
said. "I could hear a radio. Head-banging music. Heavy
metal. He or she was blasting it." He paused. "Even if the
tractors weren't running I might not have been able to
catch much of the conversation."

That was helpful. Which one of their suspects liked

head-banging music? Or had someone chosen it with the intention of drowning out his or her voice? This was a small village; George may have been able to identify the person if he'd been able to hear the monk speak. It was likely that this one had never taken a vow of silence.

"Thank you," Macdara said. "We'll need you to come into the station to get your account down in writing."

George nodded. "I'm sorry I wasn't more helpful." He held up his mobile phone. "Do you mind if I get home now?"

"Go be with your wife," Macdara said. "Happy Christmas and all the best with the baby." They fell silent as they watched him go. Macdara turned to Jeanie. "Thoughts?"

"It would be helpful testimony," Jeanie said. "The fact that the monk screeched away and afterward there was suddenly a scarf around our victim's neck is compelling. But it's still circumstantial. I'm pretty sure the DPP would need a lot more evidence." The Director of Public Prosecutions was the governing body who decided which cases to take to trial. Understandably, they wanted rock-solid cases. "But let me see what my examination finds, and if we're lucky maybe we'll find a stray hair or DNA on the scarf."

Siobhán pointed to the key still in Jeanie's hand. "At least we know where to look next," she said. "The Twins' Inn." Inwardly, she groaned. They wouldn't need that exact key to get into Michael's room; the proprietors of the inn could give them access. But a judge would have to sign off on a warrant first. Another delay and yet another person whose Christmas holiday they had to interrupt with tragic news.

"One of the care home residents had five hundred euro in cash stolen," Macdara said, gesturing to the roll of money also in Jeanie's hand. "I'd be interested to know the amount he's got there."

"I'll process everything as quickly as possible," Jeanie said. "Do either of you have an evidence bag handy?"

Macdara retrieved one and Jeanie dumped the contents into it. Doctor Jeanie Brady nodded her thanks. "I'll get back to you as soon as I finish the postmortem."

Chapter Five

Once the body was removed and taken to the morgue at Cork University Hospital, the tech team arrived and got to work. They took extensive photos of the scene, but apart from partial tire tracks of the mysterious blue Toyota Corolla, there was very little to go on. A judge had been notified that they needed a warrant to enter the deceased's room at the Twins' Inn, and guards were assigned to interview all the tractor participants. At best they were hoping someone had caught some of the number plate off the car. By the time they received the warrant from the judge, the sun was starting to set over Kilbane. Siobhán took a moment to drink in the deep oranges and reds spreading across the sky. She took Macdara's hand in hers for a squeeze. The job was a constant reminder of how fragile and precious life was, that one needed to take time each day to appreciate the good things. And Macdara was one of the good things. He didn't even make a cheeky remark. He simply held her hand for a few minutes as they watched the sun sink into the horizon. And then it was back to work.

The Twins' Inn was run by identical twins, Emma and Eileen. They were petite and cheerful women in their thirties with curly golden hair. They rather enjoyed being twins, and often dressed alike. Today was no exception; they each sported an ugly Christmas jumper. Emma's featured a gingerbread man dancing a jig, and Eileen had Santy's legs dangling in the fireplace, as if the rest of him was stuck up the chimney. Siobhán stared at their jumpers, and couldn't help but see the long, ugly scarf. At least the jumpers weren't a death hazard. Siobhán turned back to gaze at the inn. The rooms were all arranged around a horseshoe configuration, and if decorating for Christmas was a contest, the twins had everyone beat. Colorful lights were strung along the top of the roof, and miniature potted trees with multicolored lights had been placed in front of every door along with a fat red bow. Candles shimmered in the window of the motel office, and the twins' cottage and back garden had been decorated with more lights, and trees, and mechanical reindeer.

The twins were gobsmacked that one of their guests had died. Although Siobhán and Macdara did not use the word *murder*, the town was already speculating about long scarf syndrome, the blue car, and the mysterious costumed monk. Macdara requested the CCTV footage from the inn for the length of Michael Walsh's stay. "What about poor Max?" Emma said.

"We loved Max," Eileen chimed in. "He fetched me slippers every morning."

"And the newspaper," Emma added. "And a few things we didn't ask him to."

"Currently Bill Casey is looking after him," Siobhán said. "It will be up to Michael's family what happens to him."

"Took us ages to realize he'd taken our welcome mat and dragged it to the back garden," Emma said. "Put it right in front of the reindeer like he was welcoming the pack!" The two laughed in unison.

"But we didn't mind. He's a wee dote!" Eileen said.

"We'll be sure to keep you posted." Siobhán was eager to process the room and get home for dinner and a bit of sleep.

The twins opened Michael's room and hurried off to gather the CCTV footage. Macdara and Siobhán suited up, including gloves and booties. It was a possible secondary crime scene and they wanted to err on the side of caution. The rooms were simple and cheerful even though it was apparent that a messy twenty-something lad and his dog had been staying there. His luggage bag yawned open at the foot of the bed, clothes waterfall-ing out of it as if trying to escape, trousers discarded on the floor. The end table next to the bed was equally cluttered: keys, a Stephen King novel, a pack of Winston cigarettes, a box of vanilla dog biscuits, and multiple packets of Solpadeine—the fizzy kind that you dissolve in water. Most of the packets were empty. Solpadeine was a popular hangover cure, but one had to be careful as they contained codeine and could be addictive. Chemists had begun paying attention to purchases, and one could not buy a pack these days without being questioned and warned of the addictive nature they posed. "We'll need to visit the chemist," Siobhán said. "See if he bought the Solpadeine here."

They did a quick search of the room, but there was nothing out of the ordinary. "I half hoped our stolen items would be here," Macdara said.

"Me too," Siobhán said. "That would have wrapped one case up with a neat little bow."

Macdara returned to the end table and studied it. "He likes his drink, but can't deal with the hangovers."

Siohban nodded. "If he was hungover, that may be the reason he wasn't paying attention to the end of the scarf," she said. Being actively drunk was dangerous enough, but often it was the next day when folks were accident-prone.

"I just can't figure out why he would let a strange man wrap a scarf around his neck," Macdara said as they stepped outside, eager to take off their suits, gloves, and booties. They tossed them in the nearest rubbish bin. The technical team was on its way, and it was a relief to get out of the room. They were having a mild start to winter so far, but Siobhán wrapped her coat around her, feeling a winter chill in her bones. "What if our killer knew that Michael was hungover and taking a massive amount of Solpadeine? Thus making him vulnerable to not paying close attention when he or she placed the scarf around his neck?"

"Especially if it was someone he trusted," Macdara said. He sighed. "It means our killer is a lot more cunning than I was giving him or her credit for."

"Are you convinced this is murder and not an accident?" Siobhán asked.

"I don't see any innocent reason why someone would disguise him- or herself as a monk, wrap a too-long scarf around the lad's neck while he's on a tractor, and screech away," Macdara said. "Do you?"

"No." Siobhán stared at the Christmas lights, trying to keep her spirits up. "But as Jeanie said, the burden is going to be on us to prove it."

Macdara put his arm around her. "The burden on us is to present the best evidence we can find. The rest will be out of our control."

Siobhán sighed. He was right. It was a maddening aspect of life that so much was out of one's control. They wandered away from the front door and gravitated toward the back garden. Siobhán continued to take comfort in all the twinkling lights and reindeer. Their mechanical heads bowed as if nibbling on grass, then lifted into the air, perhaps watching for Santy's sleigh in the distance. There was a pleasantness in the constant motion, and it calmed Siobhán as they sat in the gazebo awaiting the technical team. Moments later, Emma hurried out with a silver tray that she set on a table in front of them. On it were generous mugs of hot cocoa with little marshmallows, and delicate curled biscuits with a golden-brown sheen.

"Bless you, pet," Siobhán said. "Like a gift from the heavens."

"You're quite welcome," Emma said. "These are Irish Lace Biscuits. Baking is my favorite thing about Christmas. I have a booth at the market this year."

"After tasting these we'll be sure to stop by," Macdara said.

He was right. The Irish Lace Biscuits were light, crunchy, and heavenly, and the hot cocoa warmed Siobhán's insides. One could almost forget there was a possible murderer on the loose.

"We have the CCTV ready to review," Emma said. "Would you like to hear what we saw on the tapes?"

"Absolutely," Macdara said.

Siobhán half suspected he wanted more time with his cocoa and biscuits but given she did too, she didn't dare interrupt even to tease him.

Emma was eager to fill them in. "He had three young visitors this week. A blondie fella, a bald one, and a gorgeous young woman with black hair."

"Finn, Shane, and Bonnie," Siobhán said. "When were they here?"

"He checked in four days ago. They visited the day after his first full day. And nothing since." She handed Macdara a USB stick. "It's all on here. I've emailed you a link and password as well."

"Thanks a million," Siobhán said.

"Not a bother." Emma headed off with a smile.

"The four seem awfully close," Siobhán said. "What if we have a pack of thieves and one turned on the others?"

"That is a definite possibility," Macdara said. "And it will be to our advantage if true."

"How so?"

"It's hard enough for two people to keep a secret, let alone four."

Siobhán nodded. "And one of them is a very beautiful woman," Siobhán said. "What if Michael *didn't* let a man wrap the scarf around his neck? He allowed a beautiful woman to do it instead?"

Macdara frowned. "Interesting. But would he have recognized her dressed as a monk?"

"Not until she was right in front of him," Siobhán said. "He could have thought she was having a laugh."

"Or perhaps they were up to something, and he knew she would be in disguise," Macdara mused.

"It truly bothers me that the other three did not show up for the tractor run," Siobhán said. "We must speak with them as soon as possible."

Macdara set his empty plate and mug back on the tray with a sigh. "I agree, and I'm tempted to haul them into the station early tomorrow morning for a good grilling. But given what Doctor Brady said, that we need a full confession—I'm wondering if it's not more advantageous to proceed cautiously. Let them think we're investigating this as a terrible accident and keep an eye on what they do next."

The sound of cars pulling in lifted them from their seats,

and they headed back to the front of the inn. The technical team had arrived. Macdara spoke with them then turned to Siobhán. "There's nothing more we can do here this evening. Well, wife? Shall we head home?"

Home. Such a beautiful word. *Wife* was taking longer to get used to; every time he said it there was a moment when she wondered who he was on about. "We shall, husband." They headed for the car. "Wait," Siobhán said, coming to a halt. "Did you open the press in Michael's room?"

"I completely forgot," he said. "It seemed as if all his clothes were in his luggage bag. But we should still have a look." They pivoted, and made it to the room before the team had entered. Macdara asked them to hold up as they retrieved additional gloves and booties from the team, donned them, and were soon standing in front of the press. Macdara opened it. There was only a single item hanging on the rods. A long brown robe, like that of an old-fashioned monk.

Chapter Six

The next morning, Bill Casey's farm was bustling with activity. A large working farm, he had sheep, horses, and cows out in the fields, chickens wandering near the opening to the barn, and a large section of his garden that was filled with fresh-cut Christmas trees. Siobhán was looking forward to selecting one, but given they had important work in front of them, her siblings had promised to find a good one. The tractor participants were in shock but equally determined to honor Michael's passing. They asked if after the tractor was processed they could move it to the side of the road where the incident occurred, so that they, and anyone else in town who wished to do so, could decorate it with flowers, Mass cards, and other remembrances. Their request was quickly granted, and it was determined that the tractor parade could indeed follow the original route they had planned out. This way Michael's parked tractor would be honored once again, saluted as each tractor passed it by. In addition, all the monies collected for the parade would go to an animal shelter in Michael's hometown. Michael's family would be attending the tractor parade and remembrance.

Siobhán took a moment to join her siblings at their assigned John Deere. Ciarán was holding Trigger, who was dressed in a tiny Santa outfit, and from the snarl on his face, he wasn't quite getting into the spirit of it. Ciarán's boyish looks were fading, sixteen going on seventeen. Ann in her last year of school, was also nearly an adult, although Siobhán was having a difficult time thinking of any of them as grown and if she thought about it for too long it did her head in. Eoin was twenty-two, and Gráinne, twenty-three and in six months Siobhán would be thirty. How did time do this? Had it sped up when she wasn't looking? Gráinne, dressed in a sequined-green top and tulle skirt, was more decorated than the tractor. She was sitting in the driver's seat, barking orders to everyone below. James, the oldest at thirty-two, was stringing lights around it and testing the battery pack that would keep the lights blazing during the parade, while Ann and Eoin were placing garland around the front.

"We need reindeer," Gráinne said. "Pulling the tractor."

"Are ye just going to sit there like the Queen of the Tractor Parade?" James asked her.

Gráinne patted her head. "That's what I need," she said. "A crown." She pointed to Siobhán. "What about your wedding tiara?"

"No," Siobhán and Macdara said in unison.

Siobhán turned to Ciarán, taking a moment to scratch Trigger behind the ear. "How many words do you think Trigger knows?"

"Treat, brekkie, lunch, supper," Ciarán said. Trigger licked his face. "And Trigger."

"You should work on that," Siobhán said. "See if you can teach him a few more."

"He needs a job," Grainne said. "So he can be on telly."

"Why don't you lead by example," James said, swatting

her with a large plastic candy cane, "and start showing off your decorating skills?"

"I'm afraid this is where I leave you," Siobhán said as she looped an arm around Ann. "But it's a cracking tractor so far."

"It's class," Gráinne said with a grin.

"No thanks to you," James said. Eoin leapt up next to Gráinne and honked the horn, making her jump. Everyone laughed.

Ann picked up a pine garland and wrapped it around herself like a scarf. It took a moment of everyone staring at her open-mouthed before she gasped, and quickly threw it off. "I'm sorry, I'm sorry," she said. "I wasn't making fun."

Siobhán brought her sister in for a hug. "I know that, love," she said. "This is hard for all of us to process."

Siobhán kissed heads and cheeks and was about to leave when she felt a hand grip her arm. Gráinne leaned in and pointed across the field. It took Siohban a second to realize she was pointing at Finn Doyle, standing a few meters away, looking as morose as Trigger in a Santa cap.

"What can you tell me about that fella?" She had a flirtatious tone to her voice, obviously unaware of his connection to Michael Walsh.

"He's a suspect in our murder inquiry," Siobhán said.

James groaned. "Don't tell her that. She'll only want to marry him."

"You're one to talk," Gráinne said. "Your girlfriends should come with a temporary visitor's pass."

"Quit your squabbling, and the fella is off limits," Siobhán said. "Find a lad well outside of our murder probe."

"Murder?" Ann said. "Are you sure this wasn't a terrible accident?" Her siblings all stared at Siobhán, waiting for an answer.

"Please don't repeat any of this," Siobhán said. "We don't have all the answers yet. But be on the lookout for a blue Toyota, or anyone dressed as a monk."

James shook his head. "Happy Christmas," he said sarcastically.

Siobhán gave his arm a squeeze. "It will be. As long as everyone stays alert and cautious. And we really don't have any answers so it's best just to focus on trying to brighten everyone's spirits as best we can."

Gráinne fluttered her eyelashes. "Maybe I could chat him up and see what I can find out."

Ann and Eoin rolled their eyes in unison. "I have to jet," Siobhán said. "Would the rest of ye keep Gráinne otherwise occupied?"

"Buzzkills," Gráinne said, taking Trigger out of Ciarán's arms and lifting him into the air. "Now there's two words for you, Trig. *Buzz. Kills.*"

The Kilbane Players, a local theatre group situated in the town square, was in full-throttle rehearsal for the panto when Siobhán and Macdara finally arrived. They found Cara, the costume designer, in the basement of the theatre, a clipboard in her hand and a rack of Christmas costumes in front of her. Her honey-colored hair was piled loosely on top of her head held up with a pencil, and another one was tucked behind her ear. She took one look at the brown robe, now housed in clear plastic and marked with an evidence sticker. "Yes," she said. "It's ours. Did you only find one?"

Siobhán's ears perked up. "How many are you missing?"

"Two."

That was interesting. "When were they stolen?"

"I can't say for sure. They're not part of our current production and it was only yesterday I noticed they were missing."

"When were they used last?" Macdara asked.

"I believe they were from last year's Halloween party. I had planned on cutting up the brown fabric to patch up a malfunctioning reindeer costume." The panto this year was *Rudolph*.

"I'm afraid you won't be getting this back anytime soon," Macdara said. "It's part of an ongoing inquiry."

Her eyes grew wide and she patted her head, making sure the pencil was still holding. "Does this have anything to do with that poor lad on the tractor?"

"We can't say," Macdara said. "But can you show us where the monk costumes were stored?"

She gestured to the racks of clothing. "You're looking at it." She chewed on her lip. "Most likely they were taken from the town square."

Macdara stepped forward. "What's that now?"

"I took two racks of costumes out to the square when we were rehearsing. The Christmas market was just setting up and the square was chockablock. It would have been easy for someone to slip them off the rack."

"What day was this?" Siobhán asked.

"Saturday."

The same day that the residents had their outing to the market. *Premeditated?*

"Thank you. That's helpful," Macdara said. Although it meant a possible lead, it also meant more CCTV footage to pore through.

"Why don't we go to the town square and you can show us where you placed the costume rack?" Siobhán suggested. This way they could identify the closest CCTV cameras. And maybe the Christmas market would bring them a little cheer. Despite the case, this was still their first Christmas as husband and wife, and she wanted to savor it, even if it was just with a single mug of hot cocoa and a brief search for a sprig of mistletoe.

Siobhán and Macdara were meeting with their three young suspects this afternoon, and then they would return to the retirement home to follow up on conversations they had about long scarf syndrome. Siobhán couldn't shake the feeling that there was a direct relationship between the thefts and Michael's death. They were going to be very busy indeed, and Siobhán wasn't even including her usual Christmas errands. She had yet to buy gifts, or the turkey and ham for Christmas dinner. She knew her brood would be happy to pitch in; Eoin was the chef in the family and could handle dinner with ease, but she didn't want to miss out on a single thing. Garda Aretta Dabiri, a recent addition to the garda team and a top-notch organizer, would not be on hand to help them out or join them for the celebrations, and she was sorely missed. But she was on her holidays, hopefully enjoying herself in Dublin with her family.

Cara led them to the middle of the square where the Christmas market was in full swing. A chorus of excited voices filled the background and the scent of sugar and dough infused the crisp air. Although they might not get snow, the rain was also holding off, and there was a hint of sun beneath a thin layer of gray clouds, taking the edge off the winter bite. Costumed actors rehearsed *Rudolph* on a stage near them, and Christmas music played overhead. "I placed the rack of costumes here," she said, gesturing to the spot near the panto stage. "Yesterday and the day before." Siobhán scanned the area. They were in a central location; the thief could have approached from literally anywhere. Depending on how crowded it was when the robes were nicked, it was possible they wouldn't glean much from the CCTV cameras. And it was looking like they were going to have to pull footage from nearly every camera in every shop surrounding the square. Their to-do list was growing with each passing second. Suddenly, a nearby conversation became very loud as the voices of two little girls stole all the attention.

"Mam said no more candy!"

"Don't tell or I'll tell you what Santy is bringing you this year!"

"You don't know what Santy is bringing me!"

"I do so! It's socks! That's all you're getting is socks!" A loud wail followed the pronouncement.

A mother's voice soon joined in. "Girls! I can hear every word you just said."

Siobhán and Macdara exchanged a smile. They were near King John's Castle, a tower house with a passageway underneath which sat at the entrance to the town square. Most of the locals knew that when you stood at a certain spot in the passageway, your voice would amplify and everyone around would be able to hear you, even if you were whispering. It was nearly a right of passage that young ones found this out, sometimes in the most embarrassing of ways. The mother hurried out from beneath the passageway, holding two little hands as one continued to plead for confirmation that Santy was bringing her something more exciting this year than socks.

"Do you have children of your own?" Cara suddenly asked, interrupting the moment.

"No," Siobhán and Macdara said in stereo. From the look on Cara's face, perhaps they had sounded a bit too emphatic.

"We're newlyweds," Siobhán said. "And I have five siblings."

"That's child-minding sorted then isn't it?" Cara said. "Now."

"Have you had anyone from outside of your cast approach you lately?" Siobhán asked, avoiding the talk of all-things-babies. "Anyone from the elder care home or the tractor parade?"

"No," Cara said. "I've been completely absorbed with the production."

A pair of missing brown robes. It bolstered the theory that they were most likely looking at a pair of thieves. They thanked the costume designer and moved out of earshot. Macdara called in the request to pull CCTV from the shops surrounding the square. A live band was starting to set up near the bookshop Turn the Page, located at the corner of the square. The owners, Oran and Padraig, stood outside in thick wooly sweaters, clutching mugs and watching the hustle and bustle of the market. Books would make lovely Christmas gifts and Siobhán tucked the thought away for the near future.

"What do you say we get something delicious to eat and a mug of hot cocoa?" Siobhán said. "And then pay a visit to Bonnie's tent." There was another reason they found themselves in the town square today: They had learned that Bonnie Murphy would be working at one of the tents. It was the perfect opportunity to have an informal chat with her.

Macdara took her hand, and planted a kiss on it. "That's the best idea I've heard all day."

The tent for hot cocoa with or without Irish cream had an enormous line. But luckily it was run by Declan O'Rourke, a previous neighbor of the O'Sullivans, and Maria, one of Siobhán's best friends. She was a petite girl with a large personality. Her dark hair was streaked with red and green for the holidays and she wore a Santa cap with bells that jingled every time she moved her head. Maria caught Siobhán's eye in the crowd and gestured for her to cut the line. "Let the guards through," she commanded. "They're on duty. If anyone whinges about it, you won't be getting any cocoa from me!"

Declan, a hearty man with an even heartier disposition, threw his head back and roared with laughter. Siobhán and Macdara, slightly embarrassed, nodded and waved to the kind people who parted and let them move to the front of the line.

"If it isn't Herself and Himself," Declan said with a wink. "Happy Christmas."

"Happy Christmas," they echoed.

"Is it true?" Maria whispered when handing Siobhán her hot cocoa. "The lad on the tractor was murdered?"

"We're investigating all possibilities," Siobhán said.

Marie leaned even closer. "That's why I gave you a nip of Irish cream. Just a touch."

Siobhán laughed. "Macdara too?"

Maria shook her head. "Let him drive," she said with a wink.

By the time they made it to Bonnie's tent, featuring hand-painted ornaments of the Irish countryside, there was a lad manning the booth all by himself. Siobhán particularly liked an ornament featuring their ruined abbey covered in a blanket of snow. The abbey wasn't just her favorite spot in town, it was where they'd held their wedding reception. She had to have it. Macdara saw her eyeing it and leaned in. "Don't go buying anything until you see what Santy brings," he whispered.

She laughed. "Subtle, Mr. Detective. Shall I close my eyes so you can buy it now?"

"There's no fun in that, now," he said. "I'll wait until Christmas Eve like I always do."

"Do that and you might find I bought new locks for Christmas."

He chuckled and then they turned their attention back to the matter at hand. "We were told Bonnie Murphy would be working this tent today," Macdara said.

The lad nodded. "She took the morning off," he said. "We're expecting her after the lunch hour."

Macdara scribbled his mobile number on the back of his calling card and handed it to the lad. "Text me the minute she arrives."

"Yes, DS Flannery," the kid said.

Siobhán gave Macdara a playful shove as they walked away. "See that?" she said. "You're infamous."

"I think you mean famous," Macdara said, standing straighter.

"Infamous," Siobhán repeated with a gentle shove. All of their other appointments were for late this afternoon and early this evening, and Jeanie Brady had yet to finish her postmortem, so they took time to enjoy the market. They bought shepherd's pie from a stall and Macdara insisted they finish it off with a brownie with vanilla ice cream. "We'll have to come back when we're off duty and get our cocoa with Irish cream," Macdara said longingly.

"Absolutely," Siobhán said. "It's not like Maria already gave me a nip in mine."

Macdara's mouth dropped open. "She did not."

Siobhán shrugged. "I suppose we'll never know."

"Keep this up and you'll be on Santy's naughty list," Macdara said.

Siobhán didn't reply; she was drawn into a tent that made adorable wooden statues. Some were religious in nature, others featured Santa, nutcrackers, and even Christmas trees. They reminded her of Sinead's Virgin Mary statue, although she had a feeling these were much more ornate. They were painted with glorious colors. Siobhán remembered these from years past, and if she wasn't mistaken they had a secret little compartment on the bottom. "Do you have a statue of the Virgin Mary?"

"She's right here," the woman said, picking one up. Although less adorned than some, it had exquisite detailing.

"We have a friend whose mother bought one of these at the very first Christmas market."

The woman nodded. "That would be my great-granny. I've been keeping the tradition alive."

"I know it won't replace the one she's missing, but maybe it will cheer her up some," Siobhán said. "I'll take it."

The woman nodded and began to wrap it up in lovely red and green tissue paper. She stopped. "And you know all about the secret, don't you?"

"Do you mean the secret little compartment?" Siobhán grinned. "I remember. But show it to me again, it's delightful."

The woman nodded, then unwrapped the statue. She turned it over. "There's a little compartment underneath." She pushed in on the center and a little secret door opened up. "She's hollow. You can't fit much in there, maybe a secret note or some money that you don't want anyone else to nick."

"It's a brilliant idea," Siobhán said. "Have they always had that component?"

"Right from the very beginning. Did your friend's statue have something inside?"

Did it? "I have no idea. I don't even know if she knew about the compartment." Was it possible Sinead was so determined to get her statue back because of something that was hidden inside of it? Macdara came up behind her and placed his hands on her waist, making her jump. After swatting him, she showed him the statue and the secret compartment.

"I sincerely hope that sweet old woman hasn't been lying to us," he said. "Or I really will have to handcuff her."

Chapter Seven

Siobhán felt a tiny glow of satisfaction as she took her Virgin Mary statue and headed for Bonnie's tent with Macdara. One Christmas present sorted, even if it was for someone who wasn't on her list. *Progress.* Macdara's mobile phone dinged with a text. "Bonnie is here," he said. "But she's been moved to a new tent. Let's see if I can follow these directions."

They wound around the square, taking in toys, and jewelry, and food. They jostled their way through a sea of winter coats and gloves, hands full with bags and boxes. "This should be the lane," Macdara said as they turned down another path. "Down here on the right." It might have been difficult to pick out Bonnie Murphy from all the other young, beautiful women at the market, but they had been told that she had taken to wearing a red and green knitted flower in her hair, compliments of Beverly. It took a while to spot her, but they finally spied the knitted flower in the far corner, at a candle stall.

"Candles!" Siobhán exclaimed as they neared the tent. "I can buy some for our windows."

"Make sure you get the glass covers," Macdara said. "I don't ever want to worry about you and fire again."

There had been an incident shortly before they were married where Siobhán and Maria, along with their third bestie, Aisling, were trapped in the dairy barn on their property, which an arsonist had set on fire. They managed to escape relatively unharmed, but Macdara still had nightmares. "I will absolutely buy the hurricane covers," she said, picking up a pair of long creamy candlesticks. "And I can wrap the bottom in garland." She pointed to the decorative garland next to the glass covers.

"Happy Christmas," Bonnie said when there was finally a moment for her to speak. When she tucked a strand of black hair behind her ear, Siobhán noticed her hand was trembling. "Happy Christmas," Siobhán and Macdara echoed back.

"I made these myself," Bonnie said, gesturing to the candles.

"You did?" Siobhán was quite impressed. "Well played. That's amazing." She meant it. They were gorgeous. For a second Siobhán lamented all the talents she didn't possess. She wasn't craftsy, she wasn't an artist, or a chef, or a musician. She used to be able to whittle, but it seemed her special talent had been reduced to sussing out murderers. It wasn't something she'd ever dreamed of as a little girl, but on the other hand there was nothing more satisfying than getting a killer off the streets, and bringing justice to victims. Still. Had she more time, perhaps she would be a fantastic candlemaker.

"Thank you." Bonnie clasped her hands below her chin, her eyes alert and friendly. "I know you're not here to buy the candles. I'm sorry I wasn't at the ornament tent this morning. Michael's death has just been such a shock."

"We understand," Macdara said. "We wouldn't blame you if you decided not to have a tent this year at all."

Bonnie chewed on a chipped green-painted fingernail. "I thought about that. But what good is being sad all on my lonesome going to do? I'd rather be out here keeping my mind occupied."

"I'm definitely buying some candles," Siobhán said. "But first we need to ask you a few questions."

"Of course," Bonnie said. "I'm horrified about what happened to Michael. Are you investigating for insurance purposes?"

"Pardon?" Siobhán said.

"It was just a terrible, terrible accident, wasn't it? I suppose you have to write up a report, or whatever, and I don't mean to be dense, but I don't quite understand what you're investigating."

"We have loose ends to tie up," Macdara said. "Including identifying someone who pulled up alongside Michael's tractor in a blue Toyota Corolla."

"Right," Bonnie said. "I heard something about that. I wasn't sure whether it really happened or it was just a rumor."

"The person was dressed in a brown robe with a hood," Macdara said.

"How odd." Her eyes darted around as if she was looking for the nearest means of escape.

Siobhán picked out four yellow tapered candles, four covers, and four decorative garlands. "We just moved into a new house," she said as Bonnie began to wrap them up. "I can't wait to put them in the windows."

"They'll be stunning," Bonnie said. "And if you're looking for a wreath for the door, you'll want to see Oscar at the elder care home," Bonnie said.

"Oh?" Siobhán said. She was definitely in the market for a wreath.

"He makes them," she said. "And they're exquisite."

"He should sell them here," Siobhán said.

"He was supposed to." Bonnie shook her head in dismay. "He hasn't gone anywhere since his cane was stolen. To tell you the truth, I think it was more like an emotional support cane."

"Emotional support cane?" Macdara said, lifting an eyebrow.

"He was so attached to it. I think it meant as much to him as a family pet."

Family pet. Siobhán needed to get their Jack Russell, Trigger, a present for Christmas too. Beverly had seemed rather attached to her scarf as well. Did the thief take some items to cause a distraction? Creating an emotional disturbance to keep everyone off balance?

"Where were you, Finn Doyle, and Shane Boyd yesterday?" Macdara asked. "Mr. Casey said you didn't show up to the tractor rehearsal."

Bonnie dropped her fingernail and chewed on her bottom lip this time. Siobhán was tempted to buy her some beef jerky. "I'm to blame." Bonnie looked at them as if waiting to see if they would interrupt. They kept silent. "I heard of a shop in Cork that sold canes. I wanted to see if we could get one for Oscar. We tried to get Michael to come with us, but he was eager to drive the tractor."

"I find it odd that the three of you signed up to participate in the tractor parade and then missed the first outing," Macdara pressed.

"I'm glad we did," Bonnie said. "It may have saved our lives."

"Why do you think that?" Siobhán said. "You just pointed out that you think it was an accident."

Bonnie bit her lip. "Yes," she said slowly. "I did." Siobhán cocked her head and stared at her. Bonnie threw her arms open. "If it was me on that tractor, who's to say I wouldn't have had something similar happen to me?" She folded her arms. "I'm very accident-prone."

"What time did you leave for Cork?" Macdara asked. "What time did you get there, how long were you there, and when did you return?"

Bonnie chewed her lip and stared at the ground. "I said we were *going* to drive to Cork. I never said we made it there."

That got their attention. "Didn't make it there? Why not?" Siobhán asked.

Bonnie crossed her arms and let out a puff of air, sending her fringe flying. "It's Finn and Shane you need to question. They drove into town, stopped near the Christmas market, and chucked me out of the car!"

"Did they say why?" Siobhán said.

"Shane wanted to go to a pub where his mate was bartending. Said he was going to give them free drinks."

That seemed like it would have appealed to Michael as well, Siobhán thought. "Do you know if they told Michael about it?"

Bonnie shrugged. "I don't think so. Michael was mad for the drink, he certainly would have gone with them." Bonnie handed Siobhán her candles all wrapped up. "You don't think . . . you don't think someone *wanted* Michael dead, do you?"

"We're still conducting our inquiries," Macdara said politely.

"He definitely wasn't wearing that scarf at the start of the tractor practice," Bonnie said.

"That's the theory we're working on, but how do you know for sure?" Siobhán asked.

Bonne reached into her coat pocket and pulled out her mobile phone. "He sent this to me fifteen minutes after we dropped him off." She swiped through it and turned the screen toward them. On it was a picture of Michael atop the tractor, flashing two fingers and sticking his tongue out. The road was visible in the background. A scarf was nowhere to be seen.

"I'm going to need you to email that to me," Macdara said, taking out his calling card and handing it to her. "Do you have any other photos from that practice run?"

"It's the only one he sent me," Bonnie said. "Shall I send it now?"

Macdara nodded. "Please."

Bonnie seemed pleased to be useful. She nattered on as she brought up her email. "Why do you think Beverly made such a long scarf? It was more like a Rapunzel rope."

"Perhaps she enjoyed making it and didn't know when to stop," Siobhán said.

"Or she knew exactly what she was doing," Bonnie said. "And where that scarf would end up."

Siobhán stepped forward. "You're saying that Beverly wanted Michael Walsh dead?"

"I don't have any proof, mind you," Bonnie said. "But she didn't like him. I know that much."

That was news. "Why is that?"

Bonnie poked at her screen and soon a whooshing sound could be heard. "Done!" she said. She stuck her phone in her pocket. "I don't mean to speak ill of the dead, but Michael knew how to get under people's skin. He rather enjoyed pushing buttons."

"And what buttons did he push with Beverly?" Macdara asked.

"She overhead him talking to us, making fun of that scarf," Bonnie said. "She heard every word."

"Can you give us those words?" Siobhán said.

Bonnie gulped. "He said . . . he said the scarf was so ugly he wouldn't be caught dead wearing it."

Chapter Eight

They returned to the Casey farm when there was only a half hour of decorating time left in the day. Siobhán's siblings saw her coming and blocked her from seeing their progress. "It's a surprise," Ann said, wagging her finger. The youngest girl, she was getting so grown-up. She had chopped her blond hair over the summer, but it was starting to grow in now. She was beautiful either way, a spirited and athletic girl.

"Not even a peek?" Siobhán said.

"Not even a peek," her siblings echoed. Siobhán ruffled some heads, and had a gander at the other tractors. They were delightful to behold adorned with colorful lights, garland, and illuminated signs reading HAPPY CHRISTMAS. She could imagine the procession now, lights twinkling through the darkness and giving the illusion of moving through space. She couldn't wait. In the meantime, there was work yet to do. Bill Casey invited them into his farmhouse and gestured to the kitchen table. A feast was laid out before them, coffee, tea, and a full Irish breakfast.

"Breakfast for supper!" Macdara exclaimed, eagerly pulling out a chair. "That's class."

Casey shrugged. "Me wife passed on years ago. At first

I did it because it was the only meal I knew how to make. Now I just like it. I eat breakfast all day long."

"You shouldn't have," Siobhán said. Macdara was already planted in front of a full plate. Siobhán stuck with tea, toast, and an egg. Macdara hummed as he ate. When they were finished they exited the house and stood near the line of tractors in the drive.

"They would have been on their way home now, but everyone knows to wait until you speak with them."

"Good man," Macdara said. They gave Bill Casey another nod of thanks and readied their notebooks. They approached Finn Doyle first. He seemed jittery, his thin legs bounced as he tried to stand in one place, and his eyes were rimmed in red. Every few seconds as they tried to talk to him, he wiped his nose with the back of his sleeve. Siobhán was having a hard time concentrating, she was so fixated on wanting to hand him a tissue. But she wasn't his mammy and they would get more answers out of him if they gave him some autonomy.

"I never suspected," he said. "I swear."

"Suspected what?" Macdara asked.

"That Michael was the thief." He pawed the ground with his boot. "I suppose I should have, given his background." He looked up at them. "Did you know he was recently in jail?"

"We haven't determined that he was the thief," Siobhán said.

Finn shook his head as if something was stuck in there and he was trying to jostle it out. "But he had Beverly's ugly scarf."

"Do yourself a favor, lad, and just call it a scarf," Macdara said. "You wouldn't want that getting back to her and hurting her feelings, would you now?"

"You're right, you're right," he said. "My bad."

"I'm sure you've heard that a blue Toyota Corolla pulled up next to his tractor, an unidentified person in a brown hooded robe exited the vehicle and spoke with Michael for a moment?" Siobhán said.

Finn nodded. "He gave Michael the scarf too, didn't he?"

"We're making that assumption," Macdara said. "Did you see a scarf on him that day?"

Finn shook his head. "He must have known the person, don't you think? Why else would he wear it?"

Siobhán noted that he had yet to volunteer the fact that he had skipped the tractor rehearsal. Guilty conscience? "You were supposed to be on the tractor route," Siobhán said. "Mr. Casey told us you didn't show up." They weren't going to divulge that they had already spoken to Bonnie Murphy. They needed to see if their stories would match up.

"Yet you left the elder care home with Michael at the exact same time," Macdara added. "Along with Bonnie Murphy and Shane Boyd. But Michael was the only one who participated in the tractor route."

"Right, right," Finn said. "Bonnie wanted to go into Cork City to buy Oscar a new cane. We dropped Michael off." He stopped as if that was the end of the story.

"The three of you drove to Cork then, is that what you're telling us?" Macdara asked.

Finn shook his head. "Bonnie changed her mind as soon as we dropped off Michael. She got a text—I don't know who from—and asked if we would drop her off in the town square instead. And she was really the one who wanted to buy Oscar a new cane. I mean Shane and I were willing to tag along, but I don't know what kind of cane he'd like. Shane said he wanted to have a pint so I dropped him off in town and then I decided to go the chemist to sort out my Aunt Nuala's medications."

Interesting. Was Finn lying or was Bonnie? Would Shane back one of them up or add a third version to the story? By *chemist* did Finn mean *pub* and by *medication*, did he mean a *pint*? Siobhán took the next question. "What chemist did you visit?"

Finn looked away. "I didn't ask for his name or anything."

"Was it the chemist in town?" Macdara probed.

"No. I went for a drive. It was pretty far out."

Siobhán knew Macdara was getting frustrated, so she stepped in. "What town?"

Finn shrugged. "I couldn't tell ye that now." Siobhán wondered if Santy would forgive her a little slap but she managed to control herself.

"Do you think we're daft?" Macdara said. "You can't walk into any chemist and get prescription meds."

"Ah, I see. I see," Finn said. "They weren't prescription. Me granny likes her Solpadeine. They give you the side-eye if you come in too many times to the same chemist to buy them, so whenever I'm near a new chemist I stop in for a pack."

Solpadeine. Just like the packs they had found in Michael's room. Not that there was anything unusual about that. You'd find a pack in many Irish homes. Especially if there were any drinkers in the household. But what if Michael hadn't purchased them himself? Had he been snooping around Nuala's room, searching for jewels? Did he come away with Solpadeine instead? And assuming he stole them, perhaps it wasn't a far leap to believe Michael Walsh was the thief after all. But if that were the case— where were the rest of the missing items? And more to the point—who killed him? Was the killer a vigilante furious that Michael had stolen from the elderly a fortnight before Christmas?

"Do you have the receipt from this chemist?" Macdara asked.

"Nah," he said. "I never keep receipts."

Macdara was not going to let up that easy. "What direction did you travel? What did you pass, and were there any landmarks near the chemist you can remember?"

Finn swallowed hard and the twitching amped up. "Are you like . . . asking for my alibi?"

"I'd say you should be eager to provide it," Macdara said. "Given you left with Michael and are a frequent visitor to the elder care home."

"If you're looking for answers, look no further than the mystery man in the brown robe," Finn said. He frowned. "That's odd," he said to himself.

"What's odd?" Siobhán nudged forward.

Finn shook his head. "It's probably nothing."

"Go on, then," Macdara said. "Give us your nothing."

"I could have sworn I heard Cathal Ryan saying something to Nancy Martin about someone running around the grounds of the care home early in the mornings. Someone dressed in a brown hooded robe."

Nuala was seated in a rocking chair in her room, next to a window, her fingers deftly working her knitting needles. The view was sublime; from here she could see the front of the grounds with the mountains in the background. The Christmas decorations were done and dusted, and the gardens were glowing with lights and cheer. It was somewhat mesmerizing to watch Nuala rock as she knitted. "I'm making a replacement scarf for Beverly to give to her daughter," she said. "But I assure you this one is going to be very short."

"That's very kind of you," Siobhán said.

Nuala frowned. "Let's hope Beverly sees it that way."

"We overheard someone mention long scarf syndrome the other day," Macdara said. "But we can't remember who introduced the topic of conversation."

"And who else was around," Siobhán said.

"It was that Bonnie lass," Nuala said. "I've been hoping she and my grandson would have a little spark, but I think she had her eye on that Michael Walsh. May he rest in peace."

Siobhán and Macdara exchanged a quick look. Bonnie hadn't mentioned having a crush on Michael Walsh, but next time they spoke with her they would have to venture into that territory.

"Did you have any interactions with Michael Walsh?" Macdara asked.

"He and my grandson got on like a house on fire. But to tell you the truth, I thought he was a bad influence." She stopped rocking. "Maybe even the thief."

"We've processed his room at the Twins' Inn and there wasn't a trace of the stolen items," Siobhán said. "But we did find a heap of Solpadeine on his end table."

"I'm afraid that's my fault," Nuala said. "I was going through my products and had a load of it from my days where I liked to have a martini or four before bed. Those days are long gone." She grinned. "I have a strict two-martini policy now."

If she was telling the truth, and why wouldn't she be, that meant her grandson Finn had been lying. She didn't need more Solpadeine if she no longer had hangovers. Finn *hadn't* been driving to a chemist. Where had he gone instead? Was Finn the murderer?

"Did Michael Walsh steal the packets from you?" Macdara asked.

"Heavens, no," Nuala said. "And if he had, I wouldn't have cared. It's me emeralds I want back."

"Was there any particular reason Michael needed all that Solpadeine?" Siobhán asked.

"He was moaning about needing the hair of the dog," Nuala said. "You know how the young ones are."

Siobhán's gaze fell to the grounds outside the window. "Have you ever seen anyone walking around here in brown robes?" she asked.

"Are you on about Rory and Oscar?" Nuala said.

Macdara stepped forward. "Rory and Oscar?"

Nuala nodded. "They nicked a couple of robes from the panto costume rack at the Christmas market, then ran around here like a couple of children. When they went to take them back, one was missing."

"Why are you just telling us this now?" Siobhán said. "You know we're looking for a mysterious person in a brown robe, do you not?"

Nuala shrugged. "Oscar and Rory were here the entire time and I figured if you wanted to know more you'd ask, and here you are asking, and here I am, answering."

"Now," Siobhán said. *That's that*. She and Macdara exchanged a look. If the robe was stolen from the grounds, it brought them right back to their four young suspects. As Nuala pointed out, all the residents were home when the brown-hooded figure made his or her approach.

"It has come to our attention that you have a safe where you kept your emeralds," Macdara said.

There was no safe visible in the room, but the rest was lovely. A four-poster bed, evergreen wallpaper adorned with golden leaves, a dresser, the rocking chair and a cedar chest. There was one closet door, and of course a small safe could be under the bed, in the dresser, or in the cedar chest. Nuala didn't respond, she simply kept rocking. Why was she keeping her lips sealed about this safe? Did it not exist? Suddenly the door swung open and Nancy Martin stepped in.

"Pardon the interruption," she said. "Nuala has a doctor's appointment and her transportation is waiting downstairs."

"Of course," Siobhán said. She turned to Nuala. "If you tell us where to find the safe and give us the combination, we might be able to make some headway on the disappearance of your emeralds."

"How? The safe is empty now," Nuala said.

"We're going to make a round to the charity shops, in case someone tried to sell them for cash," Macdara added. "But we would still like to see your safe."

Nuala eyed Macdara. "You can see it but I won't be able to open it for you."

Macdara kept a patient smile on his face. "Why not?"

Nuala dropped her knitting into a nearby basket with a sigh. "Someone has gone and changed my combination!"

"Is there any chance you've simply forgotten it?" Nancy asked gently.

"Bah humbug," Nuala said. "It's me birthday. Are you telling me I've forgotten me own birthday?"

Nancy exchanged looks with Macdara and Siobhán. "I've encouraged her to change it. But it can be difficult to remember new combinations."

You can't teach an old dog new tricks. The thought popped in Siobhán's mind before she could stop it. It sparked another thought. Max was a young dog. And he knew plenty of tricks. She had no idea why her mind was torturing her with that right now—safecracking probably wasn't one of the dog's many talents.

"You're definitely going to have to change the combination now," Siobhán said.

"I told you, someone else has already changed it." Nuala rose from her chair. "Besides, the emeralds are gone. I don't need a safe now, do I?" She was certainly defensive. Was she worried it was her grandson who'd changed the combination?

"Why don't you show us the safe when you're back," Macdara tried again.

"If I make it back," Nuala said. "After all, there's a murderer making the rounds, a Christmas angel of death."

Chapter Nine

They found Beverly in the kitchen, on cookie duty. The air was filled with the smell of fresh baked chocolate chips and all things sugar and dough. When Macdara and Siobhán stepped into the room Beverly gasped. "Are you here to arrest me?"

"Arrest you?" Macdara said.

She brought her hands up to her face. "Is it true? Did me scarf kill that poor lad?"

"You mustn't blame yourself," Siobhán said. Unless, of course, she was the killer. In that case, she *should* blame herself but probably didn't. In fact, if Beverly was the killer, it was quite clever. Make the murder weapon with your own two hands, then pretend it was stolen a day before the murder. But given she was in the sitting room with them when the murder occurred, she was probably in the clear.

"Everyone kept warning me about the length. But it wasn't supposed to be worn by a lad on a tractor!"

"Of course not," Siobhán said. "How were you to know?"

Macdara shook his head. "If only we had all learned our lesson from the great Isadora Duncan."

"Someone is doing this to get at me," Beverly said. "Someone wants to torment me." She thwacked the rolling pin on the counter, then set upon a ball of dough, rolling it out and pounding it with gusto.

"We heard that Michael was making fun of the scarf before it was stolen," Macdara said. "Can you tell us about that?"

Beverly's eyes narrowed as she thunked the rolling pin on the table. "Who told you that?"

"We're not at liberty to say," Siobhán said. "But we'd like to hear your version of what happened."

"I don't quite remember everything these days," Beverly said. "But he said it was ugly and that he wouldn't be caught dead wearing it."

"Where was everyone when this occurred and who all was there?" Macdara asked.

Beverly sunk a cookie cutter into the dough. "We were outside in the gardens. I asked Michael if I could wrap it around him to check out the length. I suppose I should have asked someone more agreeable." She lifted the cookie cutter and sunk it down in a new section. "The foursome was there. I don't know why Bonnie was hanging around those lads—attention I suppose. And then myself, Rory, and Oscar."

"By the foursome you mean Bonnie, Shane, Finn, and Michael?" Macdara asked.

"Yes. Rory and Oscar call them the Four Horsemen but I just call them the foursome."

"The Four Horsemen?" Siobhán asked. It was rather a grim nickname.

Beverly waved it off. "Rory and Oscar are jealous of their youth," Beverly said. "Some people grow old gracefully, others claw and hiss all the way to the grave." She took a spatula and carved around the cookie. "Now," she said. "Isn't this a lovely snowman?"

"I'm sure he will be," Siobhán said politely. "Once you give him a head."

Speaking to the residents one-on-one had proven to be a bit frustrating. The residents all went on tangents, or blamed someone else. They decided it might be advantageous to give it one more go as a group. They gathered in the library around the cozy fire. Cookies and hot cocoa were served. Christmas music still played overhead, but Nancy turned it down so that they could easily talk over it.

Macdara waited until everyone had taken their seats and had a mug of hot cocoa and a helping of cookies. "Let's go over the day of the thefts one more time as a group," he said.

Nuala bit the antlers off a reindeer cookie. "It was a dark and stormy night," she said.

"No, it wasn't," Oscar said. He snapped the leg off a snowman. "It was morning and the sun was shining—we were all in exercise class." He leaned in. "That's what they call it but it's really just old folks standing in a circle passing wind."

"Oscar!" Nuala shook her finger at him.

Oscar chuckled. "Ah, now. It is. You know it is."

"Ever since they stole his cane he's been as prickly as a briar patch," Beverly said.

A tear came to Oscar's eye. "That was from me pilgrimage. You can't replace it." He looked at the guards once again. "But you are going to try, aren't you?"

"Of course we are," Siobhán said. "In the meantime, we're still trying to figure out how the thieves entered the house without being seen."

Rory squirmed in his seat, then lifted his hand in the air. "No need to raise your hand," Macdara said.

Rory extended his arm, pointing at Beverly. "This one's been leaving the back door ajar trying to woo a wee fox."

"Trying to what a what?" Macdara asked.

"He's a lovely red fox, so he is," Beverly said. "I've named him Rudolph."

"He's a wild animal," Rory said. "You're asking for trouble."

Beverly gasped. "That's the same thing you said about me scarf."

Rory threw his hands up. "I was right, wasn't I?"

Beverly dropped her head and moaned.

"It's alright, luv," Siobhán said. "Rory isn't blaming you. It's the killer who's responsible for where that scarf ended up, and no one else."

"She's right of course," Rory said. "I'm sorry, Beverly. I didn't mean to imply you had anything to do with that poor lad's death. I just don't think you should be inviting a wee red fox into the house."

"It is best to leave wild animals alone," Macdara said. "Did you leave the back door ajar that morning?"

Beverly lifted a Christmas tree cookie in front of her face as if she was hoping to hide behind it. "Will I be arrested if I did?"

"Throw the book at her!" Nuala said. "I'll sue. We should all sue!" Heads turned to stare at Nuala. She stared back and then finally broke it off with a laugh. "I'm only messing. I'm just back from the doctor and he's given me terrible news."

Everyone leaned forward, concern stamped on their faces. "What's wrong, pet?" Beverly cooed.

"He said I'm perfectly healthy and going to live a long,

long life." Nuala kept her face still as those around her took ages to catch on to the joke.

"That's a terrible, terrible thing to say to people of our age," Beverly said. "Shame on you, Nuala."

Nuala shook her head. "You'd think at this age we'd have learned to have a bit of craic."

"There's a killer running loose," Oscar said.

"And a thief," Rory added.

"Who cares about the thefts when there's a killer?" Oscar said.

Rory shook his head. "That's easy for you to say. All you lost was a cane. I lost five hundred euro and it was me Christmas shopping money!"

Siobhán's heart gave a squeeze. She still wanted to replace all their stolen items as soon as possible.

"Go on, lads, have a row," Nuala said. "That will be some craic. Do you want to put on your brown robes and settle it like men?"

All chatter came to screeching halt. Oscar froze with the rest of his snowman cookie halfway to his gob.

Rory placed his hot chocolate on the table with a *thunk*. "I suppose that's us outed," he said. "Oscar and I did borrow a pair of brown robes from the Christmas market. As Nuala said—just for a bit of craic." He seared Nuala with a look. "You seem fond of the craic, yet won't let us have a bit of our own, heh?"

Nuala pursed her lips and shrugged.

"Wait," Siobhán said. "You weren't at the Christmas market that morning. You said you were here in exercise class."

"Max scared the fox off anyway," Beverly said as if there wasn't an entirely new conversation taking place. "Came tearing out the back door barking. The fox took off. And that was a good ending to the story. As soon as I realized that Max and the fox might get into a row, I stopped encouraging the fox to come around."

Macdara nodded. "Well played, Beverly." He turned back to Oscar and Rory. "Were the two of you at the Christmas market?"

"No," Oscar said. "A little friend of ours brought the robes back for us. I'd been telling her all about the monks from days of yore. She thought we'd get a laugh at it."

She. Bonnie. Had she stolen the robes for herself and a partner-in-crime? When Oscar and Rory noticed them did she switch tracks and pretend they were for them?

"And she works at the market, so she was going to return them the next day. Only when we went to give them back, they were missing!" Rory added.

"It's obvious what happened," Oscar said. "The robes we borrowed were stolen!"

"You stole them first," Beverly pointed out.

Oscar frowned, then shrugged and started over. "I hung it on a hook right next to the bedside table where I used to have me cane."

"Why didn't you tell us about this immediately?" Macdara said.

"You were only just here," Rory said. "Now you're back. In our world, this is as immediate as you get."

"Sorry I'm late," a little voice popped up. They turned around to find Sinead in the doorway.

"Hello, luv," Macdara said. "How was the fingerprint demonstration?"

Sinead clasped her hands together. "It was wonderful. They did a fine job, I'm telling ye."

"Did they lift any prints?" Oscar asked.

"They lifted mine," Sinead said. "I put me hands all over the doorknob and they showed me how it's done."

"Were all of the items stolen out of your rooms?" Siobhán asked.

Heads nodded. "And the rooms are all on the second floor?" Once again heads nodded. "Is there a lift?" Siobhán said.

"There is," Rory said. "But we've also got a mechanical chair that goes up the stairs, and a few of us can still walk it."

"He means him," Nuala said. "He can still walk it."

"And were you all in the same location doing your exercises?" Siobhán asked.

"We were all outside for exercise class," Beverly said. "It was a grand fresh day and we had a walk about the gardens."

Siobhán turned to Oscar. "Isn't that an activity where you would normally have your cane?"

Oscar shook his head. "That's my going-out-on-the-town cane. I wouldn't want it in the muck."

Beverly joined in. "Me scarf was on the table near my bed."

"My Virgin Mary statue was on my bedside table too," Sinead said.

Interesting.

Everyone looked at Nuala. Would she say something about her safe? She took her time before speaking. "Why are you paying attention to our things when you have a killer to catch?"

"We believe there may be a link between the thefts and the murder," Siobhán said.

All five of the residents leaned in. "I'm afraid there's nothing more to say at this point," Siobhán said. "But given our victim was wearing one of the stolen items, it's obvious there might be a link."

Sinead bit into a cookie and grimaced. "These aren't

nearly as good as the vanilla biscuits Nancy's been leaving on me beside table."

"Vanilla biscuits on your bedside table?" Everyone turned as Nancy Martin piped up. Siobhán hadn't even noticed her in the room. Perhaps she would make a fine politician's wife, always there but never drawing attention to herself unless it was absolutely necessary. It sounded like a dreadful life to Siobhán, hiding in the shadows. "I haven't been leaving vanilla biscuits on your beside table," Nancy continued.

"Then where have they been coming from?" Sinead said. "Santy's elves?"

"I've been getting them too," Nuala said.

"And me," Rory added.

Oscar raised his hand. "Me too."

"It sounds as if our ant problem has been solved," Nancy said, shaking her head. "Our housekeeper has been very cross about the whole business."

Beverly bobbed her head. "I gave one to the fox. I'm sorry. I won't be doing that anymore." She reached into the pocket of her house dress. "I have a few more in here. Where are they?" She pulled out a pair of glasses and a handkerchief and set them on the coffee table. She kept digging until she pulled out two biscuits. She held them up. "See?" She offered one to Macdara and he wasted no time sticking it into his pie hole.

Siobhán edged closer. "Those look like the dog biscuits we found in Michael's room."

Macdara lunged for a napkin as if he was thinking of spitting it out, then paused as if considering it, shrugged, and swallowed. "They aren't bad, but if I start barking you can put me outside at night." He winked at Siobhán.

"Dog biscuits?" Rory sputtered. "Someone's been feeding us dog biscuits?"

A whir of black and white fur shot through the room. Max was suddenly sitting up straight in front of Beverly, tongue out, whining.

"I thought Max was at Bill Casey's farm," Siobhán said.

"We missed him terribly," Beverly said, patting him on the head. "We're all over the moon about him."

"Bill dropped him off for a little visit," Nancy said.

"Have a biscuit," Beverly said, pointing to the one on the table. Max leaned in. "Wait," she said, holding up her finger. "Wait until I say you can have it." Max eyed the biscuit but remained still.

"He's so well trained," Beverly said.

"Hold on a minute." Siobhán approached the coffee table and pointed to Beverly's glasses. "Are these very dear?"

Beverly shook her head. "Cheap ones from the chemist, luv. Why?"

"I'd like to try something. I promise I will buy you a new pair."

Beverly shrugged. "Be my guest."

Siobhán moved the eyeglasses right next to the Christmas biscuit. Without hesitation, Max ignored the cookie, snatched the pair of eyeglasses, and ran out of the room.

"What just happened?" Nancy Martin said.

"We've just learned we've all been eating dog biscuits," Rory said.

"And we just caught our thief," Macdara added.

Siobhán headed after Max. "He was trained to steal any item that was situated right next to a biscuit. Let's see where he goes." Everyone scrambled up and headed after Siobhán.

"Woof," Beverly said as she trailed behind. "I didn't see this coming."

Chapter Ten

Max was quick. He was down the hallway and whining at the back door by the time they caught up. "This door was propped open when all the items were stolen," Siobhán said. "Beverly had been forgetting to close it after looking for the fox."

"Let's see where Max takes the glasses," Macdara said. He opened the back door and Max zoomed off, morphing into a black and white blob as he streaked across the grounds. They hurried after him.

"He is super fast," Siobhán said.

"It explains how he managed to steal all the items while everyone was exercising out front," Macdara said. "Good on you for putting it together."

"Lucky for us Beverly had that biscuit in her pocket." They jogged after Max; he knew exactly where he was going. The grounds ended at a road. Max sat at the edge of the road, the glasses in his mouth.

Siobhán and Macdara stopped. "It's like he's expecting someone to be here," Siobhán said.

"A car," Macdara said. "Max brought the goods to a waiting car."

Max dropped the eyeglasses. Siobhán swooped in and grabbed them. "Unharmed," she said. Max turned and looked at them. Siobhán patted him on the head. "Little thief," she said. She turned to find the residents making their way toward them. She handed Beverly her eyeglasses.

"They have slobber all over them," she bemoaned.

"We'll still buy you a new pair," Siobhán said.

"Why is he just sitting there?" Rory said. "Where did he take our things?"

Macdara turned to face the group. "We're sorry to report we think our thieves had been waiting here in a car. Your items could be anywhere by now."

"But why?" Oscar said. "A cane? A Virgin Mary statue? A scarf? That doesn't make any sense."

"I think it was part of the training," Siobhán said. "The game. What they were really after were the emeralds. It's the only thing that makes any sense."

"You believe me now, do ye?" Nuala said.

"Yes," Siobhán said.

Nuala thrust her chin up. "I told youse I had emeralds. They've been in me family for ages."

"Don't be ridiculous," Beverly said. "A dog couldn't open a safe and carry emeralds out in his mouth."

"You're right there," Siobhán said. "I believe the emeralds were in Sinead's Virgin Mary statue."

Sinead gasped. "Whatever do you mean?"

"When we were at the Christmas market we found similar statues. Made by the same family for generations. Were you aware the statue was hollow and there's a little compartment inside?"

"I was," Sinead said. "I never used it."

"I'm afraid that Michael must have known about it. He hid the emeralds in the statue and trained his dog to take the items. I think he wanted to throw us off by stealing items that seemed to have very little value."

"How did anyone get my emeralds?" Nuala said.

"Does your grandson have the combination to the safe?" Siobhán asked. It was delicate territory.

Nuala's face hardened and she wagged her finger at them. "Are you calling my grandson a thief?"

Siobhán stayed calm. "I'm only asking if he had the combination."

She pursed her lips. "I trust him with me life."

"Perhaps he showed someone the emeralds. Perhaps he didn't realize how good that person was at reading combinations," Siobhán said. She started walking toward the house. "Follow me." She led them back inside to the library. She pointed to the binoculars on the table. "I don't have any gloves." She pulled her sleeves over her hands, picked them up, and looked through them. "I can see the security panel from here," she said. "I think our thief used these binoculars to steal that code. Perhaps the same was done with Nuala's safe."

"We need to speak with Finn, Bonnie, and Shane," Macdara said. "One of them was in on it with Michael. I have a feeling whoever was in the mysterious blue car might be Michael's devious sidekick." He glanced at Nuala. "I think we're going to need a look at that safe now."

Everyone gathered in Nuala's room as she opened her closet. On the back shelf sat a small safe. She gestured to it. "How could anyone have used binoculars to see this combination?"

She was right. It was hidden by Nuala's wardrobe, mostly long, dark dresses. "Had you taken them out of the safe for any reason?" Macdara asked. "Maybe to polish them or show them to anyone?"

Nuala frowned. "I didn't. But my grandson is sweet on that Bonnie girl. Only she liked Michael. I'm worried he may have decided to impress her. He must have opened the safe to show them to her and she was sneaky enough to watch him do it."

"Do you have any paperwork or photos of the emeralds? Any insurance on them?" Siobhán asked.

"We'd like to get any documentation we can on them," Macdara said. "Including any valuations."

"If they were the reason that young man is dead, I don't want anything more to do with them," Nuala said. "A life is way more precious than a few emeralds."

"Of course," Siobhán said. "But we'll still need that paperwork for our inquiry. And everyone has been very generous in giving to Michael's favorite causes."

"Finn has all my paperwork," she said. "And his friend Shane has been such a big help."

"What do you mean?" Siobhán asked feeling a tingle at the base of her spine. "A big help in what way?"

"He appraises precious gems," Nuala said. "Finn hired him to get an appraisal on me emeralds."

"You mean they removed the emeralds to appraise them?" Macdara asked.

"No," Nuala said. "They were stolen before an appraisal could be done."

There was something very odd about that. Neither Finn nor Shane had stepped forward with this information. Macdara and Siobhán gravitated toward the window on the far side of the room so they could have a private chat.

"Bonnie and Shane," Macdara said. "Or should we call them Bonnie and Clyde?"

"What do you make of this appraisal business?" Siobhán said. "Not one of them has mentioned it."

"They're definitely being squirrely," Macdara said. "But we still need hard evidence of a crime."

Siobhán sighed. "Unless we find the stolen items, we can't even prove my theory that the emeralds are in the statue," Siobhán said.

"The good news is that Michael's partner or partners in crime, whoever they may be, haven't had enough time to do anything with the stolen objects." Macdara gave a wave to Nuala, who seemed keen on overhearing their conversation. Nuala quickly looked away.

"I wouldn't be so sure about that," Siobhán said. "A small statue is very easy to ship. And with so many packages being mailed out at Christmas, it's not like the post office would have been suspicious."

"We could, however, find out if any of our suspects have been to the post office since the theft," Macdara said. "It wouldn't be proof but it might help us narrow down the suspect pool."

"Sounds like we have a ton of CCTV footage to go through. Shall we make popcorn?"

"Sounds delicious."

"Not to eat," Siobhán said. "To string and to make into decorative balls. For Christmas."

Macdara scrunched his face. "Popcorn on a string? In balls?"

"Gráinne saw it in a magazine. I think it would be lovely."

"I'm making a batch just to eat," Macdara said. "If you want to string yours up, be my guest."

"And, we should pop by the market for some hot cocoa. And maybe a nip of Irish cream."

"Now *that's* the woman I married," Macdara said, slinging his arm around her. "But next year, instead of hours and hours worth of CCTV footage, let's watch *It's A Wonderful Life* instead."

*   *   *

Bellies full of popcorn later, and no balls or strings to show for it, Siobhán and Macdara had gleaned nothing of value from the CCTV tapes. They had one more to go. Macdara held up the USB stick. "This little piggy went to the market," he said. They watched as another camera angle opened on the Christmas market. At first it just looked like a sea of townsfolk doing their pre-Christmas shopping and eating. Macdara yawned, his eyes drooping. Siobhán caught movement in the corner of the screen. She zoomed in on what looked like a couple arguing. It took her a moment to realize it was Nancy Martin and Cathal Ryan. She looked at the date on the tape. It was from the trip that most of the residents had taken, leaving the five behind who were exercising in the yard. Siobhán elbowed Macdara. He jerked awake and rubbed his eyes. "Sorry."

"Look at this." She pointed to Nancy and Cathal on the screen. "Didn't Nancy say she stayed at the grounds with the five who remained?"

"She did," Macdara said. "Why would she lie?" He peered closer. "Is it just me or does that look like a lovers' quarrel?"

"And remember when Cathal looked all mussed-up and was tucking his shirt in on our first visit to the home?"

"They were making up," Macdara said. "From whatever this is."

"I'd nearly forgotten about what Mr. Casey said," Siobhán said. "How Michael Walsh ran over part of his garden with his tractor."

"Looks like we need to confront Mr. Ryan with a few things," Macdara said.

Siobhán stopped the tape and stood. "He wasn't at the care home earlier, so it must be his day off."

"Let's pay the man a visit." He looked at his watch. "I think it's best if we call it a day and surprise him in the morning before he goes to work." Macdara's mobile rang, startling both of them. "It's Doctor Brady," he said. "Our plans are going to have to wait."

Jeanie met them at O'Rourke's Pub. They exchanged pleasantries with Declan and took a cozy booth by the fire. "Thank you lads for meeting me here," Jeanie said. "I'm so hungry I could eat a small horse." She winked. "Or shall I get with the season and say 'eat a small reindeer'?"

Siobhán was too full on popcorn to join her but Macdara ordered a ham and cheese toastie and crisps while Jeanie ordered bacon and cabbage. They all had a pint of the black stuff, and soon it was on to business.

"There are only a couple of findings that I thought might be of interest to you. The rest is as I surmised. He died quickly, at least there was that." She removed a roll of cash in an evidence bag and placed it on the table. "Five hundred euro," she said. "Belonging to a man named Rory."

"How do you know it belongs to Rory?" Macdara asked.

Jeanie nudged the cash forward. "He's written 'Rory' on every bill."

Siobhán laughed. "I'm so thankful we can return it to him soon." She and Macdara leaned in and waited, knowing Doctor Jeanie Brady liked to build up a bit of suspense.

"Did Michael Walsh have a girlfriend?" Jeanie tilted her head as she awaited the answer.

"There's one lass we know of who had a crush on him," Macdara said. "Bonnie."

"Have you found his mobile phone yet?" Jeanie asked.

"No," Siobhán and Macdara said in unison.

"I'm thinking he might have sent someone, perhaps this Bonnie, a little photo just before he was murdered." She made a clucking noise. "Young ones these days. They do that sort of thing, don't they? Send photos of all their bits to each other." She looked forlorn. "I suppose nothing shocks me anymore, but I do wish they had a bit more retraint."

"You think he sent someone a photo?" Macdara said. "How could a postmortem tell you that?"

"His neck," Jeanie said. "He had a giant hickey." She removed a print-out of a photo and slid it across the table. It was a close-up of Michael Walsh's neck and indeed there was a big red spot prominently featured. "I'm speculating of course, but I'm wondering if whoever handed him the scarf wanted to make sure it was covered up."

"Wait," Macdara said. He turned to Siobhán. "Bonnie showed us a selfie Michael had sent her." He dug in his pocket and brought out his mobile, then swiped through his phone. "Here." He showed them the photo. Michael had taken it from a peculiar angle, and as he was holding up two fingers. The view and his arm blocked the mark on his neck.

"The love bite wasn't from Bonnie," Siobhán said. "Or if it was—he didn't want her to see it."

"We need his mobile phone records *yesterday*," Macdara said. "I'll nudge headquarters. If your theory is correct, then whoever received the last photo from him, and rushed to bring him a scarf, could possibly be his killer."

"And the reason why his mobile phone is missing," Siobhán said. "Maybe this person realized the photo exchange could lead to his or her identity."

Jeanie Brady sighed. "Love possibly kills once again," she said. "On days like this I miss me pistachios."

Cathal Ryan's gardens were extraordinary. He seemed to have taken a page from the elder care home gardens. His front hedges had all been trimmed to look like giant candy canes. Except for the left side—what should have been three candy canes were now hacked-off. Tractor marks were still visible in the dirt. "I can see why this irked him," Siobhán said. "But we'll need more than this to connect him to a murder."

Just then a petite woman came out of the house, dressed in a fancy winter coat, carrying a handbag. "May I help you?" she said, stopping at the end of the walk.

Macdara introduced them. She cocked her head. "I'm Cindy Ryan," she said. "We didn't expect you to follow through with this," she said, gesturing to the destroyed hedges. "After all, the perpetrator is dead and there's possibly a murderer running around."

"Is your husband home?" Siobhán said. She had a sinking feeling. If one's marriage was at stake, that could be a clear motive for murder. But why kill Michael Walsh? He had been hanging around the elder care home. What if he had copped on to the affair between Nancy and Cathal and had been blackmailing him? Maybe mowing down his hedges was a warning . . .

"My husband is at work," Cindy said. "He said he needed to get a word in with Nancy."

Siobhán and Macdara exchanged a glance.

"Were you here when Michael ran down the hedges?" Macdara asked.

"I was in the house," she said. "When I heard my husband getting worked up I came out to see what on earth was going on."

"Did you hear any exchanges between them or speak with Michael?" Siobhán said.

"Why is that of interest?" Cindy asked.

"We don't have much to go on," Macdara said. "Any little thing Michael said might be a clue. I know it sounds impossible but we've broken many a case with the slightest overheard conversation."

He was exaggerating but at least Cindy Ryan seemed satisfied. She relaxed as she nodded her head. "Let's see. My husband was asking if he'd been drinking—Michael apologized and said he'd been reading a text and not paying attention to where he was going." She stopped and gasped. "I bet you'd like to know who that text was from!"

"If you think of anything else, please give us a call," Macdara said.

Cindy nodded. "Brilliant. Happy Christmas."

"Happy Christmas," they echoed, with slightly forced enthusiasm. Cindy Ryan got in her car and drove off. They stood for a moment and watched it disappear down the road.

"It looks like Mrs. Ryan has no idea her husband is having an affair," Siobhán said. It wasn't the type of news Siobhán wanted to break to anyone, let alone at Christmas. But if it turned out to be part of their case, they weren't going to have a choice.

"Bonnie and Michael, and Nancy and Cathal," Macdara mused. "Are we down to suspecting lovers?"

"Nancy is a married woman as well," Siobhán said. "Didn't she say her husband is running for mayor?"

Macdara nodded. "Indeed, she did. But if Cindy Ryan doesn't have a clue, it's likely Mr. Maybe-Mayor doesn't either." He reached into his pocket and took out his mobile. "I'm going to call the station, see if nudging headquarters about Michael's mobile has paid off." If they could get his mobile records it wouldn't include photos, but they were hoping to glean something from the texts and calls. Siobhán studied the mutilated candy-cane hedges as he spoke. Something wasn't quite adding up with this case. It felt jumbled. Like a jigsaw puzzle where they had all the pieces, just not in the right places. "Great news," Macdara said. "I've managed to charm them." He grinned. "The records have arrived."

"To the station then, Mr. Charming," Siobhán said.

Macdara sighed. "It's starting to look like there's quite a few folks on Santa's naughty list this year."

Siobhán removed a sprig of mistletoe from her pocket and held it over her head. "If you can't beat 'em, join 'em."

Macdara grinned and came in for a kiss. "What did I tell ya? Charm."

"You're full of it alright," Siobhán replied.

Chapter Eleven

Siobhán and Macdara hurried to the Kilbane Garda Station. A giant wreath greeted them from the door, Christmas music played softly overhead, and the counter had been decorated with a string of multicolored lights. They grabbed some coffee from the break room and took the mobile phone report to Macdara's office. Michael Walsh had sent three texts during the practice. The first was to Bonnie:

Why don't you dump that loser and date me?

The second text was to Finn:

You won't get away with this

The last text was to Shane:

I wish I had never met you

There was one more text, sent forty minutes before Michael died, to a number that turned out to be a burner phone. There was a notation explaining the text as an image and Macdara would need to file a request to retrieve it. There was no time, they were working against the clock. Macdara called the number. "It's dead," he said.

"Maddening," Siobhán said. "I bet the photo is of the love bite on his neck and whoever received it has to be our killer."

"Agreed," Macdara said. "An affair so illicit they needed burner phones."

"If Bonnie is dating someone else, would that be reason enough for her to murder Michael?" Siobhán mused.

Macdara rubbed his chin. "It might be reason enough for her to take him the scarf. Perhaps it was meant as a joke—one that had horrible consequences."

"I suppose we should focus on the clues we do have." She went back to the texts. "The one to Finn is intriguing. 'You won't get away with this.' Get away with what? Michael could be referring to the robberies, but it's clear he was a major part of them, if not the leader, given Max's participation."

"Maybe Finn double-crossed him. Took the emeralds for himself?"

"The emeralds already belonged to his granny," Siobhán said. "And given the two seem close, I don't think she's cut him out of the will. Finn wouldn't have needed Michael's help to steal them."

"Perhaps he needs the money from the emeralds now," Macdara said. "But his granny was saving them for later? There may be some drama unfolding in his life that requires it."

Siobhán focused on the text to Bonnie.

Why don't you dump that loser and date me?

"What loser is Bonnie dating?" she pondered aloud. "Does that mean she and Michael *weren't* intimately involved?"

"I guess you don't have to be dating to give someone a hickey," Macdara said. "I say it's high time we bring those three into the station for questioning."

"What about speaking with Cathal Ryan and Nancy Martin?"

"Let's get our three unwise men in here first," Macdara said. "If we can't get anywhere with the emeralds, let's see if we can shake some gold out of them."

Finn Doyle and Shane Boyd were set in interrogation rooms 1 and 2 while Bonnie Murphy waited on deck in the reception room. They were just about to question Shane first, when Nuala barged into the station.

"I hear you've taken my grandson into custody and I demand you release him." Her volume startled nearly every clerk within earshot.

"We're conducting interviews, love," Siobhán said. "No one has been charged with anything."

"This entire murder is somehow related to the theft of my emeralds," Nuala said. "Is that right?"

"We're looking into all possibilities," Macdara said.

Nuala scoffed. "Are you guards or are you politicians?"

"You should walk around the market while you wait," Siobhán said. "It's much cheerier than waiting in here."

Nuala waved a document. "Finn wouldn't steal my emeralds, because they were already his."

"What's that?" Macdara edged forward and Nuala handed him the documents.

"I'd already signed the emeralds over to Finn," Nuala said. "He was the one refusing to take them—he said he wanted to make sure we had a safety net—insisted I could live another twenty years." She glared at Siobhán and Macdara until they wholeheartedly agreed with the prediction.

Macdara glanced the certificate. "Why did it take you so long to bring this paperwork forth?"

Nuala dropped her chin. "I truly didn't think it was

anyone's business. I wasn't going to divulge anything unless it was absolutely necessary."

"Why didn't Finn tell us this himself?" Siobhán asked.

"Because Finn wouldn't even imagine that you'd suspect him of murder. He's very naïve in a lot of ways. But
he's the best grandson ever."

"Thank you for this. If you prefer to wait here I can
bring you a cup of tea," Siobhán said.

"You're still going to question him? Even after what I've
told you?"

"Why are you so afraid of us asking him questions?"
Macdara said.

Nuala's eyes moved ever so slightly to the left. *Bonnie
Murphy.* Siobhán thought of Michael's text: *Why don't
you dump that loser* . . . Was Finn the loser? What if
Michael had stolen Finn's inheritance, and was going after
his girl next? If that wasn't a double motive for murder,
Siobhán didn't know what was. Nuala had come here to
help her grandson, but she'd just placed a big bull's-eye on
his chest.

"Yes, the emeralds were mine. But it's still not what
you think," Finn said. "Is it possible to bring Shane and
Bonnie in?" He seemed uncomfortable in the interrogation room, which is exactly what the rooms were de-
signed to do.

"No," Macdara said. "We'll be interviewing you all in-
dividually."

"I can only hope they tell the truth," Finn grumbled.
"You have to promise me that you won't tell my granny
what I'm about to say."

"That's not how this works," Macdara said.

Finn sighed. "I invited Shane here to help me."

"Help you?" Siobhán asked.

Finn nodded. "My granny was so excited about leaving the emeralds to me in her will. She wanted to have them valuated again—she was hoping the value had gone up since they'd last been appraised, which had been when my da was around." He sighed. "I needed Shane to fake the appraisal. I told my granny that's what he did for a living. The truth is—he's just great with graphic design and was able to fake the appraisal and certificate."

This was unexpected. Macdara straightened up. "Faked? Why on earth did the appraisal need to be faked?"

"Because they're fake." Finn crossed his arms and waited.

"Explain," Macdara said.

Finn's head drooped. "My granny talked about those emeralds her entire life. How her mother had inherited them. It was her big nest egg, one she was proud to leave to her family—to me. I got some money when my da passed on. I used it to pay for Granny's place at the elder care home. Granny only agreed to it because she thought I'd be paid back when she died and I inherited the emeralds. When this last bill came due, she said she was bequeathing them to me now. What she didn't know was that when my da had had the emeralds appraised a long time ago he learned they were fake. My granny and her ma had been swindled. My father didn't want her to know. And once he passed, I didn't want her to know. They're worth nothing—except to her. And to her—they're worth everything."

Siobhán was momentarily stunned. If he was telling the truth it was a touching thing to do. Finn looked at them with a pleading expression. Macdara frowned. "Are you saying that Michael and someone else planned the robberies because they didn't realize the emeralds were worthless?"

"No. It was about protecting Granny. Those emeralds

were the world to her, her nest egg. I couldn't have her finding out they were worthless. I came up with the plan to have them 'stolen' and I was going to give her the rest of me savings, telling her the insurance had paid out on them. Shane had just read an article about Max—how Michael would tell him to go fetch his dolly or whatnot, and as long as there was a biscuit next to it, Max would fetch it. Sinead had just shown me the secret compartment in her Virgin Mary statue. I wanted to practice and see if Max would actually do it. He was only supposed to nick the cane and the Virgin Mary statue with the emeralds hidden inside. I thought it would look too suspicious if only the emeralds were stolen. I did not plan on stealing Rory's money. I have a sneaking suspicion Michael stole Rory's five hundred euro. We were going to return the cane, and statue. And, of course, if Michael didn't confess to taking the money I was going to replace that too. I was gobsmacked that it worked. Max actually took the items. We were waiting for him in me car by the back gardens. It was an absolutely eejit thing to do and I deeply regret it. But I swear to you. I had nothing to do with Michael's accident. I didn't hand him that scarf."

Macdara slid the report forward with Michael's text to Finn highlighted.

You won't get away with this

Finn sighed. "It was the last thing he ever said to me. It looks menacing but it just supports what I've just told you. When you two arrived he realized it was going to be seriously investigated. That's what he meant by me not getting away with it."

"Wait," Siobhán said. "If Shane was going to fake the appraisal, why did you need to pretend the emeralds had been stolen?"

"Because my granny was insisting on using her own appraiser. Any day now she was going to find out her emeralds were a fake. It doesn't seem too dire in the light of what happened to Michael, but at the time I thought I couldn't let that happen." Finn was starting to sweat. "I swear to you I was going to return all the items. Even the five hundred euro—although I had nothing to do with that."

"Where did you go when you dropped Michael off at the tractor parade and Bonnie off at the Christmas market?"

Finn grew animated. "I went to collect the items. They were all going to make a magical reappearance on the front porch on Christmas Eve." He paused. "There is one odd thing, and I know I should have said something when it ended up on Michael . . ."

"Go on," Macdara said gruffly.

"That scarf," Finn said. "We didn't take the scarf."

"But wasn't there a biscuit found in Beverly's room?"

Finn nodded. "I'm not saying Max didn't take the scarf, but he didn't bring it to us with the rest of the items."

And what about the fake emeralds?" Macdara said. "Were they going to make a magical reappearance?"

Finn shook his head. "I was going to tell my granny that the insurance money would pay out instead." He stared forlornly at the tabletop. "That's why we split up. One of us had to retrieve the items. But Michael thought it would look suspicious if only one of us was missing from the tractor rehearsal. We decided to divide and conquer. Michael would take the tractor practice, Bonnie would go to the Christmas market, and Shane would wait it out at a pub, while I collected the stolen items from my flat. Michael was really on edge that day. He was terrified you were going to cop on to the scheme, his involvement would be reported, and all his fancy publicity with Max would be soured."

Parts of the puzzle were shifting now, forming a different picture. *Publicity.* Michael grinning, snapping a photo of his hickey and sending it someone . . .

Finn was still talking. "That dog would have been worth a fortune if Michael had been able to attract sponsors. Worth way more than any emeralds . . ." Finn stopped talking for a moment and tilted his head, as if just now realizing something. "Max," he said, to himself. "Would have been worth a fortune." He stared at Macdara and Siobhán. Beverly's words the other day came roaring back to Siobhán, and she couldn't help but repeat them. "Woof."

Once Finn was released, Siobhán turned to Macdara. "We don't have time to interview Bonnie or Shane. I believe Finn about the robberies. It was a terrible thing to do to the residents and they may have to face charges for the scheme—but they're not the killers."

"None of them?" Macdara asked. "Are you sure about Bonnie and Shane?"

Siobhán nodded. "We need to ask Cathal Ryan a direct question, and depending on his answer—I believe we'll have our killer."

"Does it have something to do with Max?" Macdara said. "All those fancy sponsors?"

"No."

"Then what on earth are you talking about?" Macdara said.

Siobhán gestured for Macdara to follow her outside. She held up a finger as she found a private spot. The hustle and bustle of the market was dim enough for them to make the call, and loud enough so that they could be on speaker and no one else would overhear.

Cathal Ryan answered on the first ring. "I don't have

time for a lot of explaining," Siobhán said quickly. "I have to ask you a question and you must answer honestly."

"I'm always honest, Garda."

"When we first visited the care home, and you returned to the sitting room with Nancy Martin, you seemed a bit . . . out of breath. You had red lipstick on you."

"And you were tucking in your shirt," Macdara added.

"Oh," Cathal said. "And you thought Nancy and I?" He chuckled. "I see, I see. Hopefully you haven't floated that theory to Nancy's husband. He'd kill me."

"We assure you, we kept our theory to ourselves," Siobhán said.

"I had been accosted by Sinead. She was over the moon she was going to get to watch guards take her fingerprints and she ambushed me with a kiss to the cheek. I was out of breath because I was late to the sitting room so I ran. I'm madly in love with me wife. I would never cheat on her."

"Good man," Macdara said.

"There's something I forgot to tell you," Cathal said. "I found out why all the furniture in the recreation room was pushed against the walls. The staff was making room for the Christmas tree."

Another piece of the puzzle sorted. "Also on that visit you were missing your car keys, were you not?" Siobhán asked.

"I was," he said. "The housekeeper found them. I must have dropped them out of me pocket. I'm always on the go, I should be more careful where I put my keys."

"Do you drive a blue Toyota Corolla?"

There was a long pause. "I do."

"When you returned to your car that day—was there anything odd? Seat placement? Scents? Anything?"

"As a matter of fact—the radio station had changed. Horrible, horrible noise."

"We saw you on CCTV with Nancy Martin at the underpass," Macdara said. "It was the same day as the thefts. You appeared to be arguing."

"We were just upset," Cathal said. "The robberies had just occurred so she came to collect me."

"Thank you." Siobhán hung up before Cathal started asking them questions.

"Well?" Macdara asked.

"Nancy and Cathal were not romantically involved. Whoever was involved with Michael was willing to kill to keep the affair a secret." She waited as Macdara frowned. "Do you not think the future Mrs. Mayor might have wanted it kept under wraps?"

"Nancy Martin?" Macdara said. "And Michael Walsh?"

"I'd bet me life on it. She had access to everything. The brown robe. Cathal's car. Remember how his keys went missing? Don't tell me that's a coincidence. We know Michael could fixate on people. My guess is what started out as a little romp turned more serious for him. Maybe he wanted Rory's five hundred euro to splurge on her. She was in and out of Beverly's room; she could have easily taken the scarf right after the thefts. The residents had just been talking about long scarf syndrome. And then there was the loud music playing in the car—heavy metal. Prior to that she'd been blasting Christmas music in the house. Everyone commented on it. She wanted people to notice it. This way no one would associate her with someone else's car blasting heavy metal. And that way no one could hear her voice as she got out of the car and spoke with Michael."

"He must have sent her a picture of his hickey so she brought him a scarf to cover it up," Macdara said.

"That's probably what Michael thought. That's why he allowed her to put the scarf around his neck. A little joke between secret lovers. But she was around for all that long scarf talk. I think she knew exactly what she was doing." Siobhán sighed. "That doesn't mean I can prove it."

"But she was at the care home when Michael was killed," Macdara said.

"She must have snuck out. Remember—she brought all the folks who'd had items stolen into the sitting room to have a chat with us. But Nancy and Cathal took ages, remember?"

"How could I forget."

"Nancy had enough time to take Cathal's keys, then drive to her lover and back, and return the keys before we even knew she was gone."

"Doctor Jeanie Brady was right all along," Macdara said. "We need a confession. We need a Christmas miracle."

"Then let's help one along, like Santa's elves," Siobhán said. "I have a plan."

Chapter Twelve

Siobhán and Macdara stood in the underpass to King John's Castle, waiting for their opportunity. They had set up an additional tent and parked it at the end of a row just a few meters away. The tent would be set up to collect donations for animal shelters in honor of Michael Walsh. Nancy Martin had taken the bait and would be working the first shift. The tent was located in a unique position. Siobhán and Macdara could stand at the edge of the underpass and pretend to have a private conversation, but given the special acoustics in that spot, and where Nancy's tent was located, she would be able to hear every word. When Nancy arrived, they would launch into their "private" discussion and hoped it would do the trick. It took nearly an hour for Nancy to arrive, at which point they were tired of practicing their faux-discussion and the smells and sounds of the Christmas market made them long to be a part of it. But finally, it happened. Nancy was alone and in place at the tent. They were ready.

"We've got a breakthrough," Macdara said. "Can you believe the future mayor's wife is involved in something like this?" Although they could not see Nancy from this vantage point, another guard was catching it all on film and the feed was going directly into Macdara's mobile.

They watched Nancy freeze as she caught the sound of her own name.

"Nancy Martin," Siobhán said. "I still can't believe she was having an affair with Michael Walsh. Do you think she intended on murdering him?"

"I do," Macdara said. "And the Technical Bureau was finally able to access Michael's photos. Thank goodness for the cloud. We didn't even need his mobile! Let's pay a visit to her husband while she's occupied here."

Nancy was on the move. She exited the tent, and broke into a run.

"That didn't take long," Siobhán said.

"She must be headed for her car," Macdara said. "Lucky for us we have primo parking." They hurried to the car park at the back of the garda station and hopped in. It was a little over fifteen minutes to Nancy's house right along the tractor route. Siobhán and Macdara had already arranged for a tow truck to block the road in the exact spot where Michael had died. Hopefully this would heighten her distress, and weaken her lips. Unless they received a full confession, this was all for nothing. But the one thing they had in their favor was human nature. Secrets were difficult to keep inside. People tended to have a clawing need to let them out.

Their Santy outfits were awaiting them in the garda car. Siobhán changed into hers first while Macdara drove. Once they reached Michael's tractor, now adorned with flowers and wreaths and cards, another guard hopped out of the tow truck and backed up to allow their car past. They would park it behind the giant tow truck and Nancy would be none the wiser. Macdara changed into his Santa outfit and they were ready. He turned to Siobhán and grinned. "You make a great Mrs. Claus."

She laughed. "And if you keep eating the way you have

been lately, you'll grow right into that Santa tummy."
That was the end of their playful banter. Nancy Martin
screeched up in a red car. She frowned at the pair of Santas
and then laid on her horn. Siobhán put her white-gloved
hand out and gestured for her to roll down the window.

"I have to get home," Nancy said. "I have a family
emergency."

"I'm afraid you'll have to turn around and take another
approach," Siobhán said. "We've just been called in to
move this tractor."

Nancy's gaze pivoted to the tractor. "I thought it was
supposed to stay as a memorial for the tractor parade."

Macdara hopped down from the tow truck. "We just do
as we're told," he said. "But between us, it seems there's
new evidence they think they can glean from the tractor."

"Really?" Nancy said, her chin quivering. "I don't believe it."

Siobhán leaned forward. "A stray hair," she said.
"Clinging to the wheel well."

Nancy's eyes widened.

"It's amazing what they can do these days, isn't it?"
Macdara said.

"The hair of the dog," Siobhán said. "Or in this case . . .
the killer."

"Killer?" Nancy said. "Surely it was a horrible, horrible
accident."

"Not what I heard, but what do I know," Macdara said.

"If it was an accident, why would the fella have to disguise himself?" Siobhán said.

Nancy frowned. "I assumed it was an actor in the panto,"
she said.

"We shouldn't have told you about the hair," Macdara
said. "Do you mind keeping this to yourself?"

"Of course," Nancy said. Her voice wavered. "If you let me pass?"

Macdara grinned. "No can do. We need to tow this baby. Do you mind turning around and finding another way home?"

"I can't do that. Do you know who my husband is?" Not even mayor yet and she was already putting herself above them.

Siobhán pointed to Macdara. "My husband is Santa Claus. Can you beat that?"

Nancy let out a roar of frustration, turned off her car, and exited with her mobile phone glued to her ear. Siobhán and Macdara exchanged a glance. Neither of them had any idea how to tow away a tractor, so they hoped this would work. "Darling," they heard Nancy say. "Are you at home? I need you to go to Charlesville. The butcher has a turkey and ham waiting for us—and they've had a run on them so if we don't pick it up today, we'll miss out on our Christmas dinner. I know. I know. I know. I' can't—there's an emergency at the care home. Just do it. Just do it. Bye. Bye. Bye-bye-bye." She hung up, then approached the tractor.

"Did you know the victim?" Siobhán asked as Nancy got as close as she dared, eyeing it as if trying to figure out where that pesky little hair could be.

"I know I'm not the mayor's wife *yet*," Nancy said, ignoring the question. "But it would really help me if you'd let me pass, and maybe when my husband is the mayor, there's something he can do for you? Better pay, shorter hours?"

"We're actually not locals," Macdara said. "Just called in to do a job."

"I see." Nancy looked around as if trying to make sure no one was in earshot. "Then perhaps you could do me a favor that's in your wheelhouse."

"What's that?" Siobhán said.

"It's so embarrassing, but I wonder if you could look at my back tire. I think it's flat, but I'm not an expert."

Macdara and Siobhán exchanged a look. What was she up to? They had learned in this business to never underestimate a killer. Especially when she was desperate.

"Have a look," Macdara said to Siobhán.

"Not a bother," Siobhán said. She strolled toward the back of Nancy's car, wondering what the possible-future Mrs. Mayor had in mind. Luckily, she had an inkling what Nancy was up to and had already formulated an idea of her own. Once she arrived at the boot, sure enough, Siobhán heard a beep and the boot yawned open. Nancy was controlling it with a remote. Next, Siobhán felt a shove from behind and her front half toppled into the boot. As she pretended to struggle to get up, Nancy grabbed her feet to maneuver her all the way in. Siobhán waited a few seconds, allowing her entire body to be shoved inside. Then, she yelled for Macdara. He was there in a flash, grabbing Nancy as she tried to make a run for it.

"She just fell in," Nancy said, once she stopped trying to squirm out of Macdara's grasp. "I opened it to see if there was a spare tire."

"She pushed me all the way in," Siobhán said. "She thought you would come running to help me out of the boot and she could make a run for it."

"I did come running," Macdara said. "Too bad yer one wasn't fast enough."

Nancy stopped struggling and her shoulders slumped. Just then Siobhán spotted something in the corner of the boot, grabbed it, and held it up. "And then there's this." It was a piece of red yarn, presumably from Beverly's scarf.

Nancy seemed to shrink before their very eyes. "You're not really tow truck workers, are you?"

"We're not Santa either," Macdara said, ripping off his beard. "Detective Sergeant Flannery, and you know Garda O'Sullivan."

Siobhán dangled the yarn. "Belongs to Beverly's scarf, doesn't it, Nancy?"

"You can't prove a thing," Nancy said.

"But we can book you on kidnapping charges, and hold you in custody until enough evidence comes in to charge you with Michael's murder," Siobhán said.

"Kidnapping?" Nancy said.

Siobhán smiled. "You shoved me in the boot against my will."

"I saw the whole thing," Macdara said. "Kidnapping charges is spot-on."

"You two think you're so clever don't you?" She shook her head. "Fine. I gave Michael the scarf. Good luck proving it was anything other than an innocent gesture."

"You're forgetting about the affair," Siobhán said. "And the love bite."

"DNA on the neck," Macdara said. "Amazing what science can do these days, isn't it?"

"And that burner phone you tried to get rid of," Siobhán said. "I'm afraid we have that as well."

"Please," Nancy said. "My husband is running for mayor. He'll never forgive me."

"Michael Walsh was a young lad with his entire life ahead of him," Macdara said. "Shame on you."

Nancy's eyes flashed with anger. "Shame on me? He was the one who wouldn't let it go. What did he think? I was going to leave my husband? It was just a little fling."

"Did he threaten to tell your husband?" Siobhán asked. "Was he stalking you?"

Nancy was crumbling, Siobhán knew the look. "He sent me a picture of the mark on his neck and said he was going to send it to my husband." Nancy thrust her chin up. "I suppose you think I'm a joke. Having an affair with a man half my age."

She was talking and Siobhán wanted to keep it that way. "I don't think you're a joke. I'm sure you never imagined you'd have to do something like this."

"I did it for my husband. It would have ruined his chance at becoming mayor. For what? A little fling? It meant nothing."

"But Michael wasn't the type of lad to let things go," Macdara said. "Was he?"

"Being middle-aged and around all those elderly folks does something to a person," Nancy said. "Don't get me wrong. I love them to bits. But it's a stark reminder of what's coming. Michael was into me. When will that ever happen to me again? One's husband running for mayor isn't as glamorous as it sounds. He's never home. He certainly never shows me any attention anymore. Michael was different. He was so full of energy. I thought for sure he'd understand that it was never going to be more than a brief affair." She gazed at the tractor with a sad expression. "And then Cathal told me Michael had a criminal past. A *stalker*. I saw it then. My life becoming a nightmare. And then I turned around, and there was Beverly's scarf tucked under the chair in the library. It hadn't been stolen after all."

"We're going to need you to come to the station," Macdara said.

"Can I call my husband?" she said. "He'll straighten this out." He didn't have *that* kind of power, but Nancy Martin would find that out in due time.

"You'll get a phone call," Siobhán said. "I promise."

"What about my car?" Nancy said as they guided her into the guard car. Just then the tow truck started up.

"He'll sort that out," Macdara said, with a nod to the driver. Siobhán turned on the radio and "Silent Night" came on. She increased the volume. After all, Nancy was a mad one for the Christmas tunes. They rode the rest of the way with the music on high.

Folks lined both sides of the winding road as the sky turned a fiery orange before morphing into to a bluish-black. Christmas Eve was here at last. A low hum filled the air as the tractors passed by, lights moving through the darkness. How gorgeous they all were. Some had mechanical reindeer and candy canes, others bows, and bells. Even the wheels were decorated, making it seem as if the lights themselves were moving through time and space. Siobhán was wondering which tractor belonged to her brood when she saw an enormous heart made from red lights featured prominently on the bonnet of a tractor. Inside the heart, lights spelled out: *Our 1st Xmas.* Tears came to Siobhán's eyes, and just when she was starting to wonder why Macdara wasn't teasing her for the waterworks, she turned to find his were brimming as well. She slipped her hand into his and squeezed it. James and Ciarán yelled out "Happy Christmas!" as Eoin, Ann, and Gráinne, dressed as elves, tossed candy canes out to the people lining the road. Eoin had Trigger under an arm and he was sporting a little red bow. Max was in the parade too, riding with Bill Casey, and sitting up proud as he took in the crowd. Gráinne flung something at Siobhán. It whacked her in the forehead and dropped into the palm of her hand. She looked down to find a sprig of mistletoe.

"You're welcome," Gráinne yelled.

"Well," Macdara said, turning to her. "When in Ireland."

Siobhán laughed and held the mistletoe over their heads. "Happy first Christmas, wife," Macdara said.

"Happy first Christmas, husband." They kissed as bells and cheers rang out.

After the parade, Siobhán, Macdara, and her five siblings stood in front of their stone house, taking in the beauty. Jeanie Brady would arrive on Christmas Day, but the eve was just for family. A brand-new lion's-head knocker gleamed from the door. Macdara said it must be a gift from Santa. Eoin and James had brought in a Christmas tree the day before and everyone planned on decorating it all through the night. Siobhán had squeezed in the last few hours at the Christmas market and this year each of them would have a new ornament to commemorate their new home. Candles flickered in the window, and a bespoke wreath with white lights and a red bow winked from the door. Bonnie had been spot-on, Oscar's wreath was class.

Thanks to the prodding of Nancy Martin's husband, who very well might make a great mayor, she had made a full confession to the murder. Given the stolen items had all been returned, and the three young folks had agreed to do community service, they were not charged with any crimes. Mostly they were spared due to the pleading of the folks at the elder care home who did not wish to see them charged. Max had gone home after the tractor parade with Michael's family. Siobhán and Macdara planned on paying the elder care home a visit tomorrow, this time with her brood in tow. Cathal Ryan would be busy looking for a new house manager, and everyone was rallying around to support the effort.

Gráinne turned to them, a grin planted on her face. "We have another surprise."

"I don't know if I can take anymore," Siobhán said.

"Sort yourself out," Gráinne said. "Hit it, Eoin."

Eoin revealed a small remote hidden in his pocket and pressed a button. Soon, a word and a heart symbol lit up above their doorway: HOME. Tears filled Siobhán's eyes as she forced everyone to smash in for a group hug.

"*Nollaig shona daoibh*," Macdara said. *Happy Christmas to you.*

"*Nollaig shona daoibh*," they all responded.

"As long as we're all together," Siobhán said, "we'll always and forever be home."

I met Noel McMeel, an award-winning Irish chef, at a book event in Chicago a few years ago. He said I was welcome to use his recipes in my books. Here is one from his book Irish Pantry. *(I highly recommend the book.) The photo shows lacy curled-up biscuits that he notes are "eaten with the eyes first." And if the dog happens to snap one up, he or she will love it too.*

Irish Lace Biscuits

Reprinted from *Irish Pantry* by Noel McMeel and Lynne Marie Hulsman—*Shared with oral permission*

Makes about 3 dozen biscuits

Ingredients
12 ounces unsalted butter at room temperature (Kerry's
    Irish butter a great choice—my comment)
2¾ cups light brown sugar
2 tablespoons all-purpose flour
2 tablespoons milk
2 tablespoons vanilla extract
1¼ cup old-fashioned rolled oats

Directions
Preheat the oven to 350 degrees

Grease 2 baking sheets with vegetable oil or line with parchment paper. Set in oven while it is heating up.

Using an electric mixer on high speed, cream the butter and brown sugar together until smooth. Beat in the flour, milk, and vanilla. Fold in the oats. Place teaspoonfuls of dough 3-inches apart on the hot pans. Bake for 10 to 12 minutes, keeping a close eye on them so you can remove them from the oven as soon as they are fully spread and turn light golden brown.

When the cookies are done, let them cool on the pans for 1 minute or until they are just firm enough to be removed with a metal spatula. If you like them rolled into tubes, turn the cookies upside down on the pans, and working quickly with your hands, roll them into cylinders on the pans. (If the cookies become too firm to roll, return them to the oven for a few seconds and allow them to soften.) Transfer the cookies to a cooling rack and let them cool completely, then serve them at room temperature or store in airtight container for up to a month.

Follow this link for a great article on Noel:

https://www.forbes.com/sites/margiegoldsmith-/2019/03/18/top-chef-noel-mcmeel-king-of-modern-irish-cuisine/?sh=3830811013f9

SCARFED DOWN

Maddie Day

Chapter One

Ikept learning about new ways to murder people. Was it bad karma or something more random? Either way, I wished I could instruct the universe, "That's quite enough, thank you very much."

"More coffee?" I—Robbie Jordan—asked the knitting club members that mid-December Tuesday morning.

"No, thanks, hon." Vicky Chakrabarti clicked away at a green scarf. Her hands and fingers were reddened. The knitting looked like it might be painful, but she kept on. "I surely do love what you've done with your decorations."

It did look festive in Pans 'N Pancakes, my country store and restaurant. My staff and I had gone to work more than two weeks ago stringing garlands and fairy lights, hanging wreaths and red ribbons, and trimming the store's Douglas fir, which my husband Abe O'Neill and I had cut at Greasy Hollow Christmas Tree Farm. My customers seemed to enjoy the decor, even people who might not celebrate Christmas themselves.

"Thank you." I held up the carafe. "Anybody?"

"I'll take a hit, if you don't mind." Eva Kenney set down the four needles enmeshed in the multihued yarn she was using to knit a sock and held up her mug. Eva, a few inches taller than my height of five foot three, had a soft figure indicating she might like a rib-eye more than running, would choose cheesecake over calisthenics, and generally preferred eating over exercise.

I certainly wasn't judging Eva for her choices. I loved cake as much as the next girl, and my hips showed it. It was only my bicycling habit and my hundred sit-ups every morning that kept my waist in line. That, and running my tush off as chief chef of my own eating establishment.

"Me, too, please." Cole Brewster pointed at his mug with his chin, his hands being full of needles and yarn. The tall, austere-looking real estate agent was knitting something red that was starting to look like a hat.

"I do love your aunt's yarn," Vicky said. "Why, it's softer than a talcum-dusted baby's bottom after its bath." Despite her last name, her speech held the same Hoosier twang as many of the locals. Vicky had told me she was born in Bloomington, the university town to the west of us, where both of her Indian immigrant parents had been professors. She was a handsome woman, slender with only a bit of silver shooting through her dark hair.

I poured. "I'll tell her you said so. Aunt Adele takes a lot of pride in her wool." My late mom's sister, Adele Jordan, raised sheep on the outskirts of South Lick here in southern Indiana and dyed the wool herself. I made a note to ask her to bring in more. For sale in the retail area of my store, it was a popular purchase at the holidays, and I was nearly out.

"It don't make my skin itch, neither, not like some wools." Eva gazed up at me with light brown eyes bordering on green.

I was so not a crafter and couldn't imagine focusing on tiny stitches—itchy or otherwise—over and over for hours. But when these three sixty-somethings from surrounding towns had asked if I minded whether they stayed on after their midmorning breakfast twice a week to knit and schmooze, I had readily welcomed them. It was our lull time in the restaurant, when my assistants and I took breaks, grabbed a bite to eat, and got going on the lunch menu. We rarely had a line of hungry diners waiting for a table between ten and eleven-thirty on a weekday unless a tour bus rolled in.

Speaking of the lunch menu, it was smelling pretty good right now in a space already redolent with the alluring aromas of bacon and biscuits. I headed back to the kitchen area and pulled open the oven door.

"How's the Partridge in a Pear Tree looking?" Danna Beedle, one of my two employees, asked from the grill.

"If by partridge you mean boneless chicken breasts baking with sliced pears, it's looking great."

Turner Rao, my other employee, walked up with a load of dishes in his arms. "And smelling even better. But what are we going to do when we get to Twelve Lords a-Leaping?"

I wrinkled my nose. "Riffing on the 'Twelve Days of Christmas' for our daily specials seemed like a good idea yesterday."

"Nine Ladies Dancing is going to be tough, too," Danna chimed in.

"We could do a dessert with ladyfingers." Turner cocked his head.

"Brilliant. We'll figure out each day as we go along." I glanced over at the knitters.

Was Cole clandestinely rubbing Eva's foot under the table? I'd never seen those two act like a couple, and their expressions looked perfectly normal for friends knitting and chatting. *Oh, well.* Definitely not my business. None of the three wore wedding rings. Even if they did, I still didn't care what they did in their personal lives. My mission here was to provide delicious breakfasts and lunches, make customers feel comfortable and welcome, and keep the finances in the black. So far, my business had been a rousing success on all fronts for over four years.

The cow bell on the front door jangled. Adele pushed through, with a giant—and stuffed-full—cloth tote bag in each hand. I hurried over to relieve my mid-seventies aunt of her burdens. Over her slate-gray pageboy, she wore one of her own creations, a knitted red-and-green striped hat with a puffball at its pointed top.

I kissed her cheek. "Some hat."

"You like it? It's my newest design." She dragged it off her head.

"I do."

"Brung you a new load of yarn." Adele pointed at the totes now in my hands.

"Perfect. I was about to call you to say we're nearly out. Did you price them?"

"Yup, just like usual."

"And, as usual, you don't have an invoice for me."

"Nah," she scoffed. "If I can't trust my own niece, who can I trust? Just keep track and pay me for what sells. That's all I ask."

"I promise. Do you want something to eat while you're here?"

"Sure thing, kiddo. Who can't use a second breakfast? I'd take me a plate of biscuits and gravy any old day."

"It's yours." I smiled. She and I shared a love of eating, and we both worked hard enough to earn the calories. "Hey, do you know the people knitting at that table? They all love your yarn."

"Well, butter my butt and call me a biscuit."

I was amused by her colorful language, but that particular phrase was over the top.

"I might have seen them folks around town," she went on. "Yes, I do believe I have. Welp, no time like the present to renew our acquaintance. Thanks, sugar." Adele sauntered over to the knitters' table.

My aunt was one of those people who had never met a stranger she couldn't instantly turn into a friend. A friend for life, usually. Today was no exception. I headed back to the kitchen to plate her morning snack as she pulled up a chair and started yarning about yarn.

Chapter Two

I was about to lock up behind Danna and Turner at three that afternoon when my stepson, Sean, rode up and jumped off his bike. I greeted him, then wrapped my arms around myself. So far, we hadn't had any snow, but it was already frigid out. My winter uniform of long-sleeved blue T-shirt and jeans wasn't anywhere near warm enough for standing outside. I waited to hear why he was here.

"Hey, Robbie." His fifteen-year-old voice had stopped cracking and had settled into a nice baritone like Abe's. "I need help with something."

Maybe it was a math assignment for school. I could dust off my former high school math-team chops and help with that. "Come on in." I stood back and held the door open for him.

He carried the bike up onto the wide covered porch and left it. It wasn't a fancy bike and should be safe out here.

Inside I thought about what I could offer him to eat. "The grill is off and clean, but I can make you a ham and cheese on rye."

"Thanks, Robbie." He slid out of his jacket and took off his gloves, his cheeks still pink from the cold. He was already taller than Abe's five nine and was still growing. "I'm starving."

"When are you not?" I smiled at him. Sean's teenage appetite was as legendary as our local police lieutenant's. I'd never seen anyone eat as much as Buck Bird—until I met Sean. I busied myself with sandwich makings. "Grab yourself a glass of milk, sweetie."

I had slowly, cautiously, ventured into using endearments with him. The poor kid had lost his mother to a murderer last spring, and I knew I couldn't take her place. But I was quite fond of him and hoped he knew it. He'd never pulled back from my affection, for which I was grateful. He and Abe and I had been sharing a home since I'd married Abe at the end of May.

I set down the plate, plus two brownies, on the table nearest the kitchen area. "Talk to me while I do breakfast prep for tomorrow, okay?"

"Sure, and thanks."

For tomorrow's breakfast special, we were reprising an easy spinach–red pepper egg bake we'd done during a previous Christmas season, with the reds and greens reflecting the season. I brought out red peppers, butter, and milk from the walk-in, scrubbed my hands and the peppers, and began seeding and dicing.

Sean made quick work of the sandwich. He opened his backpack.

I glanced over. And stared. He had pulled out two skeins of yarn, one red and one green, and a set of knitting needles with a project already underway.

"You know how to knit?" I asked.

"Sort of." He swiped and thumbed his phone. "I mean, I'm, like, learning. I have an app, but I'm kind of screwed up right now." He frowned, holding up the needles and a few inches of loose uneven knitting.

"Is that what you wanted my help with?"

"Can you?" His hopeful tone matched his expression.

"Sorry, dude. I have never knitted and have no desire to learn." I smiled to soften my answer. "Math homework? That I can help with."

"Except I don't need help with math. But I don't know what to do with this mess. I wanted to make something nice for Maeve." He blushed as he said her name.

"Sean, honey, you need Aunt Adele. Is that her yarn?"

"Uh-huh." He nodded.

"She'll be super happy to help you. Text her. I'll bet she'll come right down, or maybe visit at the house tonight."

He brightened, his thumbs already flying with the text. He finished and took a bite of brownie.

"Is Maeve the girl from math club?" I asked.

"Yeah. We've been, like, hanging out a lot this fall."

"That's cool to want to give her something homemade. You can invite her home for dinner sometime if you want." I covered my container of prepped peppers and set it aside. We had seen a girl who was part of a group Sean spent time with, and I thought it had been a friend from math club. Until now he hadn't mentioned that Maeve was more than a friend, but it sure looked like it. "We'd love to get to know her."

He stopped short of rolling his eyes. "Maybe." He stashed the knitting back in his bag. "Hey, Robbie?"

"Yes?" I measured out flour for tomorrow's biscuit dough.

"Yesterday after school, before you and Dad got home, this guy came to the door." Sean frowned.

"What did he want?" I added baking powder and salt and stirred.

"He wanted to know if we wanted to sell the house."

"Really? Unsolicited?"

"Yeah. I told him no way. I forgot to tell you guys last

night." He pulled a crumpled business card out of his jacket pocket. "Here." He extended it toward me.

I dusted off my hands and stepped over to the table, keeping my arms bent and my hands near my shoulders. "Lay it down so I can see it. I need to keep my hands clean."

I leaned over the table where Sean placed the card. "Cole Brewster?" I straightened. "Was he a tall, serious-looking man? Kind of bony?"

"Yep. Why, you know him?"

"He's part of the Tuesday-Thursday knitting club that comes in here. He sat right over there a few hours ago." I gestured with my chin. "He didn't say anything about the house."

"Maybe he doesn't know you live with us now. You lived back there for a long time." Sean pointed to the door at the back that led to the apartment where, in fact, I had resided since I'd bought the country store, thanks to my inheritance after my mom's untimely death. Until I married Abe, that is.

"True," I said. "What he did just seems strange. Did he knock on other doors on the street?"

Sean lifted a shoulder. "I don't know. I went back to my room. We have an essay due on Friday."

"On what?"

"Yuck. *The Old Man and the Sea*. Talk about picking apart a story until it dies a slow death. If I'd found it and read it for fun, I might have liked it. Now I never want to read another word by that Hemingway dude."

I laughed and resumed prepping biscuit dough. "You know, you don't have to answer the door when someone knocks or rings the bell. It might be safer not to."

"Robbie." He gave me a look.

Sheesh. Did teenagers practice The Look?

"I'm not a little kid," he went on. "I mean, look at me."

"You're right. I'm sorry."

He was totally right. Low voice, on his way to six feet tall, hairy. Obviously—I hoped—Cole Brewster was harmless. Still, Abe and I were responsible for this young person for years to come. I'd hate to see him threatened or hurt by some random stranger.

"Be careful, okay?" I cut a two-pound block of butter into cubes.

"I will."

"And don't ever let anybody in you don't know."

This time he did roll his eyes. His phone dinged and his expression brightened. "Adele's meeting me at the house in fifteen for a knitting lesson." He jumped up and shrugged into his warm outerwear and his pack. He grabbed his dishes, setting them in the sink before rushing a kiss onto my cheek. "Thanks, Robbie. See you at dinner."

"See you then. Have fun with Adele." I followed him over and locked the door after him. Before I began cutting the butter into the flour mixture, I again peered at Cole's card, which Sean had left on the table.

"'Residential, business, and vacation real estate,'" I read aloud. The address was in Nashville—Indiana, of course—which made sense. The county seat five miles away was a much larger town than South Lick. Next time the knitting club came in, I was definitely asking Cole about scoping out our house. Something seemed fishy about it. But what?

Chapter Three

When I walked into our cottage at four-thirty, Adele was still there. She and Sean both glanced up from their side-by-side perches on the sofa. They weren't genetically related, and their ages were separated by six decades, but their grins were identical. Cocoa, Sean's two-year-old chocolate Labrador, sat in a relaxed Sphinx pose, watching them. He cocked his head to check me out, then resumed guarding his human.

"Looks like things are working out." I plucked off my maroon knitted cap and slipped out of parka and mittens.

"Hard to believe this kiddo thought he could learn to knit from some fool program on his phone." Adele winked at Sean. "The youth of today. Heaven help us."

"Hey, Aunt Adele, most apps are, like, super useful," Sean protested.

I loved that he called her "Aunt." We were a blended family, but a family, nonetheless.

"I s'pose that's true. Anyhoo, I think the boy picked up a couple few tips. Show her, hon."

Sean smoothed out ten inches of red-and-green scarf on his lap. The piece was even, the stitches regular, and the knitting tight.

"It looks beautiful," I said. "You got a mini-apprenticeship. That's really the only way to learn something you do with your hands."

"She's a good teacher. Thank you, Aunt Adele." Sean picked up his phone and muttered what might have been a mild swear word under his breath. "I promised Dad I would put in the roast beef."

"Do you need help?" I asked him.

"No, I know how. Stick some garlic in, add a bunch of salt and pepper, and pop her in a hot oven." He stood and bussed Adele's cheek, then stashed his project in a cloth Bloomingfoods bag, which he held up. "Cool, right? I went to the food co-op in Bloomington last week with Maeve."

"Very."

"Aunt Adele, want to stay for dinner?" he asked. "We'll have plenty. I'm roasting potatoes and vegetables, too."

"Thanks, sugar, but I can't." She beamed at Sean. "Next time."

"Come on, Cocoa. Want to go outside?" Sean patted his thigh.

I watched teen and dog disappear into the kitchen.

"He's a good boy," Adele murmured.

"I'll say. Want a glass of wine or anything?" I asked Adele. "Four Roses?"

"Thought you'd never ask. Samuel's picking me up at five, so I have time for some of my favorite bourbon with my favorite niece."

Samuel MacDonald was Adele's eighty-something sweetheart, an arrangement I approved of.

"Ice?" I asked. "Or mixed with some sweet vermouth for a quick Manhattan?" Manhattans always seemed like a cold-weather drink to me.

"That sounds yummy."

"Coming right up." In the kitchen I filled a couple of

glasses with ice, alcohol, and a dash of bitters. The oven was preheating but Sean seemed to be elsewhere.

I handed Adele her drink and took Sean's place on the sofa. My kitty, Birdy, wandered in and sprang up to nestle next to me, purring louder than a ceiling fan in summer. He'd adjusted perfectly well to his new home after only a couple of days. My aunt and I clinked glasses.

I sipped and let out a contented breath. "That totally hits the spot."

She tasted her own, agreeing. Sounds from the kitchen indicated Sean had gotten back to the task at hand.

"You know Cole Brewster." I sank into the soft seat. I'd been up since five. Finally sitting down and sipping an adult beverage was exactly what the doctor ordered.

"Real estate man? 'Course I do, hon. The fellow in the knitting club, with Vicky Chakra-whosit and old Eva Kenney."

"Yes, exactly. Sean said Cole was in the neighborhood yesterday cold-calling at houses asking if they wanted to sell. Why would he do something like that?"

"I'd hate to think the man's hard up for money. I thought he was purt successful in his work." She sipped her drink. "But I don't know. Maybe he isn't. What I did hear is that he's sweet on Eva."

"I might have picked up on that this morning. It was just a little thing, but that was what I thought."

"Vicky used to go out with him, but she dropped him one day like he was hotter than a potato baked the other side of Hades and blessed by Lucifer himself."

The senior dating scene around here was more active than I'd suspected.

"How do you know all those people?" I asked her.

"Oh, heck, Robbie. You know I'm acquainted with plum

anybody south of Indy, it seems like. And when I had that little chat at their table this morning, it all came back to me."

With a burst of cold air, Abe pushed through the door. "Whew, it's getting colder by the minute. Hey, Adele." He gave me a cold-lipped kiss, and leaned over to kiss Adele's cheek, too. He sniffed. "Smells like Sean got dinner underway."

"He's a good boy you got there, Abe." Adele drained her glass.

"Thank you." Abe shed his coat and hat and stuffed his gloves in his pockets. "We try."

My aunt stood. "Samuel's going to be waiting for me. Thanks for the drink, hon."

I rose, too. "Of course. Thanks for helping Sean."

"You and Samuel are joining us for Christmas Eve dinner, right, Adele?" Abe asked.

We'd decided to host both sides of the family for a feast here, since it was my first Christmas in the house.

"Wouldn't miss it for nothing. Can we bring Phil, too? His parents are going away somewheres."

"Of course," Abe said. "And if he wants to include his girlfriend, let him know that's fine." Phil MacDonald, my friend and dessert baker, was Samuel's grandson.

Adele suited up and made her way out. Abe wrapped his arms around me for a long embrace.

"How did I get so lucky to find you?" he murmured into my hair.

I pushed back and laughed. "I was about to say that myself. Sit down and I'll get you a beer."

"Gladly."

A minute later I was nestled next to him telling him about Sean's encounter with Cole.

"Sean didn't let him into the house, did he?" Abe frowned.

"No, and he says he knows he shouldn't. I find it odd, though, what Cole was doing. Sean didn't know if he knocked only here or on other doors on the street."

"I'll see what I can find out."

We sat keeping quiet company, sipping our drinks. I mused on a possibly suspicious person. And on our little town having been blessedly free of suspicious goings-on for nearly half a year. May it stay so.

Chapter Four

By seven-thirty the next morning, Pans 'N Pancakes was hopping. Nearly all the tables were full. We'd already gone through one pan of hot biscuits, and the breakfast special was proving popular. Danna poured and flipped at the grill as fast as she could, while I poured coffee and took orders at a similar pace. Turner would report for work at eight, which was a good thing.

Buck ambled in a few minutes later, all lanky six-foot-six of him. I pointed to his preferred two-top at the back. The weather continued frigid, especially with the sun not rising until eight at this darkest time of the year, and the coat rack already overflowed with puffy jackets and wool coats. The lieutenant kept his uniform winter jacket on, not shedding it until he sat. I made my way over, coffee carafe in hand, and greeted him.

"Boy, howdy, Robbie, it's colder than a bullfrog's hind leg out there, and darker than a pocket."

I smiled as I poured his coffee. "But there's peace in South Lick, I hope."

"So far, and that's the way we like it. Now, though, I got a hole in my stomach as big as two Grand Canyons." He squinted at the Specials board. "I don't need no green stuff in my breakfast. Can I get me the—" His phone made a sound. He held up a finger and jabbed at it. "Yes. You what, now?"

"I'll bring you your usual," I murmured.

He glanced up and nodded, his expression pivoting into ultra-serious.

I poured coffee on my way back to the kitchen area and scribbled an order for Buck on my pad—pancakes, biscuits with sausage gravy, two sunny-side-up, ham, and hash browns. It was a lot of food, and he would get through every single bite. I hoped his call wasn't a colleague reporting a bad accident or something worse. Except I hadn't heard any sirens.

We were so busy it was ten minutes before Danna signaled Buck's order was ready.

"Here's his blowout patches, heart attack on a rack, two sunnies with Noah's boy, and hash browns."

I loved her diner lingo. "Thanks. I think Buck might have gotten some serious news. Let me see if he'll tell me, then I can swap in at the grill, if you want."

"Cool." She folded over a Kitchen Sink omelet and flipped four whole-wheat banana-walnut pancakes before transferring three rashers of bacon to a plate waiting under the warming lights.

I set Buck's breakfast on the table, where he was staring at his phone but not holding it to his ear.

"Is everything okay?" I asked.

"What?" He shook himself. "Oh, thanks, Robbie. No, everything's not okay, not by a heck of a long shot."

I waited, even though I didn't really have time to.

"Seems an older lady died over in Beanblossom, and it weren't a natural death, neither."

"You mean homicide." I kept my voice low, but it was so noisy in here, I doubted the diners at even the adjacent tables could hear me.

"Yup. Her friend found the victim in her apartment."

"In the victim's?"

"Yeperoo."

"Beanblossom is an unincorporated county town, so that means the county sheriff's office will handle the investigation, right?"

"You got it, and Cousin Wanda's on the case. That was her on the phone."

Buck's cousin, Wanda Bird, had started out with the South Lick police. She and I clashed a bit early on. After she transferred into the county sheriff's office in Nashville, she found romance and improved health in her life, losing a bunch of weight and marrying a state police detective only a few months ago. She also became more easygoing.

"Good. Buck, I have to get back to work. Can you tell me the name of the woman who was killed?"

"I don't see why not. Knowing you, you'll start poking around, anyway. She was Victoria Chaka something or other. Went by Vicky."

No. My breath rushed in. "Vicky Chakrabarti?"

Buck pointed at me. "That's it. Why, you knowed her?" He forked in a too-large bite of pancakes.

"She comes in here with a knitting group. They were here only yesterday. That's awful she was killed. How did she die?"

"Don't rightly know yet. All I can say is, the county coroner thought it looked suspicious. And the death was definitely unattended. You know the drill by now, Robbie. They gots to investigate."

"Was the friend named Eva Kenney?" I whispered.

'That's exactly who it was."

Suddenly the world wanted me. A man waved his empty coffee mug. Danna hit the Ready bell three times. Two women pointed at their empty plates and signaled for the check.

"Enjoy your breakfast, if you're able," I said. "And will you pass along news as you get it?"

He swallowed before he spoke. "I'll do what I can."

I hurried back to the present, but my thoughts were on Vicky, murdered in Beanblossom.

Chapter Five

I was still stunned by the news of Vicky's homicide, but a busy restaurant waits for no one. Who knew a mid-December Wednesday would lure seemingly everyone in the county to eat breakfast out? And not just out, but here. The breakfast special was gone, and we'd baked additional pans of biscuits too many times to count. Buck had left the minute he finished eating without us speaking again of the death. Even with Turner on hand, he and Danna and I didn't have a moment's break until ten-thirty.

Danna made a mad dash for the restroom, and I planned to follow her path the minute she emerged.

"Do we have a lunch special?" Turner asked, neatly flipping two eggs for one of the remaining customers.

"Phil was supposed to bring a load of turtle cookies. That's it."

Turner grinned. "For 'Two Turtle Doves'?"

"Exactly."

"What is a turtle dove, anyway?" he asked.

"You know, I haven't the slightest idea." I whipped out my search device, also known as my phone. "According to Wikipedia—not always the best research tool, but a good starting point—there is a European turtle dove. The name *turtle* has nothing to do with the reptile but comes from the Latin word *turtur*, which comes from the sound the bird makes." I glanced up at him. "Live and learn."

"I guess. My next question is, what are turtle cookies?"

"No clue. Maybe sugar cookies shaped like turtles and dusted with green sugars?"

He laughed. "Not that real turtles are green."

"No, they aren't, are they? We'll find out when Phil shows up."

Danna headed toward us looking much relieved.

"Back in a flash." I headed for my own quick break.

When I came out, Danna was helping Phil carry in trays of cookies.

"Awesome." At the stainless-steel counter, I peered at the cookies, which looked like a chocolate thumbprint cookie rolled in chopped pecans, filled with caramel, and drizzled with dark chocolate. "Thanks, Phil. Is that caramel in the middle?"

"You got it." Phil bobbed his head. "I tried to approximate the candy, but in a cookie. Try them, guys."

I popped one in my mouth, chewing and savoring. "Phil, you've outdone yourself." I should have eaten something more substantial than a sweet for my snack, but I couldn't resist.

He beamed.

Danna nodded her agreement, swallowing before she spoke. "O. M. G, dude. To die for."

Turner gave Phil a high five, pulled off his apron, and headed for the restroom.

"Speaking of dying, Robbie." Phil's smile slipped away. "I heard Ms. Chakrabarti was killed in her apartment."

"She was. You knew her?" I asked.

"Sure," he said. "Who didn't? She was the best English teacher at South Lick High. It's incredibly sad that she's gone."

"I didn't know her." Danna finished tying a clean apron around her waist.

Turner returned and did the same.

"She retired at the end of the year I graduated." Phil gazed from Danna to Turner, then raised both palms. "Sure, you can cut to the jokes about how I wore her out. Not true." He shrugged. "Well, maybe a little. I asked more questions than anyone else in AP. With a name like Philostrate, how could I not love Shakespeare?"

When I'd first met Phil, the budding opera singer had told me his full name came from *A Midsummer Night's Dream*, where Philostrate was the Master of Revels.

"But Ms. Chakrabarti was awesome and responded to every single question," Phil continued. "Often, instead of giving me the answer, she would ask me what I thought, or she would tell me to go look it up. Now I realize she was the best kind of teacher, ever."

"That's quite a testimony," I said.

"She deserves it."

"Phil, where did you hear of her death?" Turner asked.

"A guy who was in my class works for the county sheriff," Phil said. "He sent around a message to a few of us who were in Literary Club. She was our advisor."

"Buck told me when he was in here eating. He said Wanda has the case." I thought. "Phil, the name Chakrabarti sounds like it fits her heritage. Was she married when she taught?"

"She had been." Phil bobbed his head. "She was actually getting divorced during my senior year. That's gotta be hard, and she was still an awesome teacher."

"Who was she married to?" I asked.

"A Mr. Kenney."

Kenney as in Eva? Interesting. Maybe he was Eva's brother.

"She never talked about him in class, but one time in Lit Club we were reading *Pride and Prejudice*," Phil continued. "It's set during an era where women were basically their husbands' property. Ms. Chakrabarti talked about why she never changed her name when she got married."

"Can you even think of a more arcane thing to do?" Danna asked.

Turner chimed in. "Don't shoot me. I know I'm a guy. But my mom told me she changed her name from Turner to Rao to kind of unify the family. She's not Indian like Dad, but she said it was a way to show her love for him, and to give everybody in the family the same name."

"Then why doesn't the man change his name?" Danna snorted.

"You didn't become O'Neill last summer, Robbie," Phil said.

"And Abe didn't change his name to Jordan, either," I pointed out. "When—if—we have kids, we can hyphenate or choose one of our names for them, or even make up a new one for all of us. To unify the family, as you said, Turner." At this point, having abandoned birth control for the last four months with nothing to show for it, I wasn't all that confident a pregnancy would happen, anyway. The disappointment tugged at my heart when I didn't shut it away deep inside.

A diner at a four-top raised her index finger as if wanting her group's check. Phil said he had to run. The bell on the door jangled, and a half dozen ladies streamed in, chattering and admiring the cookware. A full two dozen additional women poured through the door after them.

"Looks like it's tour-bus time," I said. "Thanks for the cookies, Phil. Person your stations, gang." I didn't have a quiet moment to contemplate the murder of the world's best English teacher for another couple of hours.

Chapter Six

No sooner had the ladies from Cincinnati left than the lunch rush began. That one turtle cookie, no matter how delicious, had not been the substantial snack I should have eaten, and my five-thirty scarfed-down breakfast was a distant memory. I finally grabbed a hot dog rejected for being over-charred, wrapped it in a piece of whole wheat bread, and ate it standing up.

By one o'clock, a few tables were open, and my co-chefs had been able to snatch a bite on the run, too. With the lull, thoughts of a murdered Vicky flooded back in. Buck was right. I was eager to start poking around. Except I didn't have any reason to, other than having met and served the victim. I hoped her soul was resting in peace, wherever that might be.

Eva Kenney pushed through the door a few minutes later, followed by a thickset man of about Abe's height. I hurried over to greet them.

"Eva, I heard about Vicky," I said. "I'm so sorry"

The man's nostrils flared. He pressed his lips together and looked away. What was that about? He had remained standing with Eva, so he was obviously with her and hadn't simply followed her in. In fact, his eyes were the same light brownish-green as hers. It looked like they were related.

"I know you and Vicky were friends," I went on, speaking to her.

"We were." Eva's eyes welled. She sniffed and gave a swipe at the tears. "Thank you, Robbie."

"It must have been so hard to discover her." I had come across a homicide victim or three in the last few years. I knew what a horrible shock it was to encounter a corpse who had not died of natural causes. But none of them had been my friends. That had to be much worse.

Eva could only nod.

I glanced at the man. "I'm Robbie Jordan, proprietor."

"Adam Kenney. Brother." He gestured at Eva with his thumb.

"I apologize," Eva rushed to say. "I should have introduced to you to my baby brother."

"No worries, Eva," I said. "Nice to meet you, Adam. Are you both here to eat lunch?"

"Yes, please," Eva murmured. "I'm sorry for, for this." She waved her hand in front of her face.

"You don't have to apologize. Please follow me." I led the way to an open and cleaned two-top. "Coffee?"

"Only water for me," Eva said.

"Do you have beer?" Adam asked.

"Sorry." I shook my head. "Customers can bring their own, but I need to open and serve it."

He pulled his mouth to the side. "I didn't bring any, so I'll have a Pepsi, please."

"Is Coke all right?" I asked.

"Of course." He lifted a shoulder and dropped it. "I prefer Pepsi, but you must get that a lot."

"We do." We didn't, actually, but the customer was always right. "I'll bring your drinks over in a minute and take your order when you're ready."

Eva thanked me. He stared at the menu on the placemat. I headed over to our drinks cooler, wondering if their parents were fundamentalist Christians to name their children after God's first couple. Giving siblings the names of people who went on to procreate together was kind of bizarre, when you really thought about it.

I set down their glasses. "What can I get you to eat today?"

"You wouldn't think I would have an appetite." Eva slid her cat's-eye reading glasses onto her nose to inspect the menu. "But I can always eat. I'd like a grilled cheese and ham on rye, with tomato, please."

I looked at Adam.

"Give me a double cheeseburger with onions, no lettuce, and a side of biscuits and gravy." As an afterthought, he added, "Please."

"Coming right up," I said.

Eva glanced at the Specials board. "Those turtle cookies are bound to be good. Can we get a couple, please?" she asked.

"Of course." I headed back to the grill. Adam wasn't a tall beanpole like Sean or Buck, but he'd put in a similar order. His was the kind of thickset build that looked like he had formerly been muscular, but it had mostly turned to fat with age. He didn't seem to be doing much to comfort his sister as she grieved. She'd said he was her baby brother. Maybe him comforting her wasn't part of the roles they'd played for decades. She might be the nurturer of the two. And if he was Vicky's ex, that could explain the reaction when I'd mentioned her name.

I gave Danna their order.

"You got it, boss." She glanced over at Eva. "Who's the dude?"

"Adam Kenney. He's Eva's brother."

"Brother and sister are named Adam and Eve? That's gross."

A laugh rolled out of me. "I had the same thought." My stomach gurgled at the heavenly smell of beef patties and onions frying on the grill. My stomach would have to wait.

I busied myself delivering checks, collecting money, and busing tables while Danna cooked and Turner worked the sink. When I passed near Eva's table, she and her brother seemed to be arguing. They kept their voices low, but it was clearly a dispute. About what, I had no idea. I took a surreptitious glance. Adam sat back, arms folded across his chest, shaking his head, glowering. Eva leaned forward, as if pleading. As I watched, her expression morphed, with the edges of her mouth drawing down, her eyes narrowing in anger. She began to stand. He grabbed her arm like he wanted to persuade her to sit. She sat.

Danna hit the Ready bell twice. The cow bell on the door jangled, admitting four young hunters in camouflage gear. A woman signaled for more coffee. I couldn't stand here and spy on customers. I had work to do.

By the time I delivered their lunch, the Kenney siblings seemed to be getting along again. I set down their plates. "Can I get you anything else?"

"No, thank you." Adam lifted the top bun and squirted ketchup onto the loaded burger.

Eva, having already taken a bite of her sandwich, shook her head.

Wanda Bird strode through the door. Eva's eyes widened. She brought her hand over her mouth. Wanda, wearing a black blazer and dark trousers, stood holding her elbows out from her sides, hands dangling, scanning the restaurant. Eva swallowed.

"She's the cop who questioned me for hours this morning," she whispered. "I hope she's not looking for me."

"I doubt it," I said without any basis in fact for my opinion. "I'll go see what she wants." I hurried toward the detective. The person who reported the body was always looked at with extra interest. In Eva's case, she also knew Vicky and was friends with her. Of course the police would begin by focusing on Eva.

"Hey, Wanda," I said. "Here for lunch?"

"I do have me a hunger, Robbie. But I'm obliged to do a piece of work before I eat."

"Eva Kenney says you already questioned her. I hope you're not here to interrupt her lunch."

"Nah. She can eat in peace."

"Have you learned yet how Vicky died?" I kept my voice low.

"We are not entirely certain, but it appears to have been a contact toxin in that green yarn she was knitting with."

"A toxin in the yarn? Not Adele's yarn." *No.* It couldn't be.

"In fact, it was hers." Wanda swallowed, shifting from foot to foot and looking uncomfortable. "Which is why I'm here to confiscate all the skeins you have for sale in your store. And any other products made with your aunt's wool."

"What?" I screeched. I clapped my hand over my mouth and glanced around, but nobody seemed to have noticed. "Adele *made* all that yarn. You can't possibly believe wool from sheep she raised and sheared, wool she dyed herself, has something wrong with it."

"I sure to high heaven hope not, hon, but we gots to play it safe."

"You can't just take it all," I protested. Two years ago the state police detective had confiscated all the special Mexican hot chocolate packets I'd made for sale, suspecting they'd been poisoned. That had been bad enough. Taking Adele's lovingly created skeins was a step too far. "Please don't."

"People in hell want ice water, too. By that I mean, we actually can take it. Come on, Robbie. You don't want nobody else to keel over while knitting a Christmas scarf, do you?"

"Of course not, but . . ." I let my voice trail off. What was going on? How could Vicky—"Wait. Vicky was in here only yesterday morning knitting. She seemed fine. Do you mean someone poisoned the yarn last night or something?"

"Look, alls I can tell you is that I got a guy coming right behind me to load up his bags. And you're not to restock until we give you the old go-ahead."

Sure enough, a man in the two-toned brown uniform of the county sheriff's office was next through the door, toting two big bags. But the first thing he pulled out was a white papery-looking garment.

My horrified breath rushed in. "He can't put on a hazmat suit right here in my store."

"He sure enough can. In fact, he's obliged to."

"Wanda, please wait until I close." I grabbed her arm, begging. "Seriously. I'll block off the yarn shelves. I'll lock the door to newcomers right now. Let the diners in here eat without thinking my entire store is toxic." But what if it was? *Ugh*.

She gave it one second of thought. "Joe, hang on a little minute." She headed over to the officer.

Whew. I scanned the diners. Eva and Adam appeared to be the only ones watching the action. Danna and Turner were, as well. Nothing slipped by them.

Chapter Seven

I locked the door behind the last customer at two o'clock and put up the sign I'd lettered earlier. CLOSING EARLY TO GO FISHING. SEE YOU TOMORROW! Fishing, we weren't, but folks didn't need to know that. Wanda was fishing, for sure. I could only hope she wouldn't hook anything in the rest of Adele's yarn.

I turned to the detective and her deputy pal, who had enjoyed lunch on the house while they begrudgingly waited for the rest of my diners to finish up.

"Go for it," I told them.

The dude pulled on the hazmat suit, plus gloves and a mask. Wanda stood with hands clasped behind her back, looking like a civvies-clad guard. Within minutes the two were out the door with their bags full of yarn, mittens, and hats. Adele's display shelves sat empty, forlorn, abandoned. I would need to rearrange all the retail stuff so the gaping hole wasn't obvious, but not right now. My shoulders sagged as I faced my crew.

"So much for Christmas sales to crafters," I muttered, making my way over to Danna and Turner. He scrubbed the grill while she washed pots in the sink. And so much for Christmas spirit, to be honest.

"What was that all about, Robbie?" Danna asked.

"Wanda and her sheriff buddy taking Adele's yarn and knitted stuff."

I hadn't had a chance to tell them what Wanda had said earlier.

"Don't you guys want to sit down?" I asked. "I have beers in the back."

"Thanks, but I have volleyball practice at four," Danna said.

"Rain check for me, too." Turner gave rueful smile. "Talk about holiday retail. I have to work in the maple shop the minute I get home."

His parents ran a maple tree farm as a sideline, and their little shop amid the trees was a popular destination for gift-seekers at this time of year.

"Be that way." I softened it with a laugh. "Well, here's the deal. As you know, Vicky Chakrabarti was murdered. Apparently it was by handling poisoned yarn."

Danna made a horrified face. Turner's frown lines went deep.

"Wanda said Vicky was knitting with Adele's yarn," I added. "So they took it all. I assume out of an abundance of caution. No way did Adele use some kind of contact toxin on her lovely wool."

"Of course she didn't." Danna nearly stomped with outrage.

"Contact toxin." Turner looked thoughtful. "I think that means if it touches your skin, it poisons you."

"That's what it sounds like," I said. "I don't know what it could be, though, or where it can be found."

"Do you think Adele knows anything about this?" Danna asked.

At that very moment, my phone rang—and the ID said Adele. "This is her." I held up a finger.

"Robbie, they're hauling me in for questioning," my aunt said with no preamble.

"You're kidding."

"I am not. The whole shebang is ludicrous, but what can you do? Can you come out here in an hour and check on the girls? I don't have no idea when I'll be back."

"Of course." Could I take the time to see to her sheep before dark? I absolutely could.

"Thanks, sugar. And feed Sloopy and Chloe, please. Samuel's busy."

"Of course. Do you need me to call a lawyer for you?"

"Done."

"Text me if you need me," I said. "And when you get home."

"Gotta run, child."

My "love you" was cut short by her disconnecting the call. I sat staring at my phone for a moment, then glanced up at my team.

"They took Adele in for questioning." I let an expletive slip. "Sorry."

Danna dried her hands and sank into the chair next to mine. "Robbie, we all know she's innocent. I'm sure they only want to find out if she knows the evil person who did that to the yarn."

Turner joined us. "You know what? We closed early. I think I have time for a beer, after all."

"Me, too" Danna said. "So I don't play my best game. Who cares?" She held out her palm. "Give me the key to the apartment. I'll get the brewskies."

My throat tightened as I handed her my keys. "You guys are the best."

Two minutes later we had toasted Adele's innocence and a speedy resolution to the case. The cool beer went down just right.

Now I did have a VGR—a Very Good Reason—to investigate how Vicky ended up dead. I'd listened to a podcast not long ago featuring a cozy-mystery author who had talked about the need for an amateur sleuth to have a VGR. I seemed to have become a bit of an amateur sleuth myself, oddly enough. If having your favorite living relative be a person of interest in a homicide investigation wasn't a VGR, I didn't know what was.

Turner worked his phone. He looked up. "There are a number of contact poisons."

"Ick," Danna said. "I hope they're super hard to find."

"Clearly not impossible, though." I squared my shoulders. We weren't going to solve this today. "Murder aside, Three French Hens is up tomorrow. Ideas for specials, you brilliant people? Me, I'm not feeling a bit inspired."

"Chicken stew and call it coq au vin?" Danna suggested.

"Ooh. I like that," I said. "Chicken, mushrooms, and red wine. We have the first two, plus onions, and I can pick up a few big bottles of burgundy or pinot noir when I go check on Adele's sheep."

"Don't forget the lardons," Turner said. "You can substitute bacon for that. We have plenty."

"We could do French baked eggs for a breakfast special," Danna said. "You know, because hens."

"How do you make those?" Turner asked.

"I've made them before," I piped up. "It's basically eggs poached in the oven but fancied up. You break one into each cup of a greased muffin tin, add a little cream on top, a little Parmesan, and a sprinkle of herbs. They're done in under ten minutes."

"Oo-la-la, I want a couple right now." Turner faked a French accent as he twirled the end of a nonexistent mustache.

Danna laughed and elbowed him. Our mood lightened. My crew was the best. They weren't that much younger than me. But as the business owner, I felt older than I really was. Still, they were good friends. Today they'd seen I needed some comfort and had rearranged their priorities to provide it.

Chapter Eight

I pedaled, head down, up the last hill to Adele's farm at four o'clock. Cycling the up-and-down roads of Brown County was my exercise and my mental health all in one vigorous package. It was tempting, after a hard day at work, to stretch out on the sofa at home and fall asleep. I felt much better if I fit in a workout on my bike first. I could think through problems or not think at all. I'd chosen the latter on this leg of the trip out to make sure Adele's animals were fed and safe.

The wind and the temperature chilled my cheeks, but otherwise I was covered in wicking layers. My muscles were well-warmed by the time I leaned the bike against the side of Adele's cottage. Abe and I had held our wedding here half a year ago, outside on a sunny day when all was right with the world. I'd almost never been at the farm when my aunt wasn't, and the place seemed bereft without her old red pickup truck in the drive. At least Wanda had let Adele drive herself to the station and hadn't hauled her away in the back seat of a cruiser.

Inside, I gave Adele's sweet white cat, Chloe, half of a small can of food and made sure she had plenty of dry food and fresh water. She glanced up, asking to be petted while she ate. I obliged, of course, gazing around the warm kitchen with its broad table where I had both grieved and celebrated with Adele over the years. I'd also eaten loads of baked goods here, yeasted bread and butter, sweet cakes and pies, and indulged in more than one nip of Four Roses. This was a place of comfort for me, for so many reasons.

Right now it was decorated for Christmas, which made it even more homey. On the door to the basement hung a quilted wall hanging featuring none other than the Twelve Days of Christmas. I raised my eyebrows and moved closer to examine it. For Seven Swans a-Singing, six little cygnets wore red and green caps, and the mother swan in front had a wreath around her neck. My eyes perked up at the square depicting Twelve Lords a-Leaping. The crown-wearing lords were puffy baked fellows with green belts and red buttons. We could do that in the restaurant with biscuit dough, or get Phil to create them out of cookie dough. I made a note to tell Danna and Turner tomorrow.

I shouldn't get too comfortable here. If I didn't finish my errand promptly, it would be dark before I arrived home. I had lights on my cycle and my helmet, but the temperature would drop even more, and I preferred to ride while the sun still shone. It was a lot safer when cars could easily see me, too. Speaking of light, I left the kitchen over-head light on to welcome Adele home, whenever she got here, and flipped on the outdoor light while I was at it.

I fed border collie Sloopy, who had followed me in, and made sure he had fresh water. I shot Abe a text about where I was and that I was heading for my store soon to do prep for tomorrow. I knew I couldn't relax until we were ready for the morning rush. He wrote back almost instantly.

I'll meet you there with dinner plus hands ready to help.

A smile split my face. What a guy.

You're on. And thank you!

I would be sweaty from the ride, though, and hadn't thought to bring a change of clothes on the ride. I sometimes kept a few extras in my old apartment, but I didn't think I had anything warm back there.

Bring my black leggings and UCSB fleece?

I'd picked up a sweatshirt from the local University of California campus almost two years ago when I'd been back in Santa Barbara for my high school reunion, even though my own alma mater was the San Luis Obispo campus. Abe texted back, including a winking emoji.

Gotcha.

On my way out, I glanced into the front room, where Adele had her loom. She sold her knitted products, mostly hats and mittens, but she saved her weavings for loved ones. I hated the thought of my aunt—strong and kind, fierce and fearless, competent and caring—being questioned by the police, even though I knew she could stick up for herself.

Who would have wanted to kill Vicky Chakrabarti by poisoning the strands that ran through her fingers? Adele sent her wool out to be carded and spun, but she dyed it herself. She wound the skeins and added her custom paper label. Did Vicky's murderer also hold a grudge against Adele? Had the killer wanted to redirect blame away from themself and cast it on Adele?

Sloopy kept me company as I forked fresh hay into the wire rack in the barnyard. The fenced-in space connected to the barn with a low door so the sheep could scoot inside to shelter from cold and rain if they wanted. I broke the ice in their water trough and added fresh water from the hose that ran from inside the barn. I counted the beasts, happy that all fourteen were present and accounted for. The herd grew in the summer with the year's new lambs, but Adele had always said two dozen plus a couple was a manageable size for her.

I gave Sloopy's head a scritch and locked the door to the cottage, since he had a dog door that let him go in and out at will. Gazing around the property after I clipped my shoes into the pedals of my metal steed, I took my memories back to Abe's and my beautiful wedding right here on the farm at the end of May. After the ceremony, facing all our loved ones—and with the sheep also observing from the other side of the fence—my heart had nearly burst. Eating roast pig under a tent and dancing in the barn, scrubbed down for the occasion, had provided a proverbial cherry on the top.

Now I began my trip homeward, sort of, with a detour planned to the market in downtown South Lick where I could pick up wine for tomorrow's stew.

As I rode back down Beanblossom Road through the dark and slanting shadows of a December afternoon, I thought again about Cole Brewster. Adele had said he'd dated Vicky, but that she'd dropped him. Surely he wouldn't murder her over a relationship that hadn't worked out—would he? Phil had mentioned Vicky was divorced from a Mr. Kenney. If her husband had been Adam Kenney, would he harbor long-standing resentments and now, after at least a decade, kill her? That seemed like a stretch, too.

When my front wheel hit a rut, I was almost wrenched from the bike. I kept my balance at the last minute and cycled more slowly. The daylight was already dimming into the gloaming. *Gloaming* was a word I'd loved since I'd first read it, possibly because it conjured an image of a gloomy, mysterious twilight. Which was all fine in a work of fiction. In real life while riding a bicycle? Not so desirable.

My mind didn't slow along with my wheels. Eva had been tearful about her friend's death. What if she'd faked her grief? I didn't know anything about the two women's relationship. Maybe Eva had hated Vicky and was only biding her time before seizing the right moment to kill her. Or maybe I didn't have a snowflake's chance in Phoenix of figuring out this mystery with such scant information.

Back on a more recently paved stretch of the road, I sped up again. Hard exercise automatically quieted a speeding brain. It had no choice but to focus on the job at hand.

Chapter Nine

By six o'clock I was in my comfy warm clothes, including dry socks and Uggs, both of which I needed but had forgotten to ask Abe to bring. It was no fun clacking around in bike shoes. Abe, bless his sweet heart, had included fleece socks and the furry slipper-boots with my clothes. *Tosca* played on the speakers, a loaded roast beef sandwich on toasted sourdough bread and a drinking glass half full of cabernet sauvignon sat in front of me, while a handsome husband faced me across the table. I'd picked up a bottle of wine for our dinner while grabbing the big bottles for the coq.

"I'm worried about Adele." I had to trust that Wanda was only soliciting information about Adele's yarn and would believe what my aunt told her, but it wasn't easy.

"Everything's going to be fine, darlin'," Abe said. "I'm sure Adele will be released and home soon."

"I hope so." I took a big bite, savoring the horseradish, smear of avocado mayonnaise, and thin slices of cucumber Abe had added. "Mmm, thank you." I covered my mouth as I spoke.

"Any time. What will we be prepping, besides the usual breakfast?" he asked.

I told him about our Twelve Days of Christmas project. "So it's chicken stew for Three French Hens."

"Fun. Don't know what you're going to do when you get to Lords a-Leaping, though."

"I had been worried about that, but over at Adele's I saw a quilted wall hanging depicting the song. It had twelve puffy lords who looked like the Pillsbury Doughboy wearing crowns and green belts." I shrugged. "We'll figure something out."

"You could have Phil make leaping gingerbread men."

"That's brilliant. Better that than trying to shape biscuit dough. And he could do toy drum cookies for the ninth day. I should see if I can find a cookie cutter in that shape."

Abe swallowed a bite. "I did some checking around today about Cole Brewster."

"And?"

"He doesn't seem to be the most popular real estate broker in town, for sure. A few customers weren't happy with deals he struck—or failed to—and found themselves a new agent. I didn't hear that he'd attempted anything fraudulent, at least not that I could find, but Brewster might not be doing as well financially as he'd like."

"Hmm." I sipped the wine. "So, he could be trying to drum up business door-to-door. It still seems like a strange thing to do."

"I agree." He popped in his last bite about the same time I did. "Why don't I chop and do the *mise en place* for the stew? I know you have your biscuit and pancake recipes in your head, and that way you won't have to write them down for me."

"Sounds good."

Abe stood and cleared our dishes. "Just tell me what to do, boss."

"You bet." I headed for the walk-in to grab mushrooms, onions, chicken, butter, eggs, and whatever else we needed. My phone dinged with a text from Adele before I got there. I stopped to read the message.

Am home. Thx for doing beasts. Catch you in AM.

Good. They hadn't kept her overly long, but that was a terse message, at least for Adele. She must be exhausted.

Glad they let you go. Anything you need?

No, doll. Samuel will be here by and by.

Samuel keeping her company sounded like a good idea. Adele had been questioned in a case some time ago, so this hadn't been her first go-around. Still, being grilled in an interview room wasn't a fun experience, and my beloved aunt wasn't getting any younger. I tapped out a quick reply.

Love you.

She responded with a winking emoji, which was possibly not the way she was feeling. I didn't care.

I emerged from the walk-in with my plastic mesh carrying-basket full of food. As I unloaded it on the counter, I glanced at Abe. He frowned at his phone.

"What's up?" I extracted a half dozen pounds of mushrooms and set them on the counter.

"Mom's been in an accident."

Freddy. My breath rushed in. "Is she okay?" I hurried to his side and laid my hand on his shoulder.

"I think so." He swiped through the message again. "Dad said her car was sideswiped as she was leaving Nashville after some Christmas shopping. Her air bags went off and such, but she might have a broken leg. She's in an ambulance on the way to Columbus Regional Hospital. Dad is heading there now."

"Of course." Taking her to Columbus—Indiana—to the west made sense. From Nashville, it was about equidistant from the IU hospital in Bloomington to the east. "I'm so sorry, sweetheart. What can I do?"

He glanced up from the phone, worry written all over his face. "I have to go, but Seanie has school tomorrow. Could you—"

I held up a hand. "Abe. I've got him. I can get Turner to fill in for me tomorrow early to make sure Sean gets off to class okay." I thought for a split second. "But he's fifteen, and you know how close he is to your mom. Why don't you ask him what he wants to do? He might feel terrible not going to the hospital with you."

Abe looked at me. "You are so wise. Of course that's what I should do." He gave me a quick hug and a quicker kiss. "I don't care if he skips a day of classes tomorrow, come to think about it." He turned away and spoke to Sean briefly, then faced me. "I'll let you know what happens, sugar. I'm sorry to leave you with all this."

"Go. I'll get it done. Do give your mom my love, all right? And text me how she's doing."

"I will. I'm sure we'll be super late getting home." He kissed me again, grabbed his coat and hat.

"Wait," I said. "Let me grab my bike from your car. If I don't, I'll be walking home." He'd loaded it into the car when he'd arrived, knowing we'd be going home together in the dark.

"Good thought. But be careful, Robbie. Are you sure you want to ride home? You could get a ride-share."

"I'll be fine on the bike, sweetheart. It isn't a long ride." Getting a ride-share in South Lick was always an iffy proposition. It wasn't exactly the big city. Only a couple of drivers worked around here, and they were often busy or AWOL.

A minute later I stood on the front porch holding my bike as I watched him drive off. I sent healing intentions for Freddy out into the universe and crossed my fingers for good measure. Clouds had blown in, so I couldn't wish on a star for her. I adored Abe's petite, quirky mother as much as she adored Christmas. She was going to be madder than a hopping frog missing a leg, as Buck would say, to be laid up during the holidays. I would do what I could to make it up to her.

For now? I wheeled in my bike, locked the door, and got going on my tasks for tomorrow.

Chapter Ten

I glanced around the store at eight-thirty that evening. Breakfast and lunch prep was as done as it was going to get. The usuals were ready to go, and the easy version of coq au vin was cooling in our biggest pot in the walk-in. If we started running short tomorrow during lunch, we could easily augment the stew. We always had chicken stock at hand, and it was easy to quick-sauté chicken, onions, and mushrooms, plus throw in some chopped parsley.

My phone pinged with a calendar reminder. I glanced at it, grateful for the notification. I'd nearly forgotten Monday afternoon at three was my volunteer stint at Cornerstone Connections. Last summer, I'd met a few of the cognitively delayed adults who were served by the day program. I'd enjoyed being around them. One young man had a relentlessly cheerful approach to life that was contagious. A girl I'd interacted with was intense and ruthlessly truthful. When the woman running the organization mentioned they had a need for volunteers, I'd signed up for a weekly spot on my day off.

Speaking of volunteers, I really hoped Freddy would recover easily. My mother-in-law, a volunteer at several worthy service agencies, was only in her early sixties. The older I got, the more I had a perspective on how young sixty really was. Heck, Buck's grandmother was still alive and well at a hundred. Adele and Mom's parents were deceased, but my Italian *nonna* still made her way through life, although her dementia was worsening. I hadn't been able to communicate with her very well when I visited a couple of years ago. Still, she'd recognized my similarity to Roberto, my father, and had given me fond, almost mischievous looks, plus lots of hugs and hand squeezes.

Keeping the twinkly fairy lights lit, I switched off the store's main lights. I clipped on my bike helmet, loaded my biking togs into my pack, and zipped up my jacket. Home was only two miles away. I wouldn't bother changing into bike shoes for the ride, even though Uggs, while warm, weren't exactly athletic footwear. Door locked, bike lights and headlamp switched on, I mounted my bike.

Instead of pedaling, though, I stood with one foot on the ground. My skin crawled. My neck prickled, and I hugged my shoulders to my ears. I whipped my head left and right. I couldn't spy a threat. So why did I feel as if someone or something malicious was out there? I hadn't done a lick of investigating—yet. But if someone was watching me, it could only be Vicky's killer. A killer so far without a name.

The cold night air didn't hold a hint of scent to tell me who was watching. Sniffing, I picked up only a whiff of woodsmoke from a fireplace or wood stove. I inhaled again, detecting the metallic smell of impending snow. But the goose bumps on my arm did not retreat. I kept feeling every hair follicle on my head.

I squared my shoulders. I'd been in danger before. I'd

always survived. I pulled out my phone. Texting Abe was no good. He was absorbed with his mother's health, and rightly so, at a hospital an hour away. But I did want to let someone know where I was and where I was headed. I quickly mulled over Danna, Buck, or Adele, discarding each for different reasons, and settled on Wanda. It was her homicide case, and if I was at risk of attack, she should know.

Wanda, FYI, am riding my bike from store to home. Having Spidey sense of a threat. Will text when I arrive home and am inside with doors locked. Hope it's a false alarm.

I sent the message. I seriously didn't care if the detective thought I was being silly or crying wolf. I looked around. No strange car lurked. There was no hint of cigarette smoke wafting from around the corner of a building. It didn't matter. I sensed danger.

Then I pedaled for home. I'd never ridden with such determination. I wanted to speed, but I had to watch out for potholes, patches of ice, and other obstacles barely visible in the dim light from my headlamp. I knew my bike's strong front light and red flashing rear light made me visible to motorists, but the roadway itself wasn't as well illuminated. I cycled past the bank through a mostly darkened downtown. I passed the bike shop and South Lick's artisanal bakery. Both were closed up tight for the night. Strom and Pete's—otherwise known as South Lick Stromboli and Pizza—was still open, but I could see Pete through the plateglass window wiping down empty tables, getting ready to lock the door at nine.

Few cars were out on this dark Wednesday night. I should have been glad. I'd been nearly run off the road in the past. But I still felt a deep unease as I swung onto Bow

Street a half mile from Abe's cottage. It didn't help that my sock was sliding off my heel into the Ugg, nor that my earlobes were freezing because I hadn't pulled on a watch cap under my helmet. No way was I stopping now.

I coasted for a moment, listening. I couldn't hear an engine. *Good.* Except . . . out of the void, a vehicle clunked through a pit in the pavement. My blood turned as icy as my fingertips.

I chanced a glance behind me. About a block back, a dark car crept along in silence, keeping pace with me. Its headlights were on, but it wasn't making a sound. An electric car, or a hybrid? It didn't matter. Somebody was following me. Were they planning to wait until I reached the house and attack me as I unlocked the front door?

Now I was sweating inside my fleece and my puffy winter jacket—and not from my exertions. I wasn't about to lead this person to my one safe haven. Where could I go? I thought frantically, desperately. A side street was ahead. I could circle around and make a beeline for the police station. I wanted to switch off my back light, which signaled my location with every flash, but stopping would make me too stupid to live.

I swung a sharp right. Bad choice. This street had fewer streetlights than ours. My tail followed. And sped up. I'd never be able to outrun whoever it was. Ahead on my side of the street was a well-lit house, illumination from all the downstairs windows a welcome wagon pushing into the darkness. I made a split-second decision, veering into their driveway. Surely the inhabitants would take me in. I dismounted, intending to let the bike fall as I raced to the door. Except my Ugg caught on the back wheel. Bike and I crashed to the pavement in one ugly yard sale of a heap.

The dark car pulled to a stop. As my throat thickened, I let loose a few choice swears. I struggled to extricate myself from the tangle, knowing I was so very screwed if I didn't. And even if I did.

"Robbie?" Wanda called through the passenger window, her voice a clarion call of rescue for my panic zone to stand down. "What in hog's heck was you up to?"

Chapter Eleven

I was dragging the next morning. Abe had called at nine-thirty last night, telling me Freddy had, in fact, broken her leg, but had been lucky to escape with only that injury. Sean was going home with his grandfather, but Abe was going to wait with his mom until she was admitted to a room. He didn't arrive back from the hospital until two o'clock, after I'd been asleep for several hours. I'd woken up to talk with him for a few minutes and then hadn't been able to get back to sleep for almost an hour.

I'd kept musing about my ride home and whether I'd imagined the danger I'd sensed—or not. Yes, the car following me had been Wanda, making sure I got home okay. But I didn't think I'd made up my sensing a threat. Maybe Wanda's presence had scared away whoever it was. When I'd told her I thought I was being pursued, she laughed but followed me the rest of the way home, nevertheless, and watched until I was safely inside and flashed the porch light to signal she could go.

Now, despite my fatigue, Danna and I managed to open the restaurant on time. By seven she'd already baked two pans of French eggs and had more prepped. She lettered *Three French Hens* at the top of the Specials board as I unlocked the front door and turned the sign to OPEN.

" 'Mornin', Robbie." Buck removed his hat.

"Come on in, Buck." Beyond him stood a dozen customers, none of whom I recognized. "Welcome to Pans 'N Pancakes, everyone. I'm Robbie Jordan, proprietor. Please come in and sit anywhere you'd like."

Buck ambled to his favorite table. I was almost physically itching to find out what he knew, if there were any developments in learning who had killed Vicky, but that conversation would need to be back-burnered for now.

"Your place looks so dang cute all decorated, hon," a plump woman said, her bouffant white hair a puffball. "Don't it, Gladys?" she asked the angular woman who had come in with her.

"You bet." Gladys's hair, more of a sheet-metal gray, was pulled back in a bun. "We approve."

"We came to eat," the first one said to me. "But we're also fixing to pick up some of that pretty yarn you sell."

Ugh. "I'm sorry, but we're all out right now. If you give me your number, I'm happy to let you know when my supplier has more ready."

"Well now, that's a crying shame." Bouffant shook her head. "We're down from Fort Wayne for the day. It's quite a piece of driving, isn't it, Gladys?"

"Yep."

The heck with the police. "Tell you what," I began. "The person who makes the yarn lives on the outskirts of town. I'll give you her card. Call Adele. I'd say she probably has some ready and simply hasn't brought it in yet."

"Thanks, hon," Bouffant said.

"From me, too," Gladys said.

I hurried over to my desk and came back with one of the cards I'd had to remove from the display area after the sheriff's deputy had confiscated the yarn.

Gladys took it. "Jordan. Didn't you say that was your last name?"

"It is." I smiled. "Adele is actually my aunt." I glanced at the grill, empty because Danna was out pouring coffee and taking orders, doing what I should have been busy doing. "Please grab a table and enjoy your breakfast. Right now you'll have to excuse me." I waded into my job, my livelihood. Wanda didn't have to know what I'd just done.

I thanked Danna and took over coffee and order duty. As expected, Buck wanted nothing to do with French eggs. By the time I delivered his massive order, Wanda had joined him at the two-top.

"Here you go, Buck. Good morning, Wanda. Coffee?"

"I'd love some, thanks."

"Thanks for, um, looking out for me last night."

"Just doing my job," she said.

Buck's eyebrows went up.

"I'll tell you later, Cuz," Wanda told him. "Your knee okay, Robbie?"

"Yes, thanks." Even though I didn't really have time to stop and talk, I asked, keeping my voice low, "Any news about Vicky?"

She held up her left hand, her three-month-new gold wedding band gleaming on her ring finger. "Gimme a little minute, okay? In the meantime, I'd like two French eggs, a slice of ham, and a bowl of fruit, if you please."

"You got it." I wove my way back to the kitchen, crossing my fingers for Wanda to tell me something after she ate her low-carb breakfast. I gave her order to Danna and took a moment to start another pot of coffee before wading back into the fray with the full carafe.

Every time I looked Wanda's way, she and Buck were either deep in conversation or working their phones. When I delivered Wanda's order, she barely glanced up as she thanked me. It wasn't until Turner arrived at eight that I had a free minute, and by then both Wanda and Buck were on their feet donning their jackets.

I swore under my breath before intercepting them at the door. "Wanda, do you have any, I mean, can you tell me—"

"No. I don't, and I can't. Gotta run, Robbie. Left my money on the table." She jammed her official hat on her head and set her hand on the door handle.

Sheesh. Nothing like eat and run. She'd shared the bit about the contact toxin yesterday. Why clam up today?

"Well, can Adele at least restock her yarn here?" I asked.

"Not yet. I will inform her when she can." Wanda leaned toward me. "Robbie, stay out of this for once, would you? We got ourselves a real-live murderer out there. We don't want no more homicides around here. Leastwise not before Christmas." The detective, now a much-reduced version of her former well-padded self, slid out the door.

"Nothing, Buck?" I flipped open my hands and faced him with what I was pretty sure was a look of entreaty. "Can't you tell me something? Anything?"

"I might if we had something, but goldang it, we don't, Robbie, and that's a fact. I admit to the case being a frustrating one." He tilted his head toward the door. "Which is why old Wanda was a tiny little bit short with you. It's her case, and it's the holidays."

"I can understand that. But . . . she hasn't learned if Vicky had any enemies? Or how the poison got into the yarn?"

If Buck had worn glasses, the look he gave me would have been from over the top of them.

"Okay, okay," I said. "The answer is obviously a no."

"You would be correct. And now I'm later than a—" He seemed to catch himself. "Later than the old White Rabbit for a dee-partmental meeting." He rolled his eyes. "Just another piece of buffalo patty the chief insists on."

"Good luck, Buck." I held thumb and pinky to my ear. "Call me when there's a development?"

"Sure thing." He turned toward the door, then pivoted back, looking concerned. "I meant to ask how your mother-in-law is doing. I heared about the accident."

"Thanks for asking. She has a broken leg but otherwise is apparently okay. She's in Columbus Health."

"God bless Fredericka. I'll be praying for her."

I watched the big-hearted officer trot down the steps. I hoped God blessed Freddy, or whatever part of the universe was watching over her. Meanwhile, back here in earthly South Lick, I had people to feed.

Chapter Twelve

We continued busy through the next hour. The rush kept the three of us, if not on our toes, then certainly scurrying here and there to provide breakfasts and smiles, not to mention tables that were clean and set. When previous homicides had occurred in South Lick and surrounds, the death often became the topic of the day among my diners. Not so this morning. Fine with me.

I continued to ponder, when I had the rare minute, why I'd thought someone was after me last night. Had it been my imagination at work? Maybe. If not, who could it have been? Had I already been obviously questioning likely persons of interest in Vicky's murder? I didn't think so. I'd been thinking about the case, for sure.

"Robbie, I'm going to erase French eggs from the board," Danna said. "Keeping them warm after we take them out of the oven makes them overcook, and not that many people have ordered them, anyway."

"Sounds good," I said.

From the grill, Turner nodded his approval, his backwards red IU ball cap not budging.

"By the way, I made a simple coq au vin last night," I told them. "We're set for the lunch special. In fact, I think

I'll get the pot out now to take the chill off the stew before we start warming it."

"I'm already hungry." Turner grinned as he flipped pancakes and shoved around peppers and onions sautéing on the grill.

Before I could arrive at the walk-in, Eva Kenney and Cole Brewster made their way through the door. Was it a knitting club day? I supposed it was, but eight-thirty was two hours earlier than they usually met. Plus, neither carried a bag full of yarn, needles, and whatever project they'd been working on. It didn't matter. I went to greet them and tried not to stare at Eva's arm tucked through Cole's.

"You're here earlier than usual." I smiled.

"We aren't knitting today," Cole said. "We only want breakfast."

Eva, with eyes no longer tear-reddened, gazed up at Cole with a look that was unmistakably adoring. This was new. In all the times the knitting club had eaten and crafted here, I'd never seen a hint of a romance between the two, other than when I'd spied Cole and Eva playing literal footsie. *Whatever.* They had every right to enjoy each other's company.

I surveyed the restaurant, which had every table filled. "It'll be a few minutes until a table opens up. I'll seat you when one does."

"Not a problem, hon," Eva said. "We can do a little shopping for stocking stuffers."

"Sounds good." I had an entire endcap devoted to Christmas ornaments, which included tiny kitchen implements on red strings. Mini box graters, little whisks, and tiny mixing bowls, plus an array of miniature black frying pans three inches long, each painted with Pans 'N Pancakes in store blue on the back. The smallest jars of Mennonite honey and the mini bottles of maple syrup from Turner's family farm were good stocking stuffers, as were the vinyl Brown County stickers depicting a covered bridge and fall leaves. Normally we would also have Adele's knitted hats and hand warmers in all colors of the rainbow, but those were likely locked in whatever county sheriff's evidence room Wanda had stashed them in.

By the time I emerged from the walk-in, carrying the heavy stew pot in two hands, our waiting area had filled with a dozen more customers. People dusted snow off their shoulders and shook it off hats. At least the storm had held off until now. If I'd had to ride like the wind in fresh falling snow last night, only twelve hours ago, I would have ended up in even more trouble. Not that I had been imperiled in the end, but my knee still ached from when I'd tangled with my steel steed.

That fall had been from nerves, not weather conditions or an attacker coming at me. The evening could have turned out much, much worse. In the light of day, I again wondered if I had imagined being followed, made up the sense of being watched. It was worth some thought, but not right now.

I carried the stew to the kitchen area. From the grill, Turner shot me a pair of raised eyebrows.

"Yes, we're busy," I said. "All good, right?"

He gave a single nod as he rescued a couple of nearly burnt pancakes. I returned to greet the newcomers.

We stayed busy. I found Eva and Cole a table, but I couldn't pay any extra attention to them. I also didn't have a free minute to see what the weather was doing. The rush was subsiding by nine-thirty, and no one was waiting to be seated by the time Adele and Samuel hurried in. I headed in their direction as they shook snow off their colorful Knitted-by-Adele hats.

"Good morning, you two," I said. "How's the storm?"

"It's picking up." Adele leaned in for a kiss. "You got yourself a warm cheek there, hon."

Hers was chilled and pink.

"How are you, Samuel?" My cheek got a cold kiss from him, too.

"I am well, thank the good Lord. And happy to have my lady love nearby." He squeezed Adele's hand.

"He means nearby as opposed to in the clink." Adele gave a snort and tossed her head.

"We all are, Adele." I lowered my voice. "They didn't really think you had poisoned your own yarn, did they?"

"I ain't in the business of figuring out what folks in uniforms are thinking, sugar. I surely made it clear to them that I had not and would never dream of doing such a terrible thing. Now then, I got me a hunger worse than an itch in a place that don't lend itself to scratching."

I laughed. "Please sit anywhere that's open."

Adele squinted at the restaurant area. "Why, is that Eva Kenney setting there with old Cole Brewster?"

"It is. They've been having a leisurely breakfast."

"I reckon I'll go say hello. You coming, Mr. MacDonald?"

"Of course, my dear." Samuel winked at me and murmured, "Do I have a choice?"

I watched him trail in Adele's wake to where Eva and Cole sat. When Adele arrived at their table, Eva glanced up. Even from here I could see her glare, although I couldn't hear what they were saying. Eva folded her arms and shook her head, hard, as Adele spoke to her. Adele shrugged, hooked her arm through Samuel's, and turned away.

Something was up between them. I just didn't know what.

Chapter Thirteen

By ten-fifteen things were quiet enough for me to slip a slice of cheese and a crispy rasher of bacon inside a biscuit. I pulled up a chair at Adele and Samuel's table. Eva and Cole had left shortly after Eva's encounter with Adele, and I was itching to find out what had gone on.

Samuel sat with his chair pushed back, turning the pages of the *Brown County Democrat*. Adele poked at her phone with her index finger but laid the device on the table as I sat.

"I s'pose you want to know what in heck old Eva was so het up about," my aunt began in a soft voice.

"I do." I matched her tone.

Samuel glanced over his readers at us and went straight back to his article. I'd been acquainted with him long enough to know that he rarely butted into Adele's business or even asked about it.

"Seems Eva's buying into the thought that I applied that there toxic substance to my own yarn. That's why she and Brewster weren't knitting this morning. The only yarn they got is mine, and neither wants to touch it."

I wrinkled my nose. "That's crazy, Adele." I took a bite of my snack.

"Sure it is. But what can you do? Thing is, the yarn

Wanda and crew showed me wasn't the exact same green as I use. Sure, it had my label on the skein and all such like that. But that green was a bluer shade."

"That's strange, isn't it?" I asked.

"I told em which end was up, so to speak, and one of those cops had the audacity to suggest my eyesight's going. Why, I've been using that same shade of green dye for nigh on twenty years, Robbie. You'd think I'd know when my yarn's been tampered with."

"Nothing wrong with my girl's eyes, I can attest to that." Samuel beamed at his "girl" of seventy-four.

I had to agree. But was it the toxin that made Adele's green yarn look more blue? It had to be.

"I told Eva I wadn't under arrest or nothing," Adele continued. "I said the detective doesn't have a chicken-picking thing to charge me with. Eva didn't appear to care."

"Did Wanda give you any sense of what the toxin was?" I asked. "The one in the yarn Vicky was knitting with, I mean. How it got there?"

"She suspects it was something agricultural or what-not. They were still waiting on some lab results." Adele shook her head. "It's a frustration, Robbie. No two ways about it."

I narrowed my eyes. "Something agricultural." I'd learned about a lethal herbicide in California when I was out there and had explored whether it had been the cause of my mom's sudden death. "Like an herbicide or a pesticide?"

"Might could be." Adele drained her coffee.

"So, the question is, who has access to agricultural poisons and also wanted Vicky out of the way?"

"That would be the question, all righty."

I thought for a moment. "Cole sells real estate. He could have found something lethal in a client's shed."

"Didn't he sell a farm a while back?" Adele asked. "I'll have to check. Too, he and Vicky were a number for a bit. He could still be holding a grudge against her."

"What does Eva do for work?" I asked.

"Let's see. I do believe she worked for IFCC before she retired."

Around us a few tables of customers ate. Danna cooked. Turner cleared and took orders. The cow bell on the door jangled, admitting a handful of midmorning diners. I stared at Adele.

"What's IFCC?" I asked after she didn't elaborate.

She opened her blue eyes wide. "Indiana Farm Chemical Corporation. She had a position of some power, as I recall."

"Seriously?"

"Yup. And guess what else?"

I waited.

"Her brother Adam owns a soybean farm. Shoo-ee, the chemicals they put on them fields would kill anybody."

My jaw dropped. When she seemed to be about to tell me the flies would get in, I shut my mouth. The three people I knew of who had connections to Vicky, also had access to agricultural toxins. That was stunning news. I sat there, thinking. Did Eva have any reason to wish harm to her friend? Maybe her loyalty had been stronger to her brother than to her knitting buddy.

Samuel folded his paper and cleared his throat. "Adele, we need to be moving along." He laid a twenty-dollar bill on the table, more than enough for their meals. "No need for any change, now, Robbie."

"Thank you, Samuel," I said. "We're not going to solve

this here and now, anyway." The cow bell jangled again, admitting a dozen more people of all ages looking glad to get in out of the snow. I stood. "And I need to get back to work."

"Say, I heared poor Freddy O'Neill got hit," Adele said. "Is your mom-in-law going to be all right?"

"She is." *But, ugh.* I'd been too busy to look at my phone. Now I pulled it out and swiped into my messages. "Abe says they want to keep her in the hospital one more night."

"Too bad. Well, I'll take and bring a meal by the house tomorrow for them."

"You're the best." I said goodbye to both of them and gathered up the dishes. After I deposited them in the sink, I returned to my livelihood even as my brain exploded with questions about toxins and motives and so much more.

Chapter Fourteen

Three French Hens, in the form of coq au vin, proved a popular lunch special. By twelve-thirty, Danna was already in the process of augmenting it. Buck was demolishing a hamburger alone at his usual table, and I was on greeting-and-clearing duty when Abe pushed through the door. I gave a table a last swipe and hurried over to greet him.

"Too bad your mom has to stay in the hospital," I said after a quick hug, during which my shirt was adorned by rapidly melting snow.

"I know. She really wants to be home. But she's been running a low-grade fever, and the doc wants to get rid of that before she'll release her." He glanced back at the door. "This snow isn't helping anything."

"I haven't even been out." I peered through the glass in the front door. "Abe O'Neill, did you shovel the front steps and walk?"

"Of course I did. I don't want my wife sued by somebody who slips in six inches of snow."

"You're the best. Thank you." I squeezed his arm. "Did Sean go to school?"

He shook his head. "Snow day. He's with Dad."

"Is it forecast to keep snowing?"

"I haven't had time to check. Man, it smells good in here."

I sniffed the air. It did, with the usual bouquet of fresh biscuits and frying meats, plus the background scent of coffee. "Are you hungry?" I asked him.

"I'll say."

"The coq turned out great."

"That sounds perfect. Can I have an extra-big bowl?"

"For you, anything." I turned to survey the place, which had every table occupied and six people waiting. "Go eat with Buck. He won't mind."

Abe gave me a thumbs-up and headed over. I stole another glance at the swirling white stuff outside. With any luck, the storm would keep moving and be over soon. Half the time, it seemed, the temperature warmed in the afternoon. Some of the mess melted, and then overnight the melted snow froze, so the next day all walkways were sheets of ice. I'd never lived in or even visited farther north places like Minnesota, Maine, or Manitoba, but I'd heard there the snow stayed snow until March or later.

I waded back into the fray of a busy lunchtime. Whenever I glanced over, Abe and Buck were both staring at their phones. I personally dished up Abe's bowl of thick fragrant stew, adding a biscuit on the side, a bowl of fruit salad, and a glass of chocolate milk.

"Your lunch, husband." I set down the array of dishes.

"Thank you, darling wife." He gave me one of his signature beams before slicing the biscuit and applying two pats of butter. He worked hard physically and seemed to burn up every gram of fat he took in.

I gazed at Buck, who really needed to wipe his mouth with his napkin. But I wasn't his mother, and his eating habits were his own business. Homicide, on the other hand, I had an interest in.

"Buck," I began.

"Before you up and ask, Robbie, just hang on a little minute." Buck held up a hand.

"What are you, a mind reader?" I cocked my head at him. "Did you think I was about to ask you for any new developments?" Any developments at all, actually. But the thought of asking was theoretical. I usually figured if he had something to share, he would.

"I do have a small bit we've learned that I'm willing to tell you."

Ooh. My eyebrows went up.

"Do I have to cover my ears?" Abe asked.

"Shoot, no, O'Neill. She's going to tell you, anyhoo." Buck pushed away his plate. "So it seems somebody soaked a bundle of Adele's yarn in a contact toxin."

A bundle being a skein, but so what? I didn't correct him.

Buck scrunched up his nose. "The victim had open sores on her hands, which made it easy for the poison to get into her bloodstream, although touching it even with unbroken skin woulda done the trick sooner or later."

"I noticed her red hands," I said.

"The substance is worse than the Devil's own cocktail," Buck added.

"What kind of poison was it?" I asked, even though Adele had said it was of agricultural origin.

Abe looked back and forth between us as he ate. I was pretty sure he sensed I already knew something about the means of murder.

"It seems to be a herbicide called paraquat dichloride. Kills weeds and that type of thing. It also kills humans who touch it with bare, broken skin. The whole business is a crying shame, no two ways about it."

"A crying shame and also a horrific crime," Abe murmured.

"That, too, O'Neill." Buck gave a definitive nod. "You got that right."

"Adele told me Eva worked for a farm chemical company," I said. "I assume you know about that?"

"IFCC," Buck said. "And old Adam has himself a soybean farm. Guess what kind of plants they apply that paraquat around?"

"Soybeans?" I asked

"Yeperoo."

"Adele thought Cole Brewster had been the selling agent for a farm not too long ago," I said. "He might have had access to the herbicide, too."

"I think I heard about that sale," Abe chimed in. "It was a soybean farm on the way down to Madison."

"Seems old Wanda should oughta check that out," Buck said. "Thanks for the intel, kids."

Yes, she should, and ought to, too. Now we knew what the poison was. Who had applied it to the yarn and made sure Vicky received it was still a wide-open question.

Chapter Fifteen

"Tomorrow is Four Calling Birds," I said to Danna and Turner after the last customer left. "What are we going to do about that?"

Danna shook her head, dreadlocks swinging under her purple scarf. "Cookies shaped like old-fashioned telephones?"

"How about four tiny turkey sliders, or four turkey meatballs for a lunch special?" Turner swiped at a table. "Turkeys are birds, right?"

"I like that, dude," Danna said. "What do you think, Robbie?"

"Great idea. I'm pretty sure we have a load of frozen ground turkey." I cast around for a serving idea. "How about this? We could line up four in a hoagie roll. If you squint, the roll looks like an old telephone receiver or one of those clunky early cell phones."

"Serve them in tomato sauce like a meatball sub?" Turner asked.

"That sounds good, with cheese," I said.

"Whew. I'm glad we've settled tomorrow's lunch special, but what are we going to do for Five Golden Rings?" Danna scrubbed at a stubborn spot on the grill.

"I'm not sure we totally thought through this twelve-days-of-specials deal."

"I hear you," I said.

"Pour pancake batter in rings?" Turner asked.

"They would puff up and look like bagels," Danna said. "How about onion rings, five at a time?"

"But we don't have a deep fryer," Turner said.

That was by design. I'd picked up a used fryer when the restaurant opened, but it had soon malfunctioned. I hadn't replaced it. I hadn't wanted the mess and danger of hot oil, not to mention how to dispose of old oil. The perfection of our menu was marred only by the lack of deep-fried food, and that was fine with me.

"Maybe we could batter and flash bake slices of onions," Danna offered. "In fact, I think that's a brilliant suggestion. I'll look up the best method."

"Baked sounds good," I said. "I'm sure we'll figure it out. In the meantime, I'll get out the turkey meat from the freezer." I headed for our chest freezer next to the walk-in. I extracted all the three-pound packages of ground turkey and set them on the back of the stainless-steel counter to defrost in room temperature until I left for the day. The meat would finish thawing overnight in the walk-in, and we could roll meatballs midmorning tomorrow. I might even have a few unfrozen pounds in the walk-in that I could assemble after I finished breakfast prep.

Turner frowned at his phone. "Robbie?"

"Yeah?"

"My aunt heard something about Vicky," he said. "Auntie Meena—my dad's oldest sister—is so tied in with the Southeast Asian community, you wouldn't believe it. She hears everything. And what doesn't cross her path, she digs up."

"She's the gossip-in-chief?" Danna asked.

"Pretty much. Meena means well—most of the time—but if you want the scoop, she's the lady to see. She never married or had children, so gossip is a big part of her life."

"Does she live with your family?" I asked.

"Yes and no." Turner tilted his head one way and then the other. "She has her own apartment above the garage. But she usually eats with us. Heck, half the time she cooks for us. Anyway, I know her pretty well. She came to the US about ten years ago. She was living with my grandmother in Indy and working as an engineer, but after Dadiji passed on to the next life, Meena retired early and moved in with us."

Turner's paternal grandmother had taught him to cook and had left him her Indian recipes. She was a big reason he loved making food and why he wanted to become a chef in his own right. Still, I wanted to know what scoop Meena, single snoop that she was, had uncovered. I hadn't met her a couple of years ago when Turner's father had been suspected of murder, but she must have still been living in Indianapolis with her mother at the time.

"And?" I pressed.

"And Auntie Meena thinks Adam Kenney was trying to get back with Vicky, even though they were divorced," Turner said. "Like, you know, sending her flowers and chocolates and stuff."

Adam. Vicky's ex-husband. Soybean farmer. Brother of Eva.

"I wonder what she thought about that." I loaded up a few last plates and pushed the Start button on the dishwasher.

"Meena said Vicky's cousin's wife told her Vicky was, like, furious about it. That she'd considered reporting Mr. Kenney to the police for stalking."

"Wow," Danna said. "Remember last Christmas when that reporter guy wouldn't stop taking pictures of my brother and me at the town tree lighting? I wanted to get a restraining order against him."

Turner snorted. "And instead you grabbed his camera and ended up hurting your newly found bro. Reporter Whatshisname could have turned right around and reported you for assault."

"Yeah, well." Danna lifted a shoulder. She made one last wipe of the grill before throwing the cloth in the laundry box. "Not my proudest moment."

Especially not at the holidays. Things had worked out in the end, though.

"Turner, has Meena ever been in here to eat?" I asked.

"No, I don't think so."

"You could invite her in sometime," I said. "I'd love to meet your aunt." And pick her brain about Vicky while I was at it.

"She's holding down the fort in the gift shop every day in this season." He headed over to grab the floor sweeper. "Plus, she'd probably want to take over the cooking and throw all the beef in the trash. You don't know my auntie, Robbie. She's a force of nature."

I laughed. Maybe I could get out to the maple farm to have a little chat with her after prep for tomorrow was done. If the snow stopped, that is.

Chapter Sixteen

After my staff left at three o'clock, I switched on a playlist of Christmas songs—sung in Italian—and hummed along as I set to work on breakfast prep. We'd decided to reprise another red-and-green breakfast special from a prior holiday season: cranberry-mint muffins. I whipped up four dozen of them, plus dry ingredients for more that we could assemble tomorrow.

As always, having my hands busy set my mind free. What had Buck said that herbicide was called? Panko. No, that was flaky breadcrumbs. It had been pan-something, or maybe para-something. I got an image in my brain of an inch-long oblong-shaped orange citrus fruit I'd eaten as a child in Santa Barbara, one where the skin was sweet, but the flesh was too tart to taste. *Got it.* The chemical was paraquat, which was why I'd thought of the kumquat citrus.

As the muffins baked, I mixed baking powder, brown sugar, and salt into whole wheat flour for the pancake mix. My expression turned as sour as a kumquat's insides. Siblings Adam and Eva both had access to paraquat dichloride. Had they killed Vicky together? Eva had seemed genuinely sad at her friend's death, but she could have been putting on an act.

I moved on to biscuit dough, even though my fingers were itching to do research into the toxin and into Cole's real estate sales history. My hand holding the big pastry cutter slowed. Of course we—that is, Wanda—needed to figure out who killed Vicky. But maybe it was more important to understand how poison had been applied to Adele's yarn after it had left her farm and before Vicky began knitting with it.

Had the skein been purchased here in my store or elsewhere? Had Vicky bought it? Maybe someone gave it to her as a gift, knowing her love for knitting. My brow was the thing being knit right now. Turner's aunt Meena told him Adam was courting Vicky, apparently in vain.

I stopped cutting butter into the biscuit mix. Meena had said Adam was sending Vicky gifts. Including yarn? Possibly. I hastily wiped my hands on a towel and extracted my phone. Buck and Wanda needed to know what Auntie Meena had said.

Turner's aunt, Meena Rao, told him Adam Kenney was trying to woo Vicky back, sending her flowers and candy and "stuff." Maybe poisoned yarn? Meena lives with the Raos.

I sent the text to both Buck and his detective cousin. Because Meena hadn't married, I assumed her last name would be the same as Turner's father's—or hoped it was. I'd been about to urge my message recipients to check out her veracity and sources but had stopped at the last minute. That was their job.

The biscuit dough finished, I swathed it in plastic wrap. In the walk-in, I exchanged it for the three unfrozen turkey packages I found. Now, what would be a good turkey meatball recipe? Should I go Italian seasonings or head in the Thanksgiving route? Sage and poultry seasonings might fit better with Christmas, but we were going to serve the meatballs in tomato sauce. Italian, it was.

To three pounds of ground turkey, I measured out and added breadcrumbs, finely grated Parmesan cheese, a healthy dose of dried oregano and basil, and three eggs. I added salt and pepper and scrubbed my hands anew before starting to smoosh the mixture between my fingers.

It was a good thing I did. My hands were heading toward the mixing bowl when my phone vibrated with a call. Buck or Wanda calling back, maybe? I connected without paying attention to the number.

"Robbie, you need to know something," Abe's mom said without preamble.

"Freddy! How are you feeling? I was going to call you as soon as I was done with prep in the restaurant."

"I'm fine, hon. It's a blasted nuisance, of course, that idiot running into me and my leg. I could . . . well, I won't go there. It's the holidays, after all."

"How are they treating you?" I wandered over to the door and peered out as we spoke. By some miracle, the snow had stopped falling and a weak sun was trying to assert itself through the clouds toward the west.

"Everyone here is a gem. It's just that they wake you up every couple hours at night, and the dang leg wakes me up every other hour."

"What can I bring you?"

"I don't need a thing, Robbie. They're supposed to spring me tomorrow. If they don't, I'm going to order that son of mine to take me home, anyway. Run an intervention."

"Are you sure I can't bring you a book, or a couple of muffins? Or would you like a visit sans gifts?"

"Nah, you stay put. Roads can't be too great for driving right now, anyway. Only thing I'd like is a tumbler of Scotch whiskey, and I'd bet my cello these . . . kind nurses wouldn't allow me to drink it." Freddy snorted, then whispered, "One just walked in."

"Fine. But Abe and I will make some food and bring it by tomorrow after you're settled." And maybe we'd add a bottle of Scotch to our offering.

"Sure, that'd be great. But listen, Robbie. I've picked up a little scuttlebutt about the recent incident, if you know what I mean, to share with you."

"I'm listening." She had to mean the incident of Vicky's murder. Or I hoped she did.

"Cole is in the Indianapolis Symphony with me," Freddy continued. "He plays viola. You know he also sells real estate?"

"Yes, although I didn't know about his musical abilities."

"Why would you? He's reasonably talented, but of course the Indy Symphony doesn't pay any of us a living wage. We only get a token payment and do it for the love of music, mostly. Anyway, Cole fought hard to get the contract to sell that farm down on the road to Madison."

"Fought hard against whom?" I asked.

"Nobody you'd know. Another agent. Thing is, my cousin's neighbor's brother caught Cole leaving the barn with something under his coat. Sounds suspicious, wouldn't you say?"

"If he was removing a piece of property he didn't own, I'd say it sounds very suspicious. Do you know how big this thing was?"

"Nope. But I can—" Her voice broke off, then she mumbled something away from the phone. "I'll have to call you back, Robbie. Doc's here."

She disconnected before I could even say good-bye. I stared at the phone. I still had so many questions. What was the name of the cousin's neighbor's brother? If Cole had concealed an object under his coat, it could have been a container of herbicide. Except it seemed like a stretch for him to murder a woman simply because she hadn't wanted to continue dating him, especially when he now seemed enthralled with Eva.

I hoped Freddy would call me back after she talked to the doctor. If she didn't, Abe might know who the unknown brother was, and I could ask the man myself. And if not the neighbor's brother, Abe could at least put me in touch with his mother's cousin.

Either way, I decided to be a good doobie and pass along what Freddy had said. Both Buck and Wanda were so tuned into the local populace, one of them might be able to trace the convoluted connection without even having a name. Or they might simply go interview Cole and ask him.

I tapped out a text and sent it along.

Meanwhile, those turkey meatballs weren't going to roll themselves. I plunged my hands in and squeezed the eggs into the meat, crumbs, and cheese. It smelled divine. As long as my phone didn't ring again, I could be out of here by five.

Chapter Seventeen

I sat in my car at five-fifteen. I'd finished all the prep I could do and had shoveled the porch, front steps, and walkway again. I considered visiting Meena at the Rao Maple Farm, but I didn't want to get entangled in her gossip machine. Instead, I could drive out to Adam Kenney's soybean farm. I did a quick search on my phone and found Kenney Farm on Gatesville Road, which ran between Beanblossom and Taggart to the east but was still part of Brown County.

A truck fronted by a yellow triangular snowplow attachment rumbled by, maybe one of the contractors the town hired to clear the roads. Main Street, on which my store was situated at nearly the edge of town, looked entirely drivable. I doubted Gatesville Road would be as cleared, running through a much more rural section of the county as it did. From here, it would take me at least twenty minutes to make my way to the farm, and the sun would have set by the time I got there.

Most important, I had no reason in the universe to pay

a visit to a soybean farmer on a cold, snowy afternoon. A farmer who might be a murderer. That would definitely slot me into the Too Stupid to Live category. They gave out Darwin Awards for lesser acts.

I thought. Did I have any excuse to call Adam? I drummed the steering wheel. And snapped my fingers. *Duh*. I could always invent a reason. I took a deep breath and made the call.

"Kenney Farm."

"Is this Adam?" I asked.

"In the flesh. How can I help you?"

"This is Robbie Jordan in South Lick. We met recently when you came into my restaurant with Eva."

"Oh." He cleared his throat. "I suppose you want to talk about my late ex-wife."

"Not really, no." Of course I did, but I didn't want to start with that. "I was actually wondering about soybean waste."

"Soybean waste." He sounded incredulous.

I didn't blame him for not believing me, but I forged on. "The thing is, my aunt has a sheep farm, and she's thinking about adding pigs. I told her I'd check around on food sources for them. Do you compost whatever you don't sell, or would you consider giving some away, as long as we pick it up?"

Adele would be surprised to hear she was considering adding porcines to her ovine mix, but Adam didn't need to know that.

"You do know it's December, Miss Jordan."

"Naturally. I was only thinking ahead for next year." I didn't bother asking him to call me Ms. Jordan, or better, Robbie. If he wanted to go all old-school on me, let him. I shut up and waited.

He finally spoke. "I could consider that. Have your aunt contact me in the spring. What's her name?"

"Adele Jordan. Her farm is in South Lick but it's out on Beanblossom Road."

"Heck, I know Adele. She's good people."

Maybe he knew Adele well enough to buy yarn from her and then poison it.

"Well, I'd better let you go," he added.

And I'd better give her a heads-up about my lie, stat. But . . . first things first.

"I am so sorry about Vicky's passing," I said. "I know you were no longer married, but I wondered if there were any funeral arrangements yet. I'd like to pay my respects."

"Not yet." He didn't elaborate.

"Do you know if they've found the awful person who ended her life?"

Again I was met with silence. Again I waited. It was getting cold in here, but I didn't want to start the car and add any distracting background noises.

"I've heard you're all buddy-buddy with the police," he growled. "Why are you asking me about who killed Vicky?"

I smiled, not that he could see me, but I knew it altered a person's voice quality. "I do know a couple of officers who come into my restaurant to eat, but they don't tell me a thing."

"They sure as heck don't tell me."

I thought I heard a voice in the background. His voice came through muffled, as if he held a hand over the phone, but I could have sworn he said "Eva." His sister must be visiting.

"Sorry about that," he said, his voice clear again. "Anyway, Miss Jordan, you might not believe me, but I loved my wife even after she left me. She didn't deserve to be murdered." His voice broke and the last words came out almost as a sob.

Was that sorrow real or an act? I waited a moment to let him compose himself and to be sure he was done talking.

"Of course, she didn't," I said in a soft tone. "Listen, I don't want to keep you. I'll let Adele know you're willing to talk with her about food for the pigs. Take care now."

He disconnected almost before I stopped speaking.

Me, I fired up the hybrid and headed for the warm solace of home, hearth, and husband.

Chapter Eighteen

A fire crackled in the wood stove at seven. Abe and I sat side by side on the couch, both with a bellyful of the yummy lasagna he'd baked, each with our own choice of reading material. His was a book he needed to read for a course he'd be starting in January.

Abe had decided to change careers, saying working as an electrical lineman was too dangerous for a husband and father. He was going back to school to earn a certificate in wildlife education. He loved the woods and was at home in wild spaces, so retraining in that field made perfect sense. I'd told him he had my full support.

My book was a new mystery by an author named Becky Clark, which featured a crossword-puzzle designer solving crimes. That one was right down my alley.

We had set up our fresh-cut Christmas tree on Sunday in the front windows, across the room from the stove. The tree's small white and colored lights glowed with the season, and the fir's aroma filled the air.

Sean had disappeared out the door for a library study session with his math club buddy—that is, his girlfriend, Maeve. The house was quiet. Birdy nestled happily between us. Sean's half-completed green scarf peeked out of his cloth tote a knitting bag. My sheepskin-clad feet on the coffee table were snug and warm. But I couldn't concentrate on the story.

"I talked with your mom this afternoon," I began. "I'm glad she can go home tomorrow."

"Did she tell you if they don't spring her, we're doing what she calls a 'liberation intervention' in the morning?" He laid his book facedown on his lap.

"She implied that, yes."

"Do I sense a 'but' coming along?" He twisted to gaze at me.

"You do. Not about facilitating her release, not at all. That's perfect. But she mentioned her cousin's neighbor's brother seeing Cole Brewster smuggle something out of the barn at a farm he was selling."

"And this is important why?" Abe tilted his head.

I scrunched up my nose. "I haven't had a chance to fill you in on a few pieces of information. Buck said the toxin that got into Vicky's blood via her hands—that is, the substance that killed her—was an agricultural herbicide used on soybean farms. The farm we were talking about, the one Cole was the selling agent for, was a soybean farm like Adam Kenney's."

"So Brewster might have been in possession of the poison. Why would he want to kill Vicky Chakrabarti?"

"That's the question, isn't it? I really have no idea." I stroked Birdy's long, soft fur. "This cousin intrigues me. Do you know who your mom was talking about?"

"Not really. I'll see if I can find out more tomorrow." He squeezed my hand. "And if I don't get this book read before January second, I won't have much of a place in my class."

"Go for it." I squeezed his hand in return. It wasn't fair

of me to drag him into every question I had about the latest homicide investigation. Adele seemed, for now, to be in the clear, but I still had an intense interest in the case.

I sat thinking. Adam had seemed suspicious about my asking questions. He'd also sounded broken up about Vicky's death. But had he been, really? Eva had looked like a grieving friend on the first day. She'd gotten over it fast enough, cuddling with Cole in public the following day. If she believed Cole still pined for Vicky's affections, would Eva want to get her friend out of competition in the most final of ways? I couldn't come up with a reason for Cole to kill Vicky. But he could have helped someone else do it by purloining poison—unless he'd stolen something else. That would still be a crime, just not a homicide-related one. Alternatively, Eva could have helped Adam or vice versa.

What a tangle of yarn it all was. I idly poked around the Internet on my phone, looking for more information on any of the three. Adam seemed the most likely, his sob and reports of his trying to win Vicky back notwithstanding. Maybe he was paying alimony to her and was sick of it. Maybe he didn't like seeing her thrive without him. Some men would take that as a slight.

Then we had Eva, who had worked for a chemical company. Eva—with her comfortable body and purple reading glasses on a beaded chain, with her knitting bag and homey accent—didn't look like a murderer. Except, if I'd learned anything in the last few years, it was that killers come in all shapes and sizes. I dug into IFCC, pairing it with her name.

My eyes widened. She had held a position in senior management in the company. In fact, she'd been the chief financial officer. On the surface, Eva didn't look like what one thought of as a CFO, either. More proof of the old books-and-covers adage.

What was making me stare at the article from five years ago was that she'd apparently been asked to step down, to leave the company. The news was couched in careful wording about Ms. Kenney deciding to leave in pursuit of other opportunities. I was pretty sure that was code for the company asking her to resign. That is, firing her.

I found another source saying there had been financial irregularities at the time Eva left IFCC. The mention of missing inventory really caught my attention. I kept searching but couldn't unearth any criminal charges associated with it. The board of directors must have found out what she was up to but kept it quiet as long as she went without a fuss.

I sat back. Did she still have that missing inventory in her garage? In her barn or storage unit? I was horrified to think she'd used it on Adele's yarn, a skein she knew Vicky would knit with. I wondered if I should pass along the news articles to Wanda but decided not to. Researching persons of interest would be one of the first things she and her team would do. Eva finding the body, as well as being Vicky's friend, should have automatically made her a person of high interest.

At the sound of a soft snore, I glanced over at Abe and smiled to myself. He'd leaned his head back on the cushion to read, except the book now lay collapsed against his chest. Between us, Birdy purred, knowing a kindred napper when he heard one.

I focused on my novel again, where all murders were fictional. I felt safe here, and I couldn't do anything about this tonight, anyway.

Chapter Nineteen

After I parked behind my store at six o'clock the next morning, I stretched my arms high. It was so very dark at this time of year and so cold. We hadn't gotten any more snow overnight. Instead, the clear skies let the temperature plummet. My boots crunched on the plowed snow in the driveway. I paid a plow guy to clear it, but I'd asked him not to get down to the gravel or it would all end up in the pile. Instead I had a packed inch of snow left, which made it drivable and easy enough to walk on unless it thawed and refroze, always a possibility in this neck of the woods.

A yawn overtook me. But the show must go on, or, in my case, the restaurant must open. I slid off one glove to insert the key in the lock of the service door at the side of the building. I pulled open the automatically locking door and stuck my hip in the opening so I could remove the key. My eyes narrowed at a sound somewhere behind me.

An arm wrapped around my neck. "Inside," a woman's voice ordered.

Eva. My breath rushed in. I didn't want to be alone with her in my store. She pushed at me. I dug my feet in, bracing myself with my strong cyclist's thighs.

"I have a container of something rather lethal," she

threatened in a low, gravely voice. "Do you want me to pour it on you out here and leave you to freeze to death?"

I thought frantically. Fight to stay out here where the fresh air would help dissipate any fumes? No. Better to be indoors where I knew the space and had kitchen tools I could defend myself with. And maybe call for help, too. I moved forward, leaving the key in the lock. When Danna got here in half an hour, maybe she'd know something was wrong. Would she spy Eva's car, wherever she'd left it? I didn't have time to dwell on it.

The door clicked shut behind Eva. She kept her arm firmly around my neck. She pressed on my throat. Her soft torso pushed at me, but her forearm was an iron bar under her wool coat.

"Please let go, Eva." My voice croaked.

"As if. Here. Turn on the lights." She nudged me toward the switch plate.

I flipped on all the store lights. "You're hurting my throat." At least she wasn't pressing hard enough for me to black out, but that could change in a flash.

"Listen to me, Robbie Jordan, and listen up good," Eva snarled. "I know you're about to turn in the two people in my life I actually love."

"What are you talking about?" How could I turn the tables on her? I had to escape and call for help. My thoughts raced. "Do you mean Adam and Cole?"

"Brother and lover. You think one of them killed Vicky." She pushed me into the kitchen area.

"Not at all." I was now certain Eva had. "I can't figure out why anyone would murder her." Just in time, I stopped myself from saying, "any of you," which would not go over well at this particular moment.

She snorted. The pressure of her arm lessened. Not much, but a little.

"Who wouldn't want to get that smug woman out of the way?" Eva scoffed. "She always pretended to be so self-sufficient, divorcing my brother, dropping poor Cole. Even talking about what great friends she and I were. You wouldn't believe how she looked down her nose that I hadn't kept my figure like she did. And what did she ever do for me? She wasn't much of a friend when the company I started kicked me out the back door like I was garbage."

Delusional much? "They did?" I pretended to be shocked. "That's terrible."

Her grip softened even more as she ranted.

I shot a glance at the wall clock. Ten after six. I sent out a prayer to the universe that today Danna would find herself awake and alert early and I'd see her walk through the door any minute now. Except I couldn't rely on wishful thinking. My life was up to me.

Me, who had both hands free. *Doh.* My initial terror had made me stupid. Why wasn't Eva gripping my hands behind me, or holding on to my arm with her free hand? Because she had a vial of poison in the other hand. She'd said as much. I had to free myself and get far away from her. As fast as I could. I was sweating inside my coat even though my feet and hands were cold and numb from fear.

I zipped through my options. She had pushed me up against the under-counter drawer that held a set of sharp skewers. I'd never be able to push back, open the drawer, grab one, and wield it before she counterattacked. My cell was in my turquoise cross bag, not in my coat pocket. Eva was at least two inches taller than I and heftier, but I was a lot fitter and faster.

A click came from the service door. Eva's grip slipped. I dashed toward the front door.

"Hey! Get back here," Eva shouted at me.

At the door, I whirled to see Danna appear in the service

door opening. She held up my keys, looking quizzical until she spied Eva.

"What's—?" Danna started to ask.

"Get out, Danna!" I screamed. "She has poison. Run!"

I rammed myself against the fire bar, making it onto the porch. I scrabbled for my phone, even as I raced down the steps and around the side. Danna had to have made it out. She had to have. I jabbed the emergency button.

"Murderer attacking in Pans 'N Pancakes," I said to the dispatcher. "Nineteen Main Street, South Lick. Eva Kenney has a vial of poison. Hurry!"

Chapter Twenty

I'd never been happier to see Danna jogging toward me under the street light. "Is Eva following you?" I grabbed her arm.

She shook her head, hard. "What's going on, Robbie?"

"Come on." I kept hold of her arm and glanced behind us. "Tell you in a minute after we're across the street."

I checked both ways for cars, waiting for a sedan to speed by, its driver apparently oblivious to the drama inside my store. Danna and I rushed to the other side of the road and huddled in the dark next to the now-abandoned antique store.

"Eva Kenney surprised me as I was unlocking the service door." I panted as I spoke.

"Thus these." Danna extended my keys.

"Yes, and thanks." I pocketed them. "She forced me inside, saying she had a vial of poison. She ranted about Vicky, listing all the reasons anyone would want to murder her." I shuddered.

Eyes wide, Danna brought her hand to her mouth. "That's terrible."

"Of course it is. When you showed up, her grip on me slipped, out of surprise, I think. You know the rest." I kept a close watch on both the front door and the driveway, but Eva didn't appear.

"Why didn't she come after us?" Danna's breath made little clouds in the frigid air.

"Maybe she spilled the toxin on herself? I don't know."

When the lights and sirens roared up, I stepped forward and waved. Buck jumped out of one of the SLPD cruisers, hurrying across to us. Officers piled out. The ones who emerged from the Brown County Sheriff's SUV wore SWAT gear. Wanda directed the officers, some to the front door, some to the side.

"You girls all right?" Buck asked when he reached us.

"Yes." Girls, we weren't, but I knew he, unlike some men, meant no belittling by the term.

"Gimme the high-speed version," he said.

"Eva Kenney surprised me when I was opening the side door." The words rushed out of my mouth. "She said she had a vial of 'something lethal' ready to spill on me. She pushed me inside and accused me of being ready to turn in both Adam and Cole for Vicky's murder. Danna arrived, and it startled Eva. Danna and I got away out of separate doors. We ran over here. Haven't seen Eva appear."

"Got it."

"Wait. You'll need these." I pulled out the keys and isolated one before handing over the bunch. "This is the front door. The one with the red thing on it is the side door."

"Thanks. Stay right here." Buck loped back across the road.

"Be careful," I called.

He gave me a thumbs-up without looking back. He quickly conferred with Wanda. They crept up the front stairs. Buck crouched to unlock the door, then handed the keys to Wanda. She ran with surprising speed for a woman her size around the side and disappeared. A moment later, the SWAT personnel burst into the front door shouting, "Police!" and other warnings. I assumed they'd done the same at the side. Eva didn't have a chance. Still, I crossed my fingers that no one would be hurt.

Chapter Twenty-one

"**S**orry about all this, Danna." I shivered as my adrenaline ebbed. I hugged my arms around me.

"Hey, no worries. I hope she doesn't try to spill whatever she claimed to have on the cops."

I quickly thought back. "Did you see her holding a vial or a container? She was behind me the whole time until you came in, and then I was focused on warning you and escaping. I didn't get a good look."

Danna stared at the lit windows. "Yeah, no. I didn't, either."

"Maybe she was bluffing. Somehow I don't think so."

We stood waiting together in the cold air. The homey smell of woodsmoke and pine needles jarred with reality.

I tried to peer into the store, but the porch overhang made it impossible to see more than vague shapes moving about. Had Eva crouched behind a counter and surprised them? Maybe she'd tripped trying to reach Danna or me and spilled the poison on herself. With any luck it wouldn't have landed on broken skin but on her winter clothing. She needed to be able to stand trial, that much I knew.

An ambulance sped up and braked to a stop, lights flashing but no siren. I brought my gloved hand to my mouth. Could that mean Eva was dead? I shook myself. No. Surely it was because she needed medical help but not urgently. Or maybe an officer was hurt with nonlife-threatening injuries, as the news always put it.

A thought hit me. I swore out loud. Danna glanced over with a skeptical look.

"You don't usually talk like that. Dish, Robbie. What's going on?"

"It occurred to me that we're not going to be able to open the restaurant today." I wrinkled my nose. "I think."

"Why not?"

"They'll say the whole store is a crime scene."

"Is it?" Danna asked.

"I'm not sure. Forced entry, sure, and assault? Maybe it depends on if Eva hurt herself or not."

"Hey, worse things have happened than staying closed for a morning or even a day."

"You're right." I kept my gaze on the lit windows of my livelihood, made garish by the addition of strobing red and blue lights. "I made the muffins yesterday, but they'll keep."

"Everything will keep for a day, boss."

"You're right. Of course it will."

Danna was nearly a decade younger than I was, but she often seemed older than her years. I appreciated her even-keeled approach to life, especially at times like these, when mine felt bumpier.

I pointed when the front door opened. An officer gripped Eva, whose wrists were handcuffed behind her back, by the elbow. Wanda followed close behind as Eva was es-corted to the back seat of the sheriff's department vehicle. The officer protected Eva's head as she slid in. The door clicked shut behind her. Eva didn't appear harmed, and she was docile as she went, not rebellious.

Wanda looked across the street at us. "You done good, Robbie. Catch you later."

I raised a hand in reply. Wanda climbed into the front seat. Without siren blaring or emergency lights flashing, the SUV drove off. A quiet ambulance followed. Buck peered across the road from the store's front porch.

"Come on back over." He gestured to us.

We made our way across. It had to be nearly seven by now, but the sky was still dark. The weak pre-solstice sun wouldn't rise for at least another hour to start one of the season's shortest days.

Adele's pickup pulled up, which surprised me not one bit. She loved monitoring the police radio she'd never relinquished after her last term as South Lick's mayor. If she heard of something happening that involved her only niece, she was all over it. I was a bit surprised it had taken her this long to get here.

Danna and I made it to Buck before my aunt.

"What happened in there?" I asked.

"Hang on a little minute," he said. "I might as well wait for Adele. You know as sure as the Pope's Catholic she's going to want to know all about it."

Adele climbed down from the Ford.

"What on God's green earth is going on around here?" She peered at me. "You girls all right?"

"We're fine," I said. "Can we go inside, Buck?"

"That'd be a negative."

I blew out a breath. Despite agreeing with Danna that everything would keep, I hated when Pans 'N Pancakes had to be shuttered, even if only temporarily.

An officer strode around from the side carrying a roll of wide yellow tape.

"Jimbo here's about to string up the crime-scene tape," Buck said. "He's got to establish a perimeter."

No. "Do you have to?" I grabbed Buck's sleeve. "I promise not to go inside. I'd much, much rather keep the door locked and put up a sign saying something about being closed due to circumstances beyond our control. Please?"

Buck regarded me with cocked head. "You don't want folks thinking somebody was killed in there or nothing, am I right?"

"Yes, exactly."

He thought for another moment. "All righty, then. Hold off there, Jimbo. We can make the single point of entry the side door."

The officer shrugged and headed back around the side.

"Listen up, y'all," Adele said. "It's colder than a miner's lunch pail in Antarctica out here. I got me an idea."

Chapter Twenty-two

Ten minutes later I sat around the table in my apartment kitchen with Buck, Danna, and Adele. Buck had agreed we could sit in the apartment as long as we entered by the back door.

Besides the beer and wine I kept in the fridge in here, I also had coffee makings and a small drip machine. Adele had had a notebook and tape in her truck, so I'd lettered another Gone Fishing–type of sign for the front door. I'd also texted Abe.

Had police activity at PnP. Danna and I are fine. Eva Kenney in custody. Won't be opening today. Home after a bit. XXOO

While I was texting, Danna had conveyed the news to Turner, telling him we were fine but that the store was closed, and he should stay home.

"Okay, Buck," I began after we four sat with our coffee. We all kept our coats on. I heated this space only enough so the pipes didn't freeze. "I'm ready."

"Welp." He slid sideways in his chair and stretched his legs out nearly to the door. "You girls saw the way we went inside, full SWAT and vests and all. Old Eva was just setting on the floor, arms around her knees, like she was cowering or some such. Wadn't no need for all our fuss, but, 'course, we don't know that before we head on in.'"

"So she lost her nerve after we escaped and the sirens showed up," I said. "Did she have poison with her?"

He bobbed his head once. "It appears she did, in a test tube kind of a thingy. But it was stoppered up in her coat pocket. Sure didn't look to have been opened."

"Eva must have had her other hand on it while her arm was around my neck," I said. "I wondered why she left my hands free. But she would have needed two hands to open it."

"Isn't that kind of a serious flaw in her plan?" Danna asked.

"Nobody ever said murderers were brilliant," Adele said with a snort.

"How long are we going to have to stay closed, Buck?" I cradled my hands around the warm mug.

"That'll depend on the team, when they get here and what they find. Seeing as how nobody ended up hurt at all, it might could be tomorrow or even as early as today lunchtime." He picked up his cup but set it down before drinking. "You gave me the quick summary out there, Robbie. Did Eva confess to anything in there? This ain't the official interview, you know. My cousin will be conducting that. But I'd sure as shooting like to know, and I'd bet a year's worth of nickels Adele would, too."

Adele's eyes lit up as she bobbed her head with way too much enthusiasm.

I told them how Eva had forced me inside. "She said she knew I was about to turn in Cole or Adam for the murder, then she listed all the reasons why she hated Vicky."

"She stopped short of admitting she poisoned the yarn?" Buck asked.

"I'm afraid so."

"Last night I found something pretty interesting," Adele began. "Y'all know Robbie sells my yarn in the store, but folks also come to the farm to buy it. I started going through my receipts. I'd plum forgotten that Eva had bought a dozen skeins from me way back in May. I was so busy getting ready for the wedding, it must have skipped my mind."

"Were they of green yarn?" I asked.

Adele pointed at me. "On the nose. But what I don't get is why the shade of the poisoned yarn was different from my green dye."

"I know why," Buck said. "That paraquat stuff is dyed blue. You soak green yarn in it, and it's bound to alter the color."

"That's gotta be it." Adele pointed at him.

"Turner's aunt told him Adam was trying to get Vicky back," Danna said.

"Right," I agreed. "Eva was obviously jealous of Vicky in all kinds of ways. She probably poisoned the skein, put it in a bag, and pretended to be supporting her brother by suggesting it would be a perfect gift for Vicky."

"That's exactly what happened," Buck added. "Last night one of Wanda's team finished going through the victim's trash. She found a note from Adam offering the yarn as a gift, saying he felt bad they had been arguing. But get this. It wadn't in his handwriting."

Adele whistled. I shook my head.

"They'll get a handwriting sample from Eva," Buck continued. "If she hasn't confessed already, she will, mark my words."

"Dumber than a box of rocks, as my mom says." Danna cast her gaze toward the ceiling.

"By the way, Adele, obviously you're off the hook for the crime," Buck said. "I expect Wanda'll be returning the yarn and whatnot she confiscated."

"I told you what Freddy said about Cole and the thing he took from the barn on the property he sold," I said. "What about that?"

Buck made a tsking noise. "We up and asked him. The idiot found a antique gallon jar in the barn that reminded him of his granny. Taking it was surely a stupid thing to do, but it wasn't no homicidal act."

"I sure as heck am glad this affair is over," Adele said. "It needed solved before Christmas, and you and Wanda got the job done. With Robbie's help, natch." My aunt smiled as she patted my hand.

I returned the smile. "I'll tell you, Buck. If I never learn a new way to kill someone, I'll be a happy woman."

Chapter Twenty-three

A be had gotten his mom, cast and all, nestled into a corner of our couch by five o'clock on Christmas Eve. We'd rearranged the furniture so the couch faced the room. Anyone sitting there had a sightline all the way back to the kitchen, where three generations of O'Neill men currently toiled away. The carved Italian figures in the nativity scene my father had sent me last year clustered around the manger on a bookshelf, and the lights on the tree sparkled, although only unbreakable ornaments were hung on the lower third of branches. This was Birdy's fourth Christmas, but he still loved to bat at anything hanging from a string. The base of the tree was loaded with presents wrapped in either newspaper or cloth, as we'd requested, our small gift to the environment

I handed my mother-in-law a glass of spiked eggnog.

"It's too bad Donnie and Georgia couldn't be here," Freddy said.

"I don't know." I smiled and sat in the nearest chair. "Christmas combined with a honeymoon in Puerto Rico doesn't sound too bad." Abe's older brother Don and his sweetheart had gotten married last week in a simple ceremony. It was a second marriage for both of them, and they'd decided to celebrate far from home.

Freddy took a sip. "My, my, this is very nice, and it sure packs a wallop, too. Good thing I'm off the pain meds." She chuckled.

I tasted my own small glass. "Whoa. Somebody got carried away with the bourbon." My father-in-law, most likely. I set down the glass. I'd have to pace myself or I'd be under the table before dessert.

"You got everything solved on that murder, right?" Freddy asked. "I was in a bit of a fog at the time, what with the painkillers."

"Wanda and Buck did, for sure. Did you hear what the thing was that Cole took from that barn?"

"No, I didn't."

"He stole an antique jar," I said. "An empty jar. That's all it was."

"The idiot. What kind of a real estate agent goes around lifting antiques from a property he's trying to sell?" She snorted. "Seriously."

"Agree."

"And, in the end, Eva Kenney was the murderer." Freddy shuddered. "Poisoning yarn with something that gets into the skin is just cruel, don't you think?"

All I could do was nod my agreement.

The front door opened to admit Adele, Samuel, and Phil with a burst of cold air. My aunt knew she didn't have to ring the bell or knock, at least not when a festive evening was in store. Samuel carried a wide cloth-covered basket fragrant with fresh-baked something. Phil toted a cardboard box, his eyes sparkling. In one hand, Adele held the handles of a maroon cloth carrier with wine bottle tops peeking out of the top. With her other she set down a quilted bag stuffed with soft things.

"Merry Christmas!" Adele beamed.

"And to you." Abe emerged from the kitchen, his green apron with red elves cavorting across it a perfect accessory to his red silk shirt. "Are those the rolls?" Abe took the basket from Samuel.

"As requested," Samuel said. "But baked by herself, not me."

I stood to greet the newcomers. "What are you all tickled about, Phil?" I tried to peek into his box.

"Hey!" He turned away. "All will be revealed in due time."

Birdy trotted in. He wound around Phil's ankles, then jumped up to nestle next to Freddy and survey his kingdom.

"Where's Cocoa?" Adele asked.

"I think Sean let him out into the backyard a little while ago," I said. "He's way too excited to be in here."

"Sean's actually out walking the pup," Abe said. "Trying to wear him out before dinner."

"Good idea." Adele handed the wine bag to Abe and began shedding hat, coat, and gloves.

"Let me take your wraps." I held out my arms and hung everything in the coat closet.

Abe delivered glasses of eggnog to Adele, now sitting at Freddy's feet, and Samuel, who'd settled into an armchair. Phil was laying a slender tube wrapped in red and green foil at each place on the already-set dining table.

"What are those?" I called to him.

"You don't know?" Samuel asked.

"They're crackers," Phil said.

"They don't look like any crackers I've ever seen." I scrunched up my nose.

Phil just grinned. "You'll see. It's a British tradition my mum brought here from Jamaica."

Like Samuel, Phil's father was an American Black, but I'd forgotten Phil's mom was born in Jamaica.

Three hours later we were all stuffed, sated, and a bit soused, back in the living room in various relaxed poses. Our heads were adorned with crowns from the crackers, which had turned out to be little noisemaker pull-apart packages. Each had contained a paper crown, a tiny toy, and a wrapped piece of ribbon candy.

Sean now stretched out on the floor with his head on a cushion. Beside him, Birdy was curled up next to Cocoa, all three apparently snoozing, although the cat's ears were on alert. When Adele rose to fetch her cloth bag, Birdy perked up.

"Heads up, folks." She grinned. "I took and made a Christmas Eve present for all y'all."

She started handing out red or green knitted scarves tied with a ribbon to each of us. I untied mine and spread it on my lap where I sat, Abe's back against my legs.

"Adele, I love it." She had knitted a pattern of little red skillets into the green yarn.

Freddy held up hers. She had green cellos amid red yarn. Sean's featured dogs. Phil's oven mitts, and so on. Last, Adele wrapped a thin red and green striped strip around Cocoa's neck and tied it in a bow.

"And this one might not last long." She held up a knitted orb smaller than a tennis ball. "I tucked some catnip in with the jingle bells." She threw it down the hall.

I laughed, watching Birdy race after his gift. "Thank you, Adele." I reached out my arms and gave her a big hug.

" 'We wish you a merry Christmas,' " Abe began singing in his melodic baritone.

Everyone else joined in. When the song switched to "Silent Night," I stopped singing and just listened as my eyes welled up. The murder was solved. All my most cherished people—and animals—were right here in this room, and my heart was full. I hoped the peace of the season would extend indefinitely, at least in South Lick, in our tiny corner of the world.

Recipes

Roasted Chicken and Pears

The chicken, fruit, and vegetables in this dish all roast together in the oven, and they come out golden and caramelized. It's exactly the kind of crowd-pleasing dish for Robbie to serve during the holiday season as a nod to a Partridge in a Pear Tree.

Ingredients

2 large carrots, peeled and cut into 1-inch chunks
2 small red onions, cut into inch-wide wedges
2 tablespoons red wine vinegar
2 tablespoons olive oil
1 teaspoon dried thyme
Coarse salt and ground pepper
2 tablespoons chopped fresh parsley
4 boneless chicken breasts and 4 boneless thighs (about 2
    pounds total)
1 tablespoon honey
3 firm, ripe Bosc pears (about 1½ pounds total), halved,
    cored, and cut into ½-inch-thick wedges

Directions

Preheat oven to 375 degrees. On a large rimmed baking sheet (or two small ones), toss carrots and onions with vinegar, 1 tablespoon oil, and ½ teaspoon thyme. Season with salt and pepper.

In a small bowl, combine parsley and remaining ½ teaspoon thyme. Season with salt and pepper. Carefully slide fingers under chicken skin to loosen. Spread parsley mixture under and on top of skin. (If you have skinless chicken, pat the mixture into the meat.) Push vegetables to edges of baking sheet; place chicken pieces in center, and roast 30 minutes.

Meanwhile, in a small bowl, combine honey and remaining tablespoon oil. Remove baking sheet from oven. Add pears and toss with vegetables to combine. Brush top of chicken pieces with honey mixture. Roast 30 minutes more or until a thermometer inserted in thickest part of thigh registers 175 degrees. Serve immediately.

Turtle Cookies

Phil makes these, mimicking turtle candies, for dessert on the Two Turtle Doves day.

Makes about thirty.

Ingredients

For the cookies:
1 cup all-purpose flour
⅓ cup unsweetened cocoa powder
¼ teaspoon salt
½ cup butter (1 stick) at room temperature
⅔ cup granulated sugar
1 large egg, separated
2 tablespoons milk
1 teaspoon vanilla extract
1 cup pecans, finely chopped

For the caramel:
⅔ cup caramel chips or regular caramels (about 15)
½ teaspoon water
½ cup semisweet chocolate chips

Directions

Combine flour, cocoa and salt. In a separate bowl, cream together butter and sugar until light and fluffy. Mix in the egg yolk, milk and vanilla. Stir in flour mixture until just combined. Chill dough in the refrigerator for one hour.

Preheat oven to 350 degrees Fahrenheit.

Whisk egg white in a shallow bowl until frothy. Place chopped pecans in another shallow bowl.

Remove dough from fridge. For each cookie, scoop out less than a tablespoon and roll into a small ball.

Roll each ball in the frothy egg whites, and then roll and press in the chopped pecans. Place on a greased baking sheet.

Use the back of a small round measuring or soup spoon—or your thumb—to make an indentation in the center of each dough ball or use your thumb.

Bake for about 10–12 minutes, or just until set. Don't overbake, as cookies will harden as they cool.

As the cookies come out of the oven, gently re-press the indentations with a small round spoon.

In a microwavable bowl mix the caramel bits and water. Microwave at 30-second intervals, stirring after each interval, until caramel is melted (1–2 minutes). Pour small spoonfuls of caramel into the indented cookies. Let cool.

Melt chocolate and drizzle lines over cookies.

Dear Readers:

I'm delighted to bring you another Christmas novella in the Country Store Mysteries series. *Scarfed Down* takes place in Robbie Jordan's fourth year as proprietor of Pans 'N Pancakes, her country store restaurant in fictional South Lick, Indiana.

The story follows *No Grater Crime*, which ends with Robbie's May wedding to Abe O'Neill, and *Batter Off Dead*, in which Robbie investigates not only the murder of a senior citizen during summer fireworks but also a similar homicide from decades earlier. The next book to release will be *Four Leaf Cleaver*, a book set at Saint Patrick's Day and number eleven in the series. *Scarfed Down* slots right into the seasons.

Every book and novella includes recipes, because . . . of course! Robbie is always thinking about innovative ways to feed her hungry customers. I hope you enjoy Robbie and crew's angst at following through with their Twelve Days of Christmas theme. It mirrored my own when I started writing it. Then I found my mother's quilted Christmas wall hanging, which I gave to Adele, and that sparked ideas for specials, especially for Twelve Lords a-Leaping.

I'm always interested, as we crime writers are, in new ways of killing someone on the page. For my part of *Christmas Scarf Murder*, I knew I didn't want to strangle the victim with a scarf. When I learned about contact poisons, I realized paraquat dichloride was going to be perfect. The facts that the poison is dyed blue *and* used on soybean farms, which abound in the Midwest, were extra bonuses.

Thanks so much to brilliant author—and sheep farmer—Sarah Stewart Taylor for help with details about Adele's animals. My Wicked Authors blogmate Barbara Ross came up with the term VGR, because an amateur sleuth always needs that Very Good Reason to investigate a crime. Apologies to the Indianapolis Symphony for my fictional version of their pay scale.

I hope you'll find my talented author pals and me over at wickedauthors.com and mysteryloverskitchen.com, where we talk books, food, and mystery. I also write as Edith Maxwell, and you can read about all my books and short fiction under both names at edithmaxwell.com. Happy reading, and very happy and delicious holidays to you.

DEATH BY
CHRISTMAS SCARF

Peggy Ehrhart

Acknowledgments

Abundant thanks to my agent, Evan Marshall, and to my editor at Kensington Books, John Scognamiglio.

Chapter One

A lively conversation was already in progress when Pamela Paterson took a seat on Roland DeCamp's low-slung turquoise sofa and extracted her knitting from her knitting bag.

"Such a terrible shame!" Holly Perkins had just exclaimed. "And so close to the holidays!" Absent her usual cheer, Holly barely resembled herself, despite the bright green streak in her luxuriant dark hair and her festive candy-cane earrings.

"And so unlike Arborville!" Next to her, Karen Dowling shuddered. "Dave and I and our little Lily have always felt so safe here."

"Just a few steps from the shops on Arborville Avenue . . ." Bettina Fraser shook her head. "Who would imagine a killer could be so brazen? And to think I take a shortcut through that passageway all the time."

"Not so brazen. It was snowing hard and it was dark," Roland cut in. As was often the case, his intense expression and his tone implied that his was the voice of reason. "People were undoubtedly rushing up and down Arborville Avenue trying to get their errands done and get home. The killer probably didn't think the body would be discovered until the next morning. And he probably thought the snow would cover his footprints."

"He didn't count on Laurel Lewis working late." Bettina looked up from her knitting to focus on Roland across the room. He occupied a sleek chair that matched the sofa. "How shocking for the poor woman to stumble over a corpse on her way to her car!"

"At least she didn't have to deal with it all alone," Holly commented. "So that's something."

"Yes," Bettina said. "Here's poor Mort Quigley leaving the library after a long day and all of a sudden a desperate voice screams that there's a body in the passageway."

"Convenient that the police station is so near the library," Holly said. "Mort was able to summon an officer right away—though Carys Walnutt was obviously beyond help at that point."

Pamela had read the article about the murder in the *County Register* that morning. She hadn't really known Carys Walnutt, but in the photo accompanying the article she recognized a dour-looking woman she occasionally saw around town.

A curious sound like a cross between a moan and growl emanated from the most comfortable seat in the De-Camps' elegant living room: an armchair always reserved for the knitting group's most senior member, Nell Bascomb.

Nell regarded the assembled knitters with a baleful stare, focusing her faded eyes on each in turn. "This tragic event is not gossip fodder," she said firmly. "We all know what happened last night, thanks to Marcy Brewer's report in this morning's *Register*. Now I suggest we tend to our knitting and let the Arborville police tend to the issue of who strangled Carys Walnutt and why."

The sofa trembled as Bettina, who was sitting next to

Pamela, thrust her knitting aside and flung her head back in distress. Pamela turned to see her staring at the ceiling.

"I don't think I can keep working on this scarf," Bettina moaned, fingering her in-progress knitting project but speaking as if to the ceiling. "Every time I look at it now I picture it being wrapped around someone's neck and pulled tighter and tighter, just like what happened to Carys Walnutt. I wish I'd finished it in time and was starting some whole new thing tonight."

Pamela, in fact, *was* starting some whole new thing, as were the other four members of Knit and Nibble. For most of December the group had been focused on producing woolly scarves to donate for a silent auction to benefit the Arborville Public Library. Five scarves had been completed and donated, and the silent auction had taken place the previous Saturday in connection with the town's annual tree-lighting ceremony. But Bettina had fallen behind and her scarf was still in progress. "I'll give it to them next year," she had said. "No problem."

Holly, who was sitting next to Bettina on the other side, set down her own knitting—the bare beginnings of perhaps a sleeve—and seized Bettina's free hand. "You could tuck it away," she whispered, "and get it out again next December. There really was no reason for Marcy Brewer to be so specific about how the strangling was accomplished."

"No, there wasn't." Nell's voice reached them from across the room. "And I can see why Bettina is upset. But busy fingers soothe a troubled mind." She turned her gaze from Holly to Bettina. "Tuck that half-finished scarf back in your knitting bag and come over here and sit by me. The Haversack women's shelter can always use more teddy bears for the children."

Ever the gentleman, Roland leapt from his seat, startling the lustrous black cat he had been sharing it with. He hurried across the hall to the dining room and returned with a wooden chair that he positioned right next to Nell.

A few minutes later Bettina and Nell sat side by side, leaning toward each other until Bettina's scarlet tresses nearly mingled with Nell's halo of white hair. Nell had pulled an extra pair of needles from her knitting bag, as well as a ball of turquoise yarn. She had declared the yarn to be just enough for a teddy bear and was watching as Bettina followed her instructions to cast on fifteen stitches. Nell never worried about verisimilitude in the colors of the knitted animals she turned out in such profusion.

Pamela was happy to concentrate on her own work, murmuring "knit two, purl two" as she created the ribbing that would edge the bottom of her new project, a sweater.

Bettina's departure from the sofa had left a gap between Pamela and Holly, but Pamela could hear Holly and Karen exchanging quiet confidences relating to Karen's daughter Lily and the ongoing home-improvement projects that occupied both young women and their husbands. Holly and Karen were the youngest members of the Knit and Nibble group, as unalike in appearance and personality as any two young women could be, but drawn together by a shared interest in renovating the century-old wood-frame houses that were typical of Arborville's housing stock.

Roland, as always, was content to knit in silence, looking up only when the front door opened and Melanie DeCamp entered, leading the DeCamps' dachshund, Ramona.

"We had a lovely walk," Melanie announced as Roland's greeting was echoed by the other knitters. "People have been out all day shoveling, so the sidewalks are quite clear. Good thing too, because Ramona was longing for some fresh air and exercise."

Melanie was bundled up in a sheepskin coat, caramel suede with the pale furry inside turned back to form a wide collar, and Ramona was wearing a chic doggy sweater made for her by Roland. Melanie and Ramona continued down the hall, Ramona's toenails clicking on the wooden floor.

After several minutes, Melanie returned, minus Ramona and minus the coat. Her simple black leggings flattered her long, slim legs, and the creamy tones of her slouchy turtleneck suited her blond elegance.

"What wonderful projects are you all working on?" she inquired. She surveyed the room and headed first for the armchair where Nell sat. Crouching at Nell's side, she smiled as Nell displayed the oval of pale yellow yarn hanging from her needles and explained that it was to form the body of a teddy bear destined for the Haversack women's shelter.

"The children have little enough," Nell said. "But the knitted animals are theirs to keep when they leave with their mothers."

"So you keep pretty busy." Melanie's smile grew wider.

"Sadly, yes," Nell responded. "The shelter doesn't lack clients."

Melanie crept closer to Bettina. "And it looks like you're the student tonight," she observed.

"It's going to be a teddy bear too," Bettina said. She'd reached the end of a row and held up a needle with half an inch of knitting already completed. The three women chatted for a few minutes about the shelter and about the variety of knitted animals Nell had produced over the years.

On the other side of the room, Roland was beginning to stir. He pushed back his immaculately starched shirt cuff to consult his impressive watch, set his knitting atop the briefcase he used in place of a knitting bag, and gently disengaged himself from the cat stretched along his thigh.

Apparently sensing that her husband was on the move, Melanie rose. "Do you need help with anything, sweetie?" she inquired.

"Completely under control." He raised both hands in a gesture suggesting she should remain where she was. "I've got this," he added and headed for the kitchen, followed by the black cat.

"He so enjoys serving the refreshments when it's his turn to host the group," Melanie said as she perched on the edge of the chair Roland had vacated.

She directed her smile toward the sofa and its three occupants. "Such beautiful colors of yarn you've all chosen," she said. "Pale pink, magenta, and tawny brown. Someday I'll get ambitious and become a knitter myself, but in the meantime, tell me about your projects. Something for your dear little Lily, Karen?"

Karen held up a page torn from a knitting magazine. It showed a winsome blond toddler modeling a pale pink cardigan. "And I'm using the same pale pink for my own little blond sweetheart," she explained. After the appropriate murmurs of approval, Melanie shifted her gaze to Holly.

"I couldn't resist this amazing yarn," Holly said. A prolonged knitting session in the company of her fellow Knit and Nibblers had restored her to her cheerful, dimply self. She lifted her skein of yarn in one hand and her in-progress work in the other so that the strand of yarn connecting them could be seen more clearly.

"It's like a long, long strip of eyelashes," she exclaimed, "and it looks like shaggy fur when it's knit. I've just done a little bit so far, but you can see."

She extended her needles to display the fur-like texture—though not quite the color of any known fur-bearing animal—of the several rows she'd completed.

"And your pattern?" Melanie inquired.

"Oh—I'm just inventing it," Holly responded with a flash of her perfect teeth. "It's going to be like a short jacket, sort of flared, with no collar or buttons or anything, and the sleeves are going to be flared too."

Pamela reached for the knitting magazine at her side to show what the end result of her industry would be: a simple crew-neck pullover with the fun detail of a large black cat on the front. But Melanie's attention was suddenly diverted.

It was clear that refreshments were in the offing. The tantalizing aroma of coffee had begun to drift in from the direction of the DeCamps' kitchen. Also from the kitchen came the sound of cupboard doors opening and closing in rapid succession, accompanied by explosive mutters. After a brief lull, a single word replaced the mutters: *"Melanie!"*

Suppressing a laugh, Melanie rose and hurried to the kitchen. After a few moments she darted back out, ducked into the dining room, emerged with a large oval platter, and returned to the kitchen.

Coffee and tea were served first, Melanie standing by and Roland insisting that he could handle the task himself. The coffee made its appearance, five steaming cups on an elegant pewter tray, which also held two empty cup-and-saucer sets for the tea drinkers. Next came a second pewter tray bearing the tea in a pale porcelain teapot that matched the cups, a cream and sugar set, and spoons and small napkins.

Roland made sure the trays were arranged on the coffee table in such a way that a wide space remained between them, and then he returned to the kitchen.

"He's so pleased with himself," Melanie whispered, as Roland reappeared with the platter Melanie had fetched held proudly aloft. He lowered it to the coffee table and stood back, smiling a closed-mouthed smile.

Holly was the first to speak. "Roland!" she exclaimed, clapping her hands. "These are absolutely amazing!"

Arranged in careful rows on the platter were snowmen, each constructed from three round cookies in graduated sizes. Shredded coconut made them convincingly snowy and silver dragées provided their eyes.

"I agree!" Bettina rose from her chair and stepped forward for a closer look.

"Help yourselves," Roland urged, gesturing toward the platter of cookies. "And"—he whirled around—"Nell! Let me pour you some tea."

He tipped the teapot over one of the empty cups and the bright liquid swirled golden brown against the delicate porcelain. While Roland ministered to Nell, delivering tea, cream and sugar, and a spoon to the small table beside the armchair, Melanie slipped into the kitchen. She returned with a stack of porcelain dessert plates, which she set next to the cookie platter. Roland added two snowmen on a plate to the small table at Nell's elbow, though she protested that one would be plenty of sugar for one night, Christmas notwithstanding.

A pleasant bustle ensued, with people bobbing up and down as they provided themselves with drinkables, sugared and creamed them to their satisfaction, and settled back into their places with steaming cups and snowmen ready to hand.

Roland's snowmen were sugar cookies with a sweet buttercream icing beneath the coconut, and they complemented the coffee—Pamela preferred hers black—to perfection.

Roland was happy to accept the compliments praising the tender butteriness of the underlying cookie, the convincing effect of the coconut, and the cleverness of the production process he described. He'd rolled balls of dough in three sizes and then arranged them on his cookie sheet in sets of small, medium, and large, near each other but not touching. The balls had flattened and spread as they baked, fusing together to form snowmen.

Melanie had been out walking Ramona when the topic of the body in the passageway was raised, and so she had missed Nell's admonition that gossiping about the tragic event was unseemly, as well as Bettina's anguished renunciation of her still-in-progress silent-auction scarf. And so when Melanie remarked that it was a shame the holiday cheer surrounding the silent auction and the tree-lighting ceremony had dissipated so quickly and sadly with that morning's news, she was startled by the shocked faces that confronted her.

"Did I say something wrong?" she exclaimed, raising a pretty hand to her mouth.

"It's just—" Pamela hesitated, unsure how to complete the thought.

But Nell cut in. "There's no question that a murder, on Arborville Avenue at that, is out of keeping with the spirit of the season. But rehashing the details does no one, except the police, any good."

"Oh, I didn't mean—" Melanie's chagrin was genuine. Roland's lovely wife seemed to have been born with a gift for comporting herself well in social situations. This had been a rare faux pas.

"Has anyone heard how much the silent auction made?" Holly, in her own ebullient way, was also socially adept, and she was skilled at rescuing conversations steered into stormy waters by the more opinionated Knit and Nibblers.

"I'm sure the library will send out a press release." Bettina, in the act of reaching for a second snowman cookie, looked up. "And people can read all about the auction results when the *Advocate* comes out on Friday."

The *Advocate* was Arborville's weekly newspaper. It was described by both admirers and detractors as containing "all the news that fits," and Bettina was its chief reporter.

"It's a shame that libraries have to depend on charity to supplement their funding," Nell remarked, "though I was certainly happy to donate my knitting efforts to the cause."

"I'd rather charity funded libraries than have my taxes raised to pay for services I never get a chance to weigh in on." Roland spoke from the wooden chair he had now pulled close to the coffee table, having yielded the sleek turquoise chair to Melanie.

"Roland!" Nell's expression was fearsome. "You certainly use and appreciate services other people's taxes support, people who might be just as happy if their money went for something else. Roads, for example?"

"Who doesn't like roads?" Roland seemed genuinely puzzled.

"We don't all drive the same number of miles on the roads. Why should the same proportion of our taxes go toward the roads?"

"Toll roads!" Roland looked as pleased with himself as when he'd accepted compliments on his snowman cookies. "That's the fair way to do it!"

"Should Arborville Avenue be a toll road then?" Bettina had been following the discussion and now she jumped in. She gestured with a hand that held half a snowman cookie, causing the snowman to shed a bit of coconut.

Roland hesitated. "Well . . . that—"

"Would be ridiculous." Bettina finished the sentence for him.

"In the case of local streets, yes, perhaps," Roland conceded. "But when it comes to the library, if people choose not to work hard for themselves and therefore have to freeload off the taxpayers for their entertainment, it's not my job to look after them."

"We are not all as smart and hard-working as you, Roland." Holly's flirtatious smile neutralized any implication of sarcasm.

"I choose to work hard."

"Are you sure it's a choice?" Nell inquired, her gaze penetrating. "Maybe it's genetic. Like the grasshopper and the ant. And you're the ant."

"I don't really think . . ." Roland shifted in his chair and tipped his head forward to survey his torso, his legs, and then his feet, as if genuinely concerned that some metamorphosis was underway. Seemingly satisfied that his luxurious cashmere pullover, nicely creased wool slacks, and gleaming loafers still clothed a human body, he reached for his coffee.

"Charity certainly has its place," Nell conceded. "With the budget shortfall this year, I'm sure the library will be grateful for the extra money. And I think I will have just one more of those tasty snowmen."

Soon the knitters returned to their knitting, and general conversation was replaced by quiet murmurs as Nell tutored Bettina in the finer points of teddy bear creation and Holly and Karen compared notes on the joys and sorrows of their old houses. Half an hour passed in this manner, at which point Roland checked his watch, transferred his briefcase from the floor to his lap, and carefully stowed his yarn and his knitting.

Taking the hint, the other knitters speedily finished in-progress rows and gathered their own projects into their knitting bags, Nell assuring Bettina that she would do fine continuing the teddy bear body on her own and that they could tackle the head the following week.

"How did you get here?" Bettina asked Pamela as they headed down the DeCamps' front walk. The walk was bordered by tall ridges of shoveled snow, and beyond the ridges smooth snow glistened in the light from the street-lamp. "I don't see your car," Bettina went on, "and I know how much you like to walk. But who knows when the passageway stalker might strike again?"

"The passageway stalker?" Pamela laughed and a puff of steam escaped into the chilly air. "Is that what they're calling him?"

"No." Bettina halted and turned to Pamela. "But that's what I think he was. Unless the killer was stalking Carys, how would he have known she'd be conveniently hidden from sight in the passageway right then, and he'd be able to strike?"

"That's a good point," Pamela agreed. "I hope the police have some leads."

They had reached the street. "How *did* you get here?" Bettina repeated the question. "I'm sorry we couldn't ride together like we usually do, but I was with the grand-children all afternoon and up through dinnertime."

"Penny brought me," Pamela said. "She's at her friend Lorie's, and I didn't want her to be walking around in the dark, so she's got my car."

"Hard to believe she's a senior in college already." Bettina steered Pamela toward where her faithful Toyota waited at the curb.

"Yes." Pamela nodded. "Yes, it is. She'll be off on her own soon, but I hope she'll always come home for Christmas."

*   *   *

Ten minutes later, Bettina was turning onto Orchard Street where she and her husband, Wilfred, lived directly across the street from Pamela.

"Do you mind walking from my driveway?" Bettina asked. "Or shall I pull into yours?"

"I'll be okay crossing the street," Pamela said. "I really will."

She'd be entering a house empty but for three cats. Pamela had raised her daughter alone after her husband was killed in a tragic accident on the site of an architecture project he was managing. The house, a hundred years old, with clapboard siding and a wide front porch, was a fixer-upper project that they had fixed up and cherished, and Pamela still felt her beloved husband's presence when she was within its walls. Now it welcomed her with lights glowing softly in the front windows.

"I'll be over in the morning," Bettina remarked as Pamela set out across the street. "After I meet with Detective Clayborn."

Chapter Two

The visitor was unmistakably Bettina. Through the lace that curtained the oval window in her front door, Pamela recognized her friend's pumpkin-colored coat, vivid against the black and white scheme of the wintry landscape. But when Pamela opened the door, the Bettina who stepped over the threshold was a far cry from her usual cheerful self.

She flung her arms wide with fingers extended, as if to emphasize the emptiness of her hands. Startled by the gesture, a lustrous black cat who was napping in a spot of sun looked up.

"After I talked to Clayborn, I was too upset to even stop at the Co-Op," she wailed as she slipped out of her coat. "So I don't know what we'll eat with our coffee." She had dressed for her meeting with Arborville's chief (and only) detective with her usual stylish flair, but now the bright yellow sheath that hugged her ample curves seemed ill-suited to the role of tragic heroine that her creased forehead and downturned mouth implied.

"What on earth has happened?" Pamela slipped an arm around Bettina's shoulders and drew her toward the kitchen, where Bettina slumped into one of the two chairs that flanked the small wooden table.

Pamela took the other chair and watched as Bettina swallowed and blinked a few times before starting to speak. "The murder scarf was hand knit," she said, her voice trembling. "And he knows I'm in the knitting club and all, so he took me into the room where they store evidence and asked me if I had any ideas about who might have made it."

"It could have come from anywhere," Pamela said. "Maybe Carys is a knitter herself and was wearing a scarf she had knit and the killer simply used the weapon that came to hand."

"No." Bettina's grief had bowed her head, and the whispered syllable emanated from behind a tousled mass of scarlet curls.

"Or someone made the scarf for her, or she bought it at a craft shop, or it was a scarf the killer's mother—whatever—made for *him* and he set out with it, planning all the time to strangle his victim, or—"

Bettina reached out and grabbed Pamela's hands, which were resting on the table.

"It was the scarf Holly made for the auction," she moaned. "That pretty aqua scarf with the pattern of white snowflakes worked in. And I had to tell him." Bettina looked up. "Poor Holly will be so sad—to think her beautiful scarf was a murder weapon."

"Oh, dear." Pamela sighed and squeezed Bettina's hands. "So at least Detective Clayborn doesn't think that Holly is a suspect."

"No, of course not." Bettina looked marginally more cheerful. "Someone had the winning bid for the scarf at the auction and that person ended up with the scarf."

"So," Pamela said, "the next question is, who was that person? Carys? Or the killer?"

Bettina nodded. "That *is* the next question for Clayborn. The next question for *me* is"—she gazed toward the counter, focusing on the carafe in which Pamela made her coffee—"do you have a bit of coffee left?"

Pamela rose. "Better than that. I'll make a fresh batch. Penny hasn't been down yet and she'll want coffee too."

As Pamela set the kettle to boil and measured beans into her coffee grinder, Bettina transferred the cut-glass sugar bowl from the counter to the table and poured a dollop of heavy cream into the matching cut-glass cream pitcher.

"I suppose you've already had your toast . . ." Bettina commented as she moved about the little kitchen, letting the statement trail off in a suggestive way.

Pamela pressed on the lid of the coffee grinder, and the beans whirled and clattered. She waited to respond until, with a whining growl, the grinder finished its work.

"You can certainly have toast," she said with a fond smile. "And I think I still have some of that Tupelo honey you and Wilfred gave me."

"That was ages ago!"

"I only get it out when you're here," Pamela explained.

"And that's why you're thin and I'm not."

Pamela *was* thin, and tall, and her simple wardrobe of jeans and casual tops mystified her fashionable friend, who could never understand why Pamela eschewed the fashion-forward looks her lanky frame might have displayed to such advantage.

The kettle's whistle interrupted the conversation then, but Bettina knew her way around Pamela's kitchen nearly as well as Pamela did. She fetched the honey from the cupboard where it shared a shelf with various vinegars, cooking oils, and jars of herbs and spices. And then, while the boiling water from the kettle dripped through the freshly ground beans in the carafe's filter cone, she slipped two slices of whole-grain bread into Pamela's toaster.

A few minutes later, the two friends took their places across from each other at the little wooden table. The simple meal was elevated by the rose-garlanded china on which it was served. Pamela saw no point in having nice things that came out only on special occasions, so she used her wedding china every day—and anyway, most of her other "nice things" were treasures unearthed at thrift stores and tag sales.

In a ritual with which Pamela had become very familiar over the years, Bettina first spooned sugar into her coffee and then added dribbles of cream until the contents of the cup reached the perfect shade of pale mocha that she preferred. After a sip that evoked a smile and a contented purr, Bettina set about spreading honey on the toast she had buttered when it emerged from the toaster. That task completed, she lifted half a slice to her mouth.

It was at that moment that Penny Paterson appeared in the kitchen doorway. She was wearing pajamas and a robe and carrying Bettina's stylish maroon-leather handbag.

"It's making a noise," she said. "I heard it from the bottom of the stairs. I think it's your phone."

Bettina returned the slice of toast with honey oozing off the edges to her plate, accepted the handbag, and with sticky fingers plucked her phone from its depths.

"Clayborn," she murmured after glancing at its screen. "What could he want now?" Her words trailed after her as she stepped toward the entry to take the call.

Pamela's daughter hadn't inherited her mother's height, and it was hard for Pamela to accept the fact that this small pajama-clad person with face still softened by sleep would soon be out of college and ready to take on the world. At the counter Penny filled a wedding-china cup with coffee and slipped a slice of whole-grain bread into the toaster.

"I see there's cream," she said, glancing at the table, "and honey. And I'd better grab a chair from the dining room."

But at that moment, Bettina returned. "You can have my chair," she said. "And my toast. And even my coffee, if you don't mind that I already took a sip." She stepped across the floor and gave Penny a quick hug. "We'll have to catch up later, Miss Penny. Clayborn wants me over at the police station ASAP."

Pamela had remained seated, but once Bettina identified the caller as Detective Clayborn, interest in her toast and coffee had been superseded by curiosity about the nature of the call. Now she spoke.

"Did he say what—"

"No." Bettina tightened her lips. A furrow appeared between her carefully shaped brows. "But he sounded . . . excited. And . . . oh, dear . . ." She sighed a trembling sigh. "It's about the scarf, I'm sure."

Her hands were shaking as she lifted her handbag from the table.

"I'll come with you," Pamela announced, hopping up from her chair. "We can go in my car. I'll drive."

An hour had passed, and Pamela and Bettina were standing just outside the door of the Arborville police station. The day was bright, all the brighter for the sunlight reflecting off the brittle ice that crusted the snow in the field beyond the parking lot's asphalt expanse.

Bettina looked around. Apparently satisfied that no one was listening (in fact they were the only people in the parking lot), she said, "It was all off the record, but I know you won't tell anyone."

"Of course not." Pamela was very much in Nell's camp when it came to eschewing town gossip.

"He wanted to know if I knew who 'S. Claws' was."

"Santa Claus?" Pamela laughed. "Why, everyone knows who Santa Claus is."

"Not *that* S. Claus!" Bettina grabbed Pamela's arm. "C-L-A-W-S, like *claws*." She relinquished Pamela's arm and shaped the fingers of her gloved hand as if to mime a paw with claws extended.

"*Do* you know?"

"I'm afraid so." Bettina nodded mournfully. "And I had to tell him. S. Claws is Laurel Lewis."

"I'm impressed," Pamela said. "But how did you know that? And how did Detective Clayborn know that you would know? And why on earth did he want to know?"

"Which question do you want me to answer first?"

"Why he wanted to know. I suppose it has something to do with . . . the murder."

Bettina nodded. "You're right. But let's get in your car. I'm freezing." Despite her pumpkin-colored down coat, the olive-green beret that hid all but a scarlet fringe of bangs, and matching fur-trimmed booties, Bettina's teeth were chattering and her cheeks were pale.

Once they were settled in Pamela's car—no warmer than outside but at least sheltered from the wind, Bettina explained. After the early morning conversation in which she had identified the murder scarf as the one that Knit and Nibble member Holly Perkins had made for the silent auction, Detective Clayborn had asked an auction volunteer at the library to retrieve the auction bid sheets. The bid sheet for the aqua scarf with snowflakes indicated that the winning bid had been made by one "S. Claws."

"Obviously not a real person's name," Bettina concluded.

"Obviously, and I can certainly see why he'd want to

know who S. Claws is in real life. But why did he think you'd know—though you obviously did?"

The car windows had begun to steam up as the moisture exhaled by the breathing and talking occupants condensed on the chilly glass.

"He did an internet search," Bettina said. "And an article I wrote last year for the *Advocate* came up. It was about a fundraising drive for the Haversack animal shelter and I mentioned that a cat-loving donor identifying herself as 'S. Claws' had given a thousand dollars." Bettina shrugged. "I knew S. Claws was Laurel Lewis's charitable alter ego because the shelter people knew, but I couldn't put her name in the article because she wanted to remain anonymous."

Bettina turned away and focused on the fogged-up window for a moment, though nothing was visible on the other side. "But I had to tell Clayborn because now it has to do with a murder."

"Laurel Lewis found the body." Pamela stared at the window too.

"*Claimed to*." Bettina corrected her. "Now it appears she could be the murderer."

Pamela arrived back home to find a note from Penny in the entry saying she and her friend Lorie had gone to the mall. She stepped into the living room and inspected the Christmas tree, looking for signs of cat damage, but all was well. She and Penny had brought the tree home the previous Friday and spent the afternoon decorating it with their favorite ornaments chosen from among the vast collection Pamela had assembled from tag sales and thrift stores. Now a rainbow of glittery balls interspersed with antique Santas, angels, fanciful animals, candy canes, and snowflakes dangled from the tree's fragrant boughs, and its perfume filled the entire house.

Near the arch between the living room and the dining room, Precious, the elegant Siamese cat who was Pamela's most recent feline adoptee, lounged on the top platform of the cat climber.

The morning's adventure and the revelations accompanying it had distracted Pamela from the fact that lunchtime was approaching. But now, back in her own house, she was aware that her body had exhausted the nutritive possibilities of that morning's toast and coffee and was demanding more.

In the kitchen, she peered into the refrigerator. The previous night's dinner had been meatloaf sandwiches, eaten in haste before she and Penny hurried out, she to Knit and Nibble and Penny to Lorie's. There was enough meatloaf left for another sandwich, and soon Pamela was feeling nourished and ready to go to work.

To reach her office, Pamela had only to climb the stairs. As associate editor of *Fiber Craft* magazine, she was responsible for evaluating submissions, copyediting articles chosen for publication, and—occasionally—reviewing books on topics relevant to the magazine's focus. Before Penny went off to college, Pamela had been particularly glad that all of those things could be done from home and that her job required only the occasional trip into the magazine's headquarters in Manhattan.

That morning, before she descended the stairs for breakfast, Pamela had checked her email and found a message from her boss with three articles attached. Strung across the top of the message were the abbreviated titles, each identified as a digital file by the Word logo next to it. The abbreviations were "Sericulture," "Prayer Rugs," and

"Spy-Craft." She was to evaluate them and respond with recommendations for or against publication by the following Friday evening.

Sericulture, she knew, had to do with silk, and she opened that file first. The article's full title was "Sericulture in the Cévennes: When Silkworms Had Royal Patrons." The article told the fascinating story of how a remote region in Southern France became the hub of the French silk industry. Fed up with the expense of imported silk, Henry VI offered financial incentives and perks of all sorts to the communes whose livelihood depended on cultivating silkworms and harvesting the thread they produced.

A few photos taken by the author documented what was left of the monumental stone structures that had housed extended families and their silkworms until disease and religious strife led to the industry's decline.

Pamela wrote an enthusiastic recommendation that the article be published, and looked up from her computer screen to realize that the room in which she sat had become totally dark but for the glow of the screen and a desk lamp angled toward her keyboard. When she opened her office door, the sound of Penny's voice reached her. The one-sided nature of the conversation suggested that Penny's words were directed at one or more of the cats. Pamela saved her document, closed her file and Word, and descended the stairs to greet her daughter.

Chapter Three

At the moment, Pamela had only one feline sleeping companion, Catrina, adopted as a woebegone stray, but now plump and contented. Catrina's daughter Ginger, named for her coloration, had taken to Penny right away and preferred Penny's bed when Penny was in residence.

On Thursday morning Pamela opened her eyes to find the sun bright behind her bedroom's white eyelet curtains. A pair of amber eyes in a furry heart-shaped face returned her gaze.

"Breakfast?" she inquired as she sat up against her bed's brass headboard. Dislodged from her chest, the cat leapt to the floor.

Having added slippers and a robe to her ensemble, Pamela headed for the stairs with Catrina leading the way. At the bottom of the stairs they were joined by Precious, who preferred to spend the night in the living room. Once they reached the kitchen, Pamela took a can of crab and liver medley from the cupboard, opened it, and scooped generous portions into two bowls. She set water to boil on the stove and headed outside to fetch the *Register*.

She had slept well, slumbers undisturbed by concern about the murder case. A few hours spent reading about silkworm culture in Southern France, followed by a pleasant evening with Penny, had dimmed her recollection of Bettina's visit and the trip to the police station. But back inside, slipping the newspaper from its flimsy plastic sleeve, she recalled with a jolt that the previous day's developments had certainly brought the issue of Carys Walnutt's murder closer to home.

The boldface headline, revealed once the paper was unfolded, amplified that jolt. And the kettle's jarring hoot seemed an appropriate soundtrack. ARREST MADE IN ARBORVILLE PASSAGEWAY MURDER, the headline screamed. Smaller print below added, "Laurel Lewis, who said she 'found' the body, taken into custody." The byline credited Marcy Brewer with the article.

Pamela shuddered. Marcy Brewer was known for her aggressive reporting, and she didn't shy away from ferreting out the most sensational aspects of the stories assigned to her. Pamela refolded the paper and set it aside. Coffee and toast would be necessary fortifications before reading any further.

Five minutes later, enveloped by the comforting aromas of fresh-brewed coffee and toasted whole-grain bread, and with the coffee and toast at hand, Pamela once again unfolded the *Register*.

Who would think that a pretty aqua mohair scarf with a white snowflake design could be a cruel instrument of death? she read. *Yet that was the murder weapon chosen by the killer responsible for the death of Arborville resident Carys Walnutt last Monday night between 8:00 and 9:00 p.m. As this paper reported previously, Walnutt's body was found in the narrow passageway that connects Arborville's small shopping district along Arborville Avenue with the parking lot that serves the library, the police station, and a park.*

The article was illustrated with a photo of the Arborville Avenue entrance to the passageway. Businesses that bordered the passageway were also visible: Hyler's Luncheonette on the right and one of Arborville's three hair salons on the left. Several strips of yellow crime-scene tape were stretched across the passageway's mouth.

The article went on to say that Carys Walnutt lived in a garden apartment farther north on Arborville Avenue and across from St. Willibrod's Church. Neighbors were reluctant to talk about her (curious, Pamela thought to herself, given that Marcy Brewer could be very persistent). *"She was an unusual person,"* a neighbor who didn't want to be named was quoted as saying. *"That's as far as I'll go. It's the season of good cheer after all."*

The Lifestyle section of the *Register* offered a welcome diversion, and Pamela was enjoying her second cup of coffee as she read an article about decorating one's garden with suet and birdseed "ornaments" to give the birds a Christmas treat. As she was studying a particularly charming "ornament" that featured fresh cranberries, the doorbell's chime summoned her to the entry.

Bettina swept in on a draft of chilly air.

"I suppose you saw the *Register*," she said as she began to unbutton her coat. Without waiting for a response, she went on. "So they've arrested Laurel Lewis, poor thing. And Marcy Brewer is an absolute menace. Holly called me first thing this morning. Not only did Marcy describe Holly's scarf—so everyone who knows which scarf Holly donated now knows that Holly's scarf was the murder weapon—but now she wants to *interview* Holly."

Pamela reached for the coat, but Bettina didn't remove it. "I can't stay," she said. "I'm on my way to meet with Clayborn. It's late to get something in tomorrow's *Advocate*, but I'll see what I can do. This coat is just very warm." She fanned her face with a gloved hand. "Holly called me to ask if you have to say yes if a reporter requests an interview. I told her of course not. Marcy Brewer isn't the police."

"I hope she doesn't track Holly down at the salon," Pamela said. Holly and her husband, Desmond, owned a hair salon in the neighboring town of Meadowside.

"I do too. I'm just so angry, I had to unburden myself to someone—and Wilfred has driven out to Newfield to buy a honey-roasted ham for Christmas Day." Bettina tightened her lips, glossy with lipstick in a fetching shade of pumpkin-orange that matched her coat, and shook her head until her scarlet bangs vibrated. "And that photo! Crime-scene tape on Arborville Avenue four days before Christmas! It's bad enough that people have to see it in person, but to put it on the front page of the *Register*—" She stopped, and then completed the sentence with a disgusted snort.

"There's a little coffee left," Pamela suggested, striving for a comforting gesture.

"I can't stay, really." Bettina fumbled with the top button of her coat. "But I'll drop back in after I finish with Clayborn. Or—let's have lunch together in Timberley. My treat. I have some last-minute shopping to do, and the shops there are so interesting, and I just can't face the idea of eating at Hyler's with that crime-scene tape right next door. And we can talk about the menu for my Christmas Eve party."

She continued with her buttoning task, commenting half to herself, "I'll know more too, after I've talked to Clayborn, like is there other evidence pointing to Laurel Lewis besides the fact that she won the scarf at the auction?"

A nimble ginger-colored cat darted between Pamela and Bettina and headed for the kitchen doorway. Bettina watched it vanish then shifted her gaze to the stairway. Pamela turned to look in the same direction and saw Penny standing on the bottom step.

"Good morning, Miss Penny!" Bettina brightened.

Penny, however, didn't respond in kind. Silently, her glance traveled from Pamela to Bettina and then back to Pamela. "I know what you two are up to," she said at last. "And you know how much I worry when you think you can do better than the police at solving murders."

Arborville, New Jersey, was a small, safe town, the sort of place where police spend more time responding to complaints that someone has put their tree trimmings out too far in advance of the pickup day than solving murders. Yet over the years there had been murders, not committed by strangers intent on mayhem, but rather by friends or even family members. And curiously—despite the acknowledged expertise of Arborville's sole police detective, Lucas Clayborn, Pamela and Bettina had frequently been responsible for the crucial insight that allowed the police to finger the evildoer.

With a hug, Bettina assured Penny that she had no intention of trying to usurp Detective Clayborn's investigative role and that her sole interest in the case derived from her responsibility to readers of the *Advocate*. She was on her way then, ushered out on another draft of chilly air.

Left alone in the entry, Pamela and Penny regarded each other, Penny's expression still tinged with suspicion.

"That's really the only reason we were talking about it," Pamela said. "Bettina takes her job very seriously."

Without commenting, Penny headed for the kitchen and

Pamela followed. They found Ginger waiting patiently in the corner where the cats had become accustomed to taking their meals, and Penny handled the feeding chore while Pamela set water boiling for her daughter's coffee.

Some minutes later, Penny sat at the kitchen table sipping coffee sweetened with sugar and much diluted with heavy cream, and nibbling whole-grain toast liberally spread with honey. Pamela busied herself at the counter measuring out poppy seeds for the special poppy-seed cakes she made every year at Christmas.

She poured the seeds—dark, fragrant, and so tiny that static caused some to cling to the interior of the measuring cup—into a small pot, added a cup of milk, and set the pot over a low flame. As soon as delicate bubbles began to form around the edges of the liquid, she turned the flame off and covered the pot. The seeds and milk would sit for an hour before they were ready to use. Meanwhile, though, sticks of butter could be cut into chunks and allowed to soften, flour and sugar could be measured, eggs could be separated and the whites beaten, and loaf pans could be buttered and floured.

Penny seemed content to read the *Register* without comment. Pamela was happy to work in silence, and the next half hour or so passed pleasantly enough. Penny finished her breakfast and went back upstairs, saying something about texting Lorie. Pamela launched the creaming and blending and beating and mixing that would turn her assembled ingredients into batter. When the batter had been created, she divided it between two buttered and floured loaf pans.

Once the poppy-seed cakes were in the oven, she repaired to her office, where she opened the Word file labeled "Prayer Rugs" and immersed herself in "Totemic Animal Motifs in Traditional Prayer-Rug Design."

"Heavenly!" Bettina exclaimed, closing her eyes and inhaling deeply.

"I just took them out of the oven and I'm ready to go," Pamela said, "so your timing is perfect." She stepped to the closet to fetch her coat. It was a down coat too, though not as colorful as Bettina's, and it had been a Christmas gift from Penny a few years earlier.

"Christmas Eve isn't going to be a potluck," Bettina explained as they headed out the door, "but I hope you'll bring one of your poppy-seed cakes."

"Of course!" Pamela pulled the door closed behind her and inserted her key in the lock. "And anything else you'd like me to make as well. I'm going to the Co-Op later."

"Just the poppy-seed cake is plenty," Bettina said. "There will be other desserts too. Wilfred is buzzing with ideas about what else to serve—though with so many people coming, it's not going to be a sit-down meal, so things have to be easy to manage."

Chatting about the party plans, they made their way across the street to where Bettina's faithful Toyota shared a wide driveway with Wilfred's ancient but lovingly cared-for Mercedes. They were soon cruising north on County Road, on their way to the charming restaurants and shops of Timberley, which was larger and more affluent than Arborville—though the residents of Arborville considered their town quite as nice a town as anyone could want.

It wasn't until later that the conversation between the two friends took a darker turn. Pamela and Bettina were seated at a small table in one of the two French restaurants along Timberley's main shopping street. The plates that had held wedges of quiche Lorraine and salads of baby lettuce dressed with oil and vinegar had been cleared, and orders had been placed for chocolate mousse and coffee.

Above the wisp of country lace that curtained its lower panes, the window offered a view of bundled-up people scurrying here and there, as well as storefronts sporting swags of Christmas greenery made festive with red ribbons and twinkling lights.

"Were you able to get something to the *Advocate* in time for tomorrow's issue?" Pamela asked.

Bettina closed her eyes and shook her head slowly from side to side.

"They couldn't hold the presses for such an important story?" Pamela leaned forward.

"There wasn't anything important," Bettina said sadly. "Nothing new at all—not beyond what the *Register* already reported, at least that Clayborn was willing to reveal." Her lips tightened into a disgusted knot.

"But what about other evidence, evidence significant enough to make them arrest Laurel? Besides just the fact that she won the scarf?"

Bettina continued to shake her head.

"They interviewed people who know Laurel, lots of people. Apparently they think they've uncovered a motive, but he wouldn't tell me what it is. He did say, though, that she had opportunity."

"She *was* in the area," Pamela agreed. "That's how she came to find the body."

Bettina looked up to greet the server, who was approaching with a tray bearing two cups of coffee and two servings of chocolate mousse in parfait glasses.

When the coffee and mousse had been delivered and the

server had departed, Bettina spoke. "Laurel's accounting office is above one of the shops near the passageway, and her window faces the parking lot. If Carys was coming from the parking lot and heading toward Arborville Avenue, Laurel could have seen her approaching the passageway from the parking lot end and hurried down to enter from the Arborville Avenue end. That's what Clayborn thinks anyway."

The mousse was a tempting sight, deep chocolate-brown and garnished with a puff of whipped cream. As if the motion had been purposely synchronized, Pamela picked up her spoon just as Bettina did, and each conveyed a sample to her mouth. The flavor—rich and sweet—and texture—creamy and cool—didn't disappoint, and the blissful expression on Bettina's face indicated that her reaction was positive.

Bettina took another bite and closed her eyes as she savored the dessert. At one point the tip of her tongue peeked between her lips in a motion that seemed almost catlike. But when she opened her eyes, it was clear that her brain had been occupied with more than the felicitous combination of sugar, cream, and cacao beans.

"I just can't believe someone like Laurel would do a thing like that," she declared. "With her charitable giving and her devotion to cats."

Pamela set down her cup and shrugged. She had been alternating sips of coffee and spoonfuls of mousse, enjoying the way the black coffee echoed on a more intense level the faint bitterness still lurking in the much-sweetened chocolate.

"Marcy Brewer couldn't get anyone to say anything specifically bad about Carys," she pointed out, "but she couldn't get anyone to say anything specifically good either. So maybe there are other people, maybe lots of people, who wanted Carys dead."

Pamela took another sip of coffee, caffeine seeming more appropriate than mousse to the investigative turn the conversation had taken. "There's the scarf though," she said. "Laurel won the scarf at the auction."

As if to signal that she had no wish to prolong the discussion, Bettina remained silent and tackled her mousse with renewed enthusiasm.

The lunch had been prelude to a shopping expedition, and after they had finished eating and settled their bill, Pamela and Bettina set out past storefronts whose tasteful window displays offered everything from poinsettias and amaryllis (florist), candy-bedecked gingerbread cottages (bakery), hampers overflowing with gourmet treats (cheese shop), and much, much more.

Bettina's first destination was a shop that featured crafts made by local artisans. There she picked out a string of handmade glass beads for her Arborville daughter-in-law and, after much indecision, a simple silver necklace for her Boston daughter-in-law.

"Greta has such plain taste in clothes," Bettina complained. "Even worse than you, and then there's my sweet little Morgan . . ." She sighed. "Warren and Greta are wonderful parents, I'm sure, but wouldn't a little girl want to wear pink every once in a while?"

Pamela steeled herself for the lament that she knew was coming. Bettina's son Warren and his wife Greta were both professors, and when their daughter Morgan was born they declared they were raising an ungendered child. Bettina had been forbidden to lavish on her only female grandchild the girly clothes and toys she had been looking forward to purchasing.

Bettina continued to browse as she rehearsed the themes Pamela had come to know so well, starting with her disappointment a few years earlier that the pink granny-square baby blanket she had labored over would not be a welcome gift. Pamela followed in her wake, pausing to examine a display of earrings that resembled delicate golden leaves and then noticing a card explaining that they had been cast from molds made from actual leaves. She already had several gifts for Penny—she collected gifts for family and friends all year and stored them on a special closet shelf. But the leaf earrings were so lovely that she picked up a pair.

When she caught up with Bettina, her friend was gazing longingly at a row of handmade dolls. Their bodies were cloth, like old-fashioned dolls, their hair was yarn, and their faces were embroidered. But no two were alike. One wore a puffed-sleeve dress in a flowery print, another wore leggings and an oversize sweater, a third was bundled up in a plaid wool coat with a knitted hat pulled down to her eyebrows.

"Aren't these just too too cute!" Bettina sighed, fingering the skirt of the puffed-sleeve dress. She turned away. "I can't though! They wouldn't let her keep it and they'd be mad at me besides." She mustered a smile. "Are you ready?"

Pamela held up the earrings. "For Penny," she said, and Bettina gave an approving nod.

When they reached the counter, which was staffed by an artistic-looking woman with a long dark braid and a striking patchwork jacket featuring silky fabrics in random colors and shapes, Bettina motioned for Pamela to go first.

Pamela set the earrings down and took out her credit card, aware that Bettina had left her side and darted away.

By the time her transaction was complete, Bettina had returned, carrying the doll in the puffed-sleeve dress.

"It's for Lily, Karen's daughter," she explained before Pamela could say anything. "And look"—she rotated the doll so its back was facing Pamela—"the dress comes off. See all the little buttons! So she can have other clothes, clothes that I can knit." Bettina was fairly vibrating with happiness. "Ohh! Lily and I are going to have so much fun!"

Chapter Four

Pamela wanted to be dropped off at the Co-Op Grocery, so instead of returning to Arborville via County Road, Bettina cut over to Arborville Avenue after they crossed the Arborville-Timberley border. They headed into Arborville's shopping district from the north, cruising past houses set in snowy yards and decked with wreaths and greenery.

Soon St. Willibrod's Church came into sight, and across from it the garden apartments where Carys Walnutt had lived. They were two-story brick buildings—or actually one long building, with doors opening off small porches arranged at intervals along its façade. Concrete paths leading from the doors converged into a longer path that led to the sidewalk. Despite the chilly weather, one of the doors was open, perhaps related to the fact that a U-Haul truck was parked in the street.

Bettina slowed down and veered toward the curb in front of St. Willibrod's.

"Seems awfully soon," she murmured to herself.

"Soon for what?" Pamela leaned forward and peered around Bettina, looking for whatever had provoked Bettina's comment.

"The moving truck," Bettina said, as a pleasant-looking woman, quite buxom and with curly gray hair, emerged from the open door carrying a large cardboard box. With a click, Bettina opened her car door. "There might be a story here," she said, lowering a fur-trimmed bootie onto the asphalt.

Pamela followed her across the street, but Bettina could move fast when she wanted to. By the time Pamela caught up with her, she was already chatting with the woman who had emerged carrying the box, and the box had been added to the boxes already in the back of the U-Haul.

"Sure," the woman was saying. "No reason to wait, if you ask me. Her lease is up at the end of the year and the landlord will be just as happy to rent the apartment to someone else, the sooner the better. But he wants to re-paint first."

"Just as happy?" Bettina assumed a teasing expression—a half smile, a raised eyebrow, and a sideways glance beneath a delicately shadowed eyelid—that implied a bit of gossip wouldn't be amiss.

"I think we'll all be glad to have someone else in there." The woman nodded toward the apartment with the open door. "Basically Carys was just a sour person." She paused and pushed the box closer to the others. "Not that I want to speak ill of the dead."

"Of course not." Bettina offered a sympathetic wink. "When you say *sour* . . ."

"Ill-tempered, grumpy, complaining about everything, any little bit of noise—snowblowers, leaf blowers, contractors' radios, St. Willibrod's chimes, the kid who played the drums in the apartment next door, even Christmas carolers. if you can imagine. A real Ms. Scrooge."

"Hey, Fran!" came a voice. The woman, apparently responding to her name, swiveled around. Advancing toward them was another woman, middle-aged but younger than Fran, carrying a bulging plastic garbage bag in each hand.

"Marlyn!" Fran darted forward. "Let me help."

"Getting it done," the woman, now identified as Marlyn, said. "Little by little, but there's still all that furniture to deal with." Noticing Pamela and Bettina, she added, "I'm Marlyn Walnutt . . ." The slight lift at the end of the statement, as well as the raised brows, hinted that she hoped to elicit self-introductions in return.

Pamela and Bettina complied, then glanced at each other as the import of Marlyn's last name became clear.

"You must be—" Pamela began but was cut off by Bettina's "Oh, you poor dear! Carys Walnutt must have been—"

Marlyn nodded. "My sister."

"I'm so sorry for your loss!" Bettina's mobile features expressed genuine concern.

"Yes," Pamela murmured. "What a shock!" She might have made the connection even without the last name if she'd studied Marlyn a bit more closely. The woman standing before her had a sweet, eager-to-please manner, but physically she resembled her dour sister, though softer, rounder, and younger.

"It *was* a shock," Marlyn said in a matter-of-fact way. "And now I've got this whole apartment to clear out within the next few days, as if Christmas wasn't already busy enough." Noticing that Fran was still standing there, she added, "I'm forgetting my manners. This is Fran Calvert, my neighbor. She's been helping me."

Bettina peered into the back of the U-Haul truck. "You've both been busy," she said.

"Most of this is being donated." Marlyn gestured toward the truck. "Kitchen stuff, knick-knacks, linens, clothes . . . nothing very special. But some of her furniture was nice, and it's up for grabs. My kids don't want it and Carys didn't have kids." She turned and advanced a few steps on the path that connected the apartments to the sidewalk. "Come on in!" she said over her shoulder.

Bettina glanced at Pamela and shrugged and they fell in line behind Marlyn. Fran brought up the rear.

The apartment was large and airy, with cream-colored walls and a wide window looking out on the street. A rolled-up carpet and several cardboard boxes occupied the middle of the floor, which was pale hardwood. Another box with its flaps folded back and lumpy objects wrapped in crumpled newspaper visible sat on a glass-topped coffee table. Curtains were draped over the back of the sofa, which was cream-colored like the walls.

"Take off your coats, look around, and help yourselves," Marlyn offered with a wave of the hand. "There's a small table and some chairs in the kitchen and a bureau and some other things in the bedroom. Also a bookshelf."

Fran busied herself sealing up the box on the coffee table.

Pamela had furnished much of her house with thrift store and estate-sale finds, and she still loved to discover pre-owned treasures—all the better if they were free. But she had no more need for major pieces of furniture, and looking around, she surmised that the smaller things among which she might have found a curious bowl or vase or knick-knack had already been packed away.

Bettina had strayed into the bedroom. Now she emerged smiling like a surprised shopper who, while not in search of anything in particular, has stumbled upon a lucky find.

"That trunk," she said, addressing Marlyn. "Are you really giving it away?" Marlyn nodded. Bettina clapped her hands and went on. "My son and his wife would love it."

"Take it," Marlyn said.

"I will, but I think it's too big for my car." She beckoned for Pamela to join her in the bedroom doorway and gestured toward a painted wooden trunk about the size and shape of large hassock. The ornate latch, the peony motif in the decoration, and rich reds, greens, and golds gave it an Asian look.

"Definitely worth rescuing," Pamela agreed. "It could be used as a coffee table or . . . just as a trunk to store blankets in the summer . . ."

Bettina took a quick photo of the trunk with her phone, then darted back out into the living room. Pamela heard her arranging with Marlyn to return with a larger car and a husband or son within the next few days.

"No problem," Marlyn said. "I live here too—in this same complex, I mean. Number twelve. So I can let you in anytime."

"And I'm right next door in number eleven," Fran added. "So if she's not home I can let you in."

After a last, admiring look at the trunk, Pamela returned to the living room. At that same moment, a phone lying on the coffee table emitted a shrill ring. Marlyn scooped it up and stepped to the edge of the room to take the call. After saying "Hello," she listened for a few minutes, said "Okay," and ended the call.

"I have to collect some paperwork from the Realtor who manages the complex," she said. "He's coming to me, which is thoughtful, swinging by in his car."

She pulled on a down jacket that had been tossed over an armchair, added a stocking cap and gloves, and headed for the door. Before opening it, she turned. "Keep looking around if you want—or I'll see you when you come back for the trunk." She added, "Nice to meet you both."

The sound of pots and pans rattling in the kitchen suggested that Fran had been at work there. Now she emerged carrying a teetering pile composed of baking sheets, muffin tins, a frying pan, saucepans in graduated sizes—with their lids, and balanced on top, a flour sifter.

"Running out of boxes," she commented before transferring her precarious burden to the armchair.

Bettina gave her a flirtatious smile and Pamela braced herself. Often such smiles were a prelude to questions that, in Pamela's view, Bettina had no business asking.

"Do you think she's sorry that her sister has been murdered?" Bettina inquired. "She doesn't seem terribly sad to me."

Pamela expected Fran to respond that she had no way of knowing such an intimate thing, and/or that Bettina had no business even asking. But instead, she frowned slightly, stretched her lips into a half smile, and tilted her head. The flour sifter that topped the pile of kitchenware in the armchair threatened to tumble onto the floor and she reached out to steady it.

"Carys cost Marlyn her marriage," she said.

"What?" Bettina took a step back and opened her eyes so wide that the white around her irises was visible. She did tend to overdramatize her reactions, but even Pamela felt a jolt and sensed that her own expression reflected her own surprise.

"Not the way you think." Fran waved a hand in a soothing gesture. "Carys convinced Marlyn to divorce the poor guy." In a sing-song voice she went on: *"He doesn't treat you well, the children are grown, you deserve your own life, take back your own name.* But if you ask me, Carys was just jealous that Marlyn had a husband and family and she didn't. But anyway, she convinced Marlyn to squirrel away household money for an escape fund and then make her break. So finally Marlyn did."

Fran leaned close and whispered, though no one but her intended audience was near. "Marlyn is very suggestible. And then when Marlyn leaves her husband she moves here, practically next door to her sister!"

"Maybe she's happier now," Bettina ventured. "Not every husband is as ideal as my Wilfred."

Fran shook her head. "A few months later, Marlyn had second thoughts and begged hubby to come back. But he wouldn't. Now she misses him."

"And he's off sailing, and I'm still here," came a fake-cheery voice from the doorway, accompanied by a gust of chilly air. "Midlife Crisis: His Turn." Marlyn had returned. She smiled a stiff smile.

Fran suddenly became very interested in the stability of the flour sifter, and Pamela, who rarely blushed, felt her cheeks grow warm. But Bettina stepped forward and reached out to hug Marlyn, who—surprisingly—accepted the hug and even hugged back.

"You poor thing," Bettina murmured in the same tones she used when comforting Woofus, the troubled dog she had adopted from the Haversack animal shelter. "You've really been having a tough time, haven't you?"

Marlyn dropped the unconvincing bravado with which she had greeted them and nodded dolefully. Putting an arm around her, Bettina led her to the sofa, where the two women perched at the end not occupied by the curtains.

"I loved my sister," Marlyn said, "in spite of everything. Carys was just born that way. She always had to be in charge. She thought people wouldn't respect her otherwise—like it wasn't enough to just be an ordinary person."

"Bossy, if you ask me," Fran whispered to Pamela.

Marlyn's voice quavered. "And I knew she was jealous of me. I *was* lucky, and she seemed so lonely." She sniffled and Bettina pulled a tissue from her handbag. "It's all just been *hard*, and my husband won't come back, and it didn't help that the police treated me like a suspect, at first—before they figured out where that scarf came from."

Bettina's eyes grew wide again. "No!" she breathed. "They actually thought *you* might have killed your own sister."

"They always interview the family members," Fran declared with a toss of her gray curls. "Anybody who watches mystery shows on TV knows that."

"You're right." Marlyn nodded meekly. "Of course. Detective Clayborn was nice about it, but he did ask me where I was between eight and nine Monday night."

"Where were you?" It was Pamela who spoke, the question popping out independently of any volition on her part.

"Home. Where else?"

"She was," Fran cut in. "We were both shoveling snow—getting a head start on it. We have to keep our own porches and walks clear, but the complex takes care of the rest. I heard the chimes so I know just when it was."

She stepped closer to the sofa and reached out a hand toward Marlyn. "It's time to get back to work," she said. "No point in sitting around moping when you've got plenty to keep you busy."

"Okay." Marlyn stood up.

"And what are you thinking about for dinner?"

"Hamburgers?" Marlyn's tone implied doubt.

"We ate hamburgers last night," Fran said firmly. "I'll order a pizza."

Bettina climbed to her feet. "I'll be back for the trunk," she told Marlyn, adding a quick hug. "You take care of yourself."

"She does seem suggestible," Bettina noted after they had returned to her car and settled into their seats, "though it's kind of amazing that she actually let her sister talk her into getting a divorce."

"Maybe the husband was horrible," Pamela suggested. "Maybe she just needed that little nudge—and to know that her sister would be there for her afterwards."

"She wanted him back though, so he can't have been all that horrible. But now he's gone off sailing, and her sister's to blame."

It felt colder in the car than outside, where the bright sun at least created the illusion of warmth. Pamela folded one gloved hand around the other and massaged her fingers as she spoke. "So—motive then, for sure."

"But she apparently has an alibi that convinced Clayborn, and Laurel turned up as the likelier suspect anyway." Bettina twisted her key in the ignition and the car's engine grumbled for a moment and then caught. "I just don't think it could be Laurel though"—she swiveled her head and gave Pamela a significant look—"or at least I don't want it to be." She pulled away from the curb and into the flow of traffic heading south on Arborville Avenue.

"Other people could have wanted Carys dead," Pamela commented after a minute or two. "People she complained about, like the kid who played the drums in the apartment next door, or the Christmas carolers . . ."

Bettina laughed. "Killer Christmas carolers? That's like something out of a horror movie."

Pamela laughed too. "And I doubt a kid who just wanted to play his drums loud would murder someone. Besides, he probably got complaints from a lot of other neighbors too."

They had reached Arborville's main intersection, with most of the shopping district behind them and the Co-Op on the corner across the way. Bettina waited for the light to change, navigated the intersection, and eased to the curb in front of Borough Hall.

"You're sure you don't want me to wait and give you a ride home?" she asked.

"I'm fine walking." Pamela clicked her door open and started to climb out.

"Here's something to think about," Bettina said in parting. "Maybe the ex-husband resented Carys for destroying his marriage. How do we know he's really 'off sailing'?"

Inside the market, Pamela pushed her cart along the narrow aisles, collecting the ingredients for the chicken with dumplings she planned to make that night, as well as half a pound of the Co-Op's special Vermont cheddar, a fresh loaf of whole-grain bread, and tomatoes and cucumbers for salad.

Penny was out when she got home, with a note left behind that she was at Lorie's but would be back by dinnertime. Up in her office, Pamela removed Catrina from her computer keyboard and returned to her evaluation of "Totemic Animal Motifs in Traditional Prayer-Rug Design."

Chapter Five

The next morning Pamela was back at work in her office. The article on prayer rugs, like the one on sericulture, had been excellent, and she'd given it an enthusiastic thumbs-up. Now she was tackling "Spy-Craft," whose full title proved to be "Spy-Craft: The Knitting Spies of World War II." The premise was fascinating, and the utility of knitting as a tool of espionage seemed obvious once the author pointed it out.

The knit stitch and the purl stitch could be used like the dots and dashes of Morse code, and any message at all could be encoded that way. Who would suspect, for example, that elderly Belgian women whose parlor windows looked out on train tracks were recording the times and frequency of German troop trains in the swathes of knitting that hung from their needles?

Unfortunately, though, the author's tendency to mangle the English language distracted mightily from the article's value—though there was no hint that her native tongue was anything other than English. "It would be splinting hairs," she had written, "to question motives," and elsewhere rumors were "viscous," danger reared its ugly visage, and nearly every paragraph included at least one misspelling, a malapropism, or a metaphor garbled into unintelligibility.

Pamela closed her eyes, but the image of the bright computer monitor lingered. The article wasn't to be copyedited, only read, with a thumbs-up or thumbs-down evaluation returned to her boss. Yet even just reading it was painful. She was relieved, then, to be distracted by the telephone's ring.

She swiveled around and picked up the handset.

"Are you busy?" asked a familiar voice.

Pamela responded with a grateful "Hi, Bettina."

"*Are* you busy?" Bettina repeated. "Laurel Lewis is out on bail."

"That's good news," Pamela said. "I wonder how she's doing?"

"We could know." Bettina's enthusiasm carried over the phone lines. "I think it would be useful if I talked to her, in my capacity as a reporter for the *Advocate*, of course."

"And you're inviting me to come along?" Pamela had swiveled back to her normal position, facing the computer monitor—and a paragraph in which an intrepid knitter-spy evaded death despite its being "hot on her heals." She groaned.

"Are you okay?" Bettina asked.

"Fine!" Pamela said. "And if you're inviting me, yes. I'll come."

She thought for a minute. Penny was downstairs, she knew, because she had heard her daughter talking to one or more of the cats.

"Don't come here," she said. "If we're going out together, Penny will suspect it has something to do with the murder. She has kind of a sixth sense. I'll come to you."

Happy to escape from "Spy-Craft," at least for a while,

Pamela closed the file, exited Word, and shut down her computer.

Penny was sitting at the kitchen table, still in her pajamas and robe, sipping coffee with Ginger on her lap. "Going out?" she asked as Pamela picked up her purse from the counter.

"Post office," Pamela said. "I realized I have more cards to send and I'm out of Christmas stamps. It's a nice day for a walk, so . . ."

"*Mo-om!*" Penny's forehead puckered. "It's freezing out. The paper says high of twenty degrees and that's this afternoon."

"Nice and bright though. That makes a difference." With a wave, Pamela headed for the entry, where she collected her warmest coat, the down one Penny had given her.

Laurel lived in a townhouse development at the southern edge of Arborville. The land had once been occupied by a very grand house, built at the beginning of the previous century when families were much larger. No buyers had come forward when the most recent owners died, but a convenient rezoning made the property attractive to developers. The crumbling mansion had been replaced by twelve attractive townhouses whose wood-frame construction made them blend in well with Arborville's typical housing stock.

In spring, summer, and fall, meticulous landscaping added to the development's appeal. Now a brittle crust of snow covered the lawn, and the leafless shrubs were spiky skeletons of themselves. A carefully shoveled sidewalk led from the parking area to the complex, where glittering icicles hung from the gutters that edged the roofline.

After walking several yards, Pamela and Bettina stopped

to scan the first cluster of units for the address they were seeking. A door in one of the units opened and a woman emerged, dressed for the chill in a spotted fur that was obviously fake, a bright red beret and matching scarf, and sturdy lace-up boots with thick soles. She headed toward them, apparently on her way to the parking area, and nodded pleasantly as she got closer.

She passed, and Pamela and Bettina continued on their way as well. Laurel's unit hadn't yet come into view. But after a moment, a voice behind them called Bettina's name. They turned.

"It's you, isn't it?" the woman in the spotted fur said. "Bettina Fraser from the *Advocate*? I recognize you from the senior center—you cover so many of our events."

"Why, yes!" Bettina responded with a wide smile, enhanced by the lipstick that matched her pumpkin-colored coat. She took a few steps toward the woman and offered a gloved hand. "And you're . . . ?"

"Suzanne Turner." The woman offered her hand in return, then said, "I suppose you're here because of poor Laurel."

Bettina nodded.

"I don't think she did it," the woman declared. "Laurel is a lovely person and even if she wasn't, nobody who has such a soft spot for cats could be a murderer. I was happy to take care of them while she was in jail, but they missed their mommy." She interjected an emphatic nod and then went on, her breath condensing into wisps of steam as she spoke. "I hope the police figure out who really did it— though I can't say I'll actually miss Carys."

"Really? Did you know her?" The questions were asked in an offhand way, but Pamela could tell by the way Bettina's eyes narrowed that the encounter with Suzanne was now more than an impromptu chat.

"I was in a writers' group with Carys"—Suzanne added a half smile and shrug that implied she hadn't taken the experience too seriously—"for a while at least. I'm retired now, trying new things."

"You're not writing anymore?" Bettina inquired.

"It wasn't really me," Suzanne said. "I prefer to be out and about, not sitting at a desk for hours all by myself. And I wasn't very good either, at least according to Carys. Laurel, though . . . Laurel was—"

"In the group too?" Bettina interjected. Pamela could tell from her voice that she was excited.

Suzanne nodded. "She was really good. *I* thought she was good. Carys didn't think she was good. In fact Laurel gave up on a novel she was writing because Carys convinced her that it had no chance of ever being published, and Laurel was so demoralized she dropped out of the group. I don't know if there's anybody left in it now." She laughed. "Carys might have driven them all away—and now she's gone too." She raised a hand to her mouth and added, "Ooops! I shouldn't laugh."

Suzanne went on her way toward the parking area, but Pamela and Bettina didn't move for a moment.

"Interesting," Bettina commented.

"Yes, interesting," Pamela agreed.

They continued along the sidewalk, past the first cluster of townhouses and then the second, until they reached the address they were looking for. Laurel's front door sported a cheery wreath, undoubtedly hung there in earlier, happier times—sprays of balsam intertwined with gold ribbon and studded with red berries. A few steps led up to a small porch. They climbed the steps and rang the bell.

"Hello?" Bettina spoke into the narrow gap that opened between door and doorframe. "It's Bettina Fraser. I know you from the Haversack animal shelter, and I'm so sorry about what's happened. I was wondering if you need anything—like cat food? Or something for yourself?"

The door swung back to reveal a tall woman almost as tall as Pamela, and with shoulder-length dark hair like Pamela's. She hadn't yet dressed for the day, but was wearing a long fleecy robe, pale green. Two cats peeked out from beneath its hem.

"No, I don't . . ." Her eyes roved from Bettina to Pamela and back. "But . . ." She backed up, leaving the cats exposed. "Come on in. It's cold out there."

One of the cats, a pretty calico, ventured forward. Bettina removed her gloves, bent down, and offered a finger. The cat responded with a sniff and then lowered its head for a scratch. The other cat, a Persian with a drift of pure white fur, stood aside and watched.

"Sweet baby," Bettina murmured to the calico. She straightened up and focused on Laurel. "But how are *you* doing?"

"So-so." Laurel shrugged. "It all just seems unreal." She looked around. "We can sit down, I guess, if you want to stay. It cheers me up to have company, but I really don't have the energy to make coffee or anything."

"Of course not, you poor dear." Bettina's sympathetic head-tilt, contracted brows, and sad half-smile emphasized her concern.

Laurel meanwhile had flopped into a peach-colored armchair, and the cats that had accompanied her to the door were now in her lap. They were joined by a third cat and then a fourth, also calicos. The room was charmingly decorated with a Victorian-style sofa, peach-colored like the chair, and a few pieces of ornate wooden furniture that looked very old. Several paintings of flowers rendered in an impressionistic style enlivened the pale walls.

Pamela and Bettina loosened their coats and perched on the edge of the sofa.

Laurel devoted herself to cuddling her cats for a few moments, then she looked toward Bettina. "I guess you know Detective Clayborn pretty well," she said, "because of the *Advocate*."

Bettina nodded.

"He doesn't actually listen, does he?"

Bettina made a noncommittal sound. Pamela suspected that the detective's willingness to cooperate with Bettina's reporting depended on his confidence in her discretion.

But Laurel didn't need an answer to go on. "I never actually got the scarf," she announced, leaning forward despite the lapful of cats. "And I told him that, several times." Her eyes, which were large and a startling shade of blue, lent her a guileless air that had evidently been lost on Detective Clayborn.

"You never got the scarf!" Pamela had so far been content to let Bettina take the lead, but this information was so startling that she'd been provoked to speech.

"Never," Laurel said with a tight-lipped headshake. "It was already claimed when I went to pick it up after the auction."

"How can that be?" Pamela and Bettina both spoke at once.

Laurel shrugged. "Everyone was crowding around the table where they were collecting the money from the winning bidders, and just thrusting cash at the auction volunteers. And when it got to be my turn, they said someone had already claimed the scarf. I knew I had the winning bid because I checked the bid sheet right before the auction deadline, but I guess the volunteers expected people to be honest and so they didn't ask for ID or anything."

Bettina frowned. "I can't believe Clayborn didn't follow up! If the whole case against you relies on the idea that the murder weapon belonged to you, well—" As if words failed, she concluded with a disgusted snort.

"But I had . . . I guess they call it 'opportunity' too." Laurel's expression was bleak. "My office is so close to where it happened, and then . . . who's to say—except me, of course—that I didn't just pretend to have found Carys's body, to allay suspicion, after I had killed her?"

"That seems far-fetched." Bettina laughed—though Pamela recalled that Bettina herself had raised that very point.

"Of course it is. And it assumes I'm quite the actress, which I'm not. It was dark in that passageway, and I almost tripped over her, and I tried to talk to her but she didn't answer, and I stumbled to the other end and called out to Mort Quigley—though at first I didn't recognize him because he was facing the other direction and he was so bundled up and it was snowing. And then when he turned around, he was as shocked as I was."

The fluffy white Persian had been reposing on the arm of the chair, apparently napping. Now it raised its head and twisted its neck around to glance at its mistress. Laurel reached out and began to stroke its back, her fingers disappearing into its luxuriant fur.

"Luckily I have these sweeties to comfort me," she said, and bent over until she was almost nose to nose with the cat, adding, "Mommy had to cancel her Christmas trip, didn't she?" She looked up. "A condition of being out on bail—how odd it sounds to say that!—is that I can't leave Arborville. I was going to spend the holiday with my sister and her family in Philadelphia."

"Come to my house!" Bettina exclaimed. "No one should

be alone on Christmas, and there's always room for one more at my dining room table."

"Oh, no. No, no, no." Laurel smiled sadly. "You're so kind, but I can't impose like that. I wouldn't be good company. My kitties and I will get along okay on our own."

The fluffy white cat had resumed its slumber, but one of the calicos had ventured from its mistress's lap and was investigating Bettina's fur-trimmed bootie. Laurel continued talking, as if to herself, staring ahead at nothing in particular. "I've got work to take my mind off things, the audit of the library budget and some estimated tax figures for an antiques dealer in Timberley and then there's that caterer . . ." Her voice trailed off, but after a moment she added, "Plenty of nice distracting work."

"You're sure?" Bettina leaned forward, staring as intently as a parent might stare at a child suspected of stretching the truth.

"Really sure!" Laurel tried to muster a smile that wasn't tinged with sadness. "The library thing is due right after the holiday, so I *do* have to work."

"Okay . . ." Bettina drew the word out as she rose to her feet. "If you're sure, but I'm going to leave my number so you can call me if you change your mind and want some company." She carefully disengaged her foot from the calico's explorations.

"One step forward and one step back, I'd say," Pamela remarked as they neared the parking area. They were passing a huge holly bush that offered a welcome flash of color—deep green with red berries—against the dark asphalt and ridges of piled snow that was no longer all that white.

Bettina signaled assent with a humming sound. After a

moment she spoke. "If she never even claimed the scarf, how could she have used it to strangle Carys?"

"That's the step forward," Pamela said, "assuming she's telling the truth about not claiming the scarf. We only have her word for it."

"What's the step back?"

"The writers' group."

"Ohhh!" Bettina moaned. "That's right. She has a motive now—but would somebody really kill a person who told them they were a bad writer? I don't mind it when the editor of the *Advocate* asks me to do more research or talk to more people for a story."

"But he doesn't tell you to forget about being a reporter because you're hopelessly bad."

"That's true." Bettina nodded.

"Suzanne said she thought Laurel was really good—and it sounds like Laurel was serious about her writing . . . with a novel in progress. And then she just abandoned it. If you had invested your whole self in a project like that and somebody demolished it, maybe you'd want to demolish that person."

They had reached Bettina's car. She pulled her keys from her handbag and a few minutes later they were cruising along the road that served the townhouse development. Bettina was silent until she had made the turn onto Arborville Avenue and driven a few blocks.

When she spoke, it was to say, "Clayborn must have checked with Mort Quigley or one of the other auction volunteers about who claimed the scarf. That just seems like basic police work to me."

The houses along Arborville Avenue south of Orchard Street were quite grand, many constructed of brick in a classic center-hall colonial style, and set well back from the road. This time of year, the imposing façades had

been made festive with miniature Christmas trees flank-
ing impressive doorways, oversize wreaths decking ornate doors, and garlands of Christmas greenery spiraling
around columns.

Pamela had been enjoying the scenery, but Bettina's comment roused her from her reverie. "I would think so," she
agreed. "I wonder what Mort Quigley or whoever he
talked to told him."

Bettina stopped at a crosswalk where a woman pushing
a stroller was waiting to cross. She turned to Pamela. "Obviously not that somebody else claimed the scarf."

"Maybe the person just said they didn't know—that it
was crowded and confusing."

Bettina, still turned toward Pamela, nodded vigorously.
"So Clayborn is just going on the fact that Laurel—or
S. Claws—had the winning bid, and he thinks Laurel's
statement that the scarf was already gone when she tried
to claim it is an attempt to establish that she's innocent."

From behind them came an irritated honk. The woman
pushing the stroller was long gone and the way was clear
to proceed.

"I don't know why people have to be so impatient,"
Bettina muttered as she accelerated.

A few moments later they were speeding past the stately
brick apartment building that marked the corner of Arborville Avenue and Orchard Street.

"Where are you going?" Pamela asked. "That was our
turn."

"To the library to talk to Mort Quigley," Bettina said,
her eyes focused on the road.

Chapter Six

"To what do I owe the pleasure of your visit?" Mort Quigley directed the question at Bettina, with a nod toward Pamela as well. He'd been summoned from his office by the young woman stationed at the circulation counter, which was decorated for the season with a potted poinsettia. On the wall behind the counter, foil letters spelling out HAPPY HOLIDAYS hung from a string stretched taut like a clothesline.

Bettina smiled coquettishly. The *Advocate* had given lavish coverage to library events over the years and Mort Quigley had more reason to woo her than the reverse, but Bettina had charm to spare.

"It's that time again," she said. "The new year is right around the corner, and I was wondering if you have a list of the library events you've planned so far. That way I can get a sense of what I'm going to be reporting on. And the *Advocate* will post notices well in advance, of course, so people know what's coming up."

"Good thinking!" Mort exclaimed. "Step into my parlor, said the spider to the fly." Energetic despite his bulk, he hopped to the end of the counter, pushed open a hinged gate, and beckoned them to enter. He was taller than Bettina but not as tall as Pamela, with rusty-red hair retreating from a freckly forehead.

Perched on his desk chair before his computer monitor, he brought up a file, and a few seconds later a faint chiming sound and a low purr signaled the arrival of a printout. Mort stood up, collected it from the printer, and handed it to Bettina with a bow.

She glanced over it and raised her eyes. "Lots of things to look forward to," she commented, adding a flirtatious wink and a shiver of excitement. "I'm sure we'll all be happy to put the old year behind us. Such a shame, the murder—and to have it get all tangled up with the auction."

Mort shook his head, managing to retain his affable mien while looking appropriately serious. "These things happen," he said. "Even in nice towns like Arborville."

"The auction was such a good idea too, and got such support from the community. I hope we can do it again next year." Bettina mustered a hopeful smile.

"I do too." Mort returned the smile, a wide-mouthed smile that made the skin around his pale eyes crinkle.

"So much enthusiastic bidding! And that big rush at the end, with people so excited to claim the items they'd won . . ."

Mort nodded. "Maybe next time we'll allow more time between the end of the auction and the beginning of the tree-lighting ceremony."

"Experience is the best teacher, as my Wilfred would say." Mort continued to nod and Bettina nodded too, synchronizing her nods with his. Then, off-handedly, as if the answer wasn't really important, she murmured, "I know the police are going by the fact that Laurel Lewis had the winning bid for the . . . uh . . . but it seems like if things were confusing . . ."

Mort stopped nodding. "I know what you mean," he said, "and no, I certainly didn't see who claimed it. But you expect people to be honest. We announced the winning bidders. Other people bid on that scarf. Carys Walnutt bid on that scarf. But I can't imagine somebody who bid less would show up at the end, thrust some money at the volunteers, and grab something they hadn't rightfully won."

"No," Bettina agreed. "That's hard to imagine. Especially in a nice town like Arborville."

"What do you think?" Bettina asked Pamela as they left the library and began to advance across the parking lot toward where Bettina's faithful Toyota waited. The snowy expanse of the park was visible in the background.

"I think we should have lunch at Hyler's," Pamela responded.

Bettina stopped walking. "I don't think I could," she said in a small voice. "It's right next to where . . . where . . ." Her gloved hands fumbled the air as if to capture the right words.

"The crime-scene tape is down." Pamela gestured toward the mouth of the passageway between the brick buildings that housed Hyler's on one side and the hair salon on the other. "If everybody avoids Hyler's because it's next to what was once a crime scene, Hyler's will go out of business." She bent down to make eye contact with Bettina. "You wouldn't want that to happen, would you?"

"I'd miss the Reuben sandwiches," Bettina admitted. "But I won't walk through that passageway. We're going to have to go around the long way."

*　*　*

Hyler's oversized menus were the luncheonette's trademark, listing so many dining possibilities that one could eat at Hyler's every day for several weeks with no repeat, but Bettina scarcely looked at hers.

"Now I've got Reubens on the brain," she said, "and that's what I'm going to have, with a vanilla shake." She set the menu aside.

They were seated in one of the Naugahyde-upholstered booths along the restaurant's side walls. The booths were premium spots, more private and more comfortable than the wooden tables and chairs that crowded the middle of the floor. Today, however, most of the tables were empty, and the booths as well—though it was peak lunch hour.

The server, a middle-aged woman who had worked at Hyler's as long as Pamela had lived in Arborville, approached. She was as cheerful as always, though the cheer seemed forced without the usual backdrop of laughter and chatter.

"I'll have the same," Pamela said after Bettina had placed her order. They watched the server retreat and then Bettina leaned across the table.

"Did we learn anything useful?" she asked. "I was trying to get him to talk without being obvious about what we wanted to know." She had shed her down coat, which now hung from a hook at the edge of the booth, to reveal a cozy wool turtleneck in a Christmasy shade of dark green that set off her scarlet hair to great advantage.

"Mort Quigley didn't see who claimed the scarf," Pamela said, "and the process of people claiming their auction prizes was rushed and confusing. I don't think there's a way we can know whether Laurel is telling the truth or lying."

"I believe her though"—Bettina nodded vigorously and

the carefully waved tendrils of her coiffure vibrated—"despite the possible motive involving the writers' group."

The server appeared at the end of the booth with two vanilla milkshakes in tall, frosty glasses, crowned with froth. As soon as hers had been deposited on her paper place mat, Bettina pulled it closer and bent toward the straw.

Pamela pulled her milkshake closer too, but before sampling it, she said, "I guess we're assuming that if the scarf was the murder weapon then the person who claimed it has to be the murderer."

Bettina looked up. The tip of her straw now bore the bright imprint of her lipstick. "That seems to be Clayborn's approach. How else would the scarf end up at the murder scene?"

"Think for a minute!" Pamela raised a finger as if calling attention to a lecture in the offing. As a mother she'd tried to resist lecturing Penny, but every once in a while the impulse to illuminate became too much to bear.

"I'm thinking." With furrowed brow and pursed lips, Bettina twisted her mobile features into a caricature of deep thought.

"The victim could have been wearing the scarf!" Pamela's triumphant shout would have turned heads at neighboring tables, except that the tables were unoccupied.

"Of course! Of course!" Bettina beamed across the table. "And didn't Mort say that Carys Walnutt also bid on the scarf?"

Pamela cut in. "And things were confusing with people rushing to pay for what they'd won and grab their prizes."

Bettina began talking almost before Pamela had stopped. "And based on what people have said about Carys, she seems like the kind of person who might grab what she wanted, whether fairly or not."

Then in unison, both said, "And then she was murdered with that very scarf!"

"Ironic," Pamela added.

The server was approaching, bearing the Reubens on oval platters garnished with pickle spears and paper cups of coleslaw. They were silent then, except for enthusiastic thank-yous, until the platters had been deposited and the server had turned away.

Pamela had not yet even tasted her milkshake. After a long sip that delivered a rich draft of creamy vanilla-ness, she commented, "If Carys was wearing the scarf, the killer could be anyone at all, totally unconnected with the auction."

"Like her sister?" Bettina's hand, holding a fork that bore a toasty morsel of Reuben sandwich trailing a strand of melted cheese, halted halfway to her mouth.

"She has an alibi. Remember?"

"I'm glad we ate there," Bettina said after they had returned to her car and settled into their seats. "I'd hate to think of Hyler's going out of business."

She twisted her key in the ignition, the car grumbled to life, and she focused for the next few minutes on backing up and maneuvering out of the parking lot. But as she waited to make the turn onto Arborville Avenue, she glanced at Pamela and inquired, "Have you decided what you're going to wear to my party tomorrow night?"

"Not really." Pamela shrugged. "It's not a formal occasion, is it?"

Bettina had been about to take advantage of a lull in the traffic flow but she stomped down hard on the brake instead. "Hello!" she said, swiveling to face Pamela. "It's a Christmas Eve party and you're bringing your handsome boyfriend, Brian Delano."

"He's seen me in jeans." Pamela bit her lip to suppress a teasing smile.

"Oh, for heaven's sake!" Bettina stepped on the gas, gave the steering wheel a violent twist, and the car lurched into a turn.

"I'll wear something nice. I promise," Pamela assured her. Bettina eased off on the gas.

"I don't understand why you two aren't spending Christmas Day together," Bettina commented as they cruised along Arborville Avenue. "With the Arborville children and the Boston children doing Christmas with the in-laws this year, Wilfred and I are happy that we're going to have you and Penny—but Brian would be more than welcome too."

"He's going to be with his parents in Kringlekamack," Pamela said. "We've been over this before."

"And he can't take you? And Penny, of course." Bettina sounded as indignant as if she herself was the excluded guest.

"Things aren't at that stage yet," Pamela said. "It kind of . . . means something when a man takes a woman home for the holidays." She turned to Bettina. "Doesn't it?" she asked, her throat suddenly tight as she remembered that long-ago Christmas with her husband (then her husband-to-be) and his parents.

Bettina didn't notice the change in her voice. She shrugged. "Well, at least you have someone in your life now. That's an improvement over before. And I know Wilfred will enjoy chatting with Brian tomorrow night."

Pamela swallowed a few times. She didn't mind the fact that Brian Delano wasn't ready to present her to his parents. She wasn't ready to be presented and perhaps would never be. He was smart and interesting and—yes—handsome, and having *someone* in her life was a great deal better than being solitary, especially since the prospect of her daughter graduating and being out on her own loomed so close.

Bettina's voice interrupted, seeming to arrive from far away, so deep had Pamela been in her musings.

"You're home." Bettina leaned over. "Hello?"

"Oh! Yes!" Pamela shook her head as if to rearrange her thoughts. "Thank you. And I'll bring dessert on Christmas."

"Wilfred Jr. and I are picking up that trunk at Marlyn's tomorrow," Bettina said as Pamela reached for the door handle. "Want to come along?"

Pamela stared for a moment, still not quite back in the present. "Why?"

"Why not?"

It was early afternoon, with plenty of time to fit in the two chores that awaited: finishing the evaluation of "Spy-Craft" and wrapping a few more gifts. The gifts were for Penny, and ideally the wrapping would be done when Penny wasn't around—she was out at the moment, but the "Spy-Craft" evaluation and the two evaluations Pamela had already completed were due back by five p.m.

She hadn't finished her read-through of "Spy-Craft," and even the first few pages had been a time-consuming slog, so she climbed the stairs to her office, removed Catrina from her keyboard, and pushed the button that would bring her computer to life. She enjoyed the process of wrapping gifts, and an hour or so spent with festive holiday paper and rolls of colorful ribbon would be fitting reward for finishing the *Fiber Craft* assignments.

But ten minutes later she closed the Word file for "Spy-Craft: The Knitting Spies of World War II," opened the file she had titled "Evaluations," and wrote *"Spy-Craft: The*

Knitting Spies of World War II" is not only unpublishable, it is unreadable. I suggest that the author find another line of work or at least plan never to submit to Fiber Craft *again.*

She skimmed the evaluations she had written for the sericulture article and the prayer rug article, decided they sounded fine, and saved and closed the file. After composing a brief cover message, she attached the "Evaluations" file and was on the point of clicking Send when her finger halted on the mouse. A vision of Laurel Lewis's face rose before her.

Could Laurel really have murdered Carys Walnutt to rid the universe of the person who had crushed her dreams of being a writer? A cruel critique could do things to a person—hollow them out in a way. Pamela was never sure whether her boss shared her evaluations with authors or merely took Pamela's advice into account and sent out bland acceptances or rejections. But what if she relayed Pamela's words verbatim? No one, no matter how horrible a writer, deserved to be crushed.

She opened "Evaluations," deleted what she had written, and substituted, *The author clearly is well-informed on this fascinating topic but the style might be better suited to a different sort of publication.*

Chapter Seven

The figure visible through the lace curtain was definitely Bettina, but the vehicle waiting at the curb was unfamiliar.

"It's Wilfred Jr.'s Subaru," Bettina explained Saturday morning as the door swung open. "There's plenty of room in the back for that trunk."

Pamela slipped into her coat, called goodbye to Penny, and stepped out onto the porch.

Wilfred Jr. was a younger and thinner version of his genial father. On this chilly morning his hair, thick and sandy like Wilfred's had been in his youth, was hidden by a stocking cap, and he was bundled in a puffy down jacket. He climbed out of the car and opened the back door as Pamela and Bettina approached.

"I'll play the chauffeur," he said as he gestured for them both to climb in the back.

The drive to the garden apartments was brief, just up to the corner of Orchard Street and then seven or eight blocks along Arborville Avenue. As they neared their destination, they passed the rec center and, across the way, the traffic island with the noble pine tree that Arborville decorated every year for Christmas. The lush boughs decked with oversize iridescent balls, tinsel garlands, and winking lights, illuminated even during the day, were as beautiful a sight as in years past. But now the tree and the lighting ceremony were all tangled up with the auction that had provided the scarf that had strangled Carys Walnutt and led to the arrest of Laurel Lewis. Pamela sighed and looked away.

"We're here," Wilfred Jr. announced a few minutes later.

No one answered when they tapped at the door of the apartment that had been Carys's. Through the uncurtained windows, they could glimpse sealed boxes and bulging garbage bags, as well as the richly decorated trunk with its swirling peonies.

"It looks like she's got everything packed up," Bettina said. "I'll just step down to number twelve and fetch her."

Bettina was back in a minute, trailed by Marlyn tiptoeing along the chilly path in slippers and with a jacket draped over her shoulders.

"Yes," Marlyn was saying, "all my work is done. On Monday a charity group is coming to collect the boxes, and the garbage bags are going to the curb for the trash pickup. So the landlord should have time to do what he needs to do."

"No rest for the wicked," Bettina replied. In response to Marlyn's startled "What?" Bettina explained, "It's something my husband says."

Marlyn nodded in acknowledgment when Bettina introduced Wilfred Jr. and inserted a key into the apartment door's lock.

"The trunk *is* a beautiful thing," she said as they stepped inside. "I'm glad it's finding a home. I had to squeeze a whole houseful of stuff into an apartment after my divorce, and I barely have room to turn around."

It seemed too cumbersome to be managed by one person, even a sturdy young man, but luckily it had handles on the ends, wrought in the same ornate style as the latch. Pamela seized one handle and Wilfred Jr. seized the other and together they hefted it and began to edge toward the open door.

As they proceeded down the sidewalk, Pamela heard Bettina say, "I wonder what will happen if the police discover Laurel Lewis didn't kill Carys. I suppose they'll be asking around in this complex again, looking for people who might have had a grudge against your sister . . ."

Distracted, Pamela faltered for a moment, listening. Bettina had a trick of phrasing statements in a way that made people respond to them as if they were questions.

"Are you doing okay?" Wilfred Jr. was as solicitous as his kindly father.

"Fine, fine," Pamela said. "It's not really that heavy."

A few minutes later, the trunk had been safely stowed in the Subaru's hatchback and Bettina was making her way down the concrete path that led to the sidewalk. Just then the St. Willibrod's chimes began to sound from across the street, so Pamela had to hold off asking Bettina the question she was longing to ask as she counted eleven of the reverberating bongs.

"We were here longer than I thought," she observed as the last reverberations died away.

"Less than an hour." Wilfred Jr. checked his watch. "It's only ten. The chimes must be off, probably still on daylight savings time."

But Pamela was focused on Bettina now and barely heard him. "So—did you get anything out of her about people who might have had grudges?"

Bettina shook her head. "She's very loyal, despite what Carys did to her. I wish we had run into that Fran—she was sure happy to talk."

*   *   *

Pamela had not been serious about wearing jeans to the party. Standing in front of her closet she had hesitated between the elegant black sheath that had been a gift from Bettina and the ruby-red tunic she had knit for herself from a curious pattern involving long sleeves but bare shoulders. She had finally settled on the tunic, given its Christmas-appropriate color—even though she had worn it on several Christmas-related occasions in past years—and she had paired it with slim black slacks and her black pumps.

"Very festive," Brian said approvingly as he stepped across the threshold carrying a colorfully wrapped bottle and a small box tied with a red bow. "Merry Christmas." He leaned forward to give her a quick kiss, almost platonic, and handed her the box.

Brian Delano taught photography at Wendelstaff College. She'd met him there when her car battery died in the Wendelstaff parking lot while she was attending a fashion show. He was eminently suitable, as Bettina never tired of pointing out, and handsome, with dark good looks and a wolfish air that was tempered by a sweet smile.

Pamela offered him a box in return, larger than the one he'd handed her, and flat. "You can open it now," she said. "It's Christmas Eve."

"You first." He smiled.

She perched on the entry chair and untied the ribbon. Inside the box, cushioned on a bed of cotton, was a pair of earrings, gold and silver wires twisted into dramatic spirals.

"Beautiful!" Pamela exclaimed.

"I thought they'd look nice when you wear your hair up," Brian said, obviously pleased at her reaction.

"Your turn." Pamela nodded toward the box she'd given him, vacated the chair, and reached out to relieve him of the bottle he carried.

With both hands now free, he peeled off the wrappings and in a moment was holding up a small framed picture.

"It looks like the Manhattan skyline." He studied the picture more closely. "A pen and ink sketch. Very nice." He thought for a minute and then tilted his head to study her. "You remembered!" He laughed.

"You always take the upper level of the bridge when we go into the city," Pamela said, "and you always comment on how much you like the view."

A wedding-china platter waited on the entry's small table. Under a protective film of plastic wrap, slices of poppy-seed cake were arranged in careful rows. There was no one to call goodbye to since Penny had left an hour earlier for a party organized by a college friend who lived in a nearby town. They set their gifts to each other on the table, Brian helped Pamela into her coat, and they headed across the street, Pamela carrying the platter and stepping carefully in her pumps.

Ice crystals speckled the asphalt, reflecting light from the street lamp. The night was clear and cold, and overhead tiny stars pinpricked the dark sky.

"Welcome, welcome, welcome!" Bettina greeted them, silhouetted against the brightness of her cheerful living room. The strains of "We Three Kings" drifted from within. She accepted the platter and stepped back to let them enter. When Wilfred appeared at her side, Brian presented him with the colorfully wrapped bottle.

Wilfred drew Brian aside with a hearty inquiry about his recent doings as Bettina set off for the kitchen bearing the platter. "I'm glad you wore the red tunic," she said, turning to speak over her shoulder to Pamela, who was following her, "though maybe it's time for you to think about acquiring a new Christmas outfit."

Bettina herself was in red as well, a red velvet fit-and-flare dress with a wide neckline and three-quarter-length sleeves. She had accessorized it with black suede pumps and a triple strand of pearls.

"You're the first ones here," she said somewhat unnecessarily as they passed through the empty dining room. In preparation for the guests, however, the table had been pushed against the wall, spread with a lacy cloth, and laden with delights ranging from a tempting cheese ball to fancifully garnished mini-sandwiches. Bettina's huge cut-glass punch bowl sat waiting for Wilfred to concoct the spicy wassail that was his holiday tradition.

"I invited all the Knit and Nibblers," Bettina went on, "but Karen and her husband have a family event." No sooner had she spoken than the doorbell chimed. From the kitchen they could hear the door open and then voices mingling as Wilfred greeted a wave of people arriving in a sudden rush. Bettina set the platter on the high counter that separated the cooking area of the kitchen from the eating area, where it joined a tray of carefully decorated sugar cookies and a plate of brownies. On the stove a large pot of cider simmered on a burner turned low. The nutmeg and cinnamon that Wilfred had added perfumed the kitchen.

When they returned to the living room, Wilfred was just helping Roland and Melanie divest themselves of their coats as Nell and Harold stepped over the threshold behind them. Brian had already been drawn into conversation with Holly and her husband, Desmond, and Bettina's Arborville friend, Marlene Pepper, was chatting with Wilfred Jr. and his wife, Maxie.

"Who's for wassail?" Wilfred surveyed the group, which even without the addition of spirits was brimming with holiday cheer. He himself was in fine form, with his red and green plaid wool shirt and a beaming smile that made his ruddy cheeks resemble apples.

"Me . . . me . . . me," came a chorus of voices.

He retreated toward the kitchen, followed by Bettina and most of the guests. Pamela always looked forward to Wilfred's wassail, but she didn't mind waiting a bit and, anyway, the doorbell had just chimed again.

Pamela greeted two couples she didn't know but whose female halves she recognized as friends of Bettina's, and before she could close the door voices called "Merry Christmas" from the front walk and more arrivals stepped onto the porch. Bettina reappeared and joined in the greetings. Coats were removed, guests were urged to join Wilfred in the dining room, and Bettina whisked the coats upstairs.

More and more people arrived and Bettina darted back and forth and up and down the stairs. When, after a bit, it seemed that the flow of new arrivals had ceased, Bettina returned to Pamela's side bearing two cut-glass cups containing wassail. She handed one to Pamela and looked around, saying, "I brought one for that handsome boyfriend of yours."

Brian, however, had supplied himself with his own wassail and was standing near the fireplace, where bright flames danced atop crisscrossed logs, deep in conversation with Roland.

"I'll drink it myself," Bettina said, and raised the cup in a toast. Pamela raised hers and took a sip. Wilfred's wassail, she knew, was hard cider spiced with his own special blend of spices and enhanced with a goodly dollop of brandy. It was warm in the mouth, with a nose-tingling hint of alcohol vapor and a lingering suggestion of nutmeg.

They stood in companionable silence for a bit as the sounds of laughter and conversation echoed around them, all with a backdrop of carols, as "Good King Wenceslas" gave way to "The Holly and the Ivy," and "The Holly and the Ivy" yielded to "Greensleeves."

"It's going well," Bettina commented. "Don't you think?" She surveyed the crowded room, where people dressed in their holiday finery mingled, some nibbling from small plates, others sipping from cups of wassail or glasses of wine or beer.

"Oh, very!" Pamela agreed. The wassail had eased the shyness she sometimes felt in crowds, and when Marlene Pepper detached herself from the group she had been chatting with and joined Pamela and Bettina, Pamela was happy to hold up her end of the conversation.

Marlene's topic was, blessedly, not the recent murder but rather the Arborville Players and their upcoming production of *Twelfth Night*, for which she had been on the costume committee. Pamela smiled and nodded, adding a comment here and there. More people joined them, Marlene departed, Brian replaced Bettina, Maxie stopped by to say how much she liked the trunk, and Melanie De-Camp accosted Maxie to compliment her hairstyle. With the carols and the chatter and the wassail Pamela found that she was enjoying herself.

Their whole group migrated to the dining room where they browsed along the buffet table. Ready to be spread on crackers, the cheese ball's rich cheddar-orange interior beckoned, along with a colorful paté featuring layers of red, green, yellow, and white vegetables. The mini-sandwiches, open-faced, included smoked salmon, thin-sliced roast beef, shrimp salad, herring, and prosciutto. Meatballs on toothpicks filled a platter next to a tray of bite-sized onion tarts.

Bright red cherry tomatoes shared a plate with cucumber spears and baby carrots.

Once their plates were full, Pamela and Brian stepped off to the side to sample the buffet's bounty. Pamela started with a mini-sandwich, smoked salmon layered on pumpernickel and garnished with a sprig of dill, and moved on to a cracker heaped with the cheddar-mayonnaise blend, enhanced with cayenne, from the cheese ball.

"I'll have to ask Wilfred for his meatball recipe," Brian commented after he'd deposited an empty toothpick onto his plate. "Plenty of garlic and just spicy enough."

They alternated eating and chatting, mostly about the food and Wilfred's kitchen prowess. After several minutes Bettina detached herself from a group that included Marlene Pepper and Nell and Harold Bascomb, swung by the buffet for more meatballs and mini-sandwiches, and wound up where Pamela and Brian were standing near the arch that led to the living room.

"Please have more," she urged, and then, winking at Brian, added, "We're so glad you could come! What's Christmas without friends? And any friend of Pamela's is a friend of ours." For good measure, she reached out with her free hand and squeezed his arm.

Brian responded with a smile and said, "I'll take you up on that—especially these meatballs." He turned to Pamela. "Can I get you a second helping of anything?"

"I'm fine." Pamela shook her head, and she and Bettina watched as Brian made his way toward the buffet table.

"So handsome!" Bettina sighed. "He's really a keeper."

Brian did look handsome in slim, dark slacks, a dark turtleneck, and a dark tweedy jacket. As he neared the buffet table, he stopped to talk to Wilfred, who was trading a full platter of meatballs for one with only two remaining.

In the buzz of conversation and with a particularly lively rendition of "Little Drummer Boy" coming from the stereo, it wasn't possible to make out what they were saying, but Pamela suspected Brian was making good on his resolve to ask Wilfred for his meatball recipe.

But her attention was drawn then to Holly Perkins. "Everything is just perfect!" Holly exclaimed with a smile that displayed her perfect teeth and activated her dimple. She had pulled her abundant waves, brunette streaked with violet tonight, into a loose up-do, with face-framing tendrils that enhanced her striking looks. Bold silver earrings that resembled Christmas tree ornaments dangled from her earlobes.

She shifted her bright gaze from Bettina to Pamela. "And what a sweetheart your boyfriend is—and so handsome."

Pamela wasn't sure how much credit she could take for Brian's appearance, so thanks didn't seem in order. Perhaps a smile would do, and the smile she offered in return was genuine, not the social smile she mustered on occasions that demanded smiles, whether heartfelt or not.

"I'm having such a good time that I've almost forgotten about the—" Holly looked around. "You know . . . the sad thing."

Pamela had almost forgotten too. She supposed that was the point of holidays like Christmas. Life was full of sad things, but celebrations provided a distraction that eased the mind.

"The police have solved it, I guess, so hopefully we'll soon hear no more." Holly raised a hand with crossed fingers, displaying a sparkly manicure that echoed the violet streaks in her hair. "But I don't think I'll ever forget that a scarf I knit became a murder weapon." She shivered. "It almost makes me feel like I'm guilty too."

Bettina reached out a comforting hand. "You had no way of knowing what use it would be put to. You're not guilty at all." She shook her head. "And I don't believe Laurel Lewis is guilty either."

"Who did it then?"

"Other people had motives." Bettina smiled a secret smile.

Holly's eyes opened wide and her lips parted as she inhaled deeply. "I did hear something ..." She looked around again. "I know Nell is here and I know how much she disapproves of gossip, but ..." She edged closer to Bettina.

Pamela herself did not like gossip—but in the service of solving a crime? Well, that was something else.

"At the salon," Holly said, "a lot of our customers are from Arborville and of course the murder has been on everybody's mind and we've had quite a rush with people wanting to look nice for all their Christmas activities. Today was just crazy. Anyway"—she paused and looked around—"Carys talked her sister Marlyn into divorcing her husband."

"We heard that too," Bettina said. "And then Marlyn asked him to come back but he wouldn't come back."

"He's back now!" Holly announced, then hastily covered her mouth as if aware that she'd spoken too loud, given the topic.

"Since when?" Pamela whispered. She'd just caught sight of Nell drawing near.

Holly shrugged. "Not sure." The next moment she turned to greet Nell, who had edged between her and Pamela.

Nell's ecological concerns had prevented her from adding to her wardrobe for several decades, but she looked festive in an Indian-inspired tunic fashioned from rose-colored velour. Delicate filigree earrings set with small diamonds complimented her soft white hair.

The topic of conversation shifted instantly, to Bettina and Wilfred's plan to host the Boston children over the long New Year's weekend and Nell and Harold's impending visit from their oldest son and his family.

Pamela smiled and nodded but her thoughts were elsewhere. How long had Marlyn's ex-husband been back in town—and why had he returned?

Suddenly the crowd was in motion, as conversational groupings dissolved and people backed up to create a pathway between the kitchen and the buffet table. Melanie DeCamp picked up an empty tray and headed toward the kitchen doorway, and Marlene Pepper followed with the meatball platter, still bearing one meatball with its toothpick at a rakish angle.

The seductive aroma of brewing coffee began to drift through the doorway.

"It looks like Wilfred has enough help," Bettina observed as Holly and Desmond joined in to help clear the buffet table. Soon poppy-seed cake, cookies, and brownies took their places on the lacy cloth, along with mugs and cups and saucers from Bettina's sage-green pottery set.

"I don't have enough of just the mugs or cups and saucers," Bettina explained, "but at least they're all the same color. And I think Wilfred's washing the little plates so he can put them out again."

As if on cue, Holly stepped through the doorway with a stack of plates, Desmond followed with another, and after a few more trips to supply cream and sugar and napkins, the table was almost ready for people to help themselves. The final touch was Wilfred's arrival bearing a large silvery urn with a spigot on the front.

"Please help yourselves," he urged, "and Nell, I think you're the only tea drinker. A cup of tea is coming right up."

Sipping coffee and handling a plate of goodies at the same time required a place to perch, and several people migrated to the living room after serving themselves at the buffet. Bettina's attention was claimed by Marlene Pepper and one of her friends, who wanted to make sure that the *Advocate* planned to cover an upcoming coat drive sponsored by the women's club. Pamela and Brian found themselves sitting side by side on the bottom step of the stairs that led to the Frasers' second floor.

"I think I should have a party," Brian said. "Wilfred has inspired me." He turned to Pamela. "Would you come?"

"Of course!"

He set his coffee cup down, balanced his plate on his knees, and snuggled an arm around Pamela's shoulders. "Merry Christmas," he whispered.

"Merry Christmas," she responded and turned for a kiss.

Her poppy-seed cake, she was pleased to note, held its own against the other dessert offerings, though the brownies were so intense they were nearly fudge and the cookies were melt-in-the-mouth buttery—and adorable as well. She had chosen a Santa cookie, with white beard, black boots, and a red suit complete with silver buttons.

After a bit, the party began to wind down, and Pamela and Brian had to abandon their perch at the bottom of the stairs as Wilfred and Bettina made trips up and down to fetch coats. Pausing en route to hand an eye-catching fake fur to Holly, Bettina leaned close to Pamela and said, "Don't leave until everybody else is gone." Pamela nodded.

Soon everybody else *was* gone, clusters of people trooping out into the winter darkness as calls of "Thank you" overlapped with "Merry Christmas" in a reverberating chorus.

"So—" Bettina pulled Pamela aside while Wilfred and Brian continued toward the door. "We have to find out how long Marlyn's husband has been back in town."

"We do," Pamela agreed, "and—"

But just then Brian turned and offered his arm. "Shall we be off?" he said as Wilfred swung the door back and a chilly gust of wind entered.

"We'll talk tomorrow," Pamela whispered.

Chapter Eight

The cats were enjoying this interesting variation in the household's morning routine—though they'd suspected that something unusual was afoot several days ago when the cat climber was relocated to accommodate a full-sized spruce tree. Now Precious watched from the top platform of the climber as Catrina and Ginger capered about batting balls of crumpled wrapping paper here and there and leaping for the strands of ribbon that Penny dangled over their heads.

The tree lights made the carefully placed ornaments, with their faded vintage charm, gleam, and from the stereo came the strains of "Silent Night." The Patersons' Christmas rituals included bringing out a collection of holiday LPs that had belonged to Pamela's grandparents.

"Just two presents left," Pamela said. "One for you and one for me."

"You go first." Penny offered a box wrapped in mistletoe-patterned paper to Pamela, who was sitting near her on the carpet.

"Okay," Pamela said, "but here's yours." She handed over a smaller box, wrapped in the same paper. Then she slipped the ribbon from the box Penny had given her and peeled off the wrapping.

"Ohh!" she sighed as she lifted the lid and set it aside. Cushioned on a bed of tissue was a decorative porcelain plate. She picked it up.

"It's your zodiac sign." Penny smiled. "Aquarius, the water-bearer. I found it at my favorite thrift store near the campus. It's Royal Doulton—they probably did one for each of the twelve signs, but it was such a coincidence that the only one the store had was this one."

The design on the plate showed two young girls in Victorian pinafores carrying a large pail, presumably of water, between them. A garland of violets and lily of the valley occupied the space between the central image and the plate's scalloped edge.

"I never paid much attention to astrology," Pamela said, "but I love this plate. Thank you!"

"You're an air sign," Penny said. "Intelligent and independent."

"Well!" Pamela laughed. She nestled the plate back into its bed of tissue. "Now you open yours."

Inside the small box for Penny were the golden earrings Pamela had bought when she and Bettina visited the craft shop in Timberley. Penny slipped off the ribbon and offered it to Ginger, who had been pawing at a low-hanging ornament. She stripped the paper away, opened the box, and removed the square of cotton that hid the contents.

"Beautiful!" she exclaimed, lifting one of the earrings, which dangled from her fingers as if it was a real leaf stirred by a slight breeze.

"They're cast from molds made from actual leaves," Pamela said. "A local craftsperson makes them. I'm not sure what kind of leaves she uses though."

The earring was a long teardrop shape, quite elegant. Penny picked up its mate with her other hand and held both earrings up to her ears. The effect was glamorous despite the fact that the ensemble they accessorized was a fleecy pink robe over flannel pajamas.

"Thank you!" Penny tucked them back into their box and replaced the cotton and the lid. Then she climbed to her feet and added, "There are actually three more presents. But not for us."

She hurried up the stairs and returned with a large ziplock bag. From it she extracted three small parcels swathed in brown paper and loosely tied with string. Even before she stooped to toss the parcels on the floor, all three cats were on high alert—even Precious, who usually affected a blasé attitude toward even the most interesting phenomena.

Catrina immediately pounced on one of the parcels, while Ginger circled the one that landed nearest to her, jabbing it with a paw as her tail twitched spasmodically back and forth. Precious made a flying leap from the top platform of the cat climber and landed on the third parcel.

"I didn't do a very fancy wrapping job," Penny said. She sat down next to Catrina and nudged the string loose from the parcel Catrina had chosen. The brown paper peeled away to reveal a not-very-realistic mouse sewn from blue-checked fabric. The tail was a length of blue yarn.

"Catnip," Penny explained, though she didn't have to. The cats were occasionally treated to catnip, and each time the spectacle was the same: ecstatic writhing, belly up, as paws juggled the catnip-containing object, rubbing it against cheeks and throat and chest as tongues flicked out for a lick whenever it neared the mouth.

Catrina seized the mouse and carried it into the dining room, perhaps aware of how undignified her actions were but unable to help herself. Ginger had no such compunctions. She fell on her mouse once it was unwrapped, gripped it with all four paws, and rolled onto her back, bending her head forward to rub her nose against it. Precious was more refined, but even she seemed transported by her gift, cuddling it as small squeaks emerged from her throat.

Leaving the cats to enjoy their catnip, Pamela and Penny went upstairs to get dressed.

Pamela was eager to confer with Bettina about the interesting new development Holly had revealed—the reappearance of Marlyn's ex-husband—and she suspected Bettina was eager to discuss it too. That evening's dinner would be a festive occasion, hardly an appropriate setting for sleuthing. Besides, Penny would be there, and Pamela and Bettina had insisted to Penny that they considered Carys's murder an issue best left to the police.

Dressed and back downstairs, Pamela busied herself in the kitchen for a few minutes, until she heard Penny's feet descending the stairs. She lacked Bettina's acting skills, to the point that even telling a lie was difficult for her. But the ruse she devised was simple. She opened the refrigerator and took out butter. Then she rearranged a few items, while making as much noise as she could, and closed the refrigerator door with a thud. Leaving the butter out to soften, she stepped through the entry to speak to Penny, who was sitting on the sofa watching the cats as they slept off their ecstasies.

"I need an extra egg," she said. "I have four for the cake, but I forgot that the filling needs an egg white."

Penny looked up, mildly interested.

"So I'm going to run over to Bettina's for a minute."

"Sure." Penny went back to watching the cats.

The Frasers' living room was in the same state as Pamela's, with crumpled wrapping paper and tangles of ribbon strewn over the carpet. Punkin the cat was playing with a plush ball weighted in such a way that it rolled in unexpected directions, batting it here and there under and around the tree.

Bettina was dressed for the morning in dark green leggings and a tunic-length red sweater whose front featured an elaborate Christmas tree decorated with multicolored spangles.

"So"—she led Pamela to the sofa—"what do you think about this returning husband story?"

"Whether he could be the one who killed Carys?"

Bettina nodded.

"Carys was killed last Monday night," Pamela said. "We talked to Marlyn on Thursday and again yesterday morning. Wouldn't she have mentioned that he was back?"

"I'd think so." Bettina nodded again. "He must have shown up in Arborville yesterday after we collected the trunk. News certainly travels fast through the gossip grapevine."

"What if he came back sooner though . . ." Pamela paused, distracted. Woofus the shelter dog had peeked around the corner from the dining room and then retreated.

"He's nervous." Bettina's brightly painted lips formed a sympathetic smile. "The party last night unsettled him, so it's probably for the best that the Arborville grandchildren are with their other grandparents today, though I do miss them." She shifted her gaze to Pamela. "Anyway, you were saying . . . ?"

"Suppose Marlyn's ex-husband had decided he wanted to reconcile but feared it would be impossible unless he removed the ongoing negative influence of Carys. So he came back unannounced, stayed at a hotel somewhere, stalked Carys for a bit, and killed her Monday night."

Bettina clapped her hands. "That works—and Carys was wearing the murder weapon."

Pamela nodded. "So, Marlyn's ex-husband strangles Carys and then waits several days to contact Marlyn in order not to pounce right after she has the trauma of losing her sister—"

"Though she didn't seem very sad about Carys's death," Bettina interjected.

"—and he shows up yesterday like he just flew in from wherever he'd been sailing—surely not near here in this weather."

"That all really makes sense," Bettina said. "And I'm glad because there's no other suspect. We've eliminated Marlyn because she has an alibi, and we're convinced—or at least I am—that Laurel isn't the kind of person who'd kill someone, writers' group notwithstanding."

Pamela nodded and stood up. "Penny's going to be wondering where I am . . . and"—she raised a hand with her index finger extended—"I almost forgot. I need to take back an egg, for the cake tonight."

"Ok-a-ay . . ." Bettina drew out the word and added a puzzled smile.

"That was my excuse to Penny to run over here," Pamela explained.

"And she believed you?" Bettina laughed. "Doesn't she know you're too organized to run out of ingredients?" Bettina turned toward the arch that led to the dining room and the kitchen beyond. "I'll be right back."

"Just one thing about our theory," Bettina said after she had handed over the egg. "It's all based on something Holly thinks she overheard at the hair salon. We don't know for sure that the ex-husband is really back." She continued on toward the door, twisted the knob, and pulled the door open. But before Pamela could step through it, she spoke again.

"Does the dessert you're making involve chocolate?" she inquired, joining her hands in a prayer-like gesture.

"Wait and see," Pamela responded. "Wait and see."

Back at home, Pamela returned to the kitchen, where she set about making the dessert that would complement the Frasers' Christmas menu. First she grated all the rind off an orange and juiced the orange. Then she mixed flour, cornstarch, salt, and baking powder in a small bowl and set the bowl aside. She creamed butter and sugar together and added egg yolks, orange rind, and orange juice. The dry ingredients were combined with the moist ingredients, and beaten egg whites were folded in. Soon the cake—for it was to be a cake—went into the oven and Pamela returned to the living room to knit and enjoy the tree and the Christmas music.

The dessert did involve chocolate, a rich chocolate buttercream frosting—and the filling to be spread between the layers did require an egg white, though it was primarily composed of powdered sugar and whipped cream. When the cake had finished baking and the layers had cooled, Pamela resumed her kitchen duties, making and applying frosting and filling. With plenty of time to spare, the cake was ready to be carried across the street.

Chapter Nine

Pamela carried the cake and Penny carried a tote bag containing the gifts for the Frasers. Stepping carefully, because unexpected patches of ice lurked after days of melting and nights of refreezing, they made their way across the street. Bettina greeted them at the door and ushered them into a living room fragrant with the aroma of roasting ham, accented with a spicy hint of Christmas pine. As Penny set the tote bag with the gifts under the tree, Pamela handed the platter containing the cake to Bettina and was rewarded with a happy sigh and the murmured word, *chocolate*. Both Pamela and Penny slipped off their coats.

Though the occasion was a small—very small—dinner party involving only comfortable old friends, Penny had pulled from her closet a glamorous dress she'd found on a thrifting expedition the previous summer. Fashioned from dark blue lace, it featured long sleeves and a neckline that skimmed the collarbone in front but swooped to a surprisingly deep V in back. And she had pinned up her dark curls to better display the dangling gold earrings that Pamela had given her that morning.

"Well, Miss Penny!" Bettina exclaimed. "Aren't you the fashionista! So glamorous! And Pamela—the red tunic sweater. I do enjoy seeing you in that. You've certainly gotten a lot of use out of it."

Pamela smiled. So she wasn't a clothes horse. The tunic was perfectly serviceable and quite festive.

"Too bad it's only us old folks tonight," Bettina went on, talking to Penny again. "No handsome young men for you to charm."

Penny laughed and, thankfully, seemed unembarrassed. Bettina was right though, about Penny looking glamorous. Surely there was a boyfriend up there in Boston—or home now, wherever he lived, for the holidays. Penny hadn't said anything . . . but hadn't Pamela just explained to Bettina the other day that introducing a romantic interest to one's parents was a significant step, a step that meant something serious was going on? And she wasn't ready for that for Penny . . . yet.

"I'll just take this divine-looking cake to the kitchen," Bettina said, "and you two come right along. We're going to have champagne."

Bettina herself was looking quite the fashionista in a red and green print wrap dress that hugged her waist and hips, green suede pumps, and a necklace and earrings of glittery green stones.

Wilfred was bent over the counter in the cooking area of the kitchen when they entered, but he straightened up and swiveled around to greet them with a hearty "Merry Christmas!" Lined up on the high counter were four champagne flutes and a pewter ice bucket from which protruded the telltale wire-bound cork of a champagne bottle. Next to the ice bucket was a small wooden dish of mixed nuts.

"I'll do the honors," he added. Facing them over the counter, he plucked the champagne bottle from the ice bucket, swathed it in a dish towel, and removed the wire cage that confined the cork. Careful to tilt the bottle so the cork wouldn't find a human target, he twisted. The cork came free with a satisfying pop and a puff of vapor, and he quickly tipped the bottle over one of the champagne flutes.

Bettina had set the cake, in all its chocolaty glory, on the high counter. She gestured toward the nut dish.

"I didn't think we needed much to nibble on," she said, "because Wilfred has such a fancy meal in store for us. But please help yourselves."

Meanwhile Wilfred was handing around champagne, to Pamela first and then Penny and then Bettina, and finally pouring a glass for himself.

"To the season!" he proclaimed, holding his champagne aloft. The delicate glass caught the light. Strands of bubbles like tiny beads rose through the pale liquid and vanished when they reached the surface.

"To the season," Pamela responded and took a nose-tickling sip.

They remained standing at the counter, sipping and chatting, with Wilfred chiming in as he worked, washing spinach, mashing potatoes, and slicing radishes and fennel. After a bit, the rest of the champagne was divided among the flutes to provide a few last swallows.

"I think we are just about ready," Wilfred announced as he straightened up from checking the contents of the oven. The oven door had been open for only the tiniest moment, but the aroma that wafted forth had given an intense preview of the honey-glazed ham—caramelized sweetness with a hint of smoke layered over the rich char of roasting pork.

"We're starting with soup," Bettina said. "You two go ahead and I'll bring bowls. And Pamela, please light the candles. The wine is already open—it's breathing."

Bettina's holiday table was set with a deep burgundy

cloth, burgundy napkins, and her sage-green plates. Sleek wineglasses of Swedish crystal awaited the bottle of pinot noir at the ready in a pewter wine coaster. The candle-holders were pewter as well, simple and modern in shape. A small flower arrangement in the middle of the table was composed of miniature white poinsettias.

After Pamela lit the candles, she and Penny took their usual seats on either side of the table. The head was reserved for Wilfred, with Bettina facing him at the other end.

"And . . . here we come," Bettina sang from the kitchen doorway. She entered carrying a bowl in each hand, and Wilfred followed, bearing two bowls as well.

"It's cream of pumpkin," Bettina explained as she set a shallow bowl in front of Pamela. The color and texture of the contents evoked melted orange sherbet, but the aroma promised a hearty flavor and hinted at an unidentifiable spice. As if reading Pamela's mind, Bettina added, "There's coriander in it."

Once all four bowls had been delivered and everyone was seated, Wilfred raised his soup spoon, and with a jovial "Bon appétit!" invited the others to join him in sampling his creation.

The soup was rich and mouth-filling, smooth but with a fragrant spiciness that enlivened the blandness of the pumpkin. No one spoke for a few minutes, content with wordless hums of pleasure.

"Very, very successful," Bettina pronounced at last, as her spoon pursued the last few driblets of soup around the bottom of her bowl.

"Yes, very!" Pamela's and Penny's voices overlapped.

Bettina and Wilfred whisked the empty bowls away, and Bettina took her seat again. When Wilfred returned, he was carrying a platter. The platter was large, but barely large enough for its contents—a plump and splendid ham, its glistening rind seared a deep golden brown and its spiral-cut surface a rosy pink. With a satisfied sigh, he lowered the platter to the table and set off for the kitchen once again.

"Let me help!" Penny started to rise.

Pamela, who was closer to the kitchen, jumped to her feet, saying, "Yes, please let us do something."

"It's all taken care of." Wilfred paused en route and waved them back into their chairs.

"He loves doing this," Bettina whispered. "It's like a performance for him."

Subsequent trips brought a pillowy drift of mashed potatoes in an oval bowl, accompanied by a large pat of butter on a small plate, and a dish of creamed spinach. After a happy bustle of passing plates to receive slices of ham, people helped themselves to mashed potatoes, butter to melt in golden pools atop the potatoes, and spinach. Wilfred's repeated "Bon appétit!" was the signal to lift knives and forks.

First there was silence, but for the click of utensils against pottery. Then Bettina led the way with a contented purr and a blissful expression involving closed eyes and a closed-mouthed smile. Pamela and Penny added their own appreciative sounds.

When Bettina spoke, it was to say, "You've outdone yourself!"

"Dear wife, dear friends—it was my pleasure." Wilfred's beaming countenance attested to his sincerity.

The conversation then progressed from the success of the meal to more tangential matters: the model fort Wilfred had built in his basement workshop as a Christmas gift for Wilfred Jr.'s sons, and the challenge of finding appropriate gifts for the Boston grand*child*. ("We're forbidden to refer to her as a *girl*," Bettina reminded them.)

"I could build something," Wilfred suggested. "Not a dollhouse, but maybe a puppet theater."

"When she gets a little older." Bettina nodded. Morgan Fraser had just turned two.

"Books?" Penny suggested.

"Oh, books. Yes." Bettina nodded again. "Suitable books, not girly books. No sleeping princesses roused by handsome princes. Greta made that clear."

Bettina looked so downcast that Pamela leapt in to change the subject. "I was so happy to hear that Maxie liked the trunk," she exclaimed.

"Some people appreciate pretty things," Bettina responded, still glum.

"How about second helpings!" Wilfred took his turn at cheering Bettina up. "Or shall I serve the salad?"

In the end it was agreed that justice had been done to the ham and its accompaniments, particularly given that fennel salad was waiting in the wings, to be followed by Pamela's cake.

The fennel salad, prettily arranged on individual plates, was a refreshing contrast to the rich dishes that had come before. Wilfred had cut the fennel bulbs vertically to create slices that resembled small hands with delicate pale green fingers. He had added thin rounds of radish, white but rimmed with bright red skin. He had garnished the fennel and radishes with sugared walnuts and fresh-grated Parmesan and finished each salad with olive oil and balsamic vinegar.

"Coffee and cake in the living room?" Bettina inquired after setting down her fork with a pleased sigh.

"I'll serve it." Pamela rose, and the small group followed her into the kitchen, each person carrying a salad plate.

Salad plates were stacked on the counter near the sink

and fresh plates were produced for the cake. Wilfred set water boiling for coffee while Bettina arranged a paper filter in the filter cone of her carafe and spooned in a goodly portion of the Guatemalan coffee she favored. Provided with a suitable knife, Pamela cut a careful slice of cake and transferred it to a plate.

She was delighted to see that the effect was just what she had hoped. The cake itself, flavored with the fresh orange juice and grated rind, was a delicate pale orange color, fine textured and moist. The chocolate buttercream frosting cut smoothly without sticking to the knife, and the deep chocolaty color contrasted nicely with the cake itself. The extra touch was the filling between the layers— not more chocolate, but a pale and fluffy vanilla cream.

Chapter Ten

Settled around the coffee table some minutes later, with cake and fragrant cups of coffee before them, Christmas carols coming from the stereo, and the Christmas tree lights lending a warm glow to the far corner of the room, the Frasers and the Patersons smiled at one another in contentment.

Bettina was the first to taste the cake and comment, observing that the cake was perfect and the combination of chocolate and oranges seemed to fit the season.

"It does," Wilfred said. "Oranges were a special Christmas treat up here when I was very young. My grandfather had retired to Florida and shipped us a big box of them every December."

Penny, however, had ceased to smile. "I know about the egg, Mom," she exclaimed suddenly. "I forgot, until we started eating the cake."

Momentarily puzzled, Pamela wrinkled her nose. "What egg?" she inquired.

"The egg you claimed you had to borrow from Bettina because you were all out. When I opened the refrigerator later I saw half a dozen of them." Penny shifted her gaze from Pamela to Bettina and back to Pamela. Her youthful glow made her attempted sternness more comical than fearsome.

Pamela gazed back, unsure what to say, so Penny continued.

"You two are up to something and that's why you're sneaking around."

"She's turning into a detective." Bettina laughed delightedly.

"It's not funny!" Penny returned her fork to her plate with a *clunk*. "It's dangerous."

Sensing that a change of subject was in order, Wilfred turned to Pamela. "As one cook to another," he said, "your cake is a masterpiece. Tell me about the filling."

Pamela was happy for the excuse to avoid Penny's intense gaze. She turned to Wilfred and described the simple recipe behind the vanilla cream. Meanwhile Bettina deployed her charm and soon had Penny talking happily about her plans for the rest of her break from school.

The time passed pleasantly enough then, until the plates were empty but for golden crumbs and traces of chocolate, and the cups contained only dregs of coffee.

"I think there might be a few gifts left under the tree," Wilfred said with a teasing smile. He rose and started gathering the plates, silverware, and cups and saucers. Pamela joined him and this time he didn't urge her back into her seat.

"I know you and Bettina don't accept Clayborn's conclusion that Laurel Lewis killed Carys Walnutt," he whispered after they were safely out of earshot.

"Bettina's concerned." Pamela set cups and saucers on the counter near the sink. "She really likes Laurel and can't believe she'd do something like that."

"Perhaps she didn't." Wilfred added plates and two more cups and saucers. "But who did?"

Pamela resisted the temptation to explain the role Carys had in the breakup of Marlyn's marriage and why it was interesting that the ex-husband was back in Arborville. It was Christmas and there were gifts to be opened.

Pamela and Wilfred returned to the living room to find an array of colorfully wrapped boxes waiting on the coffee table.

"For you"—Penny offered Wilfred a rectangular box whose paper featured leaping reindeer—"and you." The box for Bettina was similar in shape and size but the wrapping featured holly with bright berries.

"From the gift shop at Paul Revere's house," Penny explained as Wilfred peeled away ribbon and paper to reveal a book about Paul Revere. "I know how much you like history."

"I do." Wilfred nodded.

Bettina meanwhile was oohing and aahing over a box of note cards decorated with eighteenth-century illustrations of flowers. "The Gardner museum has a gift shop too," Penny said with a pleased smile.

The gifts from Pamela were greeted with equal enthusiasm—carved wood items from a craft show *Fiber Craft* had been involved in: a wooden paperweight depicting a robin for Wilfred and a wooden bowl in the shape of a heart for Bettina.

"And now you two have to open yours." Bettina leaned forward, picked up a large rectangular box, and handed it to Penny. Wilfred handed a similar box to Pamela.

Once the paper—chorusing angels in improbable bright pink ensembles—had been removed, it was clear from the boxes that both gifts had come from the fanciest store at the mall. Inside Penny's box was a silky robe in shades of indigo and ruby.

"Beautiful," Penny sighed. "Too beautiful to even wear."

"But I hope you *will* wear it," Bettina said, "and for many years. I still have the robe I bought for my honeymoon."

"Thank you." Penny folded the robe back up and laid it reverently in its box. "And I'll always remember who gave it to me."

"And you, Miss Pamela"—Bettina's lips curved up in a teasing half smile—"I hope you'll wear your gift—though I do like the red tunic sweater."

Pamela folded tissue paper back to reveal . . . *something* . . . made of black and silver brocade. She lifted the *something* from the box and saw that it was a jacket, a short jacket, not too fitted, with large silver buttons that buttoned up the front to a chic cowl-shaped collar.

"It's your new holiday party top," Bettina said, smiling. "Just in time for New Year's Eve with your handsome boyfriend."

"Oh, Bettina . . ." Pamela sighed. "You are really hopeless." As Bettina's smile began to falter, she added, "But the jacket is gorgeous, and I love you—and Wilfred—for giving it to me, and I'll wear it on New Year's Eve, I promise."

"Try it on," Bettina urged, leaning forward. "And take the tunic off first so you don't have six inches of red sweater sticking out down below."

Pamela stood up holding the jacket and ducked into the dining room. A few moments later, she returned wearing the jacket. Bettina jumped up and joined her.

"It's fine with the black pants you have on," she said, after leaning close to adjust the collar.

"Thank you!" Pamela hugged her, holding on a bit longer than she usually did and bending toward Bettina's ear. "Fran would know if Marlyn's husband is really back," she whispered. "We have to talk to her tomorrow. I'll call you in the morning."

Chapter Eleven

Pamela's boss seemed never to rest. Apparently she had been hard at work over the holiday weekend, because on Monday morning an email from Celine Bramley popped into Pamela's inbox the moment she roused her computer to life. The stylized paperclip opposite the sender's name suggested that the email brought work, in the form of attachments.

Celine Bramley's email messages usually consisted of terse instructions to evaluate or copyedit and return by such and such a deadline. This morning's message was longer.

The ideas in "Spy-Craft: The Knitting Spies of World War II" are clumsily expressed, Pamela's boss had written, **and I don't think any publication at all would want it in its current form. But a summer issue with a patriotic theme is taking shape and "Spy-Craft" would fit in so nicely. Please do what you can to make it readable. I'm attaching two other articles to be copyedited for the same issue. Summer is a ways away but you might as well do this work now (and return it by the end of the week) because next week I'm sending you two books to review.**

Pamela groaned. The thought of once again wading through the murky prose of "Spy-Craft" did not appeal, especially this early in the morning. She closed her email, swiveled her chair around, and picked up the phone.

"Is this a good time?" she asked when Bettina answered.

"I can't wait," Bettina said.

"I'll tell Penny I'm going for a walk. Meet me at the corner in your car. She might be watching to see if I'm telling the truth."

Downstairs, Pamela stepped over Catrina, who was napping in the sunny spot on the entry carpet, and took her down coat from the closet. Peeking through the kitchen doorway, she greeted Penny, still in pajamas and robe and lingering over the *Register*.

"I'm running out to the Co-Op for butter," she said.

Penny looked up, her lips shaping a suspicious zigzag. "We have butter," she observed, "lots of butter."

"It's for poppy-seed cake." Pamela smiled. "I want to serve it to Knit and Nibble tomorrow night and send a loaf back to Boston with you."

"Whatever." Penny raised her eyebrows, shrugged and returned to the *Register*, clearly not convinced of the errand's legitimacy.

Bettina's faithful Toyota slowed down and pulled over as Pamela neared the corner. She climbed in, Bettina made the turn onto Arborville Avenue, and they were on their way.

The journey took less than ten minutes, and soon Bettina had parked in front of St. Willibrod's and they had climbed out of the car. As they paused at the curb waiting for a break in the traffic, they were startled by the reverberating bongs of the church chimes.

"Those certainly are loud when you're hearing them up close," Bettina commented, raising her gloved hands to her ears. The purple leather gloves and olive-green beret joined the pumpkin-colored coat to create a colorful contrast to the week-old snow on the church lawn behind them.

Pamela was listening to the chimes too, absentmindedly counting the bongs. Eleven—but it was only ten a.m. The chimes were off by an hour though. Wilfred Jr. had pointed that out on Saturday when they picked up the trunk.

But if they were off by an hour, it meant that Marlyn's alibi, based on Fran's statement that she heard the chimes . . . might not be an alibi after all.

Bettina had stepped away from the curb and was waiting for one last car to pass before launching herself across the street.

"Bettina!" Pamela shouted, reaching out to grab her friend's arm.

Bettina spun around, her eyes and mouth wide. "What? What is it?"

"The chimes! They're not . . ." Pamela took a deep breath. "We have to ask Fran how long Marlyn was actually shoveling snow on the night Carys was killed."

As they crossed the street, Pamela explained what she'd just realized about the chimes and Marlyn's alibi. "That's the main thing," she said. "If Marlyn has no alibi then the husband might be irrelevant."

Bettina took the lead when they reached Fran's doorstep, raising a purple-gloved hand to push the bell. Fran answered her door in bathrobe and slippers, carrying a cup of coffee, her gray curls still in disarray from sleep.

"Good morning, ladies," she said, puzzled but cordial.

"We're so sorry to bother you . . ." Bettina smiled an apologetic smile. "But we were . . . we were . . ."

We were what? Pamela felt herself wince as Fran's expression became more puzzled. What would she herself think if two people she barely knew showed up at her door while she was still in her robe and slippers?

Bettina pushed her coat sleeve up and the cuff of her glove down to expose her watch. "Oh, good!" she exclaimed. "It really is only ten. The chimes . . ."

Fran laughed and slapped her thigh. "Oh, the chimes! That happens every year. They're off by an hour, still on daylight savings time. They're not real, you know—just a recording on a timer, and the church secretary forgets to reset them. It used to drive Carys crazy."

The front door of the neighboring apartment, Marlyn's apartment, opened and Marlyn stepped out to scoop up the *Register*, snug in its plastic wrapper. Fran edged over her own threshold to greet her neighbor.

"And how are you, my dear?" she inquired with a suggestive laugh. "Busy night?"

"None of your business," Marlyn replied, but her tone was light and a giggle accompanied her words. She backed up and closed the door behind her.

"*She* had a nice Christmas present." Fran's eyes crinkled with delight and her smile brought a flush to her pleasant features. "Hubby is back!"

"He is?" Pamela and Bettina spoke in unison.

"Yup!" Fran nodded. "All is forgiven. He flew in from Bermuda. Showed up around noon on Saturday, came straight from the airport, unannounced, in an Uber. But Marlyn was thrilled."

"What good news!" Bettina clapped her hands. "She's such a lovely person."

"Lovely!" Fran nodded again. "I'll miss her as a neighbor—I suppose they'll want a house like they had before. But I'm very happy for her." She paused, then focused her gaze on Bettina. "Now what was it you wanted to ask me?"

"Ask you . . ." Bettina studied her bootie-clad feet for a

moment. "Oh, yes. Have you been getting the *Advocate* regularly? Sometimes our delivery people aren't as conscientious as they should be."

"I guess Laurel really did it." They had been silent on the drive along Arborville Avenue, but after she made the turn onto Orchard Street, Bettina spoke.

"I guess so," Pamela agreed.

Penny was gone when Pamela got home—and a good thing too, she realized, because she had forgotten that her purported errand involved butter. A note on the kitchen table advised that Penny was at her friend Lorie's and they would probably take the bus into the city.

Pamela climbed the stairs to her office, settled into her desk chair, let her mouse explore its mouse pad until her monitor woke from its nap, and opened the files attached to the email from her boss. The two articles that had accompanied "Spy-Craft" looked fascinating, and she was tempted to tackle them first.

One—"Old Glory, Glorious Again"—was about the challenges of restoring antique flags, and the other— "From Germany, with Love"—was about American soldiers sending salvaged German parachutes made of silk home to their girlfriends for sewing projects when silk was at a premium during World War II. But there was no way of knowing how long it would take to wrestle "Spy-Craft" into readable form, so she resolved to tackle that annoying project first.

She changed "splinting hairs" to "splitting hairs" and "viscous rumors" to "vicious rumors." In the next paragraph, she made danger rear its ugly head rather than its ugly visage and sighed over "While seemingly enjoying the view from an upstairs window, the knitting needles were in fact recording vital intelligence to be passed on to the Resistance."

"Knitting needles cannot enjoy a view," she muttered to herself as she inserted "the women wielding" after the comma.

But a phrase she came upon further down the page, "a case of mistaken indemnity," elicited more than a sigh and a mutter.

"A case of mistaken indemnity." She said it aloud once to herself, and then she repeated it to Ginger, who had looked up from her nap on the floor near the radiator. "A case of mistaken identity—of course. *Of course!*"

But instead of making that correction in the manuscript, Pamela swiveled her chair around, jumped up, and ran for the stairs. In the entry, she grabbed her coat, her purse, and her keys. Normally she'd walk such a short distance, but there was no time to waste.

Five minutes later she pulled into the library parking lot and scanned the spaces that faced the wide field. Yes, there was a spot, a designated spot, but it was empty at the moment—curiously, considering the holiday weekend was over.

She circled around to the lot's exit and set off for Laurel Lewis's townhouse near Arborville's border with Meadowside.

Thankfully, traffic was light on Arborville Avenue, and Pamela had no trouble finding a visitor spot in the parking area. She hurried along the sidewalk past the first cluster of townhouses, and the second, until she recognized Laurel's unit by the attractive balsam and berry wreath on the front door.

She wasn't sure whether her shortness of breath and thumping heart were due to her rapid pace or apprehension about what she might soon encounter, but she tried to ignore them as she bounded up the few steps that led to the door. She inhaled deeply and aimed a finger at the doorbell. From within came a faint echo-y chime but no sound of feet hastening to respond.

She rang again. An echo-y chime, then silence, but only for an instant. Now a voice squealed, "Help!"

Pamela reached for the doorknob and gave it an experimental twist. It turned easily with a faint click as the latch retracted. She pushed the door open cautiously and only a few inches, and peeked through the crack between door and doorframe.

She was looking at a man's back, a bulky man with rusty-red hair, leaning over a partially obscured figure sitting in Laurel Lewis's peach-colored armchair. The man's hands were not visible, but just past his right shoulder a woman's hand flailed hopelessly in the air. A woman's slipper-clad foot was splayed out near his knees.

"Help!" the woman was squealing. The voice was that of Laurel Lewis.

Pamela pushed the door open farther and stepped cautiously inside. The man was so intent on his task that he didn't realize he and Laurel were no longer alone.

Now Pamela became aware of another sound, a muted but urgent meowing sound coming from behind a closed door off to the left. She edged closer to the door, keeping her eyes on the bulky man. When she was within a few feet of that door, she reached over, twisted the doorknob, and gave the door a shove.

With an octave-scaling yowl more suited to a creature ten times its size, a calico cat sprang through the open door. It bounded toward the man and seemed to levitate, straddling his broad back. It then clambered onto the top of his head where the orange patches in its calico coat nearly matched the tones of the man's hair.

Hissing ferociously, it began to swat the man's left ear. He raised a hand in a vain attempt to fend off the attack.

Two more calico cats had slipped through the open door. At first merely curious, they soon joined in the assault. The smaller one dove for the man's left ankle, while the other scaled his right pants leg and leapt onto his shoulder. Crouching and snarling, it raised a paw to rake his cheek with unsheathed claws.

The man raised his right hand in an attempt to dislodge the cat, but it sank its teeth into his thumb. Cursing and muttering, he reeled backward with the smaller cat clinging to his ankle and the cat that had arrived first still perched on his head.

Once he was out of the way, Pamela got a clearer look at the peach armchair and its occupant, Laurel Lewis. She was staring straight ahead, her dark hair framing a face devoid of color but for her startling blue eyes. A strip of pale green cloth that looked like the belt of her robe was draped loosely around her neck.

"Mort Quigley," she mumbled, hardly moving her lips. "He tried to strangle me. But why?"

Pamela jumped out of the way as Mort Quigley careened across the carpet toward the sofa and the lamp table at its end. The table teetered as he grazed it, and the lamp tipped toward him, landing on his chest and scattering the cats. Except for the man sprawled on the carpet and the displaced lamp, the charming room looked just as it had the day Pamela and Bettina visited. The fourth cat, the white Persian, had even joined the calicos, which were now clustered around Laurel's feet.

Pamela had fumbled her phone out of her purse as soon as it became clear that Mort Quigley was no match for three cats bent on protecting their mistress. She touched the numerals that would summon the police, spoke into the phone, and then stepped quickly toward the peach armchair.

"Pamela," Laurel murmured in a quivering voice, "what a miracle that you arrived when you did." Pamela knelt at her side and took her hand.

Mort Quigley groaned and attempted to rise, but an irritated snarl from one of the calicos made him think better of the idea.

Pamela had not realized she was hungry, but by the time the police had come and gone, and Laurel had assured her she would be fine on her own, it was approaching two p.m. Now she was sitting at the scrubbed pine table in Bettina's comfortable kitchen, eating a bowl of Wilfred's five-alarm chili.

Bettina was sitting opposite her, watching closely for a sign that Pamela was ready to describe in more detail the adventure she had sketched out in a few breathless sentences when Bettina, surprised at the unexpected visit, greeted her at the door.

Intuiting her friend's curiosity, Pamela set down her spoon. "Mistaken identity," she said. "I was editing an article for the magazine and the author had written 'mistaken indemnity' but she really meant 'mistaken identity.' I realized that mistaken identity was the key to Carys's murder." She looked away from Bettina and focused on nothing in particular for a moment. "Though I suppose killing the wrong person could be sort of mistaken indemnity too."

"What?" Bettina pulled back with a puzzled frown.

"Mort Quigley really wanted to kill Laurel. He thought the person wearing the aqua scarf with the white snowflakes was Laurel because according to the bid sheet Laurel had the winning bid at the silent auction. He knew she was S. Claws because he'd seen her filling in her bid."

Bettina nodded. "But the person wearing the scarf was really Carys, because she claimed the scarf despite not having the winning bid."

"Right." Pamela nodded back. "And Carys was tall and so is Laurel, and with people bundled up and snow falling, one tall woman could look just like another."

"So far, so good," Bettina said. "I get the mistaken identity thing, but how did you figure out the killer was actually Mort Quigley?"

"Laurel told us that when she found the body in the passageway, she stumbled out to the parking lot and called to Mort Quigley, who was walking to his car. She didn't recognize him at first because he was facing the other way, but then he turned around." Pamela paused for breath. "Mort Quigley has his own special parking space, with a sign reserving it for him. If he had really been on his way to his car from the library entrance, he would have been facing the passageway. He had actually just strangled Carys and was walking away from the crime scene."

"Oh, my!" Bettina looked impressed. "That's very clever."

"There's more." Pamela raised her index finger. "Laurel said when he turned around he was shocked, as shocked as she was. But if he had nothing to do with the murder he wouldn't yet have had a reason to be shocked—he didn't know why she was calling to him." She shook the finger rhythmically to emphasize her point. "Since he was in fact the murderer and thought he had strangled Laurel, he was shocked to see her still alive."

"One more question." Bettina responded with a lifted finger of her own. "Why on earth did Mort Quigley want to kill Laurel?"

"He'd been embezzling from the library and that's why there was a shortfall," Pamela said.

"There was a shortfall? How did you know that?"

"Everybody knew," Pamela said, trying not to sound superior. "Nell even mentioned it at our last Knit and Nibble meeting."

"I must have been concentrating on my knitting." Bettina shrugged.

"Laurel was auditing the library's books. Remember—she told us that when we visited her. She was bound to realize something wasn't on the up-and-up, and she said she was planning to finish her work over the Christmas weekend. So I knew Mort Quigley would have to act fast if he was going to prevent his secret from coming out."

They were both startled by applause coming from the dining room. Then Wilfred stepped through the kitchen doorway, followed by Woofus.

"Back from our walk," Wilfred said, "just in time to learn that Mort Quigley is actually the killer. I presume he's in the hands of the police?"

"Definitely." Pamela smiled. "And Laurel is innocent, safe with her cats, which are hero cats—though that's another story."

Chapter Twelve

Speaking to Marcy Brewer, as well as a young woman from the local TV station, had been unavoidable. But at least they had left in time for Pamela to fit in a quick walk to the Co-Op for butter before it got too dark. Penny returned from her trip to the city, and over a dinner of ham and other Christmas leftovers, courtesy of Wilfred, Pamela mentioned offhandedly that the police had arrested Mort Quigley for the murder of Carys Walnutt.

Penny set down her fork, raised her brows, and stared silently at her mother. "And you didn't have anything to do with it?" she inquired after a while.

"The strangest thing." Pamela shrugged. "I happened to drop by Laurel Lewis's place right at the moment Mort Quigley was trying to strangle her. I called the police of course . . ."

Penny continued to stare. After a longer while, she said, "*Mo-om!* Honestly, sometimes I don't know whether to laugh or to cry." At that she returned to her meal.

Now it was Tuesday evening and Roland DeCamp was just stepping over Pamela's threshold. Behind him, Karen, Holly, and Nell were hurrying through the light snow that had begun to fall only a short time before. Pamela greeted

Roland and held the door open wide to welcome the remaining members of Knit and Nibble—Bettina had arrived early to lend a hand with preparations for the evening.

A fresh loaf of poppy-seed cake waited on the dining room table, along with cups and saucers and plates and napkins and silverware, all ready for the moment when Roland would consult his impressive watch and announce that break time had arrived.

"The snow is very welcome," Nell commented as she removed her ancient gray wool coat. "Last week's snowfall had gotten so dirty. Now everything will look fresh and white again."

Pamela reached for the coat, but Nell held on to it for a moment. "I hope you're all right," she said, staring into Pamela's eyes as intently as if eyes truly were the windows of the soul. "You put yourself in a lot of danger yesterday."

"I had no idea Laurel wasn't alone." Pamela tried to smile offhandedly, but Nell could be hard to fool.

"We'll talk no more about it," Nell declared and relinquished the coat. She turned to Holly and Karen, who were lingering in the entry as they too slipped off their coats. "And that goes for both of you," she said. "Our little town's Christmas has been shadowed by a tragic event, not to mention what poor Laurel Lewis has been through, but now it's over."

"And we'll have a slushy mess, as always." Roland, en route to the living room, briefcase in hand, had apparently missed the quick exchange that took place after Nell's comment about the snow.

Bettina had already settled onto the sofa, and she beckoned Holly and Karen to join her there. Once they were seated, she presented Karen with the doll in the puffed-sleeve dress from the shop in Timberley.

"For your sweet little Lily," she explained, and Pamela held her breath waiting for Bettina to add that she was forbidden to buy such things for her own granddaughter.

But Bettina seemed happy just listening to Karen and Holly enthuse over the doll's embroidered face and yarn hair and general all-round cuteness. Pamela exhaled and steered Nell toward the comfortable armchair near the fireplace, Roland found a spot on the hassock at the other end of the hearth, and Pamela herself perched on the rummage-sale chair with the carved wooden back and needlepoint seat.

The opening of knitting bags and extracting of skeins and needles and pattern books was accompanied by a cheerful exchange of news about gifts given and received, and feasts prepared and eaten. Once it was clear that Christmas Day had lived up to everyone's expectations—and there was still the New Year's weekend to look forward to!—people turned their attention to their projects and the room fell silent.

Pamela resumed work on her in-progress sweater, happy that, with the ribbing completed, the part she was working on now required no counting or even thinking. The sweater's front, with the large cat worked in black against the tawny brown, would be much more challenging.

Lined up along the sofa, Karen, Holly, and Bettina were intent on their projects. Karen had started a new section of the pale pink cardigan for Lily, and Holly's lap was nearly covered with a swath of knitting that resembled a furry magenta pelt. Bettina was just finishing the body of her teddy bear. A rounded shape formed by strategic increasing and decreasing hung from her needles.

The silence continued for a time, interrupted only by murmured words and phrases—usually knitting directions spoken aloud by a knitter puzzling out a detail of a pattern. But after a bit, Bettina asked Karen about Lily's impressions of Christmas, and soon they were engaged in a lively conversation, with Bettina reminiscing about Christmases when her sons were young. Then Holly finished the section of her jacket she'd been working on, cast off, and crossed the room to crouch by the armchair where Nell was sitting. They chatted about Nell's teddy-bear project and the women's shelter where the bears would be delivered for the children in residence.

In fact, by the time Roland pushed back his starched shirt cuff to consult his impressive watch and announce that it was eight o'clock, the noise level had become such that he had to speak up quite forcefully to make his message heard.

Holly sprang to her feet as if she'd been poised to move as soon as she heard the announcement, and she reached the kitchen even before Pamela.

"You didn't really show up at Laurel's townhouse by accident, did you?" she whispered as Pamela seized the kettle and headed to the sink to fill it. For a minute the sound of running water made speaking pointless, and Pamela was grateful for a chance to ponder her answer. But by the time the kettle was full, Bettina had arrived and Holly had solicited *her* opinion about whether Pamela's appearance at the townhouse in time to prevent another murder had been more than a lucky coincidence.

"Of course it wasn't an accident!" Bettina declared. "Pamela figured the whole thing out and when she checked the library parking lot and saw that Mort Quigley's car was not in its spot, she knew exactly where he was."

As Pamela moved about the kitchen arranging the paper

filter in the carafe's filter cone, grinding coffee, and measuring loose tea into the squat brown teapot, she smiled to herself, happy to let Bettina rehearse for Holly's benefit the reasoning process that had led her to conclude Laurel Lewis was not the killer and in fact was going to be Mort Quigley's next victim.

"Well," Holly said when Bettina had finished, "I'm still very sorry that the scarf I knit became a murder weapon, but at least the correct person has been arrested now."

The small kitchen had been gradually filling with the spicy aroma of fresh-brewed coffee, and the tea was steeping in the teapot. Bettina poured cream into the cut-glass cream pitcher, picked up the matching sugar bowl, and set out for the dining room.

"Coffee is coming right up," Pamela heard her announce. "And tea."

She reached for the carafe and gestured for Holly to take the teapot, but Holly hesitated. "Did you know *why* Mort Quigley wanted to kill Laurel?" she asked, her nose wrinkling and her pretty lips twisting into a quizzical knot. "Or was it just that everything pointed to him so obviously you thought he must have had *some* reason?"

Bettina peeked in from the dining room. "They're all wondering where the coffee is," she reported, giving Pamela a curious look. "And the tea."

Holly held up a hand, fingernails gleaming with bright green polish. "Wait," she whispered. "It's like the end of a mystery on TV. Pamela's just about to reveal the last puzzle piece." Pamela smiled. She'd let Bettina do most of the explaining, but Holly was such a rapt audience it would be fun to provide the final detail herself.

Nell, however, had appeared in the doorway. She edged past Bettina.

"The last puzzle piece?" Nell's expression blended suspicion with amusement as her eyes narrowed but her lips struggled to vanquish a smile. "You've been sleuthing again. I suspected as much and—"

"Time is a-wasting!" came a stern voice from the dining room. The voice belonged to Roland, who went on to add, "If we don't have our refreshments soon, we're going to have to just skip them—though I do enjoy your poppy-seed cake, Pamela. I have a knitting quota to reach tonight and I would like to get back to work, and I'm sure everyone else feels the same way."

Bettina edged back from the doorway and Pamela heard her say, "Oh, for heaven's sake, Roland. Lighten up. And speak for yourself."

"The tea is just ready!" Holly exclaimed. She darted toward the counter where the tea was steeping in the squat brown teapot. Teapot in hand, she whirled around and took Nell by the arm. As they approached the doorway leading to the dining room, they nearly collided with Karen.

"Did something happen?" Karen inquired in a small voice, after she had recovered her balance. "What was everyone doing in here? And what's wrong with Roland?"

"He needs to lighten up," Nell said.

Alone in the kitchen again, Pamela laughed. Then she picked up the carafe and joined the others in the dining room, where people were transferring slices of poppy-seed cake to wedding-china dessert plates and where the arrival of the coffee was greeted with enthusiasm.

In no time at all, they were settled back in their seats in the living room with their refreshments. Pamela wasn't sure whether people were eating and drinking more hastily than usual in deference to Roland's admonition or whether that was just her imagination. But soon Holly was collecting empty cups and plates dusted with crumbs, and everyone else was focused on their busy needles.

As nine p.m. drew near, knitters in mid-row sped up, while others who had reached good stopping places began to tuck their work, their needles, and their skeins of yarn away.

Her work stowed, Holly looked up and suddenly said, "I wonder what will happen to the scarf I made for the auction now?"

"Police evidence. You won't get it back." Roland's voice was matter-of-fact and his lean face was serious. "It will doubtless be brought out in the courtroom when Mort Quigley goes to trial."

"I feel bad that Laurel didn't get the scarf she bid on." Holly's dramatic looks made her concern all the more moving. "I could make her another one. I have plenty of that aqua yarn left."

"Oh, my dear, I'm not sure that would be a good idea." Nell's words were discouraging, but her tone was sympathetic. "It might remind her of things she'd rather forget." Nell surveyed the group and added, "Things we all should forget." Her gaze lingered on Pamela. "No matter how proud we are of our detective work."

KNIT

Nell's Cozy Teddy Bear

This project is a little more complicated than the KNIT projects in the previous books have been, but it's great fun to do and the teddy bear would make a wonderful gift for a favorite child. Use yarn identified on the label as "Medium" and/or #4, and use size 8 needles—though size 7 or 9 is fine if that's what you have. The project takes about 150 yards of yarn.

If you're not already a knitter, watching a video is a great way to master the basics of knitting. Just search the internet for "How to knit" and you'll have your choice of tutorials that show the process clearly.

First make the separate parts.

Body
Cast on 15 stitches, using the "long tail" method. Casting on is often included in internet "How to knit" tutorials, or you can search specifically for "Casting on long tail method."

Knit 1 row increasing 1 stitch on every stitch so you end up with 30 stitches. To increase, use the "knit front back" technique. It's easy to find video demonstrations of this technique on the internet. Just search for "Knit front back."

Work 3 rows using the stockinette stitch, starting on a purl row. To create the stockinette stitch, you alternate rows of knitting and purling (or purling and knitting). Again, it's easier to understand "purl" by viewing a video, but essentially when you purl you're creating the backside of "knit."

To knit, you insert the right-hand needle front to back through the loop of yarn on the left-hand needle. To purl, you insert the needle back to front.

Knit 1 row increasing 1 stitch on every other stitch so you end up with 45 stitches.

Work 6 inches using the stockinette stitch, starting and ending on a purl row.

Decrease by knitting 2 stitches together then knitting a regular stitch then knitting 2 stitches together then knitting a regular stitch, and so on, to end up with 30 stitches.

Purl 1 row.

Decrease by knitting every 2 stitches together for the whole row. Now you will have 15 stitches.

Purl 1 row.

Decrease by knitting every 3 stitches together for the whole row. Now you will have 5 stitches.

Cut the yarn leaving a tail of about a foot. Thread a yarn needle—a large needle with a large eye and a blunt end—with the tail, transfer the 5 stitches from the knitting needle to the yarn needle and pull the tail through the loops.

Head
Cast on 10 stitches, using the "long tail" method.

Knit 1 row increasing 1 stitch on each stitch so you end up with 20 stitches. To increase, use the "knit front back" technique.

Work 3 rows using the stockinette stitch, starting on a purl row.

Knit 1 row increasing 1 stitch on each stitch again. Now you will have 40 stitches.

Work 3 inches using the stockinette stitch, starting and ending on a purl row.

Decrease by knitting every 2 stitches together for the whole row. Now you will have 20 stitches.

Work 3 rows using the stockinette stitch, starting on a purl row.

Decrease by knitting every 2 stitches together for the whole row. Now you will have 10 stitches.

Cut the yarn leaving a tail of about a foot. Thread a yarn needle with the tail, transfer the 10 stitches from the knitting needle to the yarn needle and pull the tail through the loops.

Arms (make 2)
Cast on 10 stitches, using the "long tail" method.

Knit 1 row.

Purl 1 row.

Knit 1 row increasing 1 stitch on every stitch so you end up with 20 stitches.

Proceed, using the stockinette stitch, until the arm is 3 inches long, starting and ending on a purl row. Alternatively, you can count 13 rows instead of measuring. Since you want your arms to be exactly the same length, counting rows will guarantee that they match.

Knit 5 stitches, knit 2 stitches together, knit 6 stitches, knit 2 stitches together, knit 5 stitches.

Work the next 3 rows using the stockinette stitch.

Knit 4 stitches, knit 2 stitches together, knit 6 stitches, knit 2 stitches together, knit 4 stitches.

Work the next 3 rows using the stockinette stitch.

Knit 3 stitches, knit 2 stitches together, knit 6 stitches, knit 2 stitches together, knit 3 stitches.

Now you will have 14 stitches.

Work 2 more rows using the stockinette stitch and then cast off.

Legs (make 2)

Cast on 20 stitches, using the "long tail" method.

Knit 9 stitches, increase 1 stitch each on the next 2 stitches using the "knit front back" technique, knit 9 stitches.

Purl 10 stitches, increase 1 stitch each on the next 2 stitches using the "knit front back" technique, purl 10 stitches. Note: you will have to knit (rather than purl) the stitches you increase as there is no way I know of to do "knit front back" on a purl stitch. Be sure to transfer the yarn you are working with from the front to the back before doing the knit and to transfer it from the back to the front when you resume purling. Otherwise you will end up with extra, unwanted, loops on your needle.

Knit 11 stitches, increase 1 stitch each on the next 2 stitches using the "knit front back" technique, knit 11 stitches.

Purl 12 stitches, increase 1 stitch each on the next 2 stitches using the "knit front back" technique, purl 12 stitches. Now you will have 28 stitches.

Knit 1 row.

For the next 4 rows, decrease by knitting (or purling, on purl rows) the middle 4 stitches together in pairs. Now you will have 20 stitches again.

Proceed, using the stockinette stitch, until the leg is 4 inches long, starting and ending on a purl row. Alternatively, you can count 13 rows instead of measuring. Since you want your legs to be exactly the same length, counting rows will guarantee that they match.

Knit 5 stitches, knit 2 stitches together, knit 6 stitches, knit 2 stitches together, knit 5 stitches.

Work the next 3 rows using the stockinette stitch.

Knit 4 stitches, knit 2 stitches together, knit 6 stitches, knit 2 stitches together, knit 4 stitches.

Work the next 3 rows using the stockinette stitch.

Knit 3 stitches, knit 2 stitches together, knit 6 stitches, knit 2 stitches together, knit 3 stitches.

Now you will have 14 stitches.

Work 2 more rows using the stockinette stitch and then cast off.

Ears (make 2)

Note: The ears are worked in the garter stitch, which means you don't switch between knitting and purling.

Cast on 6 stitches.

Knit 1 row.

Knit 1, knit increasing 1 stitch, knit 2, knit increasing 1 stitch, knit 1. Now you will have 8 stitches.

Knit 5 rows.

Decrease by knitting every 2 stitches together for the whole row to end up with 4 stitches.

Knit 1 row.

Cast off.

The end that you cast on will be sewn to the head. Leave that tail long. Hide the other tail by threading a yarn needle with it and stitching in and out with a whip stitch along the rim of the ear for half an inch or so. Cut off the short tail that remains.

Muzzle

Note: The muzzle is worked in the garter stitch, which means you don't switch between knitting and purling.

Cast on 3 stitches.

Knit 1 row.

Knit 1 row increasing 1 stitch on every stitch so you end up with 6 stitches.

Knit 1 row.

Knit 1 row increasing 1 stitch on every stitch so you end up with 12 stitches.

Knit 3 rows.

Decrease by knitting every 2 stitches together for the whole row. Now you will have 6 stitches.

Knit 1 row.

Decrease by knitting every 2 stitches together for the whole row. Now you will have 3 stitches.

Cast off.

Now, assemble your bear.

<u>Body</u>: Pull tight on the yarn tail you ran through the loops and use the tail to sew the long edges of the body together, right sides facing in. It is helpful to pin first, to make sure you line the edges up evenly. There's a photo of this step on my website. You will end up with a small opening at the end of the body where you cast on. This will be the top of the body. Turn the body right side out. Stuff the body with fiberfill stuffing by inserting the stuffing a small amount at a time through the opening. There's a photo of this step on my website.

<u>Head</u>: Pull tight on the yarn tail you ran through the loops and use the tail to sew the long edges of the head together as you did for the body. You will end up with a small opening at the end of the head where you cast on. This will be the bottom of the head. Turn the head right side out. Flatten the head into a bowl shape with the seam running down the back and position the ears on the fold about two inches apart at the top of the head. Sew the ears into place using the tails from when you cast on. Hide what remains of the tails by using the yarn needle to pull them through to the inside of the head and trim them to an inch or so.

Stuff the head with fiberfill. Position the muzzle on the face, anchor it with a few pins, and sew it on. When you have sewn nearly all the way around you can tuck a tiny bit of fiberfill inside if you wish. Hide the tail by taking a large stitch, pulling tight, and snipping the yarn, leaving half an inch or so of yarn buried inside the head.

You can use buttons for eyes—they must be shank type for ease in attaching. If the bear is for a child and you don't want detachable parts, you might want to simply embroider eyes.

Arms and legs: Right sides facing in, sew the bottoms and sides of the arms and legs together, using the tails from when you cast on and/or off if you wish. Cut the tails, leaving about an inch. Don't worry about hiding them because they will be inside when you turn the arms and legs right side out. The ends where you cast off should be left open. Turn the arms and legs right side out and stuff them with fiberfill.

Attach the arms and legs.
In attaching the arms and legs, make sure the body seam runs up the back of the bear and the arm and leg seams face the back of the bear. The open end of the arm or leg is the end that will be attached to the bear. Check the photos on my website for guidance in positioning and attaching the arms and legs. First anchor the arm or leg to the body at each end of the opening with one stitch and then go back and make smaller stitches all around. Hide each tail by taking a large stitch, pulling tight, and snipping the yarn, leaving half an inch or so of yarn buried inside.

Attach the head to the body.
The seam down the back of the head should line up with the seam down the back of the body. The openings on the body and the head are not the same size. Pick up stitches at the edge of the body opening and stitches a row or so in from the head opening. When you have stitched nearly all

the way around, you can tuck in an extra bit of fiberfill to make sure the head doesn't flop over.

For a picture of Nell's Cozy Teddy Bear, as well as many in-progress photos, visit the Knit & Nibble Mysteries page at PeggyEhrhart.com. Click on the cover for *Christmas Scarf Murder* and scroll down on the page that opens.

NIBBLE

Pamela's Christmas Cake
(Orange-Flavored Yellow Cake with Vanilla Cream Filling and Chocolate Buttercream Frosting)

Christmas and oranges seem to go together, perhaps because oranges were one of the few fresh fruits available in the winter before we could get anything at any time flown in from who knows where—though oranges themselves were imported from sunnier climes. My husband, who grew up in Illinois, recalls that Christmas always brought a box of oranges from Florida, a gift from his grandfather who lived there in his retirement. I gave this reminiscence to Wilfred in *Death by Christmas Scarf*.

Ingredients
For the cake:
4 eggs, separated
1½ cups cake flour
½ cup cornstarch
½ teaspoon salt
4 teaspoons baking powder
8 oz. butter (two sticks), softened
1 cup sugar
½ cup orange juice—about the yield of one large orange
Grated orange rind from one large orange—1 heaping tablespoon.

For the filling:
1 egg white
⅛ teaspoon salt
1 cup heavy (or whipping) cream

¼ cup powdered sugar
1 teaspoon vanilla

For the frosting:
1 cup butter, softened
½ cup unsweetened cocoa powder, sifted
4 cups powdered sugar
1 teaspoon vanilla
3 tablespoons heavy (or whipping) cream

Make the cake.

Beat the egg whites in a small bowl until stiff; set aside. Mix the flour, cornstarch, salt, and baking powder in a small bowl; set aside. Cream the butter, add the sugar a bit at a time, and beat until pale yellow. Add the egg yolks, orange juice and rind and continue beating. Add the dry ingredients and beat well. Using a rubber spatula, fold ⅓ of the egg whites into the mixture and blend, then fold in the rest of the egg whites and blend.

Divide the batter between two buttered and floured 9-inch round cake pans. Bake at 350 degrees for 25 to 35 minutes or until a wooden toothpick inserted in the middle comes out clean. Check after 25 minutes. Cool before proceeding with the rest of the recipe.

Make the filling.

Beat the egg white till foamy, add salt, beat until stiff. In a separate bowl beat the cream until it forms soft peaks, beat in sugar and vanilla. Fold the two mixtures together.

(If you are squeamish about a recipe that involves raw egg white, you can skip the filling and use some of the chocolate frosting between the layers instead. The frosting recipe makes plenty.)

Make the frosting.

This recipe makes a very generous amount of frosting.

Beat the butter and cocoa together in a large bowl. Beat in the vanilla and powdered sugar, about a cup at a time. Use a rubber spatula to scrape the mixture back to the bottom of the bowl if the mixer is flinging it around. Add the cream and continue beating. You can add more cream or more powdered sugar until the frosting reaches the spreadability you desire.

Assemble the cake.

Remove the layers from the baking pans. Center one layer on a plate large enough to accommodate it and spread the filling over the top. Add the second layer. Frost the whole cake with the chocolate frosting, starting at the top and working down the sides.

Because of the cream and raw egg white, store leftovers in the refrigerator, but the cake is tastier if it returns to room temperature before serving again.

For a picture of Pamela's Christmas Cake, as well as in-progress photos, visit the Knit & Nibble Mysteries page at PeggyEhrhart.com. Click on the cover for *Christmas Scarf Murder* and scroll down on the page that opens.